COLOURS
AND
YEARS

MARGIT KAFFKA

COLOURS AND YEARS

ENGLISH TRANSLATION BY
GEORGE F. CUSHING

INTRODUCTION BY
CHARLOTTE FRANKLIN

CORVINA

Published in 2017 by Corvina Books Ltd.
1086 Budapest, Dankó u. 4–8, Hungary

This translation is based on *Színek és évek*,
Franklin Társulat, Budapest, 1912

On the cover
Discord by Bertalan Karlovszky
Hungarian National Gallery

Cover design by
Viki Szvoboda

Second edition
Second printing, 2017

ISBN 978 963 13 5786 8

INTRODUCTION

Margit Kaffka was born on June 19th, 1880 in the provincial town of Nagykároly (now Carei in Romania). She believed her restless temperament was a result of mixed ancestry, between that of a Hungarian mother, claiming descent from among the few 'oldest and best' families who had come to Hungary with the conqueror Árpád at the end of the ninth century and a Slav father, Gyula Kaffka, whom Margit remembered as sensitive, serious and gentle. He died rather suddenly at the age of thirty-four when Margit was only six years old. His death ended her happy childhood. The young family was left destitute; her grandparents made themselves responsible for the youngest daughter, and not for Margit, the eldest. Her mother—brought up in a high provincial society, where she learned to catch men at dances, and with few other skills beyond running a household and entertaining in the proper manner—felt bound to marry again; but her second husband turned out to be unsatisfactory financially, and in other ways. Observant and sensitive, young Margit squirrelled away these memories, and years later wrote her best selling novel *Colours and Years* (Színek és évek) about her mother's hopeless predicament. The widow as object of unkind local tittle-tattle also appears in her novel, *Hangyaboly* (The Ant Heap).

Margit Kaffka was a misfit in her stepfather's household. She was sent to board in a local convent, not unlike those schools where the Brontë sisters were educated in Yorkshire at the beginning of the nineteenth century—a horrifying experience. One of her earliest short stories, *'Letters from the Convent'*, is the moving account of a little girl who suffers from neglect and lack of affection, harsh punishment, the cold, the damp and the bad food, but is always writing hopeful letters to no avail: there is a new stepfather and she dies! Today this may be read sentimentally, but it was inspired by her own experience.

Margit remained in the convent for three years. In an autobiographical short story, *'Triumph'*, she described her feelings on re-entering normal life: 'I was ten and had only recently returned in bad health from a distant convent school where I had spent three years; three years stunted, day-dreaming my sick fantasies, physically weak. There I could never see bright sunshine, flowers in the meadows or even a living dog. I must have been quite different from other children.'

After this she entered the local secondary school, boarding with relatives. Her grades in school reports have been published in Hungary; she was a good pupil, took part in performances, and wrote for the student journal.

Her home town, Nagykároly, was peaceful, remote, dominated by its feudal castle, but with an emerging middle class. Margit's maternal family felt socially superior to such upstarts; she herself was attracted by new liberal ideas and admired 'western' thought. Nagykároly had its share of other nationalities: German settlers, Romanians, Gypsies, Italians and Slovaks all appear in her novels. She loved the place, its gardens, seasons, the countryside, but found the gossip and small-town mentality of its inhabitants unbearable. Determined not to follow her mother's example in trusting herself entirely to marriage, Margit went back to her convent to gain a diploma for teaching in primary schools. In return for board and training she had to promise one more year of work as teacher at a school run by the Sisters of Mercy. She was able to transfer for this last year to the town of Miskolc (nearer Budapest but provincial) where her paternal grandparents lived.

At the end of it all, free and qualified to teach in the state system, the next job offered to her was still in a convent! To her cousin she wrote: 'To sweat it out again in a convent—when my whole soul is drawn to secular schools for new active work. The Church has become outdated with such strict prejudiced institutions. The spirit is different there, according to the Reverend Mother proposing this job, and I dared not contradict—since it's the spirit which has persecuted and embittered me these four long years.' Luckily, her mother was able to assert some influence and Margit achieved her desire to go to Budapest in 1899. She spent the next three years on a scholarship at the respected Erzsébet Training College for Women, studying for her Higher Diploma, qualifying as a secondary school teacher in the year 1902. Her experience was captured in her novel, *Mária évei* (The Years of Mary).

During this time, her poetry and short stories began to be published and noticed. Margit's mother had sent some of her early poems to a literary member of the family. The answer she received is often quoted:

> 'Dear Cousin, Your daughter's poems are not bad, indeed rather beautiful and quite good. But why should a woman write? For such an excellent housewife as yourself it would be a great pity if your daughter were to forsake the culinary arts. In fact it is a waste of time for her to become a teacher!'

In Hungary, far more than in England, the art of cooking was considered the essential accomplishment for a woman, in order to first conquer and then keep her man. The kitchen was the woman's space. One friend wrote of Margit: 'She wielded her pen as our mothers did their mixing spoons.'

In 1905 Margit, feeling she was getting on in years, decided to marry a handsome forestry engineer called Bruno Fröhlich. Housekeeping was not her forte, however; she soon felt suffocated by domesticity, and far away from metropolitan culture. She continued to write and teach. In 1906 her only child, a son László was born. Motherhood was a turning point in her understanding. Poets had seldom written honestly upon the theme. Though not in fact describing her own son, 'Petike jár' (Peter's First Steps) is a poem in Hungarian anthologies, the delightful observation of a toddler's first efforts, stumbling yet determined to reach his mother, encouraging himself by echoing her words, 'Careful, careful!' without fully understanding them. Her last stanza looks to the time when Péter, an energetic young man, will visit his mother who, anxious as ever, hobbles out to greet him. In Eastern Europe, it was always a mother's duty to worry about her children.

Poems to her newborn son (he is a miracle but what a relief when he falls asleep and 'all is well') were included in a little volume entitled *Kaffka Margit könyve* (Margit Kaffka's Book). Each poem is illustrated by Jugendstil black and white woodcuts made by her artist friend, Attila Sassy. A coloured portrait of the poet is mounted as the frontispiece. A facsimile of this pretty little book of sixty poems has recently been produced in Hungary.

By 1910, Kaffka had separated from her husband, and took up her maiden name as a writer, living in Budapest as a single mother, supporting herself by teaching and writing stories, reviews and educational books for children. Ambitious to be competent in her roles as mother, author, teacher, she was for ever rushing between home and her job at the school, 'always on the treadmill,' as she wrote in one of her poems. She was lonely, occasionally suicidal; writing was her therapy.

Though it was against convention, she sat with the men in smoky coffee-houses and became part of the small circle of writers who ran a journal called *Nyugat* (The West), which appeared twice a month. It was brilliantly edited by a poet with the pseudonym Ignotus, a name still proudly worn by his descendants. Sari Ignotus, the daughter of that editor, living in London and now in her nineties remembered Margit Kaffka: 'She was the only one of those writers coming to my father's house who knew how to talk to a child. She was a marvellous woman.' In Budapest, until recently, there was a delightful museum honouring these writers of a golden age. It meant much to Margit to be included among them, but it irritated her to be paid less than the men. Sometimes she had to sit at a 'ladies' table, and not among the contributors.

Margit Kaffka had to be tough socially. A great patron of writers and an influential friend, recipient of many of her extant letters, Lajos Hatvany, had little understanding of her problems. He was contemptuous of her untidy flat. If she put the place in order, her son quickly made it into a mess again. This little boy would also interrupt serious discussions: 'Poor Margit!' Hatvany wrote condescendingly. In 1956, when he published his book of photographs and memoirs of the literary houses of Budapest, Kaffka was the only woman among a host of male writers.

Anna Lesznai, friend and fellow-artist, recalled affectionately:

'Those Sunday afternoons of long ago at the apartment in Márvány utca! Boxes and trunks in the hall, a worn out chiffon curtain fluttering in the rush of cold air. It's dark outside, but from the end of the corridor warmth of light and sound filter back. Someone rushes to answer the bell: impossible to guess who that might be, because every Sunday brings enthusiastic visitors. One thing is certain: it has to be a writer, painter, artist, scholar, concerned for the paths of the spirit. Inside it is over-heated, making one think of a country postmaster's room. Homemade pastries fill a large tray. We sit in a circle—the oil lamp flickers among eyes of the lively

young people tracking a flow of ideas: they eat, listen, argue. They eat what Margit has baked, listen to her words—try to convince her in passionate argument… In her home, everyone relaxes, feels at peace.'

Budapest at this time was the thriving capital of a Habsburg kingdom much larger than present-day Hungary, and in close contact with the Vienna of Klimt, Freud, and Wittgenstein, just up the Danube. Its cultural life was proudly Hungarian, yet part of the European avant-garde. Successful plays from Budapest were translated and performed abroad—as for instance *Liliom* by Ferenc Molnár, which later resurfaced as *Carousel*. People from every class and background met there. It was possible fairly cheaply to be a perpetual student, travelling all over Europe in search of the new. There were salons of intellectuals, a Galileo circle and a Sunday circle meeting to discuss and solve the problems of a changing world. The 'new woman' was of course a topic for discussion, and rather disturbing to the male establishment. The idea of the traditional woman was part of this scene as mistress, muse, assistant, and wife in the background: especially admired and adored were the actresses, opera divas and dancers. From her own experience Margit could understand conventional dismay about the new woman in Ibsen and Shaw.

Margit Kaffka wrote short stories about these women who achieved financial independence but suffered many unfulfilled dreams and impossibly difficult choices. She particularly appreciated a review at that time from George Lukács. He had understood her concern with women's issues, even though she had avoided being too specific. This was in contrast with Ernő Szabó (a one-time friend) who wrote: 'For me, a country serving girl radiating vitality meant more as a woman than all the Mme de Staels, George Sands, Selma Lagerlöfs and Margit Kaffkas put together'.

Margit Kaffka explored the complexities facing different generations of these new women in three novels, of which the first, *Colours and Years*, catapulted her to success. Old Magda, an unwanted widow in a tiny apartment, remembers. This technique of the talking head unconsciously revealing her own character, her background and history, while prattling away seemed at that time startlingly original.

The book has in part the charm of period photographs, accurate pictures of a world that has passed. At the beginning one is taken aback to find that Magda 'is old and solitary; in the spring I passed my fiftieth birthday.' Many women today believe life starts at fifty. In the United States no one accepts the term 'old' at any age. Margit Kaffka records accurately the position of unwanted widows, the low esteem accorded to them in Central Europe of a century ago.

The novel starts at the end. Its interest lies in part in the subtle use of memory, hidden suppressed and emerging unexpectedly, the blending of past and present. Though a contemporary of Proust and Freud, neither of these influential twentieth century thinkers had published his work before the writing of *Colours and Years*. She does not explore at great length or long chapters the sudden tricks of memory evoked by a scent of ripe raspberries or the playing of a Polish aria; lightly, in a sentence these phenomena are recorded.

Magda had been forced to gamble her life on men and marriage—there seemed no choice; she had to learn by hard experience that the old role models of mother and grandmother were misleading. Belle of the ball in her youth, disillusioned by husbands, afraid of vulgar, sinful Budapest, Magda is reduced to tired acceptance of her fate. Her old society was crumbling, doomed. This novel chronicles the decline and corruption of her gentry class; Church and Army are represented by the two brothers of the heroine. The family's hopes for a high position for one brother as a prince of the Church are dashed as he becomes ever more unstable and ends up in an asylum. His brother in the Army takes to drink, philandering, gambling, and finds himself with debts. Both Magda's husbands are the grievous victims of her ambitious needs. The daughters whom she struggled to educate neglect her; she yet hopes their lives may be better than her own.

Mother and daughter relationships over three generations are caught without sentimentality. The matriarchal implacable old grandmother commands respect but in traditional style she favours her son over her daughter in vital matters of inheritance.

The novel plays with every permutation of possibilities for impoverished widows. She might take in lodgers, become a rural postmistress, housekeeper for an ancient uncle, or try acting in Budapest. Everything seems appalling in her social position. Finally, the most reactionary view of the true nature of women comes from Magda's stepfather, the supposedly reforming land-owner Telekdy whose worthy plans had all ended in failure. It was he who tried to help his peasants, had given full inheritance to his illegitimate brother, had introduced modern English live-stock. He bursts out to his step-daughter:

> 'The women of the species will always remain inferior; things can't be otherwise. After all, two thirds of their life-span are occupied with unconscious animal cares and duties that go with the maintenance of humankind, and instincts guide their intellect. If they liberate themselves from these, they become wayward mongrel figures who cannot find their own place. Woman is a blind tool in the hands of nature... All the philosophers, Plato, Spinoza, Kant, Schopenhauer agree about that. Only the sick culture of today struggles to play with the idea that women should be taken seriously.'

Towards the end of the book it appears that Magda might, under the influence of a charismatic priest who has come to the town, return to the conventionally religious fold. There is a nice cynical twist which brings to mind American TV evangelists.

In *Colours and Years*, Margit Kaffka wrote about what she truly knew, the world of her youth: the farmers' wives who were spent from childbirth, from preserving their produce and endless other rural labours; her mother's life, the county political circle which rested on intrigue, the petty-minded upstarts. Surprisingly, one of the few kindly characters is the Jewish doctor, Jakobi. His real-life name was Jacobovitz and he had lived next door to her family in Nagykároly. Margit Kaffka distressed those who recognized themselves in what she wrote. Her own view survives in a letter: 'The author is like an ostrich burying its head in the sand... writing is a ruthless profession demanding blood sacrifice'.

Her sure touch in changing fact into fiction astonished the critics. The book was hailed as a masterpiece. While Tolstoy and Flaubert had shown an understanding for women trapped in bad marriages, Margit Kaffka belonged to a generation of women writers who could speak for themselves. With comparable indignation at having been reared only for marriage, Edith Wharton for example, in the *House of Mirth* and *The Age of Innocence* especially, was exploring similar themes.

Mária évei (The Years of Mary) followed in 1913. Maria (perhaps Magda's daughter of the earlier book) has qualifications to earn a living and need not depend on marriage, but fares no more happily than had her mother's generation—if anything even worse. As a member of the brightest set at her college in Budapest, she is full of fun and hope, her imagination absorbed in the love of literature. Back home, a schoolteacher in a provincial town yearning for high romance, she corresponds with a famous writer in Budapest. Conflict develops between literary fantasies and the wretched possibility of marriage to a dreary colleague. After a final attempt to discover fulfilment in the capital city, she jumps from a bridge into the Danube. High hopes based on education for women have led only to disaster.

Her third novel, *Állomások* (Stations), was a *roman-à-clèf* and many characters from her artistic circle in Budapest are recognizable. Margit Kaffka was bemused by the many young second generation Jews so prominent in Budapest's intellectual life. (Later, she was to marry one.) She captures the idiom of their speech, occasional hints of Yiddish and some German, watching with fascination the working of the system: parties, patronage, jealousies—men harassing women. She reports on chattering journalists with idealistic theories for social change. Hungarians had to be fluent in many languages and were ever avid for foreign literature, busy translating everything that was fashionable in other countries. In this novel the bright young women read Whitman, James, Beardsley, Wilde and have the *Studio* on their coffee tables.

By this time, Margit Kaffka had become more hopeful about new women, their need for compromise and sacrifice. In the final chapter, Tekla explains her choice to devote herself to love of a poet at the expense of her own artistic life; while Éva, a designer, chooses work and peaceful independence, above the more romantic alternative.

Margit Kaffka was concerned with social problems and injustice, but believed in literature rather than politics. She had witnessed the suppression of the peaceful socialist demonstration in May 1912. This affected her views profoundly: she wrote about it in *Stations* and in the famous rallying poem, *Hajnali ritmusok* (Rhythms of Dawn). She had empathy with the lowest of the low in Budapest life, the servant women, and wrote particularly well about the helplessness of illiterate workers.

Literary women have often attracted younger men—Elizabeth Barrett, George Eliot and Dorothy Richardson come to mind. In 1914, Margit Kaffka, aged thirty-four, realized to her own astonishment (for she believed herself to be well past such feelings) that she had fallen in love properly for the first time in her life with an attentive Jewish medical student, Ervin Bauer, ten years her junior. His parents, both dead, had been intellectuals, lovers of literature, impoverished teachers in remote places. Margit's poems and letters at this time make for delightful reading. She discovers to her horror that Ervin is actually engaged to someone else without telling her about it! Their friendship continues, they sort things out and have a blissful journey to Italy together. Margit confides to Ervin that she is happy for the first time ever. Later, in the way of traditional superstition, she felt she had tempted the Fates: the very next day world history interrupted their idyll, in Perugia they heard of 'la guerra'. In a state of shock they returned to Budapest and married a few weeks later. Ervin, after passing his final examinations, enlisted as a doctor.

A few days later her mother in the country received a postcard photograph taken in a studio in Fiume, Italy, showing Margit in a long skirt, white blouse, a ring on her finger, standing beside the handsome formally dressed Ervin. On the back she had written:

> 'Dear Mother, thank you for your enquiry. I got back from Italy in time, though it was a terrible journey. I was there with my fiancé, Doctor Ervin Bauer, who has been called up, and after that we got married in Szeged. My husband is home for a few days for exams. We hope they will allot him hospital work—though that is quite dangerous. Ervin is younger than I am, but we get on so well: when he is back you will know him! Greetings Margit.'

Ervin adds a line: 'We don't know each other but I greet you.'

Obviously Margit Kaffka's relationship with her own mother had been described in her novel two years before this casual card. At the end of Colours and Years, Magda writes of her daughters: 'They've had no need of me, my worries and love for sometime now. They write sometimes, but their visits home are increasingly rare.'

War in 1914 was generally welcomed in Hungary. Margit's voice was among the few who cried in anguished prose and poetry against the patriotic fervour sweeping the country. In *Záporos folytonos levél* (Letter through the Storm) she first describes the vast horde of anonymous young men tramping in the cold, the fog, the mud, clothed in grey; marching to distant territory, without understanding what was happening; forced to kill, because their neighbours would do so. 'Today I live—poor fellow, he died not I!' Then she turns to the women, praying, lonely, desperate, and her personal disbelief bursts forth. 'This CANNOT be happening to us, as individuals, to you my lover and to me.'

Her story *Két nyár* (Two Summers) from 1916, was about the reality of war as it reaches into Budapest. Opening as a quiet leisurely tale, sympathetic to the urban poor, a washer woman and her unemployed husband who take a young lodger, all live their unpretentious lives. The husband is called up, the lodger expects his baby. Vera, duty bound, goes to the clinic to help look after her husband's child. She reflects on women fated to give birth in travail and blood:

> '...and so a surplus of tiny bundles of steaming bodies; in order that some lives from the womb might always survive all those destined to be exterminated with most terrible weapons, in an infinite variety of bloody ways after twenty, a hundred, a thousand, years to come. Thus there will always be an endless multitude of murderers and the accumulating dust of individual souls born to be destroyed in unimaginable numbers.'

The reader had not been prepared for this sudden outcry.

Margit spent the war years pushing herself to the limit, more frantically busy than ever, queuing for food, only using fuel when others visited her, anxious for news, following her army husband to his hospital postings whenever possible. (It was some consolation to her that Ervin was tending the sick, not involved in killing.) She continued to teach, write and review.

In 1916 she wrote her novel *Hangyaboly* (The Ant Heap). This must rank among the most lyrical and perceptive evocations of convent life. In a series of sharp, witty and warmly imaginative scenes, she exposed a closed world in which modern ideas of female education and economic independence begin to dislodge the power of religious observance and social tradition; where love, sexual awakening and the lures of the outside world all conspire to create confusion and deception. Beneath the starched white veil of serene piety and ritual order, the irrepressible demands of earthly desire find their own inevitable outlets. Some critics were shocked by her rational view of religion and sexuality, calling it a blasphemous and pornographic book. Of course the novel was a success and reprinted the following year. In modern Hungary it exists in paperback, a set book for students.

Also in 1918, *Nyugat* published *Az élet útján* (On Life's Journey), a slim volume of her own selection of her poems. It included a full range of some juvenilia and new poems written for Ervin. These wartime first editions, on poor faded paper are still poignant.

After four years, the long nightmare of war ended; but Margit felt worried by news of the terrible Spanish flu. At his hospital, Ervin had to perform autopsies. Her son seemed at risk at his boarding school. 'If we can survive the war none of us should succumb to a silly epidemic ... No more army, hospital, rural isolation, bug infested messy rooms, constant journeys in over-crowded trains. There will be peace and order. And work'. In late November 1918, Margit was preparing to write her first historical novel, to be set in biblical times, and had discussed terms, advances, deadlines with her publisher. She estimated how many pages she would need to write to earn enough money for a new dress! Without realising it she was already sickening— experiencing early symptom of headaches—the disease sweeping through war ravaged Europe. She died of it on the first day of December 1918; her only son died on the following day—a double tragedy. She was only thirty-eight years old with an impressive corpus of stories, novels, criticism, school books, volumes of poetry published; achieved while working in full time jobs, running her household and looking after her son.

The shock of this sudden death just as life beckoned was like one of the unexpected shocking endings of her own stories. A joint burial for mother and son was arranged and fellow Hungarian writers paid their tributes. Ten years later a critic, Aladár Schöpflin, wrote of it:

'At the height of the struggle and panic and catastrophe of war, the horror of Spanish flu, in the city shivering with cold, in that leaden depressing December twilight, Margit Kaffka's funeral at the cemetery pierced our hearts with numbing pain —even today horror grips me when I think of it during a sleepless night. I realised then for the first time the terrible truth of death. Everything is dying now, was my feeling...'

Anna Lesznai wrote:
'Latterly we saw little of each other. I could only catch glimpses of the Margit who had "arrived". Once she had been so happy, scarcely aware of what she wrote and then her finest poems were born. At other times she feared for her happiness with such frenzy that she cried night and day: that was when she wrote 'Two Summers', the masterpiece of her despair. Then, the last time, her life seemed so orderly that she had no time for herself; only the wounds of the world hurt her. Then she departed—her soul was fulfilled.'

The poet Ady had written in May of that year:
'Let us rejoice in Margit Kaffka because she has arrived and proves the triumph of Hungarian feminism: one need not be polite, pay false compliments to her. She is a strong person, an artist with an assured future: no criticism can hinder her true destiny, the path marked as her own.'

It is said he cried for days on hearing of her death.

George Cushing, for many years Professor of Hungarian at the School of Slavonic Studies in London, died in 1996. His translation of *Színek és évek* will now be welcomed, and the only sorrow is that he, whose introduction would have been so much more helpful than mine, did not live to see the publication of this book.

Charlotte Franklin
March 1998

I.

For some time now, I have been surrounded by a deep and pleasurable sense of tranquillity. Life goes on at a great distance from me, problems, altercations, industry and application, and when, from time to time I glance at it, I am amazed by the childish curiosity of those living in the present about what will happen to them tomorrow, and the day after. It is curious to think that for the young the matters of the world of today are every bit as novel and exciting as they were thirty years ago for me. Today I clearly see and know that there is much playfulness in all the changes and turmoil of this world, that people are play-acting; just as a child would say, I am playing at shopkeeping, or I'm playing daddy, or a storm at sea, so a grown-up will force himself into the role of an ambitious, industrious, lazy, passionate, dissolute or spiteful individual. They have to do something to pass the time; they have to convince themselves that for a time, at least, something or other is important, otherwise they would end up sitting idly by the roadside, hands clasped—which might be the natural thing to do, of course; everything else is mere self-deception and self-importance.

Be it as it may, we end up playing out our chosen roles, each to the best of his ability, except that—unlike on stage, where all action revolves around one main character, in life each person is a main character unto himself, and no one will play a minor role. We all play for our own benefit, to an audience of one. This is what gives rise to all the varied and serendipitous complications that hold us in thrall as long as we are involved—who is in love with whom, who marries whom, how someone brings up his or her children, how someone fights his way up the ladder of success, and how he falls from the heights. And once you have done all you could, and to the best of your ability, you can relax at last, provided you have a couple of quiet years left in which to do so.

I have news for the young who recoil from the horrors of old age. It is not as horrible as it may seem from a distance. You do not feel one state more acutely than another, nor do you feel the lack of things for which the desire has long since died in you.

If you are in reasonably good health, you do not feel that your body has aged; moving your arms and legs, a good hot cup of coffee, a pleasant room and a good night's sleep, these can be very satisfying, indeed, and for these delights you do not pay such a high price or take any risks; you need not go out of your way in order to obtain them.

I am an old woman. I passed my fiftieth birthday last spring. I am old and lonely, but when I think back, I see that I have lived through a great many things that were far worse than my present quiet life, and only a very few that were really good, and even that seems like a dream. I do not feel appreciably worse than at any time before, and this holds out hope that death will not seem so terrible either from up close, though at this moment it appears to be so.

Old age manifests itself in things foreign and outside the self, that gradually life passes you by, but that this does not disquiet you, for we will not allow ourselves to be put on the sidelines until we feel like it. Outside, the comedy begins—the same play, except the characters differ and so do the sets—they build up our expectation and go at it, but we are no longer interested. From time to time we'd like to shout, 'Stop it! What does it matter whether a thing turns out one way or another? It's all the same!', but we are in the wrong, it is their play now; we persued pretty much the same game with our own partners.

At this stage in life you have no definite aims or intentions, and this is not such a great affliction as the young might think; they picture old age in accordance with their own state of mind, whereas we change in life as we do nearing death—and I can not be held responsible for the deeds of the person whom, twenty years ago, they called by my name. At times, I think of her as a stranger. For example, you bend over backwards for the benefit of your children, thinking it will always be so, and the truth is, most old people latch on to life as best they can through their children. But that still comes from the love of play-acting, of playing a role. In truth, one's children are far removed from one and one's interest in their fate remains on the level of intent and self-delusion; in old age no fate and no change is important for us any more. Possibly, others feel slightly differently about this, but as for me, I find myself very much on my own.

I say this without regret—the solitude as well as the loss of aims—someone who once loved people, the more the merrier, and who was always in pursuit of an aim. Now I am sitting quietly in this warm and diminutive garden, or watch the acacia-tree lined street from behind the shutters, I rarely go out, and weeks pass until someone comes to call. It is almost too soon, I sometimes think, for the world to do so well without me. But I have grown immeasurably tired, it seems.

Who would have thought? I can sit for hours in one place with my hands clasped in my lap. My small apartment has a separate garden gate looking out on a narrow street, I use it to go to church; I don't even have to see the other inhabitants, well to do elderly Germans, if I don't want to. Yet they're close enough if I should need help, and they're kindly folk besides. I sometimes sit like this on the porch; the gentle tolling of the church bell reaches me through the blue and white of the late-afternoon summer sky, and the warm fragrance of my little old lady's flowers drift fragrantly towards me in this handkerchief-sized place. Across the way, by the blank wall of the neighbouring house, the pansies are in bloom, closer up a bed of mignonettes and another of nasturtiums, basil, love-lies-bleeding and lousewort all in a bunch, and at the foot of the porch, among the humble purslanes, a couple of red hollyhocks and three tubs of blooming oleanders. I broke off their shoots myself from the branches of other, older oleanders which had grown and blossomed in my family. Inside my lodgings—just one room and kitchen—some cheap old furniture which came with my first dowry, thirty-two years ago. And this is wonderful, too—I have scattered and cast from me so much in life, and now, even though my children urge me, I shall never again leave this little town, this nest of mine; I am too attached to these old, familiar, useless objects of mine. This is where I have spent my life, everyone knows me and knows about me; I have no need to explain to anyone who I am and in what circumstances I live. The young and the new-comers eye me with curiosity, while those few who still remain from my circle of long ago—those who loved me, or envied me, or hurt me—have all gradually become better disposed towards me. It's all so vague. When we meet on the street near our church, we are mutually glad to see each other, but surprised, too, like people from the same place who come upon each other in far-away places.

I can not say that these past few years of living without turbulence and care have not brought their share of novelty; in fact, it is only now that I am at leisure. I have read very little till now, and very haphazardly; but now, in this deep silence, I get to read a lot more, and get to immerse myself in it, too. But my daughters send me non-fiction and new kinds of writing in vain; in these I am all too conscious of change and alienation, though I understand the language well enough. I am not about to think differently about certain things, about the way things are. On the other hand, it is only now that I have grown to appreciate the inventions of poets, good novels and the like, and it is only lately that I can tell a good piece of writing from the bad. In addition, I do more thinking in one year now that I used to do in three. I think and reflect, and always about the same thing: about how things were, and how they might have been. Lord, how much time I spend like this, I veritably live backwards. Others do their thinking in their youth; I was always very active and am making up for it now. How one's nature changes! All the same, what I am today was there, all the time, but well concealed.

It is only now that I realize—some strange sort of cowardice held me back, always, from the really important things and decisions. I realize that at times I could have given my fate an appreciable push in a different direction, though now it is six of one and half a dozen of the other! Still, I had my fair share of both the good things and the bad, I have plenty to think about until my dying day. I sometimes leaf through the pages of my past like some unfamiliar, colourful picture book, and only occasionally does it occur to me that, after all, this was me. At such times I stop and say, it's all right, what's past is past. One thing is certain: I would never start any of it all over again.

As I ponder and reenact the past, time and time again in my thoughts, sometimes I can even see certain connections. Everything that happens happens for so many reasons; I don't know if I always find the most authentic when I look for just *one*, I don't even know if every little thing happened just the way I remember it, or whether I simply remembered it and recounted it that way so often that I came to believe it myself. I have heard it said that when you are travelling along a mountainous countryside, sometimes you have to take just a step or two for the scenery to change completely in front of your eyes—the relationship of the hills and valleys to each other. The panorama is entirely different from every place you stop to rest. Perhaps it is the same with events, too, and possibly, what I regard today as the story of my life is merely a picture of my life, shaped by my present way of thinking. Of course, that makes it all the more *mine*; indeed, on such church-bell ringing afternoons as this, as warm and as solitary, I can think of no preoccupation more interesting, colourful and precious than this.

II.

Red hollyhocks, mallow, love-lies-bleeding, basil, mignonette and lady's slippers—these flowers grew in the garden of the old Zimán house, too, where I spent my childhood. But that was a very big garden—the Zimán family's town estate; it formerly stretched all the way to Seven Eagle Feathers Street and Hajdú Town; later, when County Street was built up, our grandma, Granny Zimán, sold off two or three house-plots at a fairly large price. Still, when we played there, we could run a good distance from the styes, and from the ruins of the old kiln to the cool bench in the corner where the elders grew, and from the kitchen garden to the shed of the deserted bee hives. Childhood gardens can be very, very extensive, indeed, containing a multitude of things. Last year, when they finally pulled down the old house (today a Turkish bath has taken its place), I passed by and looked through the fence. The plot seemed a lot smaller, ordinary and neglected.

My two younger brothers and I ran around, ruled the roost, quarrelled and romped there when we were very small; our father had died, and we were left to our own devices, in the wild, as it were—and, I think, happy. What a pity that we remember so little of the riches of childhood; nothing but isolated scenes and insignificant events, and even those in a transformed shape, the way we have grown to think about them since then, occasionally mentioning them through the years. Now that I know what has happened to us since, I remember how Sándorka was always such a gentle and introverted child, a girlish and innocent little boy. When the two of us were together, we came up with a quite peculiar and fantastic game which we elaborated every time we played it. We said that in reality, we were both living under the earth in a maze of dark and secret roads and passages lit by blue and lilac lamps. I was Queen Vulpaverga, and he was King Rombertáró, and here, on earth, we went around wearing a disguise, and it was only by chance that we were living in grandma's house. In fact, we had very important things to do; my brother kept the roots of the trees and flowers in order down below, and also regulated the rainfall and the snow, while I had a thousand troubles and worries with perfuming the flowers and with all the lazy and finicky little fairies who were always forgetting to open the buds in time and to scrub the leaves clean by morning, not to mention their other misdeeds. Now it dawns on me that this silly nonsense originally came from a tale in a German picture book, though later we got into the spirit of it more and more; we'd spend our talking in our Vulpaverga-Rombertáró language, and we built up this dream-world in such detail, that in the end I felt it was oppressive and uncomfortable. 'Let's be Sándor and Magda again,' I'd say peevishly, but he would not give in; he could not break way from it and went on calling me 'Your Majesty,' until I had to escape from him by force.

When this happened, I'd join Csaba in a great, conspiratorial friendship, and for days I'd make fun of poor King Rombertáró. However, I never betrayed our secret. I knew that I would return to him eventually, but I needed the breath of fresh air provided by Csaba, who performed various stunts on the ladder propped against the bee hives. We'd also play acrobat, the sort we had seen in the comic shows at the market, behind the cattle permit office. He also taught me to shoot at sparrows with a catapult, and climbed with me stealthily over the stone wall by Hajdú Alley. The old bastion of the County Hall jutted out at that spot, and for a short distance, the top of our garden wall was level with it. The same stonemason must have built both way back, during the Lord Lieutenancy of one of the several Zimáns appointed to that office.

Just opposite this, a vaulted gateway opened into the narrow, musty prison corridor, at the end of which lived the jailer. We knew his wife: she sold fruit, and bought cherries and apricots from the trees off our orchard. Only the low barred windows opened on this side, and we sometimes ran all the way past them, to and fro; once there appeared some grey shadow, a long prison-shirt and a terrifying lead-coloured face. My heart pounded cruelly; I was terribly frightened, but I *had* to go. We had heard that a bandit called Gergő Oláh was there, and they were going to hang him. At that time Pali Kallós, our neighbour's son, was with us too; and I know it was I who persuaded them that we should see Gergő Oláh. It was evening by then, and there was not a soul in Hajdú Alley. But when we reached the alley I was too scared to go any further. I huddled against the stone wall, but sent the two boys ahead. 'Carry on! The third window is his!'

They set off on all fours in the dusk and between the slanting low windows opposite them, fearsome elongated shadows fell across them in the late twilight. All of a sudden it looked as if two long, transparent ghosts of inhuman size were making their noiseless way along an endless corridor, and there was silence everywhere... Now they had disappeared behind the parapet... It all seemed so inconceivably far away... I let out a frightful scream, and fell half-fainting against the doorstep; all the same, I heard the clatter of the boys' feet as they ran. Someone shouted something nasty at them from a window, then the jailer's wife came and picked me up. This caused a great ruckus at home, and we were forced to kneel on maize for a whole hour in grandma's room. I must have been ten years old at the time, but all through my life that dreadful, fearful glimmering corridor has often haunted me in my dreams, and always as nightmarish and alien as it was then, though later I sometimes went past the place in broad daylight, now grown-up and unaffected. The former prison is now gone; modern cells have been built in the new wing to replace it.

Up to that time, we studied at home with a tutor. It was around then that my mother Klári took me to Aunt Zsófi Wagner's school. It was a provincial small-town all girls-school, run by a lady from Germany, a former governess, whose two grown-up daughters helped her out. Aside from them, a priest from the Piarists came once a week to instruct us; he gave us a little instruction in this and that—I remember he once suspended a lead ball on a string saying that it was a pendulum. But what he might have said about the pendulum after that I cannot really remember. Now my daughters sometimes laugh at this; my knowledge of such things has rubbed off on me since then more by hearsay and reading newspapers, rather unsystematically, to be sure.

Although in Aunt Wagner's school the fees were the same for rich and poor, the little 'townspeople's daughters', the children of the tradesmen and shopkeepers called her 'gnä-ä-ädige fra', while we called her 'Tante'. The German language was proclaimed to be compulsory, and Tante severely chastised anyone who broke this rule. 'But suppose we don't know how to say something?' the daughters of the shoemakers in Magyar Street tried to excuse themselves.

'Then you must ask how to say it!'

'How must we ask?'

Like this : '*Wie sagt man das deutsch?*'

Gradually, we got used to putting the question at the beginning or in the middle of our sentences. We told whole stories like this: 'An' then, *wiezakmandasdeich*, you see…' And this was good enough as an excuse if we were caught speaking Hungarian. Only the Swabian girls, children of a few better-off peasants, spoke German easily in their own drawling, ugly dialect. For some of us, fortunately, German was something of a family tradition—as were one or two maids from the German-speaking area of Szepesség.

Now I often read German books. But *Tante* Sophie did take trouble over our education in other respects as well. Once I became very close with a girl called Maris Nagy, whose father was a ropemaker. The teacher summoned me to her side and explained that I must give this up, there was no future in it: a Miss Pórtelky would be unable to continue such a friendship when she went out into the world, and if we broke it up later, it would cause mutual pain and recrimination.

Today everyone would condemn such a notion, but I believe that she was quite right as things were at that time. She was a sensible woman and knew conditions here; mother Klári chaperoned her daughters once or twice to balls, as did the other ladies concerned in turn. This put her under a considerable obligation.

By this time, the two boys were going to the Catholic grammar-school too, but at home, in the garden and around the styes, we still went on undisturbed for a while, living our lives as young children. I was always with boys—my two brothers, and the boys of the neighbours—I did not really like playing with my dolls. I simply sewed big fancy hats and fashionable ball-gowns for them, the sort that mother Klári had sent from Vienna at that time. I dressed them up, but then abandoned them and went off with the boys.

From a later date I once again have a very vivid recollection…

III.

At that time, all three of us were still sleeping in the old kitchen-building that looked out on the garden. It was a cosy old room where everything reminded one of times long past, of grandmother's youth. This separate part of the building, they said, must have been at least three hundred years old: it was a squat house with thick walls, dormer windows and thick, blackened pine beams in the ceiling of the alcove. The kitchen opened to the left, and on the open veranda was an old stove with an open flue. How clearly I remember our own room! This was where they brought every piece of furniture that had outlived its usefulness in the main house on the street; there was grandma's glass-fronted cupboard with tulle-frilled cotillion-rosettes stuck inside, relics of old and far-famed balls. This was where there hung faded, gilt-framed pastels of crinolined figures and worn red brocade curtains from a village guest-room of long ago. We had big cavernous beds in which sometimes woodworm could be heard ticking, and dented, brass-ornamented cupboards stood here with deep drawers, and a cumbersome oak pedestal-table which we could not even budge. This was regarded as the oldest possession in the family.

Even in those days I sometimes wondered about these things and liked to imagine how many ladies of long, long ago must have touched the velvet tablecloths, now faded rust-red, with their hands; and imagined, too, who might have sat in the carved chairs and on the shabby old ottoman. For this room had always been the home of the Zimán children, and some twenty years before us, mother Klári had slept here just like us, with her three brothers and sisters. They, too, were just as naughty: she, too, had knelt on maize when once she stuck some tar under her young sister Marika's pigtail because they were playing 'doctor,' and she had often seen grandma putting leeches on peasants who were ill.

So old belongings, chatchkis and anecdotes cement the family together—how they make us feel that we are simply the continuation of the lives that were led before us! And all this gives a great sense of security: as they somehow survived, so shall we! Now my thoughts turn again to my three daughters; this has all been dragged from under their feet now, and somehow the world has made a great and sudden change.

Did mother Klári also know such moments of strange and confusing unease when she was fourteen, I wondered at that time? Indeed, did grandma, too, that strict and staid *grande dame*, blush to the roots of her hair at the occasional passing thought, and sometimes feel ashamed in the dark? Then I would lean forward in bed, and prop myself up on my pillows and watch the moonlight from the garden fill the sleeping room with a bluish glow. Out there on the Hajdú corner the melodious, tremulous pipe of the night-watchman signalled eleven o'clock.

Now the sound of a piano comes from the main house. They are dancing the csárdás in the big drawing-room, and my mother, my exquisite, radiant mother, is flaunting her great, mature beauty. The only other ladies around her are Aunt Ilka and the two thin and jolly Reviczky nieces; but as for male guests, every evening there are four or five young men, all surrounding mama, watching her closely and desiring her. It is to her that they speak and turn with their every movement. How affable she is to each of them, in her unforced, assured and simple way! After all, she is still the most beautiful and famous lady for miles around! But has Széchy, the one she loves, turned up today, I wonder? Will he reach out for her hand with a mollifying, casual, negligent gesture—with the usual assured, ironical or furtive desire—over the corner of the piano or the coffee-table, as I once spied him doing? And will mama, with impatient love, retire with him to the divan in the corner with reproaches stifled in excited, heated, angry whispers?... Why, that's where the real, individual life of adults goes on, hidden from us. Love, that's the most important thing, because they all talk about it, faces come to life, avidly or curiously. 'As for us children, they shut us out, the grown-ups do, and won't let us take part in anything!' I thought rebelliously, and my mind immediately switched to the chocolate cake and the raspberry ice-cream that was being brought in, though we didn't get any of that either. I was still a half-infant and half girl.

'Sándorka!' I said suddenly in the direction of the bed opposite me, only because I was so confused inside and I had to speak to someone. "Sándorka, are you asleep?"

'No!' came the immediate and unexpected reply.

'Why not?'

'No reason!'

'Don't be silly! Why not?'

'When I was saying my prayers this evening and we got to "He sits on the right hand of God the Father Almighty," well, I got tired of kneeling and sank down and crouched on my heels. So now I've got to keep thinking that that prayer was invalid.'

'Oh you idiot!' I said in a sudden and incomprehensible fit of rage. 'How can a twelve-year-old boy be so stupid!'

'That's not the only reason,' my younger brother went on hesitantly. 'I want to be awake early in the morning, when Zsuzsi comes for the shoes.'

'What for?'

'Magduska, can you keep a secret? Today Csaba and Jani Kallós caught a crow; it's in the barn under the coop, and tomorrow they want to poke its eyes out. I want to set it free.'

This rather surprised me, and I thought about it. Deep snores could be heard from Csaba.

'All right,' I said later, 'I 'll wake you up early and help you, but you've got to take me up into the hayloft, in your secret room.'

'What secret room?'

'Don't pretend you don't know what I'm talking about, you slyboots! You know very well where you keep the key. That's where mama's old piano-case is, and you've made room inside and you won't allow a girl inside. Just wait till I tell mama what you do up there.'

'I've not smoked a pipe; they never gave me one.'

'There you are! Now you've given yourself away! You smoke tobacco-leaves. If I'm not let in tomorrow, I'll tell the whole story!'

'Oh no, not that! Magduska! All right, I'll let you in.'

'Oh no, you won't!' roared Csaba with a cannibal yell. 'Traitor! Beasts! Villains! You there, girl! You nosy little goose, you should be ashamed of yourself!'

I was not scared of Csaba. The lurking tension burst out of me. In a moment I was enveloped in a feverish rage.

'You've got some nerve, you scoundrel! You eaves-dropper, pretending to be asleep! You famous lady-killer! I'll call Ágnes Kallós here to see you beaten, young man!'

'And they'll beat you too, young lady, if I tell them what I know! What you and Pali Kallós talk about in the apiary, and how once when you were wearing that open-necked jumper he unbuttoned it further down and you let him do it.'

'That's not true! All he said was that his aunt had died of cancer and… You cheeky little liar! You cur! Shut up!'

'Whine away, you viper!' sneered Csaba triumphantly. 'Whee!…'

I didn't know what I was doing. My hand lighted on an iron candlestick on the table and I hurled it towards him in the dark. The next minute I regretted it and would have liked to apologize, but he opened his mouth, howling and bellowing as he cried. Minutes passed, and he went on roaring without a break, full of fury and renewed strength. Now the maid had woken up in the kitchen next door. Someone rattled the door of the garden-house.

'Open up there! Zsuzsi! They're killing each other in there!'

It was mother. I was almost glad that she had come and that I should be punished and then things would return to normal again.

'What have you done? What's the matter with him? Why, he's covered in blood!'

I was scared to death; I wanted to run to her, cry and kiss her a thousand times, but I knew that now I was wicked anyway and I could not utter a single word.

'She threw the candlestick at me, the iron one. My shoulder's broken. It's covered in blood!'

'Stop crying! Let me have a look. Oh you heathen, just you wait!'

'He started it!' I shouted at last and burst into tears, quivering. 'He poked fun at me and scolded me. He's shut a bird up in the barn and tomorrow he wants to poke out its eyes. And every day they smoke in the piano-case.'

'Heavens above! The little heathens! Fire-raisers!'

'Yes, and she hides in the apiary with Pali and unbuttons the neck of her blouse.'

'Oh you rascal! What am I to do with you? Oh, what a curse God has laid on me! Just you wait! Where's that rolling-pin?…'

She ran right across the room to the threshold, where Zsuzsi was propping the doorpost. There grandma stood silently blocking her way. There was a nightlight in her hand, the black silk petticoat she was wearing was buttoned all the way down, and the pearl-studded lace coif was carefully placed on the shining hair that was smoothed down over her temples. She raised the nightlight and surveyed the room.

'That's just my bad luck!' my mother clutched at her head. 'They drench each other in pools of blood! I'll beat her to death!'

She made a mad dash towards me, but grandma grabbed her hand and sat her down in the chair. 'Oh my God!' said mama helplessly, and hid her face in her hands.

Grandma put down the lamp on Csaba's bed, while he let her pull his shirt to one side without saying a word.

'It's only a scratch,' she said calmly and asked Zsuzsi to fetch some cold water. 'But it might have dented his head, too!'

She went across to Sándorka's bed, where all the while he had been shivering and whimpering, stiff with cold. She stroked his head gently, almost imperceptibly.

'Whatever am I to do with her?' mother asked later, pointing at me resignedly and bitterly.

'Just leave her alone,' said grandma severely, as she carefully bandaged Csaba's aching arm. Then she came over with the lamp and illuminated my ravaged face.

'She's reached an awkward age,' grandma said slowly and thoughtfully, then turned away. 'She's a big girl now!' she added again somewhat later.

I did not get a beating, and as the night slowly relaxed into peace, roused from the soothing calm and the quick breathing of slumber, I saw the gentle yellow light of grandma's lamp still glowing on the big oak table in the dark alcove. They were still sitting together; my mother was leaning on her elbow, and the wide sleeve of her flowered, billowing batiste dress had slipped back in wrinkles, exposing her dainty wrist and her beautiful rounded arm where the old gold snake-bracelet hung. The straight, gaunt figure of grandma sat stiff and tense against the back of the wooden chair; brown shadows stretched out around her as if in some old grease-stained picture depicting a scene illuminated by a night-light.

'You're thirty-one years old, my child!' she said quietly but firmly into the silence, in support of some earlier argument.

Mama gazed into the light, her face impassive.

'There's no end to long drawn-out love affairs like this,' she went on relentlessly. 'For a good while I thought something would come of it, but as things are, enough is enough. It's been all of four years...'

'But mother! After all, it's my own...'

'All right! All right! Up to now it's been your own affair, and

I haven't interfered in it, Klári. Look here, my child; you've been here at home now for more or less ten years, and I've never bothered you about these matters. At first I let you be: you, too, live your own life, you had a pretty bad luck with your husband. When the four of you came home, though you were a widow, you still had the mind of a child.'

'And whose fault was that?' My mother shrugged her shoulders in a half-defiant, half-fearful movement.

'Nobody can look into the future, Klári. You know that two more children were growing up after you; you were young when your hand was asked for, so I gave my permission. You were sixteen years old then and your husband thirty-five at the time, it's true, but he was in good health and well off. He was a leading lawyer with four assistants. And that was the time when the Pórtelek estate was divided with Ábris. In the confused world then, the law was the best profession. Who could foresee that he would take to drink because of his acquisitions and feverish night work? It's a good thing that pneumonia carried him off, poor man, before everything else would have followed him.'

I had a good view of mother's illuminated face in the darkness of the alcove, but grandma could not have noticed the despondent convulsion that shook her whole body.

'Well, yes,' she went on in a milder tone, 'you were so very beautiful I didn't regret it. Live your own life! Enjoy yourself! By that time I'd married off my two other girls; your father was dead, too, and your brother was still at school. There was room for you here. You had no worries about a house or for the children; I took those on myself. I was an orphan, and my fate was to struggle beside your father till the end. I'm not complaining. I was cut out for it. In a lifetime we doubled the little that we had and lived and brought up children decently.'

Now mother's movements became almost impatient.

'So for years now I've never interfered in your affairs, Klári. People's tongues have wagged, but I have been here; sometimes I've sat among your guests and preserved decorum. Nobody has dared ridicule *my* house. Make your own choices, I thought. First of all there was Bojér. You strung him along for awhile, and in the end you said he was too old. True, he was a widower, but he was the leading landowner in the county. The Gebey boy came along, and that didn't come to anything either. You speculated about Kendy, a married man; true, his wife had had a stroke and couldn't move, but she's still alive today in a wheelchair. And now there's this Széchy—sometimes he's here, sometimes he isn't. I hear he took the actress out for a ride the day before yesterday.'

'How much people think they know!' My mother banged the table petulantly. She straightened up and her eyes glinted angrily. Grandma watched her unmoved, almost with indifference.

'All right then,' she said, 'don't let's talk about him. There's something else I want to say. You know that I have a son.'

Mother Klári turned to her in astonishment.

'Look! Today István is deputy district notary. But in a couple of years' time old Bélteky's sure to retire, and he'll get his job. That's a fine thing for someone so young. Yes, indeed! Well, if István gets married, they'll live here.'

'Aha!' said mama with a touch of bitterness.

'Yes. I shall keep an eye on my daughter-in-law.'

'Well, is it true, mother, that… the little Kallós girl…'

'Don't you worry about her just yet!… But there's something else, Klári. I've found decent husbands for all three of you, haven't I? You also know that since your father died I've cleared up the Bere land. When we bought it together, it was half encumbered. What the tenant pays has since gone to that. Now my only concern is to provide for the three of you. For Bere will belong to my son, I'm telling you that here and now.'

There was a sudden silence… I think my mother was not unprepared for this.

'When you were widowed, you received ten thousand forints by right… I don't know how much of that still remains. Here you've only spent money on clothes— quite a lot, to be sure! I am giving each of my daughters fifteen thousand. Your children will have eight thousand each.'

'Why are you telling me this, mother?' she asked rather sensitively. 'I can live somewhere else, separately too.'

''That's empty talk. You know it's impossible. *Here* I'm the one who's looked after you… at all events… I want you to get married, Klári.'

'With a rabble like this?' Mama nodded towards us sullenly and despondently.

'They're nothing! You're very beautiful… The boys will leave home and go away to study. The girl… She's a big girl now. In a year or two…'

'Will she be pretty, I wonder?'

'She'll be interesting! She's just developing… She's over four-teen. Next winter you can take her to balls. As I see it, that puss won't be a trouble to you for long.'

She stood up and silently crossed the room; she had a look beyond the curtain over the alcove. We were all breathing peace-fully and deeply. 'They're asleep,' she said.

She stopped for a minute at the head of my bed.

'Starting tomorrow, she will sleep upstairs in your room, Klári!'

She stayed there for a moment and I felt the beam from her big, serious eyes as it shone on my closed eyelids. Then she turned round, quietly took the lamp, nodded and went out.

I still seemed to see her as a tall, beautiful figure, straight as a ramrod. She was a complete person in every sense of the word; her love was fair and shared, her will implacable, restrained and shrewd; she was by nature a real monarch. She had a single desire: to promote the family; and for this she worked and struggled with composure, superiority and dispassion through her whole life, while she herself was always certain of her choices and aims. As she dealt with enemies, friends, business-people or her own family, I never saw her question her own words, think something over twice, in two different ways, take the wrong course or start something again.

My mother still sat there for a time, staring ahead in the dark. Her face was ruminative but calm; I could see that she harboured not a single rebellious or hostile thought against what she had heard. 'Grandma's right,' I thought with calm and simple conviction.

At that time we—mother, grandmother and child—were still able to understand each other so naturally, steadfastly and trustfully. Maybe we were no more humble or better than people today, but just somehow more like each other.

IV.

Those little high-heeled shoes of mine with their old-fashioned adornments, that beribboned baby hat, that first teenage girl's outfit, the stays and a tunic—my God, what becomes of the rags of old dresses, the actions of our former selves, the traces of betwixt-and-between days, the unassuming hours that have long fled away? How good it would be to seek out everything again: the colourful minutes of our youth, the lilt of our words, the old colour of our clothes and hair, and the hue of the rays of the sun that danced and shone on us back then; the forgotten or unknown reasons for all that happened to us, reasons that lie concealed in the grey depths of those long-lost or distant days, behind some secret blind in our souls. It would be good now—for of all the things in this great wide world the most interesting to me, after all, is myself—if everything here were suddenly to lose its colour and the scene around us were to turn grey; only those days are really lost to us which we cannot remember...

Pointed, polished shoes, ribbons and a tunic; a velvet vanity case on my arm—this was how I tripped along County Street to the sewing-school. And from behind the half-closed shutters the reproof, criticism, knowing or appreciation of women's eyes sharpened with close observation, blazing furtively after me. 'Why, there goes little Magda Pórtelky!' could be heard on those quiet noondays as the bells rang by the winking window-eyes of the old familiar houses. They had already taken me into account and initiated me into the ranks of those with whom they might occupy themselves, as someone who would be talked about in this way or that; slowly and cautiously a row of green blinds or two would rise higher behind me and I sensed how these glances fixed on my heels, above the curve of my waist and the pleats of my skirt, and how they ran all over me like the cautious probing of needle-sharp hooks.

From the dimness of these window-niches this was the way the concealed pairs of eyes measured the passage of time for decades; they measured values, possible connections, the appearance on stage of new figures—life itself. It was along the length of County Street that one had to—first and foremost—be accepted, accustom oneself to the role of newcomer, or one who has outgrown childhood or someone who was going somewhere in the world, from the Hajdú Town all the way to Castle Garden Street. This, and no more, was my own world, and perhaps deep down within me the colours and rules of this world still exist today; but now I know that nobody's world is any wider than this. It is merely different.

'She's a shapely young lass with tiny feet, the sort who can dance!' Kind Aunt Bélteky's window blinked indulgently after me from under the curious gabled stone eaves. 'Her little girl's breasts have the shape of her mother's; just let that little chicken-neck fill out a bit and become a plump pigeon!'

'She's got the Pórtelky bump on the bottom of her little nose,' Mother Reviczky's window commented, giving half a twitch like a shrugging shoulder. 'To be sure, her mouth isn't exactly small either, but there's something odd about it. Like a gypsy girl with a snow-white face, that's it! It's her eyes that do it...'

'And she knows how to use them too!' retorted Ilka Zimán's ancient sunken house on the corner, with its cunningly raised, pointed eyebrows.

It was as if the two shifty windows or the wary eyes of their mistresses kept beckoning me with secret malice. 'There, she's a clever little thing already, that's all I'm saying; good blood, lively—not letting the grass grow beneath her feet—' she is always on guard, so that her words can be turned into a compliment in case the news somehow gets back to grandma.

For everyone here was scared of grandma; they feared and respected her, and we, her family, consciously and gratefully took advantage of this, the prestige and significance that she radiated over us, her life, intelligence, haughtiness, money or prudent behaviour. I quickly became aware of the small correlations of life that in due course I should have to get along with. I grew from strong, dominating, totally unsentimental stock, and all my talents were destined for life and vitality. The network of family connections heard from childhood, family animosities or obligations generations old—all these I had at my finger-tips, so to speak, and they vibrated instinctively in the tone of my greetings and calculated precisely how deeply I inclined my head.

'Good day!' I said with impeccable graciousness but lengthening the vowel to give it a formal edge when young Vodicska, as was his custom, raised his round, urban businessman's hat with a deep flourish; but he also must have seen that at the same moment I was smiling and turning my head away as I nodded lightly but intimately across the road to return some 'country lad's' greeting. 'Good day!' my own voice re-echoed inside me while I judged whether it was correct—and all of a sudden I was struck by his greeting, 'I kiss your hand!'—the odd, endearing, jesting, indulgent or malicious intimate tone of it. 'Just look at him!' the blood flared up in my face with the sudden anger of a little girl. 'What an arrogant breed!' For he came from beyond County Street, from the outer, neighbouring world.

Beyond the Castle Garden and the vast estate park are the new-style, showy, stone-turreted estate houses where the Count's officials lived—manager, bailiff, steward and others, families who had foreign-sounding names—who knows where they had been picked up—and with an unknown past. We knew that some, at the whim of their patron, had promoted their great-great grandfathers from being stokers or grooms or the like. Vodicska's father, the old surveyor, had been a kind of companion to the counts, so they said; the young gentlemen were inspired to study through his diligence. And after that he went with them to foreign parts, too, and to this very day shrewdly maintained this semi-friendly link.

I knew that in his own circle this ancient, foxy-faced man was highly regarded; the inspector himself courted his favour—only through his cunning was he able to push through the crafty schemes of the estate to seize all kinds of land for distribution and marshy tracts. And his son, alas, would continue this; he had come home after his law examinations and was now solicitor to the estate. And now he displays his newly-fashionable bowler hat, his brilliantly-polished elegant shoes and his silk necktie. To me, of all people! Just look at him!

The men in our family nevertheless wear leather gaiters, bushy cravats and soft light hats; these they snatch off with a swift, angular fling, suddenly and briskly, with the brotherly delight of a playmate: 'We kiss your little hand, Maggie!'

My pedigree—every trait and strength of my own powerful, fine, distinguished family that preserves its position at the top—I proudly felt to be fresh and unbroken still in myself. Except that I already had a conscious knowledge of a great deal that my forbears had discovered only by instinct, and that I had now learned. Chiefly the trademark of the gentlewoman.

Standing in front of the mirror, I sometimes watch a new line or two in my face and stared at it, fascinate... a long time as I was with an unpremeditated telling expression or a pretty movement of the head; then I took note of it and used it, keeping it in reserve like a useful weapon. I observed my mother's great, complete, unsurpassable and simple beauty and was not depressed by it. 'I shall be different!' I thought. My nature was altogether more lively, mobile, compact and excitable. It seemed as if the ancestral womanliness of our family had still blossomed out in me for the first and last time, for liveliness and joy, but also for trouble and the threat of change. I contemplated the unusual line of my volatile mouth, the thin, quivering sides of my nostrils as my fathers' hawk-like hard hook of a nose narrowed and acquired refinement above them, and the coquettish, satanic black strands of hair fluttered in curls around my head, and I knew that it was with my eyes that I could do what I wanted. I sensed that others could look at me for a long time without feeling bored, that I rarely looked the same twice, and that anyone describing me would need a large and varied vocabulary.

My mother's life was open to me; I loved her and was proud of her. In her I saw a bold contempt, a fine, strong libertinism that was watched for and envied—and secretly censured. For us, this was possible! The famous Klára Zimán might drive out on Sundays before High Mass with the old mogul Bojér in his carriage and four; from her window she might send teasing and open signals in the direction of the young county clerks in their office opposite to us, just as a joke. Last year, in broad daylight, Széchy's half-mad rhymester of a manservant brought her expensive camellias every day, and half the town looked on and discussed it. And now that this was over, nobody could see a trace of repentance remaining in her; she was merely possessed by a haughty, impudent anger, a full-throated jocularity, as she nonchalantly captured a new man for each of her fingers. Never was there such a procession of suitors to our house, not even when she was first of marriageable age!—so grandma was wont to say sometimes, severely but without protestation.

The Telekdy boy, that clean-shaven young dreamer who had come home after studying abroad, was the most recent to haunt the house. One bright summer morning, on his way back from some party, he suddenly turned up in our courtyard with Bankó's entire band and positioned the gypsies under the eaves of the kitchen-block. 'Play away, damn you! A beautiful woman like that deserves it when she's mixing flour with her snow-white hands!'

I can see it now! Red and yellow roses were bursting into bloom, and the glass balls on the stakes in the big flower-bed reflected the burning heat of the noonday sun with their varied colours. From the direction of the garden-gate, sucking pigs squealed hungrily in the sty, the effervescent aroma of ripe raspberries floated around and the stifling warm steam from the dunghill quivered in gentle ripples in the torrid air. The band played in front of the privet shrubs.

Telekdy, leaning against the door-post, turned his intoxicated, unusual, but attractive face and greedy eyes to follow my mother's every movement; she displayed her white arms, bare to the elbow, petulant, laughing and blushing as she baked scones. 'Today everyone will be talking about this,' I thought with a thrill of delight. The eyes of County Street are on us! But that's all to the good—for us it's permitted! To flourish, peacock around, accept homage, and in our youth, to live out everything that is beautiful to our pleasure, with dancing and style! Live out love—*beautifully*!

For since those days I have known many kinds of people from other parts of the country, but I really believe that nowhere else in the whole wide world do they know how to live out love with such lovely play-acting, such dynamism, sadness, impetuosity and pageantry as they did long ago in these parts. People since then have learnt more; they possess all kinds of knowledge, but in achieving this they have grown coarse. Their rambling words are shot through immediately with crude and relentless straightforward desire (their theatricality is a gauche, declamatory pose), with the hideous yearning of a lovelorn cat devoid of pride, or with the arrogant and false, shameful clumsiness of their contempt for women. A beautiful and refined culture has been lost by degrees, they might say in modern parlance; nowadays they have no time to learn the art of courting women. And they have forgotten how far the delightful, frenzied, defiant and bitter bravado of the love-battle outweighs the 'end,' which in itself is commonplace and disillusioning.

Nowhere have words so many shades of colour and perfume, nowhere so much hidden meaning, than when they spring, briefly and significantly, from a thousand repressed emotions. Nowhere does grief hide itself in such fine haughtiness, nowhere do they know how to sacrifice a life to a person for a single minute of superiority as in those days, in this region bounded by ancient marshlands and unruffled reeds and streams. Once in the half-light of evening, I saw my mother's face, the haughty twitch of her mouth, when on the way home from some walk or tea-party, she boldly threaded her hand under young Telekdy's arm, because at that moment Széchy, who for months had not crossed her threshold, was suddenly seized with the desire to escort her home once again. 'Yes,' I thought with a sudden blaze of emotion, 'a moment like that counts for a very great deal!'

'Men almost always come back,' said grandma about that time. 'They give it a try; they won't resign themselves to the fact that women, too, may forget them. But such new beginnings never bring any reward.'

She was knowledgeable about things like this. In her clever head she kept turning over these odd games of life, which may be life's chief meaning and explanation. But here everyone concerned themselves with the affairs of lovers. Mother Klári and Széchy went around in broad daylight in the public gaze; their affair was common knowledge, it was discussed and put into song. There was sympathy even in the scandal itself, respect and compassion for them, as if they were acting on stage, perhaps half for the sake of the observing eyes. There was something peasant-like in this, but here, to this day the whole style and speech of the gentry are close to those of the peasant, though more colourful and flowery. Sometimes, even now, I myself find it difficult to string words together as they do in books, though they say the literary language itself came from this region. I've seen many fine, upstanding peasant lads in my life, some of such good appearance and jaunty manner, with blazing eyes and self-confidence, that all they needed to do was change clothes with one of the young district administrators. I know that this area produced the most songs; and nowhere has given birth to so many minstrels, rhymers, literary lights and famous people throughout history as our county. At least, that's what I've read somewhere. And nowadays, I've often contemplated the stone statue of the poet Kölcsey* with his elongated forehead and clouded eyes—one of them was blind— and it was as if his head bowed in grief as he sat there now for a couple of years surrounded by the railings in the acacia-shaded corner of the square. He came from this part of the world, too, and was a close relative of ours.

Oh dear! How I've been rambling on, as old women do...! It occurs to me now that in those days long, long ago when I was a little girl, I was just as able to ruminate and lose myself in daydreams as I can now in the peaceful autumn days of my life. Except that then it was still about life to come, as now it is about life that is past, but both are just as coloured with conviction and imagination. In between these times, I lived in the hub of life; I looked neither to the right nor to the left, but simply made my way through things as if I were battling some turbulent flood, or fluttering up above it for a time in fickle prosperity on the sunlit surface. But then from the beginning, I seemed to be living a truer and more introverted life.

Sometimes I was still allowed to go down to the old nursery, among the great worm-eaten beams, with the centuries-old furniture, the crinolined portraits and the peculiar cotillion figures. How strange the silence was here sometimes! I gave the two boys their coffee and drove them out to school with bossy kindliness. How much I had grown out of their company! 'Viper!' Csaba still hissed at me on occasion in his rage, but he already boasted about me to his school friends because the priests who taught in the grammar-school greeted me first at the corner of the church on the way from mass. I no longer pestered him about the 'room' in the piano-case either, and sometimes I would filch one or two real cigarettes for him from the guests' table.

'There you are, you rascal!' I hit him on the back to make up for it. And I would tell Sándorka to leave his books out for me if they went out.

It was a peculiar delight to rest like this, and instead of dusting sometimes I would peep inside the books with the hungry mind of a girl. I discovered drawings with secret, strange signs and unknown numerals, and I mused that once upon a time

---

* *Ferenc Kölcsey* (1790–1838), poet, critic and politician, was the author of the Hungarian National Anthem (1823). He was chief notary of the county of Szatmár and represented it at the Diet of 1832. Nagykároly ("Szinyér") was the county town where he worked, hence the statue.

there must have lived people who devoted their lives to this business of discovering them, and even today they must surely be doing it still in the far distance. What distant, strange aims and fates there must be in the faraway great world, of which we may never hear anything at all here!... Then I came across texts of Latin translation, and I cut the pages which had been left untouched by schoolboys' pencils and dirty fingerprints. The poems told of an old maritime people, of the world of battles, and of the destroyed or rebuilt walls of cities. 'If I were a boy,' it once struck me, 'might I perhaps get far away from here?'... This thought, the dream of distant places in the world, was so incredible here, so foreign to all that surrounded me. In the midst of the great rich abundance—carts full of wheat, tubs full of lard, serried ranks of bacon-sides, fattened geese, the world of name-day parties and feasts—travelling without necessity seemed to be some incredible foible and a mad waste of money. Nor did the idea really enter anyone's head: wicked old Telekdy was criticized throughout the county for banishing his only son to distant foreign parts when his mother died, under the pretext of a study-tour. He knew why he was doing it! 'An honest man has most honour in his own nest!' said Ábris Pórtelky, my paternal uncle, who never crossed the county boundary in his lifetime, though he was sixty years old or so. And he only left Pórtelek, the ancient village tucked away behind the marsh, when there was a county assembly or family get-together; it was said that he had never yet travelled by train.

Distant, foreign worlds, unknown roads! All the same, I sometimes thought about them at this time. If only someone would take me! If only a man would take me...! And I clasped my hands idly, dropping the duster, and looked out over the leaves quivering on the fruit trees and the silent, sun-drenched garden. During this first awkward and astonished period of growing into womanhood, there are such marvellous surges of emotion. How suddenly does all the arrogance and the frivolous ribald curiosity of a girl disappear with the swiftly-maturing consciousness of virginity! With shamed vexation, I thought of Pali Kallós and of our petty, improper talks with shame and vexation, and for the occasional minute, I saw the affair of women and men with each other in an entirely different, clearer and more serious light. If I had been sent to a convent-school or something of that kind, I wondered, might not I have become at this time just such a silent and withdrawn woman as Ágnes Kallós, grandma's goddaughter, thanks to their domestic severity?... 'If only someone were to catch sight of me and fall in love with me,' I thought in these rare, solitary moments of day-dreaming, 'someone from far away, someone who lives a different life, and who would carry me off to the unknown!' For just as with the terrifying adventures in the prison passage when I was a little child, so now I could only imagine this and everything else happening through *someone else*, through a man. 'If some very great gentleman were once to catch a glimpse of me... Count Lajos, the younger Szinyéry maybe..., if he were to survey the county ball, supposing they take me there for the first time...' Suddenly I threw up my head in shame and shrugged my shoulders, mocking myself at the same time. A Count Szinyéry? Who was he? I recalled my Uncle Ábris's sourly haughty affirmations about our own older and more genuine nobility, as opposed to the owners of estates acquired by accident and corruption.

Royal servitors, bowing and scraping pro-Habsburg loyalists, courtiers ready to lick the boots of foreigners—none of these could be found in that branch of the Pórtelky family that remained lesser gentry. The other branch, the cousins whose degradation had raised them to the barony, whose father had stooped so low as to join the government commissaries after the defeat of the 1848 revolution, were scorned and anathematized by the ancestral marshland that gave them their name and the wrathful, haughty dynasty and estate that remained here. 'Oh!' I thought, my face suddenly blushing scarlet, 'What's a Count Szinyéry to us?'

'On with the dusting, young lady, hurry up!', my mother burst in with a rush. 'The housemaid's ironing collar-frills for you. It's your job today to dust the drawing room.'

Startled, I recovered myself and went upstairs to dust the leather-bound albums, the silver salver for visiting cards, the porcelain match-holder with the two gold-tailed peacocks, and the shiny black legs of the big piano. I shook the duster out into County Street, and with the scattered specks of dust there came forth from me all the idle, dreamy thoughts that could not be harnessed to words. Perhaps only now, in the twilight of my becalmed days, will they swarm back again and gather in my greying head.

I shook out the duster and leaned out after it for a minute; from under my red head-scarf tied at the back, I shook forward all the curly black ringlets of hair and propped open the upper shutter. I leaned forward with a smile, stealthily and with backward glances, as if followed by the gaze of a stern mother. This was an instinctive piece of hypocrisy; after all, I knew my mother would not mind and now even grandma would not say a word against it. I nodded to the young sheriff's secretary, who at that time was reputed to be the best dancer; with my head on one side and leaning on one arm against the window frame, I returned his gaze without stirring. With delighted surprise, he turned his face sideways and gazed back, then suddenly halted and hurried over from the other side of the street. 'It worked!' I exulted secretly, and quickly leaned out on my elbows for a couple of smiling words, rapid and playful questions. I could see very well that Jenő Vodicska was just turning the corner—costumed in his gleaming shoes and fine new grey suit.

V.

They sent the Gách silk dresses from Pest, and quivering with delight, we knelt around the big brown box on the floor of the drawing-room. My mother's was a loose creation in grass-green with a garland of tiny, strawberry-red roses; mine was the compulsory white. There were the gold-speckled, pointed evening shoes too, and flowered hair-ornaments.

It was Hanika who took them out with her long, pale, freckled fingers—our ugly little red-haired seamstress, who for weeks clattered away on the machine in the corner of the glass-roofed veranda. What a kind, good, poor little soul she was, hollow-chested and tall as a lamp-post. Only now do I realize, looking back, what a difficult thing it is to observe the good fortune of others from close range in silence and calm. But she was devoted to us; for a few kind words from us she melted into fidelity and love. What devotion and intimacy there was in the way she lifted out the dresses, masterpieces from foreign craftsmen, holding them on both sides with the tips of her fingers and lifting them up high until red blotches appeared beneath her two tiny greenish eyes from enthusiasm. 'Oh, aren't they splendid! There isn't a single incorrect stitch in this one! Oh my!' she would say as she helped us on with it, and ran her narrow, bone-dry palm right over the cloudy tulle pleats, along the proud line of our hips and bosoms.

At first we waited for her to unpack them, excited and full of wonder, then we clapped and my mother and I embraced each other, laughing and rolling on the floor of the room. And when all this splendour and beauty of a master's hand was upon us, how we stood silently, backs straight and eyes gleaming, pale with excitement in front of the full-length mirror! My mother took hold of the green billows of the rustling, swaying train, turned and bowed, advanced and then sat down suddenly. This was something I still had to learn, to handle gracefully, be able to throw it over my arm with ease, or make it flow behind me in a snaking curve. How easily movements in this kind of dress might have become comical! For this very reason it was a refined and noble art to deal daintily with it, in the feverish turns of the dance, floating, twirling or tiptoeing on the spot, never forgetting ourselves totally, or what we owed to external appearances and to our superior status.

We joined hands and floated in a waltz around the big dining-room, swaying gently and smoothly with our supple waists. Hanika hummed a tune for us in her stifled, colourless little wisp of a voice and hurried to push the chairs out of our way. 'They're the most beautiful of all! There's none like them in the world!' she sighed feverishly and exultantly. Grandma opened the door on us; she stood there nodding and observant.

'Five hundred forints for the two of them... for that they should be pretty, too!' she said half to herself. 'But they really are magnificent, so they are,' she added more enthusiastically. 'They fit both of you like a glove!'

She swiftly turned around and went back into her big room overlooking the courtyard. In recent days, she had not had much time for us. She sat in the alcove of the window where the floor was raised, as if on a throne, and held audience for her own clients—those who obtained small sums of money from her at a good rate of interest, applicants for leases or agents for cheap plots of land, solicitors, tradesmen and merchants. The most frequent caller was Lipi, our nimble and clever Jew who was good for anything; he was her client and her business confidant. Now all her energy was devoted to her life's great desire: the elevation of the family through the one and only male heir.

István, indeed, was thirty years old and deputy public notary; next door Ágnes, grandma's favourite, smoothly groomed and in a white muslin dress, grew imperceptibly into a gentle church-mouse of a girl; she was two years older than I was and so very different. 'As for this lot here, just let them get on with things quickly and as best they can!'—this thought was obvious in the whole way grandma treated us. She felt that our style and everything we employed to achieve it were quite different, and she did not pester my mother over the expense of the dresses. She knew they were our armour, with which we had to be victorious and conquer an all-important battle of life.

When Lipi left grandmother, he would look in on me cheerfully as I sat in the covered terrace. 'How grown-up you are, Miss Magda! You've grown beautiful too! There's a new factory in Kolozsvár that makes the most splendid walnut furniture. I'll get hold of some for the price they sell it to me!'

Trézsi, the gypsy rag-and-bone woman came along and marvelled at me. 'Oh you darling! Oh you beauty! How my little brother's going to play at your wedding!' Old Náni Spach brought along a knapsack full of Transylvanian skirts, embroidered white linen underskirts and kerchiefs; she, too, might put down her bundle on the veranda if she had found my mother in a good mood, have a cup of milky coffee and tell tales of the damask tablecloths and three-year old home-made embroideries of that year when there was a good crop of flax, which the merchants from Lőcse were taking to the market at Debrecen the following autumn. 'Just in time!' she said and ran her old, fawning eyes right over me.

So now I was in the public eye; everyone observed me and took notice of me. It became my duty to stir things up a little in this small world in order to ensure that something would happen to me that would settle my fate quickly.

But all the same, I know that there was much that was fortuitous in the success of my first public appearance, and at the same time of my whole life as a debutante at the various balls. I knew that grandma, guided by a good instinct at that time, smoothed over all the little resentments among the Pórtelky clan in the country, whose unmarried sons came in and set the tone at carnival festivities. Maybe that was the first time when one or another of the young men who passed by my window may have begun to mention it.

'As sure as I'm here, Maggie Pórtelky's going to take the place of honour among the girls this season!'

My mother gave a few dinners at the beginning of the winter, and with her graciousness impressed and distinguished herself even among those whom in earlier times she had not given a second glance to. She was very charming in this new role of an attentive and anxious mother. A few of the 'extra special' men from the estate were also invited once or twice; Scherer the inspector's son excused himself; he would not make peace. Behind this lay an old and very sad story: the tragic death of their beautiful young daughter Ilonka, whom around that time the famous Pista Széchy began to court madly on a peculiar impulse and against all convention. It was then that my mother, either from sheer feminine malice or vanity, or even possibly from a real surge of love, boldly and deliberately enticed him into her circle and bound him to herself, while the romantic, lovelorn girl got hold of some strychnine from her father's veterinary medicine chest. That was six years ago, but it is difficult to forget things like that...

But Jenő Vodicska was there. I remember he was talking about legal matters with grandma, and she said he had a good head. Then later she aroused a passionate sympathy in Telekdy. The latter always had the reputation for being an eccentric with his rather exaggerated ideas about equality and the unique status of the mind, his foreign, 'good for nothing' knowledge, and his philosophical books.

'How he stands out in these surroundings, but all the same what an unpleasant mixture there is in him!' I sometimes thought, but mother Klári had a naive admiration for him and I saw that she was proud of him. For her it was unusual for anyone to talk of such matters with her; yet his courtship of her was marked by its elegant pace and traditionally fine homage.

I was taken to the county ball first. I wore my tuberose-ornamented white silk dress with a train. When Hanika had brushed, arranged and put up my hair in curls, and my mother had gently enveloped my shoulders in clouds of fine powder, and I stood in front of my mirror in full array with my slender figure, in the dignity and proud finery of my youth, the belief that I should be second to none gradually developed in me into utter certainty. Perhaps there might have been reason for me to fear and doubt, to consider that among so many other similarly finely-arrayed beautiful young girls there I, too, might fade into the shadows. But it was with the glow of this stimulating and exultant belief in my eyes that I stepped into the room beneath the luxurious radiance of all the lamps. This gave all my movements confidence and harmony; this was why I was bold and direct in the language of the eyes, both giving and receiving, and this was how there came to my mind swift, appropriate, original and clever notions, genial questions and fresh, witty retorts, too, that later were to be passed from mouth to mouth. I never looked at the other girls with calculating, envious glances or worry in my eyes; I felt that *I* was the only one here, and all was for my pleasure. Maybe this was wrong and by no means fair, but it paid off.

A lovely, intoxicating whirl of a carnival; a being fêted, light, glittering and freed from care, the ball, the ball!... The hazy, jumbled memories of it radiate a rose-tinted gaiety, a soothing, calming, womanly consciousness over a long life. That was me, that was what I was once upon a time!

Those fleeting times were joyous and lovely; those bright and radiant colours, those light and hovering years. They seemed to fly past me to the rhythm of a waltz amid sweet and profound day-dreams. Sometimes even now I float and whirl like this in my dreams; the tunes of the old waltzes that were fashionable then come back—and then I wake up in a happy mood.

Yet the vitality of the long, hot supper-csárdás was more suited to me. Near to the gypsies, with one or other partner of like mind, passionately whirling and pulsating, only through some sparkling, golden fiery mist did I sense that everyone around me in the ballroom was growing weary and silent, that only a few couples were still dancing, and that even they gave up in the end, and then gathering around us, they watched us—they watched me; the way I lost myself and merged with every movement, the pulsing of my blood, even my thoughts, in the music and the bewitching, mad spirit of the dance.

There can be no more delightful intoxication than this; and even if love gives its all, it cannot surpass such total forgetfulness of movements, eyes and passions…

'She's very flirtatious! Like quicksilver, she is! She'll pick a quarrel with anyone!' remarked one or two sharp-eyed women, but rather, it was for something to say, simply as a statement of fact. For it was absolutely unthinkable that anyone should dare to express a hint of disapproval or reproof to us. Behind us stood a protective band of male relations ready to fight a duel—a sheriff brother-in-law, an old friend of a deputy-sheriff, a public notary cousin, grandma's clientele, mother's courtiers, and country relatives who would close ranks in case of trouble. Everyone silently noted all this. 'She's her mother's daughter!' said Ilka Zimán, with an indulgent wink. 'Just see, everything looks splendid on her! If she were to wear the little chair as a dress, if she were to turn cartwheels… For a beauty, everything is permissible!'

My mother and I danced a quadrille in the same *colonne*, and she was always opposite to me. This was my wish; I sensed that this way we made an attractive, original and pleasant sight. 'Has mama got a partner yet?' I asked my admirers zealously.

By the end of the carnival season we were used to having Jenő Vodicska as our obligatory shadow. We entrusted him with the cloaks and fans; he handled them with gentle solicitude, and while I was dancing I often saw him standing in the doorway or leaning against a pillar, gazing at me warmly and observantly with delight. But in the meantime he chatted with others, too, sedately and pleasantly; he did not make himself conspicuous. His well-groomed—too well-groomed—figure and attractive, somewhat dimpled masculine face were not bad accessories.

At dinner he sat at our table but not usually next to me. 'What's that domestic tutor of a boy keeping you company for, Maggie?' the Kehiday boys, my second cousins, sometimes whispered with fretful jealousy. I shrugged my shoulders with a coquettish laugh. Then they told little malicious tales about him; once he had plucked up enough courage and tried to go on a spree, but it was quite out of keeping and after the fourth glass of wine he got a stomach-ache. And the only way he could dance was to start off on the left foot from the right-hand corner of the chest of drawers at home.

I did not listen to them. I dipped my tongue in champagne and gazed into the eyes of Bankó the gypsy bandleader as they shone with slow fire at me. He was a fine figure of a young gypsy, and it was for me that he played, head bowed, grateful for even a single smile, and with resignation and humility. Slowly and deeply affected, he came closer to me, put on a mute and struck up an ancient, difficult lament for the tárogató.* Everyone grew silent and stared ahead, spellbound; the old, stifled grief of distant generations hovered above the table full of revellers, drawing people of the same type into a community of secret understanding, towards each other. I gazed at him once again, and in a trance my eyes became dazzled by the diamond fire of his ring. It sparkled as it danced on the lean brown hand that plied the bow; I knew that on a trip abroad, an English royal princess had once sent it to him through her master of ceremonies, for out there, our own pampered and much appreciated violinist, the young brother of Trézsi the rag-and-bone woman, was an 'artiste'.

He was a distinguished figure here at that moment, virtually the only totally sober man among the champagne-quaffing gentry, with his deferential artistry and well-curbed emotions; with a sudden delectable current or warmth I sensed the man in him. 'Bravo!' I said very softly; I nodded and clapped my hands almost imperceptibly. He dropped his bow, and bowed deeply

* *tárogató:* a reed instrument of the clarinet family.

and retreated while the second fiddle went around with the plate. Coins of large value dropped into it, and involuntarily I turned to observe Vodicska; very good indeed, he put a ten-forint piece in! Without the least trace of emotion or excitement he calmly returned my gaze with his warm, intelligent eyes.

I could not tell now which ball this was; it may have been at a May feast. Maybe the memory of several glances like that on various occasions has become blurred in me now. It was so long ago!

'You see, that's the only thing people here know how to do,' Telekdy was saying to my mother behind me as he escorted us home. 'They clasp hands and leap about in order to be able to embrace each other legitimately, or with stupid and senseless outbursts of grief they prick up their ears to listen to an antiquated, undeveloped and childish music while methodically pouring all sorts of harmful liquids into themselves until they go wild or become as dumb as cattle. Hungarian folk will never amount to anything...'

'How can he say such things now?' I thought angrily and wearily, and hurried ahead so as not to listen. 'Why didn't he stay out there where everyone is so scholarly, sober and upright? After all, he too drank champagne, and his yellowish clean-shaven face was bloated with the poison of alcohol—I saw him. If he didn't dance, that was because of the little defect in his foot. He's no better than the rest of them!'

'He's read a lot of things, not very systematically, and now he's mixing them up a bit,' said Jenő Vodicska slowly at my side. 'But he's a noble soul and a great enthusiast. He's going to be disappointed.'

I turned towards him. His voice was gentle and moving in the quiet spring night as he uttered such grave, simple, pacifying words. It struck me that now he was the only one accompanying me home. The rest were all totally drunk.

'How good it would be to go to bed now and have a good sleep for once!' I thought then for the first time with a sudden attack of depression.

I soon got over this among the good comfortable pillows until noon next day. For that evening we had another invitation to a party at the Béltekys.

At home the running of the household revolved around us, our late nights, our sleep and our dressing. Sometimes our uncle,

Pista Zimán, burst in on the two boys in the kitchen-block; he ranted and screamed and even beat them now and again, and then there would be peace again for months. Nobody took any interest in their studies and their unfettered wanderings. Once or twice my mother would give a passing sigh when it occurred to her that Csaba had failed again in three subjects; once she was really scared and sad for a few days. Sándor was attacked by some kind of peculiar nerve-trouble in his neck which caused him to hold his head to one side; from time to time he would twitch, uttering a strangled hiccup of a sound.

'Adolescent change', said old Jakobi, our doctor, but he took a long, contemplative look at the boy's emaciated face and restless eyes.

He had to be sent to a distant spa for iodine treatment that summer. It cost a lot of money, but grandma herself insisted on it. Of all of us, it was Sándor she favoured most, and she had long treasured a scheme for him: he was to enter the priesthood, so that for once there might be a bishop, a rich, important, elegant and genteel prelate in the family.

'Of course, a Papist fox, a hellhound in a cowl!' my father's brother, Uncle Ábris, would sometimes rage, suspecting her intentions. The Pórtelkys had always been Calvinists, and according to the law, the two boys should have been Calvinists too. But grandma Zimán and my mother respected their own Catholic faith without devotion or piety. They felt it to be distinguished and powerful, as well as full of beauty; moreover, all in all, it had a real relevance in this world.

'A splendid mess there is where a woman rules the roost!' my Uncle Ábris battled on sternly, tugging at his white beard. 'I've heard what you're cooking up, what your plans are for this young chicken. Some Kicska... Vodicska—he's going to be your son-in-law, isn't that so?'

'If I find a husband for her, you'll get an invitation to the wedding, brother-in-law! It's up to you whether you come!' replied my mother rather waspishly. 'At the moment there's nobody at all in mind.'

'Oh, of course not, course not!' said the old man with a wicked laugh, and looked keenly at me. 'I can still remember very well, my child, when I was a tiny little boy at the Normal School. My school-friends said at the porter's gate as we were coming out, "Come on, lads, let's go to the little square: old

Vodicska's getting a hiding!" D'you know, my little dove, who it was? The beloved grandfather of the present haughty old land-carver. A serf, poor as a church mouse, who was caught from time to time by the warden because he stole a pigeon's egg in the game-forest. The whipping-post was there in the market-place!'...

At last my grandmother raised her head and with stern anger and defiance, stared the guest straight between the eyes. It was the eternal opposition of the Zimáns, the noble family of lesser importance, that flashed in her glance, facing the family of her son-in-law, that more powerful, more cocksure mob.

'Let's have an end to such foolish talk, sir! That young man was an invited guest in my house and was a credit to it. As for my granddaughter's future husband, that need be no concern of yours; there are quite enough of us here to make the choice. We're looking for someone who can keep a wife to his dying day whatever may happen in this bad world of ours. After their father—you can rest assured—they'd never live in splendour!'

From a corner of the room, I listened in silence and gloomy defiance to this acrimonious outburst of many long-simmering, tiny irritations. I was also well aware of all that neither side mentioned: the hidden springs. Ten years ago my uncle Ábris had asked for the hand of his beautiful young sister-in-law immediately after she became a widow. He too was widowed, with one daughter. Since she had unexpectedly turned him down, he had never quite rid himself of his captious, hostile attitude, though later he pretended that it was only for the sake of his dead brother's children and the well-being of the family that he wished to marry my mother. And on top of that, Vodicska! Yes, the estate surveyor, as judicial expert, had recently put a stop to one of his dubious little schemes for redistributing the property.

But I also knew full well why grandma had risen so fiercely and suddenly to the defence of the Vodicska boy. At the end of that winter she already had some scheme for me to marry the lame Elemér Kendy, who had eleven hundred acres in view. It did not succeed; they thought my own personal fortune was too small.

That was the first time I was overwhelmed with a sudden feeling of despair at my helpless state; as a girl, I was at the mercy of others. But this feeling could find no outlet; it was soon stifled in the comforting order of family discipline and respect for convention, a comfort because there was no higher court to appeal to. 'Grandma knows best!' I thought, finding relief at last.

VI.

This was still only my second carnival season; I had just passed my eighteenth birthday.

Only very gradually, like waking up with an unpleasant taste in the mouth, did a little momentary, faint nausea afflict me once in a while.

That season more or less the same young men attended the dances, but one or two of them had become engaged at the beginning of winter: local officials, who quietly became betrothed to undemanding little girls who were hardly noticed anyway. One relative fetched a wife from another county; for the sake of the older Reviczky girl, a fair, good-looking captain with a foreign accent resigned his commission.

A few new girls were introduced and scared, I watched to see whether they were more beautiful, more clever than I was. But no, my circle of admirers remained more or less intact, for all that. But somehow everything seemed to have acquired a different colour since the previous year, more faded, more ordinary and poverty-stricken. I was still the reigning queen, but I was no longer regarded as a novelty; nor was the whole thing new to me either. I was still able to enjoy the giddiness of the dance, but afterwards I was sometimes reminded of Telekdy's tart comment: 'What's the point of this half-witted prancing, this twitching night-stint? Has it any purpose?'

And this was precisely the problem. The whole affair was not just for the sake of the delight of brilliance, role-playing and waltzing in and of itself. Coming to the surface from unconscious abandonment on the way home I often had to consider now whether that day I had furthered my own cause and got closer to the compulsory purpose—a husband, a marriage.

At home, the atmosphere slowly altered; sometimes it was full of irritation and tension. It was increasingly rare for my mother and me to sit on the edge of our beds after a night's festivity, and enjoy discussing with each other the events of the night—remarks, compliments and little occurrences. Now we sometimes maintained an obstinate silence, as if each were pursuing her own selfish interests separately, and alienated from the other. Sometimes with malice, my mother made fun of one or other preposterous character at the ball; yet earlier she had no time to observe such things. The two poor, aging Tyukody sisters, distant relatives of ours, with their petty nobility and haughtiness, their ridiculous, noisy provincialism! They became the target of our jokes: they had stuck leeches from the marshes on their necks in preparation for the ball. 'To make us pale, my dear, not coloured like certain village rustics!' And then they told everyone loudly and clearly, in case they now might think so too, 'We've got tuberculosis, my dear!' And our coterie had a good laugh after recounting the way in which Erzsus, in the middle of the long, silent csárdás-gallop suddenly shouted at her partner in a good thick Ecsed accent: 'Ee, look you, the dawn's come!' And at how she once called her sister over sorrowfully from selling parsley towards the orange-seller's stall as bitter consolation : 'Come 'ere, do come! Let's at least eat a bit of decent lemon!' And laughing loudly, mother Klári imitated the way in which their mother looked Jenő Vodicska up and down, with her turkey-neck extended, and her haughty eyes, when we introduced him to her, and turning away, she asked in a stifled, rasping voice,' My dear, I didn't quite catch the name. *Is it family?*'

To me it was strange and something new that in our house people should make fun of the family haughtiness with such loud peals of laughter. 'It's Telekdy's example,' I thought, 'and mother so easily gets carried away by all this.'

Yet out of it all, other things, too, became clear: that some compulsive self-delusion was making all those at home warm to the idea that Vodicska was to be my accepted fiancé. 'What stupidity,' I sometimes thought in astonishment, 'that my future, my whole fate, should depend so much on chance! On whoever happens to be on hand. On the fact, that for the moment there's no more suitable man for me among those of the right age!'

If only I could wait a year or two! But now nothing was as it had been at first. Sometimes I had a strange sense of unease: suppose they were to become accustomed once and for all to my nature and my exclusiveness, suppose I was to lose my glamour and go stale, suppose someone else were once to occupy my place? For me it would be a deadly shame too, if there were not two or three partners eagerly waiting all the time to dance with me.

A celebrated girl whose great reputation had preceded her should not allow herself to attend balls for more than a year without becoming engaged.

Now, from the distance of three decades, I once again see the destiny of my own daughters and keep comparing it with my own. The youngest is eighteen years old now, preparing for her diploma, struggling hard, giving lessons and begging funds for herself, poor little thing. Yet all the same she writes, and sometimes I feel that she may be right, that her life is a more honest life, and her youth a more honest youth. She is still on the threshold, she can wait, make plans, rejoice in the future she feels has been put into her own hands. I suspect she has some exchange of letters and affairs of love, but as yet she has no plans or intentions to follow up on them; she continues them just for the sweetness of little thrills, festivities and tears. We folk of old knew nothing like this…

For the summer months, I was sent to stay with my mother's younger sister, who ended up living in a village. The big, higgledy-piggledy collection of buildings that made up the country mansion at Hirip, with its many rooms, was a permanent stalking-place for the family in those days. There were always two or three girl-relatives of marriageable age temporarily settled there, and every day there was a host of guests from miles around. The prevailing atmosphere here was one of great and pleasant comfort and rustic abundance. It was old-fashioned and did not bother much with outwardly appearances or fashion. Guests were treated in a wise, kindly way that left them in peace; the tables were laid all day long on the two vine-clad terraces, and everyone got up, went to bed, lived and roamed about as they wished. My Aunt Piroska would spend half the day out of sight in the apiary, the orchard or the flax-fields; her husband settled down by the threshing-machine, in the granary or in the 'smoker', while the many tiny children disappeared among the farmhands, under haystacks, or round the horse-driven mill. It was an old-fashioned, interesting kind of agriculture that went on here; nobody was miserly or stingy, there was good living in abundance, with hosts of diners, crowds of guests, lots of servants and a great band of children. Since their wedding, they had not spent a penny on luxuries or furniture; crockery and glasses were brought by a Transylvanian Rumanian in his knapsack;

even the everyday dishes were mended with wire if they got broken, and on the scrubbed floors there were striped rag-carpets. All the same, the whole household kept hard at work all the time. The dairy, the barnyard poultry, the orchard, and the bargaining with the market-women took up all my aunt's time and energy, and meanwhile she had a new infant each year. Uncle got up at dawn and was on his feet or on horseback till nightfall. He swore at the farm-labourers in Rumanian and Hungarian, the long stem of a pipe for ever in his mouth, and then there would be long intervals of silence again. Pencil and paper hardly existed in the house; the number of sacks, the workers' wages, loss and profit and prices he simply kept in his head or maybe just settled at random. By and large they did not consume all that was produced; everything went on in the same way as it had been a century earlier. Here they still manufactured candles at home out of mutton-fat; they made soap, ground barley, dried fruit and made pasta while the servant-girls sang by the light of tallow nightlights as they spun and wove till dawn. But even at that time in the town shops there were cheaper and good-quality examples of all these things; they, however, just went on working out of habit, for the sake of working, since resting, daydreaming and reading novels were only for lazy great ladies in towns. Yes, I even became accustomed to this kind of life, this world!

But they did not engage us guests in work. With tolerant contempt they left us to live our own lives as we wished. At the end of the enormous garden there was a big, cool, covered skittle-alley, where a group or two or a single couple could always retire from the heat. The leaf of the rickety painted wooden table often carried not scores, but confessions or tender queries in black chalk. Question, banter, answer—then they scribbled all over them in nervous fright; if that ancient garden table still exists somewhere, and if someone were to begin to wash it carefully and gently, the tiny stories of whole generations of girls might be read from it, written in layers on top of each other.

That summer, too, there were always a lot of local young people there; I knew this was mainly for my sake. This again was a delightful period, which I shall never forget. Boys whose acquaintance I had made during the winter came along, or those whose families I had heard mentioned from my childhood. They treated me as one of themselves, a likable companion, an attractive, jolly, good-looking creature, with whom it was right and proper individually and altogether to be in love—fashionably, sweet-and-sorrowfully, smilingly, prettily and quite hopelessly, during beautiful sunny summer afternoons and music-filled, merry evenings.

A line of dark old poplars leads from the house towards the main road; one night all of us strolled the length of it in the beautiful light of the full moon. Above the distant threshing-floor the wheat-scented summer dust glinted silver. We all kept perfect silence while the crickets chirped; an occasional gaunt young Rumanian woman came from the other direction, greeting us softly and lowered the rake on her shoulder. Endre Tabódy and I were walking well ahead of the others.

'See,' he said suddenly in a strange tone of voice, 'see, I could walk like this to eternity, walk happily along a white road like this. You would link arms with mine, we'd step out together, swaying like two boats moored alongside each other. Going along like this oblivious and bemused, and the road would never have an end! For once we wouldn't have any further thoughts of anything!'

His voice dropped to a stifled or awe-struck whisper. And with great care and gentleness he took hold of my wrist above my bracelet. So we went on like this, calmly and delightfully, treading softly. I too felt a strange sense of lightness. A kind of gentle dizziness enveloped my head, a silvery veil of mist, as we just continued on our way. We were at the end of the avenue, and the hedge of the stockyard hid us. Then Endre slowly turned to face me, and with a pleading, sorrowful, deep gaze he bent tenderly and carefully over my face. Even today I cannot tell how it happened that in stupor and pain my head nevertheless sank back further on his arm, escaping his lips; I stepped back and with sunken head went back into the road. 'You're right, Magda!' he said then, panting for breath, while we waited for my aunt and the others.

I remember that we were both very silent that evening. It was the first time in my life that I had felt such a strange sense of seriousness, though I myself did not understand it properly. I was overcome by a delightful sense of weakness, an inner and irrational desire to cry and a tremulous curiosity. 'What is this? Will there be more of it?'

By next morning all this had passed. The company gathered on the veranda late that morning; a new guest was expected as well as other neighbouring families. In the afternoon, Endre had his horses harnessed and drove away with his younger brother. When he said farewell, he clasped my hand rather tightly and tried to gaze into my eyes. I felt that to be something of an insult; after all, the affair had been settled yesterday. I did not respond to either.

That same week, Jenő Vodicska also paid me a visit. It was the deputy-sheriff who brought him in his carriage and introduced him to the household; they explained that they were on an official journey in the district, consolidating land-holdings, and brought greetings from my grandmother and her family. My aunt received him graciously. I knew that they had already heard about the business in a letter from home. But my uncle treated him with reserve, all the same, and was very courteous indeed; he called him 'my young friend' or 'my dear sir', but did not go so far as 'my boy' or talk familiarly to him as he did to the rest. At lunch, I kept looking in astonishment and speculation at his neatly-brushed figure, his fine tie-pin, his white hands and well-manicured nails, his carefully-trimmed beard and side-whiskers. 'Would he be the one, then?' I thought. 'But I shan't fall in love anyway. No, that I can't do!'

'Are you glad to see me, Maggie, just a little?' he asked, when we were left alone that afternoon and strolled the length of the garden path among the gooseberry-bushes.

'Yes, of course!'

'But not more than anyone else?'

'That's something I don't know.'

'You don't know? How can that be?'

I shrugged my shoulders and had the distinct feeling that now each of us thought the other stupid, though we were not. But he had not discovered what he ought to say to me. What should he have said anyway?

Later in the arbour he recited a poem which began, 'What is it that absorbs the light of thy fair eyes?' He knew it by heart and explained where its beauty lay and what it meant. It was the very first time I had heard that poem, and I think I quite liked it too, but I felt rather embarrassed by its high-flown language. He asked me whether he might copy it out and send it to me. I really felt composed and at ease in his presence, but was upset somewhat by the antipathy of the household and the others towards him. Maybe they despised him and because of him, me too.

Yet when I returned home that autumn, I had no reason to complain about this. Grandma and mother were now more than considerate and almost intimate with him.

Before Christmas old Telekdy died at last, the haughty, spendthrift, far-famed landowner. 'The old devil,' they said throughout the county and even at the funeral too. Even during the lifetime of his poor wife who died young, he was a dissolute, prodigal, coarse man. Every attractive peasant-girl in the village was kept hidden from him, well out of sight, because if he glimpsed one he would order her to the courtyard, and woe betide anyone who resisted him. His tubercular young wife's diary, discovered by her relations after her death, frequently contained the entry, 'What will become of my only son when I close my eyes forever?' The boy was growing up then; he observed the way his father lived, so the old man always kept him at a distance from him. He sent him to Kolozsvár to learn German, then to Pest to study law; he provided him with money and never asked whether he was taking his examinations. Later he sent him to foreign lands with the Calvinist minister's son, and kept him travelling simply to prevent him from being at home. 'He's ruined the unlucky lad!' was what everyone said unequivocally—though I never understood exactly why or how. Meanwhile, the old man made a gambling-den out of his country house and organized mad orgies at which the farmhands' young wives and girls acted as waitresses. In my presence, these things were mentioned only in whispers, while faces displayed shock and horror. A few years ago he had had a stroke. He was completely disabled, and lost the use of all his limbs; they pushed him around in a wheelchair. But his fine, wicked old face remained unaffected, with his glittering eagle-eyes and poisonous tongue, so that he could curse and proscribe his big adult son and threaten to disown him, so they kept telling us, because he had heard a rumour that he was pursuing my mother, a landless widow with three children. Now he was dead and buried with great pomp. So that would be the end of his prohibition!

VII.

That would be the end of it. This was the urgent, surprised message conveyed since then by my grandmother's silent antipathy and near-hostile behaviour. There was a kind of selfish, irascible, quarrelsome atmosphere now in the family, a feeling of tense calm before the storm. We felt each other to be almost enemies. Grandma said not a word; mother was on edge and unpredictable. Often she criticized my treatment of men in a bitter and cruel way; she said I was clumsy, and they had learnt all the feminine arts I possessed by now, that I was incapable of tying down or holding on to anyone, not even this man Vodicska. How often these two phrases kept occurring in women's vocabulary in the old days! Did they never think, I wonder, that a woman too, may become bored with a man, have enough of him and send him on his way? But why did I feel this accusation to be outrageous and so much more insulting than anything else? I knew that it was unjust.

So we started on the treadmill of dances once again. Now Telekdy was in mourning and occupied with his own affairs; they, so it was said, had all landed on his head in confusion after his debt-ridden, profligate father's death. My mother did not do much dancing now, but she was really not the right person to be a self-sacrificing guardian and escort to me. As for myself, I was often wild and overbearing, loud-mouthed and determinedly jolly, and secretly I was afraid that they were already tired of this and maybe would gossip about me and condemn me. Possibly this was indeed so. One day, out of the blue, on the sudden inspiration of my mother, we went down to the great jurists' ball in Debrecen. This was a great event for me—my first journey to an unknown, larger town, and the newness of different kinds of people. At the expensive and elegant hostelry where we stayed, the invitation was addressed to Baroness Pórtelky, and we did not protest. We let them believe this and danced the quadrille in the magnates' salon. Then a Pongrácz kept company with me, a good-looking, pleasant, distinguished lad. Yes, these people were different, perhaps superior to those at home; they talked more quietly, and moved lightly, with a somewhat feminine grace; their accent was strange, and I was afraid that they would sense that I was an outsider. Sometimes I took a long look at the shirt-fronts that were unbelievably immaculate even around dawn, at the well-tailored dress-suits that fitted them like a glove, with the tails lined with the finest silk, right down to the gleaming patent-leather shoes which clearly evidenced their quality and which were now being worn for the very first time. 'This is a different world, way up above ours!' I felt then, with eyes wide opened, and I was not sorry that we left for home the next day. Grandma regarded this business as senseless, irresponsible foolishness and spoke her mind angrily about it, though it was not her custom to begrudge us. She said the whole town disapproved of the way we were living and now at last we had unleashed people's tongues against us.

Perhaps mother wanted to make Telekdy jealous with this episode, but it appeared that she had made him really angry. He did not come to our next dinner. But Vodicska was there and sat beside me on the little corner settee where previously, long ago, my mother had retired with one or other of her admirers; now by tacit consent we were left to our own devices. So it was my turn. A few girls and married women gossiped and fooled about; one or two army-officers were there too, but today everything went more quietly than at other times. Besides, at the piano sat Ágnes Kallós, István's fiancée, in a white dress, her luxuriant hair in a Madonna-braid. My uncle was tenderly attentive to her, though their betrothal was not yet publicly announced. Grandma made herself amiable to her mother. 'Well,' I thought bitterly, 'so that's what they've been doing behind our backs!' It flashed across my mind that in the past few days, István had been talking about the finances with my mother one evening after dinner as he smoked his pipe, while grandma's knitting needles had glittered in the lamplight with regular, calm movement. I furtively took note of the figures: how much our money had diminished under the heading of educational expenses, travel and balls, and how far the share my mother had received as a widow had dwindled. And how much her and her two sisters were going to be payed in their share of the inheritance. Mama made an effort, forcing herself to listen seriously to him and sometimes nodding rather confusedly. She would have to sign something, they said, but I could see that she did not really understand. They ought to put it more clearly, I thought with my child's mind, and they ought to mention, too, how much the whole fortune is. And for the first time I had the sure feeling, that my mother was not a very clever woman. Yes, they were manipulating us very well; the two boys were at the seminary and military academy just as they wanted, and it was easy to deal with my mother. This was the first hint of disillusionment I had concerning the highly esteemed older generation of my family.

'Why don't you want to talk frankly with me?' Vodicska pursued the question several times in that quiet corner of the salon. 'Do you think I haven't noticed for some time now that there's something upsetting you, Magda?'

I could not have explained on the spur of the moment whether his solicitude appealed to me now, moved me or embarrassed me. But I should very much have liked to weep.

'No, nothing's the matter with me,' I replied. 'Maybe I just look tired from travelling.'

'Tired and sad. I've been watching you for a long time now. Shall I tell you what's upsetting you, dear, dear little Magda? Come now, don't be ashamed of those tearful eyes! Just see—after all, I'm the one who knows you best of all here. You're head and shoulders rise above your surroundings, you were born more precious, more refined; your place isn't in this dissolute, swaggering, cynical world. You've always had around you nothing but carousing, ignorant, coarse men and haughty-spirited strutting peacocks of women; and whether you know it or not or want it or not, you're looking for something else. They call it goodness, work, vocation, Maggie, and real family feeling.'

I gazed at him with eyes that were suddenly dry and astonished. At that moment I was in an incredible state of confusion. 'Maybe that's it, that's the truth!' something leapt within me. Never before had anyone talked to me so seriously, in such a fatherly way... But immediately a kind of scornful mortification welled up in me because of my tears and my momentary weakness, 'Oh come! It's absurd to preach like that, like some old professor!' my other self argued impatiently. 'How dare he sit in judgment on my nearest and dearest? He can be glad if... Oh, it's as if up to now I've been some kind of devilish creature and he's converting me! No, he ought to have said all this in a different way, more simply, more briefly and not talked down to me like this. Who is he?'

'No,' I said swiftly and defiantly, 'there's no way in which I measure up to your tastes. Why do you bother about me anyway? There are girls you can find ready-made for you, types like Ágnes, for example. Yes, indeed, I *am* bad; don't bother yourself with me!'

'You're a child, an infant!' he said and nodded his head silently. 'You misunderstood me. All the same, some day you'll realize that I was your truest friend.'

And he offered his arm, perhaps a little reluctantly, because he was unable to continue, since everyone was standing up now and he had to escort me to the table.

'What went on between you today?' asked my mother when everyone had gone. 'Did he ask you to marry him?'

'Just leave me alone!' I said and banged the door. In the darkened room I sank down over my piano and cried.

A couple of days later there was the Farmers' Union soirée, an innocent name for the first large ball of the carnival season and the most select one. Hanika, the younger sister of Lipi the broker, and our seamstress, once more frantically remade, altered and freshened up our magnificent dresses after the ball at Debrecen. The night before it, my mother woke me from sleep because I had forgotten to put lemon crême celeste on my arms and neck, to do my hair in ringlets and to wear a pair of old gloves for the night.

All the creme of society from three counties was at the ball, but the towns were represented only by us, the Kallóses, Reviczkys and Zimáns. Every year it was the custom to send invitations to the estate officials for the sake of propriety, but as usual not one of them came on this occasion either. Yet for once grandma herself had spoken to Vodicska, and had managed to arrange a welcome for him from a few influential families. But he did not come. 'Mummy's tied him to the table-leg; she won't let him go!' said my mother crossly.

At that ball I was in a foamy blue silk dress with a lot of lace about it, my mother in a yellow brocade embroidered with gold thread. When we entered, my heart leapt once again at the realization that we were still among the leaders.

Guests from the neighbouring counties entered in a single group after the first few dances. At first glance I caught sight of Endre Tabódy among them. I looked at him with a compelling, long, passionate female gaze, questioningly and encouragingly.

With a thrill of amazement I saw that he felt it; he looked around with restless and searching eyes, then with a changing, surprised expression caught sight of me and immediately made his way towards me. 'What do I want with him? What's happening to me and in me now?' I suddenly asked myself.

We began to dance, and I sensed that once again I was an attractive sight; people stopped to enjoy watching us. With half-closed eyes I floated on the arm of the slender, good-looking young man, and thought that till today the delight of dancing had been only a shabby and stupid piece of play-acting; this was the real thing, and only now did I learn its true meaning. Up to now only my body swayed and became dizzy, the glamour of my blood floated around me only in deceptive ecstasy; but now in the depths of my soul something opened and sprang up with utter reality, and this fusion was so intimate, wonderful and pure that it would be impossible to give it a name. How good, I am now, how true, serious and precious! Why, he does care for me, he has not forgotten me! And even then, in the summer, he took me seriously.

I deliberately conjured up once again the vision of the poplars and the moonlight, the silvery dust and the far, far distant fields. Now a distant, precious, mythical blueness played over this vision; here music played and everything—youth and joy—flew and floated in glittering light and perfume... Once, just this once again!

Dizzy with weariness and ecstasy I got back to my chair. Endre exchanged a few polite words with my mother. 'Oh of course, one of the Tabódys from the Nyírség! Surely not Anna Pásthy's son? Impossible! Your mother and I were together at boarding school!'

The band struck up a csárdás and once again he was my partner. A few local acquaintances who were standing around waiting for me, went up to my mother, pretending to be annoyed. Once again Telekdy sat beside her the whole evening and only allowed her, with great condescension, to dance the quadrille. Only when the supper csárdás came to an end did my mother, scandalized, take me to task. 'What are you doing? Do be sensible!' she whispered, stifled and somewhat confused. She herself did not seem to be certain what to think about the affair.

'I love you, I love you, I love you!' he kept saying to me passionately and stubbornly as he squeezed my arm close to his.

This new confession made me angry, and glad and pained, as surprising and peculiar as if I had never heard it before. 'Like two boats moored alongside each other,' I thought as I walked the length of the ballroom on his arm.

'Magda!' he whispered into my ear at dinner, when the first champagne-glasses had been filled, and for a minute our precious, silly, emotional and clumsy words and behaviour were not being watched. 'At last, Magda, my only one, wait for me! For a while. I don't know what's going to happen—I myself can't yet envision how…, but I'll wrestle with anyone for you. Wait while at least I can think about it… They say you're engaged…'

'All this doesn't depend on me, Endre,' I replied resignedly, sorrowfully. But this great, piercing, sacred distress shot through me with a very strange sweetness. I would not have given it up for anything in the world.

On the other side of the ballroom, my mother was talking in whispers with Telekdy. They looked at me and I saw they were discussing me. What Endre Tabódy and I said to each other beyond that was irresolute, touching, almost welcome resignation. We knew nothing certain about our own and each other's future, but we scarcely dared to touch on the problem. We felt that all this had come very suddenly indeed, and perhaps we ourselves did not really trust in it. 'A lovely dream!' I thought, 'nothing more! This, too, had to come now!' Listless music at dawn, stifling perfumes, drooping lace—a beautiful, sad, precious memory of those few foolish hours has been preserved in me my whole life through.

At three o'clock, though the ball was still in full swing, my mother beckoned firmly to me that we were to go home. Tabódy had already observed her disapproval. He escorted us to the door, kissed my hand there and looked long into my eyes. I knew that this was farewell. It had lasted up to then. Now it was over.

Telekdy got into our carriage, and it was he who accompanied us home. My mother lit a candle, and in her slippers softly brought it to my bedside.

'Are you asleep?—Crying? Magda! There, there, my dear little girl! My darling child!'

Fiercely I blew out the revealing candle in her hand and with a sudden, determined hug threw my arms around her neck. This, I knew, was a very rare moment between us, and something to be kept secret next day, never to be mentioned; our kindred affection had to be buried in frigidity and everyday sociability. We hugged each other in the darkness and wept.

'My darling little creature, you clever little thing, just look! For us this just isn't possible; you can't do this! It's a long, uncertain business and so much can happen in the meantime. These folks are wealthy, you can be sure they'd find it difficult to allow it. And all this is just talk, my dear; words, a sudden flame—they're nothing! Just one evening. Tomorrow he'll go home; the next day he'll say it to someone else, who knows who, from goodness knows where… Such affairs happen to every girl, but they're not serious. You're a child; just put an end to it now.'

Yes, yes! How sensibly she was speaking now. And exactly, precisely how my grandmother had spoken to her a few years before. And she was right; mothers are always right, I knew perfectly well. And I was far too sensible to take anything crazy or impossible into my head. And through my tears I said. 'But of course I know that, I know it! Do stop it!' All the same, I cried my eyes out for once.

'Today we've cleared the air between us,' she said later, more calmly. 'I'm not saying that Telekdy wouldn't suit me either; I'm a bit older than he is, and he's a clever man, a fine one, too. And I've got to get married and get away from here! Today he mentioned Vodicska. And what battles he's had with his parents over you—he told him this—and that now they've come to terms with the idea… Well, that's how it is… He's a handsome, pleasant lad with a fine future. It's madness today to bother about a name… Maybe you might not settle down well either with a stepfather, and you've had quite enough of girlhood. Up to now you've come first, don't wait until your sun begins to set! Who knows whether anyone better will come along? Such things all depend on chance!'

This was how she spoke, so wisely, so maternally, and for quite a long time.

Next day Jenő Vodicska turned up in his black Sunday best and asked her for my hand.

My fiancé was the first man to kiss my girlish, haughty lips ceremoniously, tenderly and solemnly.

VIII.

'Maggie, my darling, aren't I going to get any skin on my milk again?'

'Oh heavens, Jenő! Is it the skin now? Haven't you had enough of that? The milk from the woman at Börvely doesn't have any more on it!'

'You let it boil over, my love!...'

He muttered this in a stifled voice and rather indecisively, slowly measuring out the white milk with his beringed white hand.

The wintry morning sunshine gleamed cold as it played and glinted on his ring, on the silver handle of the ladle and the porcelain rim of the cup. The white brightness of the snow-covered world filled the fresh-smelling new dining room; in the big iron stove, wood crackled and spattered flames, and hot red flashes were reflected from the round eyes of the door and flickered playfully on the gleaming varnished side of the cupboard.

My husband had just gotten up. His moustache was still pressed down and his hair, wet and tousled from washing, stuck to his forehead; the whole man was fresh with well-perfumed water and soap. But just now I had seen him cutting his corns, standing with his legs wide apart and puffing in front of the washbasin; I had seen him clumsily filing his nails and cleaning his silk tie with a brush dipped in spirits. And now he was about to leave here tidied up, breakfasted, satisfied and smiling, while I picked up the rubbish after him, made the bed, carried away yesterday's dirty clothes, wiped the coffee-cup and immediately started rushing around again with the servant, so that by the time he returned at midday there would be order, neatness, cleanliness, lunch, warmth and everything. 'What would the master say?' we sometimes asked each other. The servant and I! Goodness, how crazy life is! And a year ago he looked after my invitation to the ball and carried my fan for me!...

Now—and it has been like this for almost a year, every day is more or less the same. I get up early and until this hour, rush right through the kitchen and the little three-roomed flat in a running battle; in the drawing-room I have already dusted all the porcelain figures on the tiny shelves, cleaned the cups and the lamp on the sideboard, then polished the silver with chalk-dust, swept and dusted and put everything straight. Till noonday it will be the same again: I beat carpets, polish door-handles, clean the vegetables and drive, stand over, curse and train the cook, who is also my lady's maid and only servant. And this—well, this is how it will be now for ever. How long?... As long as we live!...

Jenő drank up his coffee, ran his eyes over the newspaper, put on a coat and lit a cigar; then he came over to kiss me. But now I turned away in sudden dejection. 'Why, what's the matter?'

'Nothing!' I replied, tightening my lips. He gazed at my face for a while, then suddenly embraced me, forced my head back and planted a forceful, jocular kiss on my stubborn mouth. I burst out laughing; I was not one to put on an act. Then he pulled a lock of hair from under my red head-scarf and waggled it comically, gave me a slap on the thigh and suddenly let go of me as if something urgent had suddenly occurred to him.

'You're in for it next time the milk boils over, my little witch!'

The front door had already closed behind him, and I drew away from the window so that he could not see me. For a while I looked at the snow-covered roofs of the houses and the frozen morning silence of Hajdú Town Street, and then at a frosty well-sweep in the yard of the Swabian house opposite, which creaked as it moved. How monotonous everything was, today, yesterday and for ever!

We had taken a flat in a cheap and out-of-the-way street, away from Jenő's office, because we had to economize. He did not get much when he married me; there was scarcely anything left after buying the trousseau, furniture and some fine silver. And so our life consisted of great monotony, quiet and with a little comfort, just as when something is complete: it exists, and there is nothing to strive for, nothing to expect. 'Now he's gone,' I thought; 'till noonday he'll be among people, hearing news, exchanging a few words, dictating in the office, going off to see the inspector, dropping in at the finance office, involved in a case at the law-courts, then towards noon he'll have a drink at the Stag, and cross County Street in front of grandma's house where my flower-filled window opened on to it in my girlhood. Then at noon he'll come home for a good lunch and a comfortable nap, to a homely, tranquil embrace in the clean and pleasant rooms, and maybe he'll not give a single thought to how much I gallop around here, hurrying and bustling about all the time. This is the unavailing, odd-jobbing drudgery that begins anew each day, the mechanism of housekeeping! Just for a man!'

At home on County Street there existed an emptiness when I was a child—a father, the dominating, all-important head of the family, and inwardly I still sometimes rebelled against him—perhaps even more now, after the end of the honeymoon, the period of adaptation and compliance. 'The girls,' I thought, 'this season's girls are just starting the carnival round of dances, plans and dresses and little vivid secrets, while as for me, my fate is sealed now. I've been abandoned entirely to his mercy. My mother, now Mrs. Péter Telekdy, is living in a village with her husband, and my brothers are studying away from home, while grandma's only concern is for István's family and Ágnes' little child has more of her affection than we do. How they handed me over to this man! My life's already come to an end! Soon... maybe... I shall become ugly and shapeless, and then again and forever be like the other women! But isn't it wicked of me to get angry about such things? I'm certain they never cross Ágnes Kallós' mind!

Suddenly jumping up, I set to work in a mad frenzy. I felt that housework was slavery, but inwardly something drove me on and compelled me to put into it breathless passion and urgent exaggeration; this state of mind, at that time, became a hallmark for the rest of my life. My small household gleamed and shone; every conceivable place was polished, waxed, washed, scoured and brushed. Even the heads of the carpet-tacks were cleaned with brass-polish, the handle of the coal-shovel with boiling potash-water and the invisible recesses behind the cupboards were dusted with a tiny, long-handled brush every day. Yes, this is what I had become. I sometimes wonder now, after all this time, whether this wild desire for action, this crazy ambition that I spent in beating the carpets might not have been good for something else, something more important... I had in me a strong desire to be first, to be distinguished and famous—and yet how else could I have achieved this? And then that exaggerated mass cleanliness gave a sort of genteel, refined, exceptional lustre to our life and to the atmosphere of my little dwelling where everything was new and carefully preserved; and I had always possessed a natural aptitude and taste for arrangement and beautification. Who knows if I might not have made something of this, too, in another position?... Pah! That's how my daughters talk! They don't understand my world, the old world and how it worked, or my life. They're different!

'You little witch! My little witch of a daughter!' said my mother-in-law with her attractive foreign accent. 'Why, you could mix an omelette on the floor of your room, it's so clean! You'll tire yourself out by doing too much! Never mind, you'll give up some of it when the little ones come along.'

She smiled and nodded when reports reached her of what a great reputation her twenty-year-old daughter-in-law already had as a housewife, and how the ladies of the town liked to get their servants from me. Every afternoon when she came to visit me, I too sat opposite her, thoroughly cleaned up and dressed in a beautiful little tea-gown among the porcelain figurines in the drawing-room with its newly-fashionable golden-legged chairs whose backs had plump amorettes worked in silk, trumpeting among the clouds. I saw that she approved of this scene, and she too fitted in well among the big vases full of dried flowers, the flower-baskets, lace curtains, full-length mirror, and the delight-fully haphazard scattering of colourful silk cushions, tablecloths and knick-knacks. The attractive little Frenchwoman with her slender, ring-laden, snuff-stained fingers, a delicate lace collar on her rustling black dress, her grey hair carefully crimped in waves beneath the pearl-studded bonnet.

'Do you know, Jules, would you believe it—this silk is still from that end we rescued from my father's factory at Lyon at the time of the crash. It was from this same roll that the dress came in which you first saw me in Paris with my uncle the hotelier, indeed it was! I lined it twice and last year had a little lace put on it, and the pearls, too, come from my old mantilla!'

'Well, to be sure, we've always economized,' her husband assented, not entirely without a touch of malice, and looked at my new tea-gown, which Hanika and I had conjured up brilliantly at really very little cost here in the house. At times like this, my sense of justice troubled me and gnawed at my conscience. Impossible, it must be, however excellent old moiré silk is, it can't last for forty years! That's how she can delude this austere old man.

'A life of peace!' whispered my mother-in-law, 'my child, that's the main thing, isn't it? There's no need to bring every-thing up, explain it all and take it seriously!' And she ran her shapely little hand amicably and roguishly down my arm. 'The main science in marriage is a little bit of cunning. Pass lightly over things, show a little graciousness—and then you can do what you like. The chief thing is not to keep up one's end in an argument, but to remain free inwardly and live an unruffled life. Men are there for us to delude a little, out of love. They suspect this, but they need it and indeed they can desire us to bother about them just so much. Just do things nicely and prettily all the time!'

The little lady smiled and I thought she was probably right. But if I told a lie it was written all over my face, and would have sounded clumsy in my mouth. It was only with suitors and in flirtations that I was able to use a bit of cunning, not in everyday life. That would have offended me, nor did I want to do it. Yet maybe it was a good thing, a difficult and necessary thing, to lie with good intent, nicely and sensibly. But that's something that can't be learnt.

'See, father, what a proper little bride we've got, how hardworking and how tidy!' the lady would keep saying kindly and triumphantly, for it was she who finally managed to reconcile the old man to Jenő's marriage. 'Very nice, very nice!' nodded the old man, but even in his smile there was a hidden, stubborn hint of malice. Or was it simply that I thought it was there? Like someone who for the sake of others is compelled to keep some evil omen to himself, who only suspends, but does not renounce his worst convictions. 'Let's see how it ends!' he seemed to be forever thinking. Oh, the old braggart! He always had to be right in everything, with his ancient, fat, implacable cunning head! What petty-minded vanity was the source of it all! That when he greeted my mother with the fussily genteel 'Your humble servant, ma'am,' she always replied with a brief, somewhat haughty, brisk 'Good day!' like a well-known beauty, and did not give a deep bow or stand out of respect to age, or reply graciously, 'I wish you good day, Mr. Surveyor-in-chief!'... And that must have been about the sum of his personal objections to us. And before our wedding he said, 'It's like going to a funeral!'; something it was obvious he never forgot for a single minute, and all the more because he was clearly in the wrong. Oh how I detested him!...

Jenő's birthday was in February, and that was when we first invited our close relatives from both sides. My husband wanted us to give a dinner, and something of that kind was right and proper then. The two families had not been officially together since the big triple wedding.

I made preparations, rushing around and wearying myself days beforehand, with a new lease on life and full of ambition, for this was my examination, and my reputation as a housewife was at stake. I summoned Zsuzsanna Képíró, the cook famous for her wedding-feasts, to come at dawn and help me; we prepared roast sucking-pig and dumplings baked on cabbage-leaves, and heavy food like this guaranteed to put a wife to the test. I sang as before nightfall I laid the table with my finest damask tablecloth from Lőcse, set out the new monogrammed silver and the ranks of slender cut-glass. Jenő came home, shouldering bottles of wine in a pannier-basket; he lit the candles in the big chandelier, surveyed the table, then suddenly thought of something and rushed out again. He came back with a big bunch of fresh flowers; they were primulas, yellow and lilac-coloured ones, and he had to buy them with their pot to make the astonished gardener, the only one in the town, pick them. How beautiful they were, how pretty! Jenő separated them, singly and in bunches, strewing them here and there among the silver and gilt-bordered porcelain dishes. Yes, that was exactly how I had seen them on the tables laid for supper at the magnates' ball in Debrecen, and Jenő must have seen them, too, somewhere in Pest. But how well he had learnt the art! What taste he displayed! We laughed at each other with satisfaction and delight, and at that moment, we really belonged to each other. He gave me a sudden embrace in front of the beautifully laid table, and I returned it happily. Then the confectioner's boy arrived, bringing the pièce de résistance of the celebration, an imposing, towering, magnificent iced cake, the so-called *croque-en-bouche*. We set it in the middle and sat down on the corner settee with hands in our laps, day-dreaming in silence about distinction, radiance and refinement.

The first to come were grandma and her family, talking loudly and guffawing with laughter even under the window. We hurried to greet them. My uncle István was there, too, with Ágnes; they brought Ilka and the younger Reviczky girl. Later Pali Kallós came with Csaba, who in his cadet's uniform was at home on leave. The old Vodicska couple brought up the rear, somewhat ceremonially and in total silence.

The first half-hour was difficult, perhaps because I myself had been fearful in advance of this herding together of two sorts of relatives. But my little French mother-in-law could be so attractive, exotic and surprising, bubbling with chatter and yet cautious: I saw she would soon win over my relations. Now I almost regretted having left this test for so late. Why, even grandma, too, was being gracious to the old man, with somewhat coarse, high-handed witticisms and the coquettishness of a grande dame; they were talking about their old age and laughing— why, even my father-in-law could be flirtatious and attentive like that! And the part would have suited him quite well, too; it was a pity that it kept flashing across his mind that he was the universally respected head of the family and in a single minute he deliberately froze into seriousness once again.

At dinner, I remember, everything went delightfully smoothly; Zsuzsi served everything nicely and without pause. The courses were a triumphant success; I knew already that they would not be able to find fault with me and I grew calmer and happier as the food dwindled. And the mood grew livelier, too. At the other end of the table Ilka must have let fall some naughty but witty double-entendre. Ágnes blushed like a girl, while the boys in the family roared with laughter. Tilda Reviczky jingled her pendant-studded bangles and talked a lot, too, vigorously and coquettishly, and took small sips of the sweet wine. The old folk praised the food, while Jenő clinked his glass with István and made a pretence of drinking, too. Then I noticed that my father-in-law had not touched a thing after the second course. Frightened by my forgetfulness, I was about to offer him something, but Jenő gave a quick shake of his head in my direction: we must take no notice of it, his glance said to me.

'This capon's good, father-in-law! Do try some!' grandma spoke across to him at that moment in a rather provocative, bold way.

'No, thank you. At dinner I'm used to eating only one kind of meat.'

This again was a frigid, unpleasant, ill-intentioned remark, and I was suddenly seized by a fit of fierce anger at it. 'So he can't be placated, then won't he leave me in peace?' I thought, secretly fuming with rage. Jenő changed the subject of conversation. Ilka gave another guffaw; grandma watched Csaba, who was red as a beetroot by now and was talking loudly into his neighbour's ear. Around midnight, my grandmother gave me a nod, and with a dignified, housewifely motion I shepherded the ladies into the drawing-room.

Here the air was warm, smoke-free and pleasantly perfumed, and once more a jolly mood of gossip prevailed. Grandma went quietly into the bedroom in order to put a compress on Ágnes's breast, for she had just fed her baby and was sitting with us pale and suffering. We called Jenő in for a while, because his mother produced his birthday present. It was a fine large silver cup with a lid, that would look good in a display cabinet, with a seven-pronged, crowned coat of arms on its base. We examined it and praised it.

'Where did you pick that up? How beautiful! Was it a present from the Count, maybe?' grandma asked in a perfectly natural way.

'No,' said my father-in-law with equal detachment,' it came into our possession in '48. A Hungarian regiment was stationed near Erdőd for a fortnight, and the officers ate at our house. They didn't want to stay for free, so they gave it to us for payment. They had acquired things like that from the altar of the home-land—on service; that's the way to put it, isn't it? There were beautiful, fairytale things in a big chest in the colonel's quarters… The officers regularly divided things like this among themselves…'

Later my mother-in-law unpacked something else, too: a little ebony box studded with pearl flowers, to give to me. This she had brought from her homeland, France, and someone had given it to her when she was a girl. It was like a tiny coffin.

By now in the dining-room, my uncle István was getting on famously and loudly with the boys; he talked politics with Kallós, who could have been his son. Csaba, stumbling over his words, kept on mentioning Bankó and his gypsy band. I was not unaccustomed to high spirits induced by drinking, but now I could have done without it. Grandma, too, talked about the preparations. It was then that my father-in-law revealed himself to us; he had been sitting all this time deliberately silent and totally sober in the noisy group. He waited for a little, then settled down next to me on the little divan, saying that he would like a serious word with me.

'Carry on, father.'

'Just one question, my girl. I want you to give me an honest answer to what I'm going to ask you.'

'Of course! Gladly!' I said and was seized by a fit of nervous laughter.

'You'll have to put up with an old man's good intentions,

even if you can do without them,' he continued, and held my hand in his with a long, unctuous, irritatingly slow grasp. 'Tell me, my dear—that cake there in the middle of the table, how much did it cost?'

'I beg your pardon, father, but…'

'If you refuse to answer me, I've no right to go on. I can't compel you to listen to me.'

'Oh… why, it was six forints, if you must… But…'

'Good! Now, how much did you pay for the sweet wines? There were ten bottles, if my eyes don't deceive me.'

'I don't know!'

'One and a half forints a bottle. Never mind now about the three kinds of roast meat, I'd just like to know, too, how much those trumpery flowers cost. In the middle of winter…'

'Oh come! I simply don't know, father! What's the point of all this?'

'Well, my girl, just look here. According to my calculations today your completely superfluous expenses have been about twenty-five forints. For just a single evening. Just so that the close relations can be together for a couple of hours. Look, the cake's hardly been touched. Who can bear to eat so much? And what's the point of the expensive wines? And flowers!… Even in the most aristocratic houses they think twice about spoiling their greenhouses at this time of year. My dear daughter, take the advice of an experienced old man before it's too late. This was something I've always feared, you see, and now I can tell you so. This is a slippery slope leading to ruin. You're still young; come to your senses before it is too late. That's what I'm telling you.'

I listened to this high-flung sermon with a face that was stubborn and set. What could I say? If only Jenő were here! Was there some truth in what he said, I wondered? But to talk like that, in such a hateful way! And when I knew very well that in any case he could not stand me at any price. I suddenly lost my patience and snatched my hand out of his.

'Father, stop it, please… We know this… we thought it was a good idea. I can't bear to listen to sermons.'

I broke off suddenly and felt myself growing pale. Now I had said it. I knew he would never, never forgive me, even if he lived a hundred years; he would keep mentioning it until his dying day. 'So be it, it doesn't matter!' I thought defiantly. I saw him stand up and beckon to his wife.

'But father! Why so soon?' Jenő fussed around him. 'They're sending a coach from the stables anyway…'

'There's no place for me in your house, my son!' he said in an icy, cruel voice, and said a brief farewell to the others. I buried my head in the cushions of the divan and sobbed nervously, while Ilka, who had had one ear on our conversation, breathlessly related the shocking story to grandma.

'You must allow me to say, father-in-law, that you might have chosen another time to say this, that's for sure!' grandma said emphatically and gravely.

'My dear,' interrupted my mother-in-law, too, in her light feminine voice as she quickly put on her lorgnette, 'my dear, Jules is a guest here, after all. And your husband's father.'

'He was wrong to say that.'

'But it should have been put differently.'

The two old ladies looked at each other, as estranged as were their whole beings, their type, their life.

'Magda,' said grandma with a maternal severity that betrayed the greatest possible solidarity, 'you must see them to the door!'

I got up immediately to follow them. They were outside on the cold, snow-covered veranda; the others had also followed them there silent and uncomprehending. My father-in-law was already lifting the frozen latch of the gate.

'Make up with him!' I heard his wife whispering in a pleading, almost humble voice as she timidly stroked her son's shoulder. But at that moment Jenő realized that I had come out into the cold without a wrap. Scared, he stepped across to me to take me inside.

Then I saw my younger brother, Csaba. He was staggering drunkenly along in front of the others and at one point turned to face the Vodicskas, trying pugnaciously to stop and look them in the eyes.

'Why are you so pi-pi-pigheaded? Why are you so b-b-boorish…?'

The old man stepped around him in silence. Then the boy tripped and fell against the fence as he grabbed hold of it. His head drooped and with disgusting belching sounds he became violently sick.

'Just look at that!' said Vodicska to his son. 'That's how things are in your house! That's what you've come to!'

They went away.

In the confused, indignant, wine-sodden, noisy company of my relatives, I suddenly felt cold and estranged. I could scarcely wait for them to go too.

'What kind of new fashion is this? This rotten, twopenny-ha'penny world!' István's voice was heard giving vent unrestrainedly to his wrath in the street under the low window. 'All these new strictures, just because a young lad enjoys a drink!'

'Well, a home-made cake's cheaper, that's true, and there'd have been enough wine from our own vineyards, but it's only once in a while! Her intentions were good! They'll make up for it by going hungry,' said grandma in what sounded like a tiny bit less resolute tone than usual.

'And they have big parties in their house, too, but of course it's easy for them; it comes from the Count's estate!'

'To upset the poor little wife like that! How can they know that it won't do her harm at this stage?' I heard Ilka saying with an edge to her voice as the group was breaking up and saying farewell. Silence fell at last. Jenő sank into an armchair and chewed his cigar, dejected, silent and tortured.

IX.

We were getting ready to go to Mrs. Bélteky's dinner, and all that week Hanika made alterations to the little cherry-coloured gown I had been given last year for my trousseau. It had to be let out a little, and the neck cut to a heartshape; it became an attractive, serious, housewifely garment. I had a sense of expectancy at that time; was that peculiar, sweet pang a foreshadowing, I wondered, or merely impatience, a thirst for life? Sometimes it happens like that: either way, one's inner self is prepared for something to come along and, whatever it is, wherever it comes from, it both grips us and enthralls us.

I met Endre Tabódy at the Béltekys.

It was bound to happen. Fate brought him along and the intervening time, too, the year spent in duty, chrysalis-like, spent at home, the usual lethargy of the first year of marriage, the fear that nothing would ever happen, ever again, and yet our little story was still unfinished. Indeed, even the surroundings seemed to favour what was happening, wanting and intending us to do something—that familial sense of romance that thirsts for a good story. Something like this sparkled then in Ilka's enthusiastic, mercurial eyes and in her suddenly lively thin face which displayed an odd, rather crazy kinship, and, I am certain, there was something in Aunt Bélteky's condoning, apologetic smile and in the solemn hush as everyone turned their eyes on us then. They seated him next to me at the table.

Nothing special happened that evening. I simply felt the excitement and delight of a certain expectancy and I knew that he felt the same way. Yet I hardly looked into his eyes. He sat beside me and we quietly exchanged innocent, simple remarks, yet all the same concealed swift, brief words in the twinkle of an eye; the secret, the sin and sweetness lay merely in the way we stole glances at each other when nobody was watching us—like two old accomplices preserving a common secret.

'So you're happy, are you?'

'I've got a good husband!'

'You at least must be very certain of that. You must be.'

A little while later, it was I who again put a quick question to him.

'What are you doing here? How long are you staying?'

'The whole world knows I'm looking for an estate to buy in the neighbourhood, because we've divided the inheritance.'

'And for a wife?'

'That's what people think.'

'And the truth?'

'I'm looking for something. What it is, I don't know. Last year, perhaps, or some old wickedness... Someone.'

'Someone who doesn't exist any more?'

'Maybe just for me to be able to remember her better. The sort of thing one goes to a cemetery to find. You need pain sometimes.'

How strange and shameful a thing it is in old age to write down the old, simple words marking the beginning of love! They bring a bitter laugh. After all, they are mere banalities; why, they can be learnt, and such simple pathos would be shoddy even for drama school! But are there special words of recognition for real emotion and deliberate shallowness? Just as there cannot be two kinds of mouths for kissing and as no woman ever has any means of measuring a man's love. 'All love is sensual,' they say today, yet even the most shabby escapade might be called spiritual by the same token, because while it lasts, it must include imagination and emotion. For after all a *total* lie would demand of a man the kind of exhaustion and sacrifice of which he is quite incapable. Why should men do it? There is no telling. I am fifty years old and I have taken a good look at the world, but I am quite certain I do not have sufficient knowledge of men.

On that occasion... well, on that occasion every hint, every panted word pierced my soul with expectant, thrilling delight. His words raised the temperature of the air around me to a fever heat and I, without really knowing why, wanted it and longed for it, and perhaps for nothing else.

When we parted, Ilka gave me a passionate embrace and whispered in my ear that she would come and see me two days later. I spent the entire afternoon combing my hair, day-dreaming and smiling to myself; I slipped into my lovely yellow velvet house-coat and spent a long time polishing my nails. 'So you see, the life of a housewife,' was the way my thoughts went, 'isn't a final withdrawal and break from everything; it has its prospects, happenings, desires—even perhaps its grief, too.'

When Ilka came to our house, she was accompanied by Tabódy. The three of us sat at the small table in the drawing room under the fashionable standard-lamp, for which I had made a frilly shade from rose-coloured tulle. I remember well those minutes; they were the most beautiful, perhaps they were everything! To sit protected like that in the silence of a lovely, warm, homely room, with soft pangs of sadness,… romantic, unattainable, separated… and with a mysterious, exciting, secret bond of belonging to each other, and to sense each other's feelings through conscious or unconscious movements, through words that slipped out, but were understood.

Not for a moment did I think something like, 'If only Aunt Ilka weren't here!'; indeed, I was more willing to talk to her, confidentially and with the seriousness of a married woman; at moments we mentioned life and destiny—Ilka sighed and I stared hard into the lamplight. Endre became grave and sank into the armchair, watching me assiduously and almost the whole time uttering not a single word.

My husband came home, fresh and cool as a cucumber, and greeted them graciously. I offered my cheek to him, and did not worry about this—I wanted Endre to see when he kissed me.

Minutes later, the two men were deep in serious conversation. I listened for a while; they were talking about the land that the estate was going to sell or lease.

This was the excuse that made Tabódy frequent our house for a couple of weeks; he came quite often and always before Jenő arrived home from the casino.

'I can't help it. I can't leave the town. I know I can't expect anything, but just bear with me for a little while longer, so I can see you, see you both.'

I nodded and drew my hand over the tassels of the armchair. The lamp hissed softly, the fire leapt into flame now and again; outside footsteps clumped with a hollow sound on the snow-covered cobbles, while far off in the kitchen the maid clattered the dishes. How dear to me were these quarter-hours, and how lovely! A man who loves me, yet with whom I can happily be alone like this, perhaps just because he loves me—but in thought or dreams he is certain to have thrown himself at me, kissed me, embraced me. And at that time, as a wife of eighteen months, I felt totally satisfied after such a silent, ardent half-hour. Jenő came in, kind and friendly, and pressed the guest to stay to dinner.

'I feel at home here with you!' Endre kept repeating in a daze after one or two glasses of wine. 'It's good to see genuine happiness!'

'Well, we're genuinely happy, aren't we, my little witch?' laughed Jenő, reaching for my hand. 'So follow the good example, old chap, and you, too, get married as soon as you can. That's real happiness, say what you will!'

'I don't know whether that will ever happen.'

'Oh come! Was it that someone was snatched away from you?'

'Something like that.'

'Why did you let it happen?' I, too, entered the game boldly.

'Sometimes a man is cowardly, foolish. Then he must bear his troubles till he dies.'

'Oho, my lad, there are plenty more where that one came from!' laughed Jenő, the truly unsuspecting husband, as he filled his glass.

'But even this miserable little bit of happiness must come to an end soon,' said Endre next day in dejection. 'I'm scared to continue coming here, in case people begin to notice.'

'As far as I'm concerned, I feel quite at ease; let them gossip!' I replied resolutely and now with a hint of fear.

'It's easy for you! But as for me, I can't bear it. What kind of a person do you think I am?'

He fell silent for a time, taking rapid, audible breaths, then he suddenly got up and left. I did not see him for some days, and every night I lay motionless and wide-eyed, listening to Jenő's gentle snores. One afternoon I set out to pay a call on Aunt Bélteky. On the corner of County Street in the twilight and silence of winter, I recognized his footsteps behind me.

'Where are you going?'

'To your aunt's.'

'I'll be along there in ten minutes, by chance. I must talk to you.'

We must have sat there for half an hour in tense, distracted and impatient conversation, then we set off at the same time. 'Now it's sure to be obvious and they'll talk about it,' I thought, 'but now, this once, I don't care! It's all the same to me!'

Beneath the veil of dusk, we slipped quietly along the alleys; only the snow lighted our way now among the frost-covered trees on the path. Then we arrived at the foot of the castle garden, where a mile of iron railings borders the park belonging to the estate. In summertime this is where people stroll, but at this time of the year not a soul was about. Far away winking lights of lamps from the bright doorways of the row of shops pierced the mist, while behind us the massive oak trees and the white-clad little pines stood silent under their blanket of snow. We sat on a bench, and Endre kissed the white of my hand and wrist above my glove. 'Oh, what a long way from home I am,' I thought, rather scared.

'Magda, please don't think I'm mad or wicked. But it's impossible, simply impossible, for one mistake to wreck my life. Our lives. Come with me!'

'Endre, you...'

'Divorce him, and be mine!'

'Endre, how can you say such a thing?'

'Yes, come with me! Just as you are, Magda—I've no regrets now. Neither of us will ever love like this again. Go with me!'

His words fell on my spirit like strong, glorious flashes of real life—possibilities that had now revealed themselves, strange, stirring drams, like some *complete* experience. But not for half a moment was I tempted to follow what his words implied. I was able to separate the stage-scene of beautiful moments from the everyday, ordinary ones of reality. 'After all, he too is certain to have different thoughts tomorrow morning!'

'Look here, Endre,' I said gravely and with conviction from the depths of my heart, 'I've got something to tell you that will make all the difference. In seven months' time I'm going to have a little baby and... I can't be free now...'

A great silence settled on us, delightful, touching, painful. But there was a sense of liberation in it, too. I felt that this little life, as yet hardly stirring, was already protecting me, shielding me from some possible fearful, critical, violent change, deed or decision. That would have been too much for me. But acting like this was something I needed—it would be a memory for me, of a beautiful and rich evening.

He accompanied me home in silence, with bowed head. In the narrow Jews' Alley he suddenly looked about him and squeezed my arm.

'Look at me just once more!'

When I turned towards him he pressed his mouth to mine so

swiftly and forcibly that I could not stop him. The next moment, upset and ashamed, I pushed him away from me in terror.

'Go away this instant! I don't want to see you ever again!'

I ran out of the alley. In the Hajdú Town, ours was the third house. Inside everything was clean and warm, and the maid was laying the table for supper. Panting, I threw off my outdoor clothes and corsets; two minutes later in my ample, familiar tea-gown, I was sewing beneath the shaded lamp, feigning calm as I waited for my husband.

'Have you been anywhere today?' he asked offhandedly at one point.

'At Ilka's,' I said, hiding my great inner fear in indifference. I was lying, yet there was no trace of a lie in what I said.

'Just imagine!' said Jenő at lunch the next day, 'our Endre has suddenly gone away. He came into the office to say goodbye; he'd had an urgent call from home. He sends his greetings.'

I sat at the lunch-table relieved and almost happy. That afternoon the maid came in to ask me to come out for a minute. Someone wanted a word with me.

'Whoever is it?' I asked with an instinctive fear.

'The newspaper boy.'

'Well I never!' I laughed in surprise and relief. 'You go, Jenő, please.'

'He's brought a letter for you, just look! Isn't Endre's writing? What a fool he is! This is the way he says goodbye to you!'

He handed it to me and unfolded the great big Pest news-paper. Only minutes later did he speak from its depths.

'Well, what does he write?'

'Nothing special.'

'Where is the letter?' And he fixed me with a questioning glance, still innocently surprised.

'I've thrown it into the fire!'

'Into the fire? Without reading it? Why?'

'Just because!'

'Magda!'

Very pale, and trembling in every limb, I leaned against a cupboard.

'Magda, do say something!'

He stood up and came closer; he stared into my eyes with a scared, changed expression.

'Say something! Was there anything... anything between

you? Why are you being so secretive? There must have been some reason for you to throw it into the fire before I could see it. You know what he's written!'

'Leave me alone!' I groaned, trembling, but with defiant anger rising in me. 'Don't ask questions! I can see you wouldn't believe me anyway! I don't care!'

He grasped me by both shoulders, his face distorted and snarling with impotent rage; he shook me, and then restraining himself suddenly pushed me out of his way with loathing. Whether by accident or not, I happened to fall full-length on the Turkish divan. He went into the bedroom and locked the door behind him.

For a while I sat there recovering, trembling and full of loathing. So was that the end of everything here? This was the other side of life, of those romantic, interesting, tender delights. Jenő like this!... Oh, poor man, poor man! But he had hit me—and at this time—and without asking me any questions either! How frail men are in such things, hidebound, helpless and almost humorous! What was he doing now in there? I stood up and my legs shook as if with deadly tiredness. I tried the doorhandle and waited a little; I spoke, but there was no reply. Then in a daze I put on a fur coat and hat and left the house, making for grandma's house without a further thought.

It was Ágnes who let me in. I sat down and could not utter a word in the turmoil of emotion I was trying to hide. She did not notice. In her usual quiet, awkward way she chatted about domestic cares, about the child, how István was irritated when the baby cried during the night, and how she had to hide him away because he might even beat him, maybe. She sometimes had to rock the baby for half the night. And the second one was already on the way. But what could she do: that was life... And she nodded with her beautiful little madonna-head beneath the rich crown of hair.

'I hear you had a good time at the Béltekys,' she later said.

'Why didn't you come too?' I asked, just for something to say.

'Grandma didn't want us to. She said a new dress now was a waste of money. And that it wasn't good for a young wife to be seen everywhere.'

I listened with a kind of odd spiritual nausea. Why, she was a secret enemy! She envied me!

My ears were buzzing and I shut my eyes from time to time. I was glad that I did not have to think about anything for some minutes. It didn't matter, all the same! Don't let them ask any questions! Don't let them upset me! Let them decide whatever they like about me! They know! What does it matter to me!...

'How's your husband?' asked my grandmother when she came in later.

'Well!'

'When are you going to Telegd to see your mother and her husband?'

'I don't know.'

'As far as I'm concerned,' she said slowly, with an unusual burst of intimacy, 'I don't particularly want to go and see them. I've heard some odd things...'

'Really?'

'Well, your stepfather Péter's a weird and wonderful creature. He ought to be shut up in the madhouse, and all his daft, nonsensical books burnt on a pyre in the marketplace. He spends his whole time buried in them; that's what's devouring his whole life.'

'Really!'

'And your mother's small fortune—do you know, they've used it all up with all sorts of useless expensive machinery and buildings! He says that the agricultural labourer—that's his name for the peasants—must have healthy, and dry and the devil only knows what else kind of accommodations. Every labourer's family must have a detached house with a little garden, wooden floors, very elegant—the sort of thing he's seen in a picture somewhere. Yes, and the old grain-store that belonged to his father, he's rebuilt it because the window isn't facing the direction of the "prevailing wind". He's such an idiot!'

'Good gracious!'

'And then he treats his peasants as if they were patients in a hospital. He doesn't lay a hand on a single one of them, and even the stable-boy doesn't get a rod to his back. Because that's an offence against human dignity. During the winter, they even stole his fence and chopped it up for firewood. Then he had the serfs summoned into the yard and preached some tear-jerking sermon to them about rights and "property." What do you say to that?'

'Awful!'

'And in the future, he says, he's not going to sow wheat,

because that's what's killing the Hungarian soil, since everyone's doing it. So he's going to switch to root crops. Roots! For heaven's sake! And for your mother, too, he had some new kind of hen's eggs brought from a German zoo; each one of them had printed on it which hen and which cock were responsible for it and when it was laid; that's what he wants her to produce. All the expensive chicks were hatched and all of them died, too, though they were fed on tender greenstuff dipped in milk like young ladies of quality.'

'Indeed!'

'Yes, but the craziest thing of all's yet to come. You know, that heathen old father of his had a bastard child by a maid he kept there. She's dead now, and the boy was apprenticed to a cobbler there in Váralja, a hard-working, decent apprentice if his nose was kept to the grindstone, said his master. Well, he sent for the lad—even at the old man's funeral, I'm now told, he put him at the foot of the coffin while he sat at the head of it, saying, "You're of my father's blood just as much as I am!" Well, now he's taken him away from his trade and keeps him there like a parasite, so that he can have his share of the inheritance; the lad's gone bad, he drinks, smokes a pipe and flirts with the servants all day long, swatting flies from his legs, and your mother puts up with this and everything else, too, everybody can do what they like with Klári. She's such a fool! She's in love with him. But how's it all going to end?'

'How indeed?...'

'And as for you... whatever's the matter with you?'

'I don't know, grandmother! ... My God!'

Everything suddenly whirled in front of my eyes and went dark... then began to revolve slowly... something trickled gently in my ears... It was so good to let myself go and fall back, to forget and be released from words and burdens—from all the rigours and very great difficulties of life.

Later, perhaps a good while later, I was only half aware that I was lying on the settee in the dining-room; the big clock was ticking away, a lamp was alight, and Ágnes was walking softly around me. Then the opening and closing of doors outside, hushed and passionate voices talking.

'My dear, my little wife!' Jenő's scared and tender face bent over me. He was kneeling on the floor beside me and stroking my arms and face with pleading affection.

'My little witch, my poor little thing, my one and only little mama! Don't be angry! I know everything! My mother happened to drop in today just at the right moment. You see, you confided in her more than you did in me, your own husband, didn't you? Do you think that's right? True, she gave the best advice, to send away that poor crazy boy instantly, the one who had a sudden passion for you. But why didn't you say something earlier? What a misunderstanding there might have been if mother hadn't known everything, if she hadn't explained it all! But it was wrong for you not to say anything to me. You were afraid of a duel or something like that. Well, now we must take care of you and look after your health, my little witch!'

And I accepted all this in silence—a benevolent lie, tender care and concern, the gentle, natural return to normal life around me. I tranquilly put up with his caresses, endearments and fussing around me, showing his truest nature, paternal and giving him pleasure as well.

And this was how I saw him once again much later—in the endless semi-wakefulness of long, wearing, sick, feverish nights as I lay motionless amid the smells of medicine, deep shadows and dull pain. And he moved around noiselessly in his white dressing-gown in front of the nightlight like a large, warm, living statue, like something that kept me here, entreating me to stay, caring for me, and so long as I could see him, there was no need to be afraid. Pacing through the rooms in the hazy glow of the nightlight, he softly embraced in his white gown, a restless, weeping little mite, his son, carrying him around busily, hushing and rocking him.

X.

By the time I was cured, Pityu was already a year old; he crawled around on the floor and rode on his father's knee. And the first word he was able to pronounce was 'daddy'.

As for me, I began once more to move around in the world from which I had half withdrawn. 'Just live yourself back into life!' old Doctor Jakobi kept saying. But life, or a piece of it, had already slipped from beneath me, and now I found it difficult to regain my foothold. I remember that for months I just pottered around and felt with dim fearfulness that one beautiful, youthful year of mine was missing, indeed lost, and I sensed the lack of it in everything, including my development as a mother. The little one was not a pretty child; he was wizened and pale. While I was ill in bed or being pushed in a wheelchair at the little spa in the next county—someone else looked after him—it was his father who watched over the wet-nurse's timetable and later his baby-food; it was he who taught him to play, look at things and put his tiny hands together to pray 'for mummy to get better'. But they dressed him in dowdy and tasteless baby-clothes and rather spoilt him. 'As soon as I'm able,' I thought, 'the first thing I'll do will be to make Hani sew nice little embroidered white piqué clothes. And a red silk coat with big gold buttons the size of walnuts!'

My husband was good to me and very compassionate. Oh, now, after so many years and so many experiences, he is often on my mind; was I able to appreciate his devoted love sufficiently? Yet—though it's a crime to think of it, all the same!—there was something clumsy in this, something stodgy and rather boring, a frequently irritating stuffiness in his goodness, something too contrived, deliberate and unctuous. If only he had not reminded me sometimes of his father!

His parents no longer lived here. They had retired. The old man had been advised to breathe the air of a larger town in Upper Hungary, and they had moved there.

In other respects, our life now was unruffled and free from all financial worries. 'Respect that good husband of yours,' grandma kept saying, 'for keeping you in such style; the little money you might still have had was spent on your illness, to be sure.'

Yes, Jenő was doing very well at the time. We moved to a larger dwelling in Church Street, where his office was, too. On market-day mornings, there were swarms of litigious countryfolk arriving, linen-trousered Hungarians from Börvely and Germans in broadcloth jackets from Erdőd. The wives brought chickens and geese, and supplied the household with eggs. Sometimes, however, Jenő had to calm me down when I began to grumble about the smell of tobacco and the mud they brought in with their boots, for they had to cross the carpeted hall. 'Hush, my dear, hush! They're our livelihood!' he would say at such times.

And now he became more willing sometimes to talk about his work. Perhaps he was pleased that it interested me, and he would explain odd legal cases, the spirit of the law in general, the cunning, clever and devious ways of defending justice. I became quite familiar with the technical terms too. And gradually I became quite certain that my husband was indeed a talented, very learned man of swift judgment in his own sphere.

'How's Péter Kendy's case about the division of the inheritance going?' I asked on occasion. 'Are you straightening it out?'

'It's a very tricky affair,' he gave a dejected wave of the hand. 'The estate's involved in it, too.'

'All the same... he put his affair into your hands by right of kinship; you know that means a lot from such a haughty man.'

We fell silent—this was during lunch—but the affair would not leave me in peace. The Kendys were indeed the creme of county society and very distant relatives of mine, and somehow I felt it important, a particular stroke of luck, that they would be indebted to my own husband, who had married above himself. Afterwards, when we were having coffee, the whole idea burst from me with suddenness and surprise.

'What do you think? All those folk, the whole county—wouldn't they be of more worth to you than those arrogant counts of yours?'

'What's that you're saying, child?'

'Yes, and Scherer the inspector, who detested your father, too—do you think he really wishes you well?

'I don't depend on him!'

I could see that he was thinking about this, and I surprised myself, too. So he really did take what I had said with only a dimly-perceived aim seriously—perhaps it was only a wife's instinctive idea.

'Now at last my own little wife has finally recovered,' he smiled later. 'She's getting a taste for politics.'

'I'm not very much concerned about politics, Jenő,' I replied, growing bold, 'but you know, I want to be *somebody* here in Szinyér, the wife of a leading personality, whom nobody may so much as dare to despise. Do you understand? There you are then! It certainly looks as though I've regained my health!'

I burst into laughter as I said this; Jenő took me on his lap and kissed me again and again. 'We'll see, my little witch, we'll see!' And my spirits soared at this almost chance exchange of ideas. Why, it might be possible sometime to be freed from this estate gang, with whom now I must remain in contact somehow! Through courtesy visits, unavoidable invitations and social functions, I was bored and irritated by their whole way of life—well-to-do, solid, diplomatic, restrained and restricted—and their topics of conversation and interests; the one eternal focus that drew them together was the Count's family, their internal and external affairs, their intimate gossip and little romances. They repeated the words of their masters, they passed their silly jokes from mouth to mouth, and made guesses of all kinds to explain their deeds, sometimes with really great excitement. 'They're more contemptible than my maids,' I thought. 'At least, they live their own lives!' I was often reminded of my mother-in-law, who indeed was the most distinguished of them: she read, she had travelled around, and in and of herself was pleasant, easy-going and natural. While she was here, the old dowager Countess would often invite her in if she were alone on a winter evening, and they would play piquet till midnight or play the piano; the Countess would ask her about the gossip in the town. But wasn't this just what my own grandma had done with Náni Spach the linen-peddler with her knapsack, or Trézsi the rag-dealer? It was a real servant's destiny! And I could not forget, because of Jenő, that after our wedding, he took me to pay a courtesy call on the dowager Countess so that he could introduce me. On the estate everyone regarded it as natural that there was no question that these visits would be returned; I knew this, too, but I was always seized by a fit of rage when it occurred to me. I would not have gone at any price to see Count Lajos's young wife whom he had just brought home then, though the others, including the older wives, too, all went up to greet her. I had taken things so far at that stage that Jenő did not even ask me, though he often went out on the marshes with Count Lajos to shoot wild duck, and he always came home afterwards in good spirits. 'He can do it,' I thought; 'he's an official of the Count's.' And I knew he treated him as the son of his father's old friend and had a high opinion of his intellect.

Now I really flung myself into life once more; but in the meantime my spirit, too, had somehow grown up out of childhood. I began to take an interest in certain things in a different, adult way. Holding a cushion I was embroidering, I would often listen intently when after dinner Jenő had a lively discussion with my stepfather, Péter, who now visited us quite frequently, always staying with us, in order to discuss his complicated affairs.

'Things are quite impossible here, quite impossible!' he said passionately, pouring out his soul to Jenő. 'Believe me, you have no idea what a degenerate country ours has become! All of it, but especially these parts. The county wants a bomb under it, a bomb, lock, stock and barrel! It's all old pals together; a clique reinforced by haphazard marriages designed to hide their laziness, ignorance and tyrannical wickedness. The bands of robbers in Southern Italy are better than they are; they at least want to do something and act on it, too: they want to stir things up. Do you remember Eötvös's novel, *The Village Notary*?* And how it's all described there? Well, as you can see, nothing's changed since then!'

'Oh, but there are a few changes! Believe me, even here you'll find a few people with good minds and honourable intentions, for example.'

'Oh, come off it! Don't tell me that! The whole place is a hive of narrow-mindedness. Do you really think that in the whole wide world there's anywhere else with such lazy and senseless farming, such wasteful, haphazard and superficial methods of production, without any eye to the market, as in this famous, wheat-and-wine land of Hungary? All right, all right, just wave your hand like that! It's easy for you, young man; there will

* *The Village Notary: A falu jegyzője*, a novel by the social reformer and statesman József Eötvös (1813–1871). First published in 1845, it castigated conditions in a fictitious Hungarian county.

always be plenty of lawsuits, land-divisions and long drawn out cases. It's an eldorado for lawyers, that's for sure, and it always has been.'

'Come, come, old chap!'

'Of course the committee voted down the scheme I put up last year for an association to buy agricultural machinery for cooperative use. If only they'd at least made sensible objections! If only they'd discuss it seriously! But they didn't even bother with it; they gawked at it and avoided it like any idea that's new and bold. They regarded me as a madman for bringing it up.'

'If I may say so, my dear fellow, you really don't know how to speak so that the folk will understand, that's all there is to it! It would have been a sensible thing, but you ought to have stated your case in a different way; it should have been more suited to them, with a better description of the practical solution and the details. You always remain at the level of generalities and theory.'

'Indeed? Oh well, all right, that's a little thing. But now there's the question of the draining of the marshes. It's as clear as daylight: it would bring clear profit to everyone, it's a problem that can be solved in a couple of years, and it's a burning necessity from the point of view of the national economy. You can see how it's been struggling to come to the surface for years, and now it's sunk without any trace again.'

'You can't blame the estate; they were the first to put it forward, and that was in seventy.'

'Ah yes, your father worked it out... Don't get me wrong, the old man was well aware of what he was doing, but that was not a fair scheme. Everything for the Count! No, the way the previous government tried it up yonder, sharing out proportionately according to the old land-holdings, that was a more honest plan, all the same. But, well, they fell. Every government begins to hurry on with its sensible, civilized aims when it feels it's going to fall.'

'Look here, my dear Péter,' Jenő began to take it all rather more seriously, 'it's certain that the estate would get the greatest benefit from the whole drainage plan. That goes without saying. But all the same, there would be a great deal in it for the farmers, too. The only reason why they're making a fuss is because of their traditional opposition to the counts, and because those who have land along the Szinyér would certainly be burdened with the new tax.'

'Damn it, for heaven's sake! Don't I myself live along the Szinyér? And aren't I just as much tied up with it all?… All the same, I tell you…'

'You're a great idealist, Péter, that's for certain! Well now, you see… Count Lajos is going to stand for parliament in the autumn. We'll see what folks have to say to that!'

'What? Are you sure?'

'If he sees no future in it, he'll withdraw, but there's no doubt about it, that's his intention.'

'Is there anything to him?'

'He's modern, intelligent and knows where he's going. He'll cause a few surprises! If not here… then elsewhere; it would be better for us if he were to remain with us.'

'Hm. We'll have something more to say about that, old chap. There have been rumours already, but I didn't think he was serious. His father was driven out of politics.'

'But his wife's family will take him in.'

'Do you know what? My peasants don't even need a half litre of wine as a bribe, that I can tell you! They'll follow me through fire and water!'

A few glasses of light wine had inflamed him a little, but Jenő was sober and calm as usual.

'You know,' I said to him when Péter had left, 'you mustn't believe much in what he says about his peasants and everything. The estate might make concessions in the Kendy affair! And you yourself, too…'

'Oh you little schemer!' he laughed and drew his finger across my forehead. 'Why, of course we'll get down to that in time. But do keep watch on that little tongue of yours now that you're so much involved!'

'What do you think of me?' I said, offended. And I proudly kept the secret. Half playfully, I was glad that I was initiated into 'serious affairs', and after that, Jenő discussed many things with me. This was a new bond between us.

It was about that time that old Bélteky died, the former public notary who had also been the guardian of my two younger brothers. Then the family asked for my husband to take on this task in his place. This brought a great deal of trouble in its wake, since Jenő took his duties very seriously. He often had to deal with Csaba's debts and minor breaches of the law, and from time to time, with Sándor's sickness.

Sándor was a slender, girlish theological student with a fine face. When he came home on vacation from the seminary, we fed him and stuffed him with all kinds of good things; we also wanted to show him a good time, but he walked around with downcast eyes and read his breviary, and at the sound of the noonday bell, wherever we were, whoever was with us at home, I saw his lips move as he murmured the angelus.

'What a sour face!' Uncle István sometimes struck him on the back. 'You'll never make a bishop like that, lad! You still haven't gone through one kind of baptism!'

'He's still not anointed with one kind of oil,' laughed Ilka. 'And he's got to light the devil's candle, too!'

He blushed to the roots of his hair, so that I took pity on him. Sometimes I took him aside and talked to him like a sister, a good comrade.

'Tell me the truth, Sándor. Do you believe completely in the faith, the way it's written?'

'Magda! How can you ask me a question like that?'

'It was only a thought. Look, all those nice, clever, worldly, elegant priests around don't behave like you. Yet they're good priests; they get on in their careers. I wonder, is there some secret agreement among them about the truth?'

'But Magda, are you really serious…?'

'It was only a thought. Perhaps you don't know yet. Suppose you were to realize some time that the whole thing was a secret conspiracy, of course out of sheer goodwill to mankind. That you're taught about the wafer and that we are resurrected alive. Suppose you were to learn the secret…'

'Magda! For God's sake, I beg you, stop it! I can't bear to listen! If I were to learn that nobody believed, even then I would. Because it's true, that's why!'

'But where do you get that certainty?'

'From myself! Because it must be so! If it were not true, so many of us wouldn't have felt it to be so for so many centuries. The Church is such a perfect, magnificent organization. My faith is part of me, it's within me. A man's lost if there's no certainty above every contact to which he can cling. You haven't got to ponder everything; thought is a secondary thing. You've got to know how to cling to something. But no, I can't talk very well about it; I'm only an ordinary soldier of the faith.'

'I think I understand you, and you're right!' I said swiftly, because someone happened to come between us and this put me off. 'He may be a bit stupid,' I thought to myself, 'but how good he is, kindly and pure!' It was to him that I felt the closest kinship in all of my family, and I think my little son resembled him. When he played with little Pityu and walked him in his pram, he was like the holy young monks attending the baby Jesus in old pictures.

The person who interrupted our routine was the French language teacher who turned up in the town at that time, and my husband immediately engaged him to give me lessons. For a whole winter we wrestled with conjugations and grammar from a book; M. Bardeaux had a dusty suit and dirty fingernails; his past was obscure and his existence peculiar. He always wiped the inky pen in his thick strands of black hair and sometimes reeked of brandy. As spring came, he was sometimes discovered in the morning drunk on a bench beneath the Castle garden. Then he lost his pupils and as suddenly as he had arrived, he disappeared from the town.

In those days, Jenő was fond of these kind of extravagances. Once when I had a toothache, he fetched the most expensive dentist from Debrecen. The result of this was that I had a fit of nerves, wept and refused to let him pull out the tooth, so all the expense was in vain. Things like this soon became topics of conversation at tea over there in the estate officials' houses. 'Just let them envy me! That's good!' I thought sometimes in a fit of haughtiness.

During the following autumn, with a great deal of commotion, many banquets, wine and speeches, Count Lajos Szinyéry became a member of parliament here. Péter Telekdy kept his peasants up to the mark at his own expense, while Jenő created the right atmosphere in the town; and Péter Kendy also added his considerable support, for the estate did indeed settle its case with him. Yes, this success was due to Jenő through my relations; the Count himself knew this and wrote him a fine private letter of thanks in a tone that was almost friendly. 'So much for the Scherers!' I exulted in triumph.

XI.

That spring saw the arrival of deputy sheriff Jolsvay, whose wife was my second cousin, Melanie Pórtelky, a baroness in her own right.

I awaited their first visit with some trepidation and was prepared for anything, in case the lady tried to impress me with the superiority of her wealth and famous title—gained by intrigue during the Bach era.* 'I'll not bow down to her!' I thought; 'Why, not even her great-great grandfather has ever seen Pórtelek, the backwoods village in the marsh, and the colonnaded ancestral house where the parents of my own father lived, and where I can still return with dim childhood memories and visualize the threshing-floor, the horse-driven mill down below, and the gabled front of the "castle" with its stone eaves.' I resolved to be very much on guard so as not to appear too ready to make friends, a social climber counting on her high-ranking relatives. But it turned out differently. She disarmed me completely with her slightly strange, particularly great charm.

Melanie was a beautiful, blonde, mature woman; only the characteristic curve of her nose betrayed her Pórtelky ancestry; but her face was soft and pure, slightly imperious like Maria Theresa's, but more attractive.

She asked about Uncle Ábris, with whom we had had very little contact recently because of all the minor differences between him and grandma. Then she went on to say how much she would need me and my friendship, so that I could tell her about people and conditions here. She was especially gracious to Jenő; she gave the impression that she wanted to win him over completely. There was no trace in her of the family haughtiness or prejudice. 'She's a different sort; has she risen above it, or is she just good at hiding it?' I wondered.

Her friendship meant more comings and goings, social appearances and entertaining for me. One servant was now no longer sufficient for me to be able to keep my house clean and

---

* *The Bach era* was the period of Austrian rule after the collapse of the Hungarian revolution of 1848, so named after the Austrian Minister of the Interior, Alexander Bach.

presentable, so I had a series of stupid little fifteen-year old Swabian lasses fetched from the nearby villages, who after a fortnight of my training, all turned into splendid housemaids. I took a lot of trouble over precise, genteel preparations at the table, and this was how Jenő liked it, too. We took great pleasure in showing this off chiefly to the country gentry who now became our guests ever more frequently. Their affairs were mostly in the hands of my husband, and now, seen from close proximity, the famous Széchys, Kendys, Rábas and others did not impress me as such great folk as they had done in my childhood, through family title-tattle and unfounded esteem. They seemed to have lost their sparkle—or was it I that had grown up? Seen like this, full of worries and cares, helpless in the hands of their solicitor, surrounded by their families, pipe-smoking and complaining about the weather—or reminiscing about horses, dogs and old escapades of their youth in their usual slow, awkward manner of speech—not really at home in my pretty, sparkling, clean rooms with their sand-filled, paper-decorated spittoons, oh how clumsily rustic they were at times!

But now it was of them that Jenő said, 'Just treat them gently and nicely; it's in their footsteps that we trod!' Six months later, we moved into our third dwelling, near the County Hall and the inn, for it was now the county, and not the market-place that brought in most of the clients. How many contentious land-adjustments there were at that time, and what a harvest the lawyers reaped! The draining of the marshes was only in its initial planning stage, but so many wayward calculations, worries and speculations gathered round it; separate claims, appropriations of land, a hundred types of greed for the promised land which still lay dormant beneath tussocks of reed and duckweed and only provided nests for water-fowl.

So we rented a whole house, a large and newly-built one on the corner of Seven Eagle Feathers Street, near County Street. The old ones were low, with beamed ceilings and wooden lintels, but ours had been constructed by the new foreman-builder, who made tall windows with wooden shutters instead of latticed blinds; he fixed a showy veranda on the yard side in front of all the fine, spacious rooms. Oh, it was a delight to settle in here; we both suddenly felt a sense of liberation, we were in our element here. Yes, now that I recall these things from the distant past, I want to be fair to myself, but I know for sure that not only

I, but my husband too, loved and required all the refinement and beauty, the newer and more affluent habits and more advanced way of life that it brought.

'We'll plant beds of flowers in the courtyard,' he started planning with great enthusiasm; 'We'll put rose-stocks right in the centre, about a hundred of them in a big circle; we'll have honeysuckle running up the wall of the stable, and over there at the foot of the lilacs there's a place for Pityu's swing and sports gear. We'll plant lots of oleanders and pomegranates along the little veranda, and a nice pergola covered with vines in the corner. The lease is for ten years, and we can settle in it as if it were our own. Maggie! Suppose we might be able to buy it by then!'

'That's a long way off yet! But now, oh dear!, what a lot of work there'll be with all these rooms! How ever shall I manage, for heaven's sake? True, they're lovely! What a beautiful pattern this wall has, gold and lilac! Yes, this is going to be the salon!'

For that is what we called the drawing-room now, since Melanie had introduced this new French-sounding word here.

'That little separate room at the end of the veranda, Maggie, we'll furnish it for your brothers, so that they can always feel at home here whenever they come on vacation. And do you know, that Zsuzsi Képíró, the one who cooked for our wedding, I'm told we might be able to get her as a cook. Of course she would ask twelve forints. She worked for the Kendys on their farm. What do you say to that?'

'Oh, she's... a wonderful cook! I suppose she might come. But a noblewoman from Magyar Street... in our house?'

'What do you mean, "in our house"? Dear, dear! But of course she must have her own little room. She would be a kind of housekeeper.'

Well, I settled down with a new sense of delight and enthusiasm to getting the house straight. The furniture we had was insufficient, so I had to get a lot more, enough for a whole guest-bedroom, a nursery and a little blue living room. The legs of the chairs with the silk amoretti had to be reguilded, as had the mirror; the piano had to be tuned, and silverware and candle-sticks to be bought. 'Well, you know, this is an investment for us now,' Jenő kept saying with a serious expression.

The stable-master happened to mention to him that he had two handsome ponies. The estate at Erdőd had sent them over because the little countesses were now grown-up. He sold them very cheaply, and in any case there was a stable attached to the house; we also had to employ a gardener to do the watering and path-sweeping anyway, so we bought them and I enthusiastically and roguishly drove the attractive decked-out little old animals all the way along the foot of the Castle and out towards the vineyards. Now I was blossoming out a little and I was not in the least worried that the route took me in front of the row of estate officials' houses.

But my husband then received a long, censorious, admonishing letter from his old father, as harsh and emotional as the letters of the apostles in the Bible. It may well have taken the old man three days to draft it. Jenő handed it to me to read, too, then put it away without a word and maintained a stubborn and rather morose silence when I began to talk, argue and justify ourselves against the charges. For a couple of days this caused some tension between us, but then I helped to make it pass. A wife has only one office-manager, her husband; and he, if he loves her a little, can always be bribed.

But now at least we could see clearly what a treacherous, envious, scheming gang the estate officials were. Yes, it was they who had corresponded with the old folk, making charges and exaggerating our 'madly prodigal' life-style. Pah! 'Right, I'll do it just to spite them!' I thought, enraged. To me this intrigue, cloaked in the guise of goodwill was loathsome.

And I was even more annoyed that grandma, too, had become cooler towards us of late; she visited us more rarely (she had aged a lot now), and she often made short, sharp comments on our life-style. 'You must be doing very well if you've got money to spend on a thing like that!' And, 'My own house was no convent, but I've never known such a plague of locusts as you have here! They come, all and sundry, as if to a pure well!' 'Of course,' I thought, 'for her now the way her daughter-in-law Ágnes lives is the only good way; she's expecting her fourth child, she goes nowhere and her youth has gone quite numb with boredom, worry and spineless obedience!'

'I've come on a serious errand!' began Melanie in her rich, fresh, attractive voice, smoothing back her thick fair hair. 'I'm depending on you again; do help me, dear! We've got to organize a woman's society here. It's a disgrace that until now there hasn't been one in such a big place or even in the county town. I thought the two of us might head it—at the beginning, of course, till someone more suitable takes my place. And we'd persuade the dowager Countess to be honorary president. That would be Jenő's job, to smooth our path with her.'

'I shall be only too pleased, of course!' said my husband politely.

'But there's something else, too, rather more boring, in store for you.' She turned to him with an attractive smile in her clear, glowing eyes. 'The society must have a secretary who'll be close to us to give advice and deal with formalities. After all, we're only helpless women! And this important and noble aim would draw together elements that are being pulled apart here. You must be sympathetic to such a cause! Look here, we'll do our best not to burden you with things, we'll deal with them, we only need your name and personal prestige and your advice sometimes. Well now, Vodicska, don't have any second thoughts! You'll agree, won't you?'

I saw that Jenő had no way to escape now, but I was not sure whether it was to his liking. But after all, why not? It was time for us to play a part now, and this could only be to our advantage.

'How old is your little boy?' Melanie asked quickly later, pretending as usual not to have seen him. 'Not yet four? And he talks so clearly already? Look, what he ought to have now is a foreign girl; if you like, we can fetch one from Switzerland; I'm going to write about one now—I want one for my little girls.'

'Oh, you'd do us a great favour, Melanie! That's really very good of you!'

When we were alone later, Jenő was very worried about this. 'That makes four servants now; whatever will they say to that?' But in front of Melanie it was impossible to refuse, and secretly delighted, I thought how nice it would be for me to drive out in the pony-cart with Pityu and the nursemaid seated behind me in their Sunday best.

It was about that time that Melanie brought the game of lawn-tennis into fashion here; by now it is probably well-known throughout the whole country, but at that time it was not even played in Pest. Some English dancing-master had been staying with the Jolsvays during the summer, and he had taught the little girls to play. And Melanie had the first court laid down in the courtyard of the County Hall.

Certainly we were clumsy; it was not the usual thing here

for folk to leap and run about and pant unless they had to—and after a coloured ball like a child. We married ladies did quite enough trudging, bending down and getting hot with the housework in the morning, myself in particular. By the afternoon all one wanted was to sit down prettily dressed and corseted, not to disturb the hair we had put up, not to make our carefully-tended complexion suffer perspiration before strangers and men, and not to let our fine, pointed shoes get covered in dust. I certainly did not make any great effort to play, but it was a very good excuse for socializing and enjoying myself.

One late summer afternoon I had just returned home from Telegd, where I had spent a few weeks enjoying the coolness at my mother's house, when a new man was introduced to me at the courts. He had arrived while I was away and had already made the whole round of visits. His name was Horváth (names like that reveal nothing, even when they are written with a final *h*); he, too, was a solicitor and by no means young; he must have been the same age as my husband. 'Melanie's far too willing to accept anyone!' I thought in those first moments, but later, since the stranger did not play either because there was something wrong with his hand, I got into conversation with him all the same.

If only I could remember clearly now how I saw him at that time and how he impressed me!

I think he struck me as strange, different from the rest and quite congenial; but it was with a little vexation and scorn that I thought of those women who were almost immediately enchanted with him.

He had a peculiar way of looking into your face with a kind of pleased and gentle delight that does not desire or seek anything more, and is full of grateful devotion just for that. Just that women exist, and that they are beautiful, well-groomed and kindly.

'I keep looking at your hair-style,' he said quietly and thoughtfully. 'If instead of brushing it upwards you were to draw it all to one side, even that hidden under your hat, yes, more would fall over your face and it would look all the more effective. Of course, there's a lot of it as it is, it might be a bit exaggerated, but it would be tremendously impressive. What splendid hair you have, the rarest kind! That it curls quite naturally and needs no curling-irons is immediately obvious, and in such great waves, and not unpleasantly ruffled strand by strand!'

'Are you such an expert in women's lore?'

'That's not expertise! I'm only spelling it out. In any case a whole library of books wouldn't be sufficient to describe your appearance. It's quite distinctive, but all the same you do resemble someone. Yes indeed, very much so!'

'Really? Have you known someone like me?'

'Yes, if you were to dress and behave like her, definitely. But you're far better as you are!'

'Who was she?'

'A famous German actress, a very famous one.'

We fell silent and later, furtively and out of the corner of my eye, I had a good look at him. He was a fresh-complexioned, clean, fair-haired man with a lively mouth and white teeth; his face was somewhat red and his hair visibly soft and fine. His face was almost regular, his hands manicured, and there was a hint of some very excellent, unusual light and delicate perfume about him. All the same, he did not appear dandified or one of those unpleasantly foppish men; his whole image was somewhat neglected and crumpled.

'True, you've seen a lot of the world,' I plunged once again into the flood of words, watching the players; this I had heard about him. 'Won't you be bored here amongst us?'

'Not at all! I find here everything that is worthwhile in life, believe me! The sun shines, there's a glow in the eyes of delightful young ladies; you can come across kindly, sincere, friendly people; life is convivial, people know how to enjoy themselves wholeheartedly and well. What else do you want? And then there's no need for me to say that the prospects are good for me here. The solicitors themselves complain that there are too few of them and they can't keep up with the work. They're good, straightforward, fair, profitable and transparent cases. Yes, after all, for ten years or so now I've been nothing more than a little rural solicitor.'

'You'll wreck our business!' I smiled, pretending to be angry.

'Oh, you've nothing to fear from me,' he waved my remark aside candidly and laughed. 'It was Jolsvay the deputy sheriff himself who tempted me to come, saying that they'd be only too glad to give me the odds and ends, the boring, superficial, too simple things, small cases that the three solicitors here would be reluctant to bother with. Your husband, Jenő, who's the best of them, is by the way, almost too good for this place! And anyway I don't have any great pretensions; I'm my own man. Just so long as the sun shines so beautifully, I'm very fond of that.'

'Has it been so many years ago,' I asked, returning to my thoughts, 'that you gave up playing?'

'Eight years, yes; I began to get rheumatism in my arm and after that I couldn't hold the bow properly. But that didn't really matter much, believe me, I wasn't any great loss! I simply accompanied Perényi, the great artist; since then someone else has done it instead. He was very fond of me because I adapted myself to his style and to that lovable, wild, whimsical artistic nature of his. But as for me, on my own, that was nothing special. When I was very young of course I believed I was special, but when I went abroad and appeared in public, I realized the truth. I watched and admired the master, and after that I didn't make any great effort for myself—it wasn't worth it! Maybe a lot in such matters depends on laziness, but sloth is an original sin anyway.'

'The way you talk about these things!' I looked at him in amazement and almost in exasperation. 'You, who have seen the world, foreign lands, life, and known famous and wonderful people, lots of great cities and all kinds of beauty.'

'Oh heavens! When you go on like that, with an impresario breathing down your neck! At night you had to play and make acquaintances, by day travel and rest. Who has time to visit the old churches and museums and famous sights? But even if you do visit them, it's not anything special; nothing's great when you're close to it. Or rather it's not the publicly proclaimed things that are really splendid, the ones that every passer-by defiles with staring at, opening their mouths wide and lying in their embarrassment that they completely understand. From the window of a train, I've sometimes seen a sparkling sheet of water appear suddenly in the depths of a rushing, moving landscape; or I've found, in a nook in bare rocks a rose-tinted apricot tree standing alone and very young. At such times I was struck by a thought: that's beautiful! That attracts me! Only I saw these things, and then only once like that; if I were to go back, I'd not find them again.'

'Once in Switzerland, or somewhere, I slipped out to the shore of some lake and came across three little boys, all barefooted, as they were playing dice with these round pebbles. I sat down with them; I didn't understand what they were saying, but it was marvellous how they screamed and leapt and rolled around in delight when I made a mess of things and they won my silver coins. Next day I told the master, and so he had a sudden desire to see them.'

'Take me there too, let's find them, let's look for children like that playing dice!'

'Except that the rascals never materialized again, or even ones like them. If you force things like that, it's unnatural and tasteless. But is this confused and ignorant talk annoying you?'

'Not at all, not at all! I 'm only thinking. It's so odd! But all the same, how about the great and famous people?'

'Oh, don't give them a thought! They know what they need to know for everybody, but in and of themselves they're very simple. You know, they act or play or write out of themselves what makes them interesting, what they've assembled from all their choices, so to speak. Beyond that they're weary, they retire into themselves, they're shy, too, afraid that they're wanted like leeches and they think, that's enough of the public stage, now I'm my own master! And so, you see, even in such a small place as this town, I've only been here a matter of weeks and already I've seen so much more that's interesting and colourful. And in a more pleasant and self-evident way. Great people! My master's father was a ropemaker, one great actress—like most of them— was the daughter of a concierge or a grocer in the slums, and that sort of thing makes itself felt through everything.'

'But all that money?'

'Yes, yes, it's delightful, but it disappears. Mine's all gone.' Here his face was childishly penitent and mournful, as was his voice. 'Money like that doesn't stay! You think it's going to be like that forever; you like good things, and women—there are fleeting women everywhere, beautiful, kind and expensively dressed. I always had more money going out than coming in. And, damn it, that's something I haven't been able to get out of my system to this day! But I won't upset you any more with all this; you're not angry with me for spoiling your pleasure? Will you allow me to pay my respects to you at home? I know Jenő well by now, and I hold him in a very high regard.'

On the way home, I remember, my mind was occupied with the news that I had heard previously, that my Aunt Ilka Zimán, the widow, had captured this Horváth as her own personal suitor. 'All right,' I thought, 'she can't be a day younger than he is, if not more ancient!' Then it crossed my mind that here in Szinyér it was always the fashion to try and win over new people. Even the occasional base language tutor or lady piano-teacher would be invited and entertained by folk who were very haughty to the locals, the natives who were making their way up in the world. 'He's only a flash in the pan!' I gave a shrug. But all the same he was a likeable character, odd, too frank, untheatrical, a take-it-or-leave-it man.

XII.

The little green-shaded lamp slumbered on the table in the nursery and the clean steam from the bathwater that had just been carried out floated around the bed from the little sleeping body. Jenő looked in on his way from the casino; this was where he found me, and somehow both of us sat down without a word beside the child. That day we had no guests and it was something of a relief to have a quiet and casual evening for once, to bathe the child and have cold meat and vegetables from lunch served up at dinner. For a while we gazed at his little cropped blonde head, his rather thin face and thick eyelashes over his closed eyes. He seemed to sense this, and gave a little wriggle and crowed with pleasure. Then his father carefully, and very gently, turned him towards the wall, pulled the clean nightshirt neatly over him, covered him up and smoothed him down. Then we took each other's hands and fell silent.

'How rare it is for the three of us to be together like this!' said Jenő suddenly.

I drew my hand out of his and made no reply. Perhaps this was a kind of reproach, however timid and gentle; it occurred to me that Jenő often looked with melting, pitying glances at the child, and I had a maudlin feeling of injustice at this. It almost vexed me. Though a little stricter than he was, I knew I was not a neglectful or bad mother; Jenő almost spoilt him and this had to be counterbalanced. And after all I was more often with him at home than Jenő—and always in the mornings—and I supervised his meals, clothing and walks, and everything went like clockwork. Doctor Jakobi was always praising me for it. And as for the fact that we were living like this, with a lot of entertaining, could I help that? Was it only I who wanted it? In any case I had to shoulder all the worry! Jenő sensed that I was about to say something like this, because he suddenly turned away and pointed to our little boy, whispering. 'Look how pretty he is like that in a white nightshirt! That delicate, slender boyish form of his, that intelligent little face! The nanny's right: he is like the baby Jesus! You know, he already knows the letter 'm'; he says it's got three legs!'

'He's going to be clever,' I said, brightening up. 'Why shouldn't he be?'

'After his father and mother!' whispered Jenő, and we laughed. 'Oh , there's something I haven't told you yet, Maggie. Yesterday he was in the office with me; I was lying on the couch while he was sitting on the floor leafing through the German lexicon. All of a sudden he asked, "Daddy, what's this little ball?"'

'"That's the sun,' I said, 'and this little dot here's the earth, because it's so much smaller than the sun, you see.'"

He took a long look at it and asked, 'Is it smaller than the moon, too?'

'No, Pityu, the moon's even smaller than the earth.'

'Well, how would they draw that in here?'

'Well, that would be a dot, too.'

'That would be a baby-dot, wouldn't it, daddy?'

Stifling our mirth in case we woke him up, we laughed together for a long time in rare, delightful intimacy in the lamplit warmth and darkness of the little room. Later, Jenő became pensive once again.

'At any rate he got through those illnesses,' he said with a worried expression. 'That first year was a trial. I sometimes thought that both of you were going to desert me—both wife and child, two sick people. What a good thing that we got over that!'

'Even now there are quite enough troubles and worries,' I replied, falling in with this serious mood.

'It will all come right one day, you'll see! Just let's have good health! We shan't always have to spend so much, Maggie, and our income, too, will always increase. It's no use, at present we've got to do a little canvassing to win over people, relatives. Once we've got there…'

'Indeed, Jenő, that's all that counts. The county, that's it!'

'Well, after all…'

I looked at him queryingly and a little startled. This was the first time we had put it into words like this between us. With sudden emotion I put my arm round his neck and thrust my head under his arm.

'My God! My dear, if only I could reach that height for once! To be a lady *there*! That would be everything, the climax of my life; then I wouldn't desire anything more!'

'Silly, silly little woman, you witch!' He kissed me all over and hugged me; I panted and chuckled in his lap. But meanwhile it occurred to me that this would lead immediately to some instructive, rather serious talk, as always happened after such moments of foolishness.

'You see, my little donkey, it's after that we'll begin to work for him and save up for him, the little imp. Believe me, I've given it a lot of thought. Ever since I saw that your stepfather Péter is on his last legs at Telegd, I've been turning over in my mind what might be done over there. Maybe raise something to add to the two boys' money; with a bit of luck we might get something for the three of you at an auction, and then when the boys come of age their claims can be paid off in money. After all, there'll be a tidy sum from home sometime, from my parents, too. If only Péter can hold out for another two years or so!'

'Oh come, it's all up with him! Mother, too, thinks it'll be auctioned by next autumn. Even before harvest.'

'How everything goes downhill, and how quickly, too, once it's started ! At least let us keep our heads above water, Magda! At all costs! Believe me, we've spent so much already!'

'Does that mean there's been another letter from Kassa today? Yes, it's true, Jenő, it's only when that happens that you start going on like this! Well, what am I to economize on, just tell me that! Before I was married, you know, I got my clothes from Gács, while now I run up everything with Hanika. You'd soon see how any other woman would be able to clothe herself from so little, to be in public everywhere and keep up with Melanie. Well, do you want me to give up now? Shall we take a back seat?'

'I know, my dear... Of course not, of course not! Why are you talking like this? After all, I'm not complaining. Someday... Maggie... someday it's all going to be different! Look here, I've got some really great news to tell you! A secret!'

'Oh, my dearest! Out with it, quickly!'

'Only if you deserve it first. A good dinner, hot tea, hazel-nut cake, my dear little wife.'

He rocked me, petted me, scolded and teased me like a little child. I had to agree: by all appearances I was a quite stupid and childishly-lisping creature sometimes, and this had some effect in real life, too. I was energetic in my housekeeping and superior in society, but I never went beyond ten forints in buying and selling; I never had more than this amount in my possession at one time, nor did I ever discharge more important things in life, like choosing a dwelling or even ordering wood for heating, of my own responsibility and of my own free will. And all the same there was something so good and intimate about this, always asking someone, getting the occasional rebuke, appearing a little helpless or sulky, and always taking it for granted that everything would be accomplished properly and well by someone else and even against my will.

After tea, I settled down next to him on the sofa in the dining-room.

'Now then, the secret!'

'Right, listen to me—but don't tell anyone.'

'Of course.'

'Well, first of all Jolsvay's going to get the vacant high sheriff's post this very spring. That's certain now.'

'You don't say! Melanie…'

'Will shortly be the high sheriff's wife; Count Lajos is bringing the nomination in April.'

'Then what about the deputy sheriff?'

'All in good time! Unless something happens between now and then, the young heir to the throne's coming to visit the Castle in the autumn. There'll be a hunt here.'

'Oh! Really? Here in Szinyér?'

'Yes, but not a word about it for the time being! Today I'm the only one to know; the Count told me. And in that case, you know, it will be rather difficult to do anything about county politics, just before the elections; the Count himself is fully aware of that. The future king's coming: that's a great thing at all events. A chance like this for him to make friends with the Hungarian magnates is almost of national importance! Of course, we'll need to have a very fine, very imposing reception. The estate and the town aren't enough, the county's got to play its part, too, a mounted escort of nobles or something of the sort. But you know there's a lot of huffing and puffing here now because of the regulation of the river. The mood towards the squire isn't unanimous. Well, that's got to be… somehow… up till then.'

'And how?'

'Well, Jolsvay and I and you and Melanie! Create a little atmosphere, do a little canvassing—after all, in the long run it's mainly a question of relatives and clients. Why, all those pig-headed folk, all those "yoke-pin sharpeners" as the Count calls them, have got to realize that in the end they'll be the losers with their obstinacy. We've got to make every effort with them now, because as things are they're still capable of some kind of passive demonstration, of obvious hostility, too. Now we'll see what we're capable of!'

'And what's going to happen to us, all the same?'

'Oh you little gypsy! Just imagine! Immediately after the occasion, and still in November, there'll be the elections. Jolsvay will get instructions for the nominations, and the Count, too, will get things moving in the committee; up to now he's always carried through with what he wanted in matters like this. And in the end, if we can win over the county to his side, we shall have won it over for ourselves at the same time. In that case the deputy sheriff's post would be a small thing, it seems.'

I gave a little shriek of delight, clapped my hands and wound both my arms round his neck. I felt that all my dreams and ambitions would be fulfilled, and after that there was nothing more I could wish for. I should have liked to hurry this man, push him and stimulate him; his calling was to fulfill and accomplish in this world what my own ambitions desired. Yes, yes, I thought, with a man everything can be achieved; through them you can achieve everything, you only have to encourage, desire, pester, doggedly and cunningly, that's a woman's job.

The bell rang in the hall; it was Dénes Horváth, Jenő's new colleague, who had arrived. 'Oh well, we can't be by ourselves today either!' grumbled my husband at first, but when he caught sight of him, he brightened up and went happily to meet him.

Since the summer these two men had come to like each other without reservation, and spent a great deal of time in each other's company; after all, they were very different. So Horváth always turned up after dinner, if at no other time; Jenő sent for a bottle of wine, and while I took out some embroidery, they smoked cigars and chatted until after midnight.

Horváth could talk amusingly and animatedly, though rather slowly, keeping his audience waiting, but in his own peculiar, half-hearted way he nevertheless managed to inform us about things that were faraway or unusual for us: foreign people, the wider world, theatres, life, women. We liked listening to him, because he was not conceited and he kept on saying (and so it emerged anyway) that he never looked at anything in depth, 'scientifically'; a great deal had now escaped his memory. Perhaps his chief claim to wisdom could be found in something he often kept saying: 'All the same, this crazy life and everything in it is rather nice, after all!' It was good to hear him say this during those quiet, murmurous winter evenings; he was a soft-voiced, pleasant, clean-cut, blonde man. The things that occupied Jenő were not subjects of interest to him; with cheerful indifference he seemed almost to be above them. He listened to Jenő's judgements with interest and consideration, like a stranger, and approved them, too, from public administration to the inertia of the present régime, but he had no axe to grind. All he wanted was a quiet life here, straightforward little lawsuits, good company and pleasant gossip.

'He lives in the world like a fish in water,' said Ilka Zimán, and half jokingly, half enviously, tapped him on the shoulder with her ever-present black ostrich-feather fan.

He always accompanied Ilka courteously home from our house as well as from everywhere else, but somehow he was too familiar, jestingly mocking or provocative towards her in public. Most of all, perhaps, in front of me—and Ilka showed signs of jealousy, too—because he always treated me with respect and discreet tenderness. He often came rather early in the evening too, before Jenő was at home: then we would sit in the little blue room; I sewed and he looked on in peace and contentment. Then he wound cotton for me or threaded my needles with his slightly deformed hand. When Jenő came, Horváth had to hurry to hide the slippers or cap that were destined for his name-day or Christmas... And I got used to him in this way; I treated him like a kindly relative, a tame friend whom one warms to through his affection, but with whom one can be composed and intimate, on whom one can count. 'You're still an infant, madam; you're living the life of a child!' he would keep on saying, and usually I would give him a scolding for it. It was he who first saw my dresses, my needlework and all the small changes in the arrangement of the rooms or the reception of guests. I was very pleased when he praised me, because that was my highest ambition.

By that time, ours was indeed the principal house in Szinyér after Melanie's. Whoever was new to the town—army officer, official or stranger—came to pay us a visit immediately after seeing them, and only after that visited the others. If we had company in the evening, Jenő himself would light all the candles behind the dried-flower arrangements and Japanese vases in the big salon. The lovely new piano stood open, revealing its row of snow-white teeth, with Horváth's violin-case beside it (I had sewn pink roses on its velvet cover.) All the little restless, animated, warm lights flickered and glittered on the gilded wood of the chairs and mirrors. Young girls—relatives of ours, sang and flirted, while men bustled around me and paid their respects. On occasions like this, I was really and truly in my element, in a crowd, in the public eye, actively playing a part, scintillating and surrounded by respect and envy.

It was always Dénes Horváth who provided me with delicate French perfumes and magnificent hand-creams. And these things were something I greatly needed, because I really worked hard every morning at my household chores. The big dwelling had to be tidied, there was only one housemaid, after all; Jenő would not allow the nursemaid to leave the child. On my part, I refused to put up with work half-done. The china ornaments, which had multiplied to legendary numbers had to be dusted every day, and the floorboards, too, were all right only when I myself got down to stain them. Before eleven o'clock, nobody saw me except servants, tradespeople, daily charwomen, beggars or one or other of my husband's simpler clients, and that was only by chance; but from professional people and townsfolk, I hid away or pretended to be a servant. But then I stood in front of a mirror and with three-quarters of an hour's determined work transformed myself into a lady. I was rather pleased with this dual role; what an achievement it was on my part! In the afternoon I often went to the women's guild, or skated, or went visiting or for a drive with Melanie.

This lady was always very kind, indeed almost too gracious and obliging to me, but she was never intimate. I sensed a peculiar kind of superiority in her, and sometimes this caused pride and anger to seethe in me, but I knew that for the time being there was nothing I could do to change our relationship, for after all we needed the future high sheriff and his wife. And now it would have been impossible for me to ignore Melanie in social life too; she was my wealthier and higher-ranking relative, whose incomprehensible and unaffected talent had led her already to dominate the whole town and district. Unlike me, she had no enemies and attracted no jealousy; this astonished me most of all. People of all classes and ranks were unanimous in praise of her: she was beautiful, good, clever, kind and virtuous. She brought new, unfamiliar customs here and everyone accepted them and imitated them immediately without a second's thought. It was she who introduced people to tea-parties instead of the previously fashionable big afternoon meals with café au lait, preserves, milk loaf, cream slices and cake. Right at the beginning of winter she gave three large tea-parties, and in turn she sent out separate invitations for the first one to 'society' (naturally including us first and foremost), for the second to the estate wives and daughters, and for the third to the larger tradespeople and Jewish wives under the pretext of the women's guild solidarity. I really could not measure up to this kind of bid for popularity. How well she was able to talk to everyone in their own language! And whether I liked it or not, I too had to imitate her in all of my appearances. How annoyed I got with setting small tables all over the place in the salon and stumbling over them! It was easy for her in the barns of rooms in the County Hall, when for such occasions she dressed all the wives and daughters of the attendants as parlourmaids. 'Oh well, I'll be able to do that, too, some time!' I thought then, full of hope, and despair, and joy, which almost gave me palpitations. Would this really happen, I wondered?

What an incomprehensible, confusing, discordant little memory of that time thrusts itself into my mind now!

Once in the fever and enthusiasm of cleaning the house from top to bottom, I tipped over the waste-paper basket in my husband's office, and all its contents fell out. Why did I poke my hand, playfully and curiously, into the torn shreds of draft-documents, printed papers and crumpled envelopes?… 'My humble and sorrowful homage, of which you must know, Melanie, and which I would never, never dare to call anything else…' Lines crossed out, a blot of ink… the impression of angry or impatient fingers, lines of hard, confused creases in the shred of paper, the rest of which I searched for in vain. My God! After all that happened later, I have almost forgotten this; perhaps I had never given it a thought in all my life, or had deliberately buried it. After all, it was so out of character, a single peculiarity, which had never made itself obvious; even now it appears almost like an unpleasant and annoying dream. Jenő was a model husband, the most caring head of the family and—I know this for certain—loved me very much right to the end, much more than I loved him; and that was how the world knew him and so did the town, and that was how the family regarded him too; and this was what gave me my place in life. Was it tenderness or fear, I wonder, good taste, shrewdness or convenience that restrained me from mentioning this affair to him and demanding an explanation? Was it my rightful wifely instinct that prompted me to keep it a dead secret and bury it in forgetfulness? Had a letter like this ever been sent, I wondered? Was it a whim, a dream, a romantic affectation, an imagined or genuine sentiment, or nothing, a cliché, the pursuit of an interest for the well-being of the family? Who could know this man... this person? Even now it causes some strange, reluctant feeling of shame to rise in me... Oh, what foolishness!

That spring, my mother and her husband moved in from Telegd, quietly and unobtrusively. The auction was announced. They took lodgings in the Cifrasor behind the big market-place in the 'gentry-wing', overlooking the street, of a large peasant-house with mulberry trees, grazing geese and many children in its courtyard (it belonged to some dyer). Even at that time, nobody talked about them; the subject of poor Péter Telekdy had long ago been exhausted together with all his foibles, his notorious great intellect, even if he had a screw loose, and his difficult, abrasive nature. All the same, I was rather surprised at the way it all went, a straightforward eviction from the ancestral land that went with his name, from the house of his father, his great-great grandfather—and the world just went on turning! The peasants in his village must have felt something similar, too: they gathered in a crowd in front of the house and vowed rebelliously not to allow any other landlord into the fields; they would drive him out with cudgels and 'reoccupy' the mansion. Péter was hardly able to calm them down. They escorted the four ox-carts carrying their personal possessions past the third village, stopping at every community and saying a tearful farewell—mayors, town-criers, counselors, farmers and all. Péter asked them to turn back, but they simply started off again. Such was their journey, their last journey from home. Mother Klára kept telling this story in her own colourful, humorous way, half laughing, half grumbling at her husband. She was still a beautiful woman with a clear complexion and perfect teeth, magnificent eyebrows, greying hair and a corseted shapely figure, which had filled out evenly and stylishly since she had reached the age of forty. She had always had a penchant for joking and almost rash joviality, and now this developed even more with the passage of time. Maybe this was her good fortune; she was incapable of fretting, of making a tragedy out of the business, she saw the comical, bitter-sweet side of everything, and together with others laughed at things which other people conceal in shame and distress. Since they had moved into town, she spent a lot of time in our house drinking coffee, knitting stockings or smoking cigarettes; at home she must have grown bored with the company of Péter, who was expecting some post he had been promised in the land registry and would not stir from his den, 'among all those musty, daft bibles, those devilish tomes—oh, if only a thunderbolt would strike them!' If Telegd came into the conversation my mother sometimes admitted that she did not really regret leaving it; at least she had been freed from the burden of playing the big village landowner's wife, from the boring and isolated life and the peasants, and could return to her own folk in the town where she had spent her whole youth.

And summer came round again: long, sultry, hot days, enervating and sweet scents of flowers in the basil and verbena-filled gardens of the town, lovely bright cheerful batiste dresses, a kind of great and unusual physical effervescence. My figure filled out, and my whole being grew marvellously beautiful at that time; everyone noticed it. They said that now I had really become a mature woman. I was twenty-six years old.

The memory of that summer has always remained so vivid in my mind; in a strange way it is connected with the smell of ripe raspberries, of which we had a lot in the garden then, and it drifted as far as the veranda where I would sit in the bronze sunshine of the beautiful late afternoon. Almost always, Horváth sat with me, or behind me at such times.

That is how the picture is fixed in my memory. Down below Jenő bends over the rose-stocks in the big flower-bed, a long green gardening-cloak covering his increasingly corpulent figure; the servants cart watering-cans for the length of the paths, and further away the wheel of the well creaks. Little Pista in a white suit runs about playing football with the white-clad German girl; the sun sinks lower and the spray of water from the rose of the watering-cans drifts in gold and rainbow-hues diagonally, in the slanting rays of light above the carpet of flowers with their myriad of colours. And the sweet, all-embracing perfume of ripe raspberries floats upwards. Dénes Horváth sits beside me: like me he gazes over the courtyard, above the plum trees in the garden and over the wooden fences and the distant gardens beyond at the sky with its rose-coloured stripes. 'Your house is paradise! Everything you touch, all that surrounds you, becomes beautiful, attractive and agreeable. And we all have a share of happiness here, madam; even I, who hide myself away in the nook so decorously and just look at you!...' So spoke Dénes Horváth that summer in the evenings and I nodded with a smile, full of a great and simple joy at all this. Later Jenő came up, changed and sat down with us for coffee and cream. 'Now I ought to have already confessed my love to your wife, Jenő, but silly old fool that I am, I waited for you to come!' We laughed, and that is how it was. 'Why isn't my husband jealous?' I thought for a moment, after this occasion, when he withdrew once again to the office, and had the lamp lit for his work, leaving us to our own devices until dinner. And I recalled the few visits of Endre Tabódy years before. He was different, an exciting, passionate, young, demanding lover, with a latent and secretive hostility towards Jenő. This man here, it was true, had no fire left in him... yet he was only a year or two older than Jenő. And as for me... since that time I too had become *different*. It is not on the night of your marriage that you become a woman; in my case, alas, it took seven years. Yes, I was no longer a child-wife, I had learnt a lot, I had come to realize a lot of things just by thinking them through. And I *dared* to think things through, and I dared and sometimes wanted to have passionate and secret escapades, right to the very end of things. True, I was not in love; that's different, perhaps... but why didn't this ever occur to Jenő? Was it that he was too trusting, or simple-minded, or was it all the same to him? Maybe... Melanie?... It's his great good fortune that I am what I am, all the same...

'There's no more noble or distinguished man, none more diligent or talented, Magda, than that husband of yours, perhaps in the whole wide world!' Horváth said then, with a touch of sad sincerity. I looked at him for a minute and suddenly, without any warning, I was reminded of Ilka Zimán. Of course he would choose the widow, an independent woman, comfortable and harmless! That's the right sort! I'm only to be looked at, to exchange playful glances, so that there shouldn't be any complications... Faugh! The ugly, old-maidish opportunism of men, to take from every woman just as much as they can without running into trouble... After all, I'm sure I'd never allow things to go a fraction further, but it would be necessary for him to *want* me, to make an effort, or at least to pretend to!...

'How strong that smell of raspberries is from the garden!' he said slowly. 'It's like the smell of fermented, sweet heavy wine; it makes your head reel!'

XIII.

The raspberries were past their best; it was August, and Hanika sat sewing for weeks on end in my house. The poor little queen of freckles, as my younger brother Csaba called her mockingly, was to be married; Mr. Feinsilber, a clockmaker from Pressburg, had asked for her hand from the head of the family, the broker Lipi, after he had seen her picture. So Hanika was getting ready for her betrothal, expectant, panting and almost stifled by inner, concealed, joyful excitement; enraptured and grateful for some imagined kindnesses. She copied the style of my own clothes with passionate devotion—cheaply, beautifully and artistically.

By then it was the beginning of autumn, and we were ready to face expected events, the great changes, struggles and victory we hoped for.

Jenő buried himself completely in his affairs; sometimes it was almost impossible to have a word with him all day long. There were times when he even sent Pityu out when he asked to go into the office. Yet sometimes I watched him; he was not always at work, but would walk up and down the room for hours on end.

So much happened at that time. Csaba was a captain somewhere down in Temes, piling up debts left and right, and Jenő was harassed to pay them. He replied that there were only three more months before Csaba came of age, and then everything would be settled. We had to work now for our own interests. We counted a lot on grandma and her closer and older connections in the countryside, but at that very time she took to her bed. She had been ailing for some time but concealed it and would not allow a doctor near her; now, at last, old Jakobi reported sorrowfully that most probably she had cancer of the stomach. And this was the last thing we wanted to cope with and lament now, because we had so much to worry about.

Jenő dictated some letters to me—to my Uncle Ábris and to Piroska's husband, my mother's brother-in-law—and even to old Tyukody, father of the two eccentric old spinsters. He himself wrote to others, going to see Kendy, his former client and the younger Kehiday himself. For the time being he trod carefully, talking more about the reception of the Archduke than about our own affairs, but we told our close relations of everything in confidence. In some places I know that Jenő cautiously let it be known that not everyone in the county administration would accept the ideas of the estate once he finally broke free from the Count's sphere of influence. But he had to go very warily with this electioneering strategy, because Inspector Scherer and his cronies were spying on us and nosing about ever more frequently. Had they betrayed any such talk, I wondered, to the old traitor?

There was the case of the sale of some lands divided into plots, something that Jenő had negotiated: he kept pestering him with letters and sending his son Imre. He must square the accounts by the time harvest was over. In the end, Jenő wrote to the Count and of course obtained an extension of time with no demur. If only I could have looked on this lanky Imre with a smile just once, if not exactly like *that*, at least to flatter his vanity! How easily he would have relaxed all his official reserve, the family coolness! But it was easier to do on anyone else: I so detested that stubborn German peasant lad, for that is what he was like, with his uncouth yearnings badly cloaked in crude frigidity and sometimes offensive impropriety, too. All he needed was a single nod.

Time rushed on. We could not even get to the neighbouring cathedral town for my young brother Sándor's first mass; mother Klári went alone. He was a splendid young priest and stood at the altar as gentle and white as the Lamb of God; he trembled and raised the consecrated host. After the elevation, he collapsed in a faint. 'He's neurotic,' said the doctors. 'He'll have to have treatment.' Yet he was in line to be deputy secretary in the bishop's palace.

So many confusing, muddled events! Telegd was indeed put up for auction, much earlier than we should have liked. And Endre Tabódy bought it for himself. His aunt, Mrs. Bélteky, brought me the strange news straight-away. By then he was already married; his wife was little Anna Pongrácz who had come out at the County Ball in the same year that I was married. At that time, she was a nice little body with black eyes, well-padded, like a fattened goose. So Endre Tabódy was the new landlord, the new leader of the landowners along the Szinyér valley! They were the ones of whom the greatest sacrifice was demanded by the coming flood-regulation that the county administration created for the sake of the Count—Jolsvay and soon my husband would be compelled to carry through in whatever way. But after all, Tabódy himself was not in debt—he had come into money with his wife, too—and in fifteen or twenty years those costs could be covered six times over! I wondered, oh how I wondered, how he would behave as far as my husband's affairs were concerned!

A slowly-gathering opposition was already beginning to make itself felt: the Tóthfalussys, the Ecsedys, the loud-mouthed Gábor Berey and Széchy, who had once courted my mother. Somebody had already mentioned something about him being their man for the deputy sheriff's office.

But our own camp, too, was firmly united. At the end of September we gave a private dinner, but a very brilliant and imposing one. Apart from the new high sheriff and his wife, all those who supported our cause, relatives, friends and clients, came along and met together. It was then that Uncle Ábris first approached the family again after many years of vindictiveness. We received him with demonstrative graciousness. And here, too, were the Hiripys, the family of relatives from the village with whom I had last stayed before my marriage... in the moonlight, beneath the poplars. How the years turn folk around with other dreams, aims and changes of scene! Now the old man was a councillor for his district and he meant a great deal to us. Just before the meal was served the carriage of the powerful Péter Kendy drove up too; he had been invited, but hardly expected. He was the only person in the county invited by the Count to the forthcoming hunt for the Archduke. But he had a shrewd suspicion that this, too, was secretly the work of Jenő.

At first the mood at the flower-decked table, glittering with silver was rather strained, distrustful and chilly. Instead of the gossipy, arch townswomen who all knew each other, there were only two or three elderly aunts or young village wives, oddly haughty in the fear that they would be forgotten; they were relatives who had grown apart and distant from us. And the men, too, danced around the issues, shying away from the 'business', and the question of the noble escort was not immediately broached. As a matter of family policy, partly out of trust and even recognition, they were prepared to press my husband's case with the county, but why should they be the ones to play into the Count's hands now, when it would be the ideal opportunity to demonstrate effectively their ancient, three-hundred year-old opposition?

The Szinyérs' ancestor, who had acquired the estate, had also licked the boots of the Austrians like this, all those imperial servants, all those shifty pro-Habsburgs!; in this way they grabbed a third of the county, the real or imagined patrimony of kinsmen who were co-heirs and of nobles who even today were struggling to live on seven or eight hundred acres or had become impoverished. 'But at any rate we've always been independent! We're taking no orders from him!'

I was trying to entertain the ladies, and could only give half my attention, albeit with astonishment and appreciation, to the skill with which Jenő changed the subject—and the irritation—to the national government. Cursing or supporting Kálmán Tisza* and the rest was something in which their spirits tended to agree, unite or find release. The two County Hall attendants summoned over by Melanie began to open the champagne.

About midnight I retired with the women to the salon. By then the men were raising their voices, the tobacco-smoke was growing thicker and the arguments more lively. Many of them were talking at once now, and with different aims, deviating now and then from the subject with impassioned gestures and all trying to convince their neighbours. Some time later I looked through the door for a minute when the maid carried in a tray of black coffee. My Uncle Ábris was almost shouting as he held forth in the stifling cloud of smoke, denouncing the liberation of the serfs; he banged the slender glass so often on the leaf of the table that it cracked and crumbled to pieces in his hand. 'I've never swindled or stolen anything!' Péter Kendy kept repeating in a voice choked with sobs, though nobody was contradicting him.

'As God is my witness, I've not willingly laid a finger on what belongs to someone else! I'm not lying, old chap! What happened was that I was passing by someone else's field after harvest, when the corn was all in stacks. I got out of the cart and pulled out four, five or six stalks of wheat just to see what the crop was like there. That was all I stole my whole life through. That's not too bad, is it?'

---

* *Kálmán Tisza* (1830–1902) was founder and leader of the Party of Free Principle, and Prime Minister of Hungary 1875–1890.

Meanwhile, one of the Kehidays held the Galgóczy boy's neck in a close embrace and leaned on his shoulder, vowing, 'I'll never leave you, old chap, never!' I looked at Jenő. With the dejection of sobriety he was sitting in his chair as he usually did at times like this, bewildered, helpless, weary and almost shame-faced. And at that moment the thought flashed through my mind for the first time, 'How incongruous he is among these folk and how out of place here! Where I have dragged him!'

Melanie's carriage arrived; I put up my Aunt Piroska and the other two wives in the guest-room. A grey dawn was breaking when I stopped once again, dead tired, in the doorway of the dining-room. Now only old Hiripy, stern and stiff, was sitting there in silence; at the other end of the table there were still two others in the twilight leaning back in their chairs with sagging mouths and heads lolling as they dozed. One of them was snoring gently; it was Tibor Gencsy, and the other one was Galgóczy. All the lamps had gone out now and the flowers, rumpled and drooping, lay dead, strewn all around on the wine-stained, cigar-soiled tablecloth. Jenő was slowly, gently and sadly stroking the head of Sport, the brown-spotted retriever as he lay in his lap.

There were still some weeks left, and I threw myself with passionate enthusiasm into preparations, concerning matters of dress and detail in order to kill off the oppressive uncertainty and strained anxiety that filled me and set my nerves on edge. Most of all I was tormented by the thought that I had no way of knowing for certain everyone's intentions and real opinions; I could not be in every place where there was talk of the election, where moods were swayed and casual interests were brought together again and again. And I observed the way my husband took this business so seriously, as if it was a matter of life and death, as if he had staked everything on this venture.

I often saw Lipi the Jew, the agent, go in and out of the office and I knew that it was always a question of money, an urgent loan, even if it meant usury. I was well aware now that Jenő had no cash to meet the election or other expenses. But it couldn't have been much he needed! There were a few fairly large dinners, a public lunch, a few journeys so far, my dresses (I had got one of them from Gách, all the same), and a few public appearances during the royal visit. It appeared that he did not have enough money at hand even for these things.

'Jenő, my dear, I want you to tell me the truth! Is there something wrong?'

'Of course not, dear! Indeed... I think... Jolsvay summoned the committee members to a private discussion to iron out their differences. I think that's how the situation's going to be resolved in our favour. All the signs point to that.'

'But... all the same, there's something troubling you. Don't deny it! I saw you had a letter from your parents.'

'Yes, I did. It's nothing special.'

'Show it to me!'

'I think I've already thrown it away.'

'What do they say? What's upset you? If you don't tell me this minute I'm going to believe there's something in it about me! Something bad! That Scherer and his cronies have been slandering me!'

'Magda! How could you think of such a thing? Why?... For what reason?... After all, they've no reason to.'

'Well, in that case show me your father's letter. I'll not put up with you hiding important things from me. After all, I am your wife!'

Without a word he put the letter from Kassa in front of me. I wasn't mistaken! It was a reply to Jenő, who apparently had asked him for the loan of a rather large sum, three thousand forints, it appeared. But why so much? The old man refused him categorically, rebuking him sternly and harshly. He warned him to recover his senses if it was not too late by now, to give up his pretentious extravagance and work, like him, to save money for his old age and to provide for his child. Well, he had known in advance what ostentation and stylish living would lead to; he had warned him often enough, and he could not be blamed for anything; for he had been plunged into this by the dissolute surroundings in which he lived and whose depravity had rubbed off on him. Here he meant me, alas, and my family! And it was with this loathsome, yes, loathsome torrent of words that he dismissed his only son's vital, serious concern. Can such a man be a father?

'I'm sure my mother doesn't know an inkling about it,' said Jenő softly.

'Then let's write to her! Tell her the truth!'

'No! I don't want that! Don't you try, Magda! She couldn't do anything anyway; the money belongs to my father. We'd only upset her.'

'But what's going to happen to you, Jenő? Tell me the truth, can you look after things yourself? Isn't there anything else you can do? After all, you might be able to get someone.... a bill of exchange, maybe!'

'Certainly not! That's out of the question especially before the election. Afterwards... in any case..., then things will be easier, says Lipi. For a deputy sheriff, the director of the flood-regulation scheme, it is easy to lay one's hands on any amount, and then other channels will suddenly be open for as long as it takes me to get things straight. The whole thing's mere child's play, a question of time.'

'But until then?'

'Until then Lipi will give me just as much as I need for the time being. A Jew like him is worth more, you see, than one's nearest and dearest!'

Pityu dashed in with a big paper kite stretched out high in his thin little arms. The fringed tail rustled as it dragged behind him over the threshold.

'Daddy, look what Mitru, the duty-attendant's made for me! When the wind blows, it goes up and up right to the sky. But now there's no wind, and we've got to wait. In the meantime I'll put it here in the corner behind your table, so you can look after it, daddy!'

'Come, come here, my dear little son! Yes, put your arms around me tight! I'll look after it, of course I will, until the wind comes. Your daddy will be the guard of the kite!'

XIV.

A radiant October morning. The little railway-station is filled with flowers and movement, ladies in lovely new autumn dresses, a black host of gleaming top-hats and morning coats, the glitter of uniforms; an almost childlike festal polish on everything. In the town—and this made me smile—the windows overlooking the street had even been cleaned in most houses; fresh pots of flowers had been set out, and Chinese lanterns were hung up to be used for illumination in the evening. And outside, as far as the lodge in the deerpark, along the route to be taken by the band of huntsmen, about an hour and a half's journey, they had rolled the cart-track, at the expense of the county, and plastered and whitewashed the fronts of the peasant-houses facing it in three villages along the way. 'A State of prosperity!' said Péter Telekdy with sullen asperity from behind his Rousseau.

The decorated special train rumbles in. The mass surges forward; deputations, indiscernible words in the distance from one or two short speeches, the sudden measured blare of three cheers breaking the subdued silence of the huge crowd. Now I can hear Melanie's freshly-resonant, attractive voice speaking as she turns towards the royal lady, her face white and serious, her golden hair brushed back in thick waves and sparkling in the morning sunlight; her impressive, decidedly simple pure beauty shines through the delicate light green colours of her dress. She holds the big bouquet of camellias high in her tiny gloved hand; I am standing beside her and without yet taking my eyes off the speaker's face I instinctively feel for certain that the unknown man is glancing at me. Now the shadow of the flowers protects me and I return the look with a simple and exultantly hazardous idea born of determination—a glance querying and searching, understanding and dismissive, for which sometimes mere will, mere sporting instinct is not enough; naturally it requires rare elation and the certainty that this is *all*; the doubt or risk of any continuation cannot disturb one. 'The royal prince!' I thought in an unguarded moment with strange surprise. I saw a man's pensive blue grave eyes, the tired whiteness of a long, soft-featured face and lips that gleamed almost unhealthily red beneath the dark blonde moustache. The two golden eagles glittered blindingly on the lapels of the cornflower-blue braided tunic and the red stripe ran right down the slender youthful figure. There, now they hand over the flowers, the women's guild behind me raises a cheer; a couple of words in bad Hungarian, and they leave.

The whole town on the streets; ladies in new dresses parade beneath the castle garden; the privates in the garrison stand in a motionless line in painfully gleaming dress uniform. Now comes the line of carriages; oh! how they sweep past: the dowager countess, the young one with the major-domo, grey-haired military dignitaries and then the escort. Beautiful caparisoned horses trotting along, fastidious creatures all decked out, how lovely, how lovely!

Horses are gorgeous, living instruments just right for men; how impressive they are, especially to the female spirit! There's the young Hiripy, the magistrate, my aunt's son. How magnificent Kendy is! The two Kehidays together, the Galgóczys, father and son. Oh, there's Tabódy! Is it really him? He's done it... what does it mean? Oh look, there's the grey-haired Bojér in his beautiful violet-coloured, gold-braided jacket, with a big turquoise plume, and four horsemen following him! Tibor Gencsy and one or two more. That's all! No, there weren't many of them, to be sure; an imposing but little remnant!

After that, the whole day was governed by preparations—sleeping, doing one's hair, dressing—for the evening entertainment.

In the women's guild we started up a charity bazaar, thinking of all the country families with well-filled wallets seeking pleasure during their stay in the town. Of them, only Péter Kendy and the old Bojér had been invited to the castle for the magnates' dinner, and even them without their wives.

We had Rumanian homespun cloths for sale, children's wooden toys made by peasants, fringed skirts, gingerbread men and other fripperies. There was a hot-food stall, a cigar-stall, a sweet-kiosk and a champagne tent. This was where I busied myself with two girl relatives; it was an imitation gypsy-hovel, a den in silk drapes and gold, and we sat in front of the entrance in red puckered silks, decked out with gold coins and oriental ornaments of many colours, our hair let down and studded with jewels.

Dénes Horváth came over right at the start. He tucked himself away on a stool behind me and asked Jenő for permission to stay there, even though Ilka Zimán was across the way at the cigar-stall.

The evening was full of pomp and splendour. Is it only I who have such a vivid memory of it, I wonder, that I have not forgotten any of it after so many years? All the folk from the country were there, but the more well-to-do townspeople also had free entrance; the crowds swarmed around the great chamber of the County Hall, surging between the pillars right along the carpeted path bordered by booths and stalls. My two young cousins distributed the champagne, while I told fortunes with cards and read palms. But this was not for anyone and it was not cheap.

'Aren't you frightened, making a game of Fate like that?' murmured Horváth behind me in his characteristic slow, somewhat plummy voice. 'You can even get away with that unscathed. How terrifyingly beautiful you are as a gypsy! It's almost too much, nobody should be allowed to be like that! Provocative and searing like a flash of lightning! It hurts to look at you!'

'You don't often compliment me,' I waved my hand at him with a laugh, but looked him straight in the eyes, 'but when you do, you give it all you've got. So that you can remain in peace for another six months.'

'And what do you know about that? My great peacefulness, indeed!' he said, withstanding my stare with a grave face. I turned around, but even now in the midst of all the admiration I felt it was good to have his continual, steady devotion.

It was approaching midnight. The room was crowded, perfumed and hot. The outsiders, folk from the town, gradually withdrew and left of their own accord; the entertainment now began to assume the tone of the usual private evening party. Now Széchy was standing in front of me, his arms hanging down as he waited for me to shuffle the cards.

'Pick them up!'

'Which hand shall I use?'

'The left one!'

I looked boldly into his face. He was beginning to go grey now about the temples, and the rather carelessly-tailored formal suit made him look less dashing than he had been in the morning in his Hungarian gala-uniform on the decorated dancing steed.

But even so, his hard, dark royalist head was still interesting, with that hooked, high-bridged nose and the keen gaze of his bird-like eyes; and that somewhat coarse, somewhat melancholy cocksureness that had kept my mother in thrall ten years ago and had driven a dreamy young girl to death long ago, still remained. A man like this would still be able to wreak havoc even now!

'Well, have I still got a long time to live?'

'Longer than you'd like! But let's take things in order. As for the past: a lot of turmoil, of stirring things up, but rarely a real rest, a real forgetting. As for the present: a kind of sour repletion now and the sort of expectation when someone sprains his ankle and stops and says, "Right, now it's either not a single step further or else *everything* all over again, but whatever it is, it can come of its own accord; I'm not going to stir an inch for it!" As for the future…'

'I'll not let you finish, you witch!' With a single movement of his hand he clutched the deck of cards lying loosely in my hand and with it grasped my wrist as well; I felt two brown fingers press down hard on my bracelet. Then he took the cards out of my hand and put them down on the bench.

'There's no need to drag it all out like that in words and keep track of it. Believe me, as far as I'm concerned, it really doesn't matter! I'm an easy opponent these days. Things just sweep one along; it's too much trouble to swim against the tide, so I let them, and it really is all the same to me.'

He put some money in the box for orphans and went on his way. Young lads, army officers, came and gathered around the Reviczky girl and her sister; the icy foam on the champagne frothed and bubbled white and ran down one of the officers' dress-jacket sleeves to the elbow; the girls laughed and jingled silver coins. A new group came along.

Then in an unguarded moment Endre Tabódy suddenly appeared in front of me. I was leaning sideways against the red velvet of the tent pole and turned to face him. I just looked at him gravely without stirring, not reaching for the cards. It was as if nothing else were needed and nothing was lacking: here he was, and we gazed at each other in silence.

'Can you still predict some future for me, Magda?'

'None at all!' I said softly in a tone betraying deep and sur-prising tenderness, and I bowed my head. That was all I needed.

'But how lovely it would have been, all the same!'

'It *was* lovely!'

'And I still know that it was the real thing.'

'Two foolish children at play. We've gotten beyond that.'

'There will still be a time when both of us will think back on it, maybe when we're old, and we'll realize what it was.'

'At least there'll be something to look back on. All the same, it's a good thing it stopped there. Let's save it for our old age!'

He bowed over my hand and kissed it with a tender movement for some time, though hardly breathing on it. Then he left me.

A little while later as I involuntarily sought him with my glance, I saw him leaning against a pillar, furtively and gravely watching a couple deep in intimate conversation. It was his wife with her dancing-partner of old, the younger Kallós boy. 'Now he's jealous!' a wry feeling of discouragement flashed through me. How hopelessly entangled feelings and bonds become!... As I turned around I saw Dénes Horváth once again sitting there close by me; his eyes following my every movement with quiet delight.

At that moment a strange, silent throng began to stir around the entrance. It was a long way off and I could not see as far as that along the double row of pillar-bases lining the center of the chamber. The music stopped, then I saw the second band of gypsies coming down from the other platform; they had been playing here till now because Bankó and his band had been engaged to play at the dinner in the castle. They now appeared in fine new red uniforms with gold buttons and took their places. All the movement subsided to a soft rustling and the thronging crowds quickly parted to open a double line between the pillars on the broad carpet. 'Their Highnesses!' they whispered beside me in tones of scared amazement.

I saw the little group approaching, passing along the line of stalls. The archduchess buys some peasant embroidery, then chooses some toys, and from where I am I can hear the dowager countess joking as she bargains for her. Some of the men come a few steps closer and look around at other things. It was then that the prince reached my gypsy tent. He recognized me. His bored face lightened for a moment, and with a swift nonchalance in his movement he suddenly turned, smiled and held out his hand to me. His major-domo, the Italian count, stood two or three steps further back.

'*Meine Zukunft!*' he said with an almost timid gentleness, almost whispering it. I supported his hand lightly but boldly with my outstretched palm; I held the tips of the fingers of my other hand playfully pointing in the middle of his palm, but I looked into his eyes. I particularly wanted to hide my prejudice and collected my senses with swift determination. I could feel everyone watching out of the corner of their eyes, even from a distance, though they could not hear what I was saying.

'A perfect life!' I began, mustering my German knowledge with reasonable success, my voice only slightly trembling. 'A secure and strong life, like a locked, splendid, white tower on a great mountain that has been raised high by the superabundance of the hearts of many millions of people, by tiny particles of superabundance. It is a fine life, a splendid tower, but not for an instant must you desire to come down or dig further into the depths of the beautiful diamond-studded sand from the superabundance of those hearts.'

'And what about me?'...

'You'll never want to, Your Highness! You'll be strong, for you know already... and I can tell you for certain that it's not really worthwhile!'

With the last of my words I let go of his hand. I cannot forget the long, serious, musing look of surprise with which he gazed in wonder at me for a minute; not like a man playing a game, but rather someone waking wonderingly from a dream. The eyes of someone who has solitary, pensive hours—it was a brotherly look. He bowed and his spurs clinked with military precision. 'Thank you, madame!' he said in Hungarian, and he saluted and then went off to join the company of ladies.

During my life since then I have often thought with surprise, indeed almost incomprehension, about myself at that time. What sudden impulse was it that brought together in me all those vivid thoughts that had occupied me for days, and which I then used to depict and establish in my knowledge of life a picture of a royal fate, princely joy and particular royal misery? And I wonder whether 'it's really not worthwhile!' and the bitter and disillusioned certainty with which I flung it at him was so ready to come out because of the experiences of those few hectic weeks and their effect on my young self, which had, not so long before been childish and utterly pampered. Or was it that my own future haunted me?

Now that I am old, I know that even the worst thing is not bad enough to make it worthwhile for us to scare and protect ourselves and each other with it.

For a minute I still stood bemused, looking after the Archduke. He went on his way with the group; his cornflower-blue jacket still appeared receding into a blur of colour, and I thought I could see the glint of the two big golden eagles. He addressed a question to the bishop and the colonel; the major-domo reached towards me for the silk-fringed charity purse and stuffed a large note into it. At a nod the gypsy Bankó once more struck up the prince's song, 'Spinning by night, washing by day...' Now he was at the far entrance of the courtyard, where the carriages were waiting; the braid on his shoulders gleamed once again but was lost in the dazzle of my eyes; he went to meet his unforetold, unknown fate...

All of a sudden I was surrounded by a swarm of people. Curiosity, envy and wonderment crackled around me for minutes on end, and with a smile I enjoyed it once again with the mind of a former inexperienced and dazed young wife. Only the Count and his family had left with the court; the other dinner-guests now stayed behind and surrounded me, ten of them at a time waiting to hear my predictions. I talked, now even deeper in the mastery of the cryptic nonsense of the sibylline style. The diocesan bishop also put his hand into mine. I spoke to him of incredibly high elevation—a cardinal's hat, great palaces—and favoured him, acting in turn as a believer and a daughter, warming the big, fat, white fingers a little more closely. 'This ancient priest is of no consequence to me,' I thought with simple clear-headedness, 'he'll be off tomorrow and perhaps I'll never see him again. But it may be of use to my poor young brother!'

In the end I also read the palm of the gypsy band-leader Bankó, my old, silent admirer—in gypsy fashion. He extended his hand to me in silence and with the irreproachable reserve of a gentleman; he thanked me with a more refined bow than did any of the gentry there. The editor of the local paper came up and excitedly plagued me with questions about what I had pre-dicted for the heir to the throne. I told him something quite different, commonplaces about military glory and a happy family; let him put that in his newspaper. Now my husband too kept close to me; maybe he saw signs of weariness in me, feared for my health or was worried by something else; he kept on urging me to come home, which was unusual for him. Dawn was already breaking and I did not want to dance in my costume; he put me in a carriage. Even today this celebration night of long ago is as full of colour and life to me as some brilliant mirage.

Then it was over. It was followed by a sour and dreary day, as usual.

After that for three whole days I still sallied forth for an evening stroll beneath the castle garden, each time in a beautiful brand-new dress, with the other ladies in their new finery, and for three evenings more, the carriages returning from the hunt clattered right through the town that was bathed in light, under the illuminated triumphal arch. But now nothing happened. Yet the town was full of movement and people. The folk from the countryside mostly stayed in it for the election-day at the end of the week; and in the streets and squares then, I found many unfamiliar faces, and hiding my agitation, I searched for signs of their feelings towards me, towards us. And a sort of unexpected, searing, restless uncertainty took root in me, and I was astonished at myself for having been able to await the shift in my fate with such calm and confidence.

I could not have explained it even to myself why it was so, but all of a sudden I began to feel it frightfully important, a life-and-death decision amid everything else, that my husband should be deputy sheriff at the end of the week. This desire arose not from frivolous wifely ambition, but from a very serious and terrified responsibility for my husband, too. 'I've propelled him into it,' I thought; 'now he's exposed his hand, it's impossible for him not to succeed.'

Dénes Horváth ferreted out news of the general mood and brought it to me. The distinguished guests had departed; I did not bother to go to the station to see them off, and the town, too, seemed to have forgotten them the next day. Now all the attention was turned on the new sensation, the election. The counts withdrew to recover from the burden of entertaining and maybe from all the extravagance too; rumour had it that they were soon going away. Jolsvay had been summoned to the castle once, perhaps for information about the state of affairs, but nobody knew what had been discussed.

'Endre Tabódy's stayed on, too, hasn't he?' I once asked Horváth suddenly.

'Oh no! He's not on the committee yet. After all, he's only just come here two months ago. The others from the Szinyér valley are here.'

'That's bad enough!'

I was timid and thoroughly uneasy by now and I dared not openly draw out of Horváth his frank opinion—was there a chance of losing? Now only two days were left. The folk from the country idling their time away in the town organized big carousals; they were certainly campaigning. Almost every day we had one or two relatives or acquaintances from the country to lunch at our house, and they took Jenő off with them in the evening; we hardly had a chance to speak to each other. My Uncle Ábris had not been in town to see the heir-apparent; we expected him only on the morning of the election. I did not even feel like stepping out of the house till then.

Around nine o'clock that morning, Jenő's supporters came for him with a great hullabaloo. It was a chilly morning, and they had plum-brandy and scones unexpectedly in the dining-room; they were euphoric, elated and confident, and all of a sudden they instilled courage and joyfulness into me, too. 'We'll soon be bringing His Excellency the Deputy Sheriff back!' Galgóczy shouted from the gate when they set off.

Once again I dressed with care and zest in the lovely grey silk dress I wore at home. 'Have you brought any news?' I asked as I ran to meet Horváth, though scarcely half an hour had passed.

'For the moment I've only come to see you. How are you? I'm off now; I'll try to run up into the gallery. Did Jenő have a word with the attendant? Maybe I'll be able to get in. I'll bring the news when I can.'

It was a whole hour before he returned.

'What's happening? Quick!'

'Nothing yet. And don't be so on edge! It's not a matter of life and death!'

'What have you found out?'

'It looks as if Jolsvay was compelled, all the same, to support Széchy. Despite that, I think we shall have a fair majority. But there was one thing that Jenő overlooked, all the same: the big taxpayers in the town, like the rich dyer Korporák, Korbuj the doctor and son of the Rumanian priest, and Hankó the draper. There are quite a few of them and they've all joined in. Széchy himself hasn't gone up there, but his party's banging the big drum. But there's nothing to worry about. Jolsvay's had the doors shut already; maybe they've proclaimed Jenő the winner by now.'

'Just go along then and find out something for certain, for God's sake!'

'Oh do calm yourself down! And if I do bring good news, will you treat me better?'

'Why, don't I treat you well?' I asked, suddenly putting my hand in his. At that moment it must have been feverish and trembling, but perhaps a new, different womanly emotion quivered in this movement. However slowly and imperceptibly, my feelings towards this man whom I had seen almost every day for the last six months had nevertheless grown and developed in some direction, and I sensed his tolerant, gentle and deferential love close to me. I am certain I began to feel it as an *asset* during those last weeks. And, well, he was an *outsider* of pleasant appearance, accepted and favoured in every society, and he treated me with such distinction.

'Oh yes, yes, you're very good to me, Magda!' he said several times, passionately kissing my hands. 'And I'm already grateful simply for your existence, simply that you are. Yes, I'm going now. I'll bring you the news.'

He was rather more uncertain when he came to see me again at about half past ten. His forehead glistened with perspiration from the hurry. But the County Hall was not far away.

'There was a public acclamation, in favour of Jenő, I think, though it's difficult to tell, it really is! Jolsvay was on the point of announcing it, but Széchy's party suddenly demanded a roll-call vote. They'd prepared the list with signatures for it in advance. I'll dash back so as to be able to give you some definite news at last. I only came to tell you this to put your mind at ease.'

'No, Horváth! I beg you, don't go back now!'

'Why? So that…'

'Stay with me. I can't be alone. I'm so exhausted.'

'Oh, you poor dear, you dear, beautiful little witch of a wife! You dear good lady!'

'Sh! No, don't talk now!'

He sat down beside me, close up on the armchair and taking my hand in his he held it tightly for a long time in silence. My pounding heart gradually became stilled and a pleasant dreamy numbness enveloped me; I remained sitting motionless like this and almost forgot all my worries and the anxiety that arose from outside, from alien causes, until they came back.

It was exactly noonday when they returned. Old Hiripy, Jenő and my stepfather Telekdy, were overwrought with excitement and silent despondency. When I saw them I came to my senses as if from some dream. Failure… was this what it was like then? And pity sent a stab of pain through me: 'My poor, poor dear husband!'

Now I only have confused memories, as in a dream, about what happened next… We were seated at the table; a very simple lunch was prepared, a fiasco, I was just thinking—after all, the arrangement was that Jenő was to join his victorious party for lunch. Old Hiripy snorted, angrily talking about an 'injustice', of course. Péter philosophized bitterly, but in just the same way as he always did before, and this apathy almost roused anger in me. Horváth sat in silence and I did not look in his direction. Little Pityu played and rattled his spoon; I spoke sharply to him. 'Don't upset him, just let him play, poor thing!' said his father quietly. He still seemed agitated, but all the previous colour had drained from his face and brow; he was very pale, and spooned his soup quickly with a trembling hand. 'He must have been hungry since morning,' I thought, and was glad that he was having a good meal. When the plates were cleared away, he got up, saying that he had to go into the office for a minute.

I signalled to the servants to delay the meat. The company sat in silence. I looked through the courtyard window and saw the unkempt autumnal garden, the bare yard with the carpet of flowers all nipped by the frost; it was such a sad, sad sight. It was a chilly day and the housemaid was just fetching in a shovel of live coals to put in the stove. When she reached the hall with them, I saw her give a sudden start in the open doorway and drop them all on the floor. She heard the sound of the shot more clearly.

They all jumped up… I collapsed in the doorway… I don't know anything else…

At that moment… everything, everything came to an end.

XV.

Yes, yes, I must not stop here if I now want to trace my whole life in memory, avoid and omit the horror of that day and all the terrible thudding blows that rained down on me in those few, very few weeks, the great change, the great crash that like the wheel of a pulverising mill ground down and crumbled what I had been till then, my fate, my life, everything… and I must declare that this was a new chapter, a new life-story, for in it is written the state of a different person, a transformed, changed soul, the course of a newly-begun life, and I do not know, I do not know how all this could have been happening with me, and in me.

Yet that's the truth! I do not know. At that time life broke over my head; it shattered me to pieces, drove me to destitution, tore me from my roots, displaced me from my place in the world and hurled me far away, pulling the earth from under my feet and the roof from over my head; and I never discovered again, however much I tried, the self I had once been; I could never live myself back into the old, real self-assurance I once had. What I had been before came to an end and ceased to be. But I never had the strength any more to become new and different, to breathe a different air, to find a significant place even in my changed circumstances, as perhaps I might have been able to do at that time. Yes, this—this effort, all the strength I wasted on it and all the suffering and cruel interruption may be the best explanation for my subsequent fate and my whole long, long and difficult life. Now it doesn't matter, I know; now even if I had a wholly fortunate and healthy life I could not be anything else than what I am: a peaceful, unconcerned old woman; indeed, in that case maybe I should not be able to remain tranquil like this, peacefully enduring this great loneliness before death.

I no longer feel those old tortures as fresh pain, and at the present time a good little cup of warm aromatic coffee perhaps comforts me the most. Let only those dare to recall their whole past critically and searchingly who can do this as if they were concerned with another person, outside themselves. Yes, we must be able at least to face the past squarely if we have not always been able to do this with the present and the future. I was twenty-seven years old when the first appalling blow fell, and that sent my whole life into reverse.

Yet even now I cannot, no I cannot, think of that black-smudged, bloodstained little death-wound from the shot in his temple without terror and agitation... And what followed it: the singing at the funeral, the smell of death, wreaths, the stifling and cruel deluge of tolling bells, swooning tears and over everything a kind of dull half-stupor of the sort felt perhaps by someone suddenly struck on the head. Like a sleepwalker, I allowed myself to be led by the arm, comforted and encouraged, while my eyes, swollen with weeping, watched through the thick widow's veil the shocked bustle of people around me as if it were a dim and improbable shadow of a pantomime.

Perhaps it was a week later when one day my mother said, 'Now you'd better pull yourself together a little and start thinking about the future!'

About the future?.... Me?

It was then for the very first time that these words of my mother made me realize keenly and startlingly how very much I was left now to my own resources. 'Think about your destiny and your child's,' people said to me, knowing perfectly well that I'd lost everything, myself included, that pampered somebody, provided with everything, and so well suited to her situation up to now, who to the age of twenty-seven had always been looked after by someone else. But can they give me anything other than this hesitant, irresponsible, evasive advice? Do they really want to do something for me and help me? The family, that famous, sympathetic, loyal dynasty then, at the time of my misfortune, for the very first time demonstrated what a disintegrated, weak and indifferent link it had become. There I was, left on my own, helpless and broken, and I could hardly believe my fate, I still kept expecting some marvellous awakening,—that the whole thing was just a bad dream and nothing had changed.

At that time I was living at my mother's in the Cifrasor; it was a temporary arrangement, for I severely dreaded my old home where the blood of my poor dead husband had trickled on to the floor. I was also oppressed by an obscure self-recrimination; I could not put a name to it, but sometimes it even woke me suddenly from sleep. It did not arise from within me; the eyes of strangers rammed it into me; it rose up from the masked glances of evil-wishers and former rivals and the whispering behind my back, and I was startled into making excuses to myself. Could I have been the cause of it?... No, no, that's not possible; I know that for certain today. He, poor man, who has been at rest so long now, perhaps set out on his fated road when he chose me to be his wife, but he chose and desired me for what I was: different from his family, the prejudiced and narrow-minded daughters of sober, temperate burghers. He wanted me because he wanted his destiny, and it was only a terrible accident that caused it to turn out differently from what we expected and wanted. No, those 'deficiencies' mentioned in whispers and accompanied by wicked head-wagging were not so great as to have been able to lay his life in ruins. True, there were irregularities concerning the money belonging to my younger brothers, and Jenő would not have been able to account immediately for the price of the plots divided up by the estate, but, for heaven's sake, he should have had a word with the Count, or asked my Uncle Ábris for it, or borrowed it from the Hiripys or whatever. But he did not have the strength to do this; it would have been uncomfortable and difficult to admit it for a man who was proclaimed by everyone to be so precise and uncorrupt. He did not possess a sufficient desire for life to put this behind him and start again from the beginning on the slow upward path in the estimation of other people.

At that time, my poor young brother, Sándorka, could not have been declared of age as he was mentally ill, while Csaba with airy, gentlemanly simplicity, without argument or explanation, renounced all that was missing from his portion, too. Yes, the thought of these embarrassments must have been terrible to him, but he could have extricated himself! But that was the time when he was driven to distraction by the business of the election, the doubt, the expectancy and then the failure which after all was unexpected; and it only takes a momentary attack of nerves to decide all this. If I could have been alone with him then, at that last lunch, if he had been able to unburden himself, if we had shared our sorrow and he had been able to confess everything to me... it is dreadful to think on what tiny chances one's life depends!

It was strange and surprising even to myself when I gave it a thought that it was Dénes Horváth to whom I spoke most about this. It was he whom I plied with questions, he from whom

I expected consolation, relief and assurance. 'It's not true, is it? It's impossible! Did I really drive him into it? Why, am I truly so despicable, such a monster? The best thing would be for me too to follow him!'

At such times he would explain and talk to me with affectionate zeal, with his own peculiar fatalism in whose depths there was a kind of simple, childlike optimism. I felt a particular comfort in that for weeks he never grasped my hand, even accidentally, while we were talking, as he had done on that fateful day when it rested intimately in his hand for hours. And he came to visit me every day. He did not stay long at my mother's, but brought me my hat and coat and took me for a walk. We went to the cemetery together practically every day, on frosty, misty, damp cold evenings or in the gloom of early afternoons. We stood together, side by side, at the head of the grave and in silent devotion allowed ourselves to grieve. We seemed to want, to help to release in our souls the whole torrent of grief that engrossed us, justified us, and bound us together, but at the same time beneficently kept us apart and forbade one from the other. It was as if this was some justification for both of us, an apology to the dead man, when we were able to face him like this with true hearts and without self-accusation, the man of whom in pious faith we cherished the hope that he was alive somewhere and knew about us, that he looked with clarified vision and understood everything. We had never committed any offence against him! And with painful emotion I felt such a high regard for Horváth's reserve—it was so fine, noble and tender—that since that luckless morning he had never tried to grasp my hand in his as he had done then for the first time. Yet his whole being, his every word displayed anxious and self-sacrificing love.

'You will tell me, won't you,' I begged him on the way home in the misty dusk of the quiet little peasant streets, 'you will tell me the truth? Be frank with me, I want to know what you think about it. Is it true that I too… that I was partly the cause of it? That I was prodigal or… I don't know, I don't know. Do say something, for God's sake!'

My words were stifled in a fit of tormented sobbing. And he spoke to me in tones of the most intimate sympathy; he comforted me almost as if I were a child. With gentle devotion he would mention the inevitability of fate, the particular destiny of the dead man, the imbalance between his ideals and resources; that he was superior to his surroundings here and cut out for better things, but had insufficient energy either to break away or to rise above them. This was what he said, always with the reserve of a respectful outsider and with endless consideration for me in his own unassuming, almost deliberately simple words.

'He's the only true, faithful friend I've got!' I thought then with deep emotion as I felt some slight relief and a warm surge of thankfulness and trust with my whole heart. 'How good it is that I've got a man like this, at least! And the despicable, mean, evil-tongued world would deprive me of him too!'

For the world—and this word, pronounced with venom, still meant to me mainly the wives of the estate officials—the world had already begun to make itself felt in our sacred relationship. As we went around the big market square, walking like this side by side with quiet steps in the hazy darkness of the evening, it was with uneasy and hostile emotions that I looked through the mist of the big grassy square towards the row of brightly-lit uniformly large windows where the castle garden ended in a sombre group of big dark pines and the old Water Tower with its stiff, cumbersome stone cone loomed spectrally in the dark sky. 'That's where they live! It's from there that their common, rigid and narrow-minded way of life extends over this miserable town with ever-increasing influence. And now I'm the focus of their attention: they investigate my past and dog my footsteps with prejudice and ill-will. 'They've scarcely laid her poor husband, the victim of her ambitions, in the grave, and she's already going walking with her suitor, making herself ridiculous!'

I could almost hear their wicked, cruel comments, and with terrified anger I thought of them in bitterness and hatred—but no longer with that scornful disdain of old. Of old? Of three or four weeks ago! My God! Was it I who in the sunny mornings and mild evenings of early autumn paraded myself here among the celebrating crowds in bright colours, all dressed up, haughty, filled with a nerve-tingling zest for life and laughing as only a woman conscious of her beauty can? What had suddenly become of that world of mine, the old social circle, the old interests and connections? A few brief lines of sympathy, the occasional dutiful visit which amounted almost to a farewell, and my whole past receded from me—how far it receded!—in a matter of days! And today I cannot bear to think of the condemnation of my enemies with the belittling, I-don't-care attitude of the old days. It excites me, terrifies me, saddens me as if now I were everyone's concern, as if now everyone who could, might harm me, a poor widow dependent on others; there was a moment when I would have longed to appease them like a coward. After all, my father-in-law stayed with them when he came here to the funeral and escorted the coffin of his only son in grim, un-communicative grief, boldly keeping apart from me and my family. Who knows what they told him about me, what mean lies! But it was his opinion that was most important to me now, for he was my fatherless little son's rich grandfather. Merciless God! How much He piled up at that time on my poor inexperienced head!

'The best thing would be for me to follow him, too!' I kept saying in quiet, stubborn despair, and Horváth, running out of assurance, fell silent; and with helpless, heavy grief he kissed my hand as we parted in front of my mother's house.

The window of the brightly-alit kitchen was open when I passed it on my way along the veranda; I heard the rebellious, tearful, complaining voice of my little son coming from it and I glanced momentarily inside. The big peasant maid stood facing the stove with a sullen expression, taking some sort of meat out of the sizzling saucepan. Pityu sat behind her on the kitchen bench and the wall-lamp shone on his pale little face stained with tears. 'I'll tell my mummy about you!' he kept wailing with monotonous, listless childish stubbornness, and it was such a terribly sad sight. 'A fat lot I care about your mummy! I don't take orders from her!' the maid guffawed coarsely, and the boy stared at her uncomprehendingly, with his confused, tormented little face. Oh, poor, poor little fatherless child! A week ago the nursemaid was still looking after him, accompanying him, wiping his little nose and keeping him occupied with games. Now he was on his own in a strange house and had to keep quiet whenever his mother was mocked in front of him.

'Come here, my little son, my darling, I'm back!' I said with an unusual burst of affection, and I wept as I covered him with kisses. I took him in, washed him and heard him say his prayers in the cot and stayed with him till he went off to sleep. It wasn't so long ago that his father and I had sat beside him like this, I thought as I kept looking at the thin slumbering face. How he loved him, how he could fondle him and what delight he had in him! And yet how had he the heart to abandon him like this? To what fate had he destined him and me? What was I to do with him and with myself? It would be best for both of us to die together.

But this nightmarish idea dissolved in weeping and copious tears that brought relief. With great sadness and tears I pondered how I too was now going to say farewell to the boy, maybe for a long time. His grandmother, who had become very ill from mental shock at the time of the funeral, was coming here to visit her son's grave and to take the child home with her until, as she wrote, my own life was straightened out. There was nothing else I could do except let him go with her, and she, poor woman, was good, tender-hearted and kind, and was very fond of the hapless little boy. But I wondered whether the old man had been driven to make this provision for him by a kind of repentance or prick of conscience, or was it only from detestation and hatred of me, that he did not consider me worthy to be entrusted with the boy?... And yet now, even if this were so, I had to surrender him. What else could I do?

Eyes red with crying, I sat for a while at dinner, opposite my mother and her husband who sat silent in dumb estrangement. My situation had already taught me to be warily suspicious; I already sensed that they had been discussing me today before I got there, and that they had come to some kind of agreement about me.

'Ah well, life's difficult nowadays, it gets more and more difficult every day!' Péter began at last, on the feeble and artificial pretext offered by some newspaper article, as he gave up reading it. 'Today everyone's got to use their own resources to cling to life; there's no room in today's circumstances for hangers-on, either men or women. Today everyone's own burden is quite enough for them to bear.'

Mother's expression was indecisive as she nibbled in silence at an apple that remained from last year's crop in the orchard at Telekd. And I realized with chilling certainty that they were united now against me. And Péter went on with increasing generalizations, deviating more and more, as was his custom, from the case under review and from the thought of some practical solution.

'The ideal wife in the developing social order will no longer be the petted and maintained puppet of old, rocked on her husband's knee and left to eternal immaturity. The age of independent, strong women capable of fighting is coming, women who can stand firm even in trouble, responsible for themselves and for those entrusted to them by nature, as mothers. In the old days, when there was an abundance of produce around the house and a simple mode of housekeeping demanded more female labour, a single or widowed female relative might stay behind in the odd family and vegetate there till her dying day. But all that's come to an end now. Today everyone's their own master, but compelled also to stand on their own two feet. I'm not one to condemn an independent unmarried woman either if she chooses to live her own life with someone else, as long as she maintains a certain decorum, and if she is able, in particular, to regulate her own life and not be dependent on anyone. But to live in idleness is the greatest immorality. Indeed I believe we're now seeing the development of a totally new type of woman, a great mass of females who are left cold by the caprices and weaknesses of love and who absolve themselves from the problems of bearing and caring for children in order to devote their powers entirely to the community of mankind, like the superfluous but naturally degenerate undeveloped females in the beehive, the workers. And it is necessary for this to be the way of development, because ever more women are born and ever fewer men...'

'Oh, how you skirt around the issue like this! Listen to me and stop it now!' my mother broke in ungraciously as she turned away and went to the sideboard. Mortally offended, I bade them goodnight tonelessly and brusquely.

'Oh, they're afraid, afraid they're going to be stuck with me', wounded self-esteem seethed mutinously in me when I was on my own and it drew forth new bitter tears. 'No, there's no need for my stepfather to be afraid, I would not eat the bread he begrudged for long! But all the same, I must have a place here in my own mother's home now! What do they want? Where am I to go and what am I to do? Why don't they say something sensible, something concrete? This crank here who has frittered away my mother's fortune with his bad management simply pumps out empty maxims as usual, the things he has read most recently in some book and wants to express in any way, shape, or form. Why, I've had no time to think about this yet. I do not know this side of life, the value of money, how much I can live

143

on and how to acquire it. There was so little talk about such things at home, and my house was always open for months, six months at a time, for my younger brothers, for example, when they had grown up, without keeping accounts and not even noticing or ever considering that what they had to eat was also worth money.

All this was new to me, totally new, and it struck me as dreadfully wrong, hideous and not genteel... 'Why, is everyone so wicked and common when it comes to the crunch?... That's impossible, there must still be some real tenderness and sacrificial love such as my poor good husband possessed. But where? Dénes Horváth?... But after all, he only showed it in words... No, that's an ugly, evil thought! He's an outsider, just a good friend whose reserved respect cannot allow him to entertain such thoughts. But how good he is to me, how much he sympathizes with me and worries about me, how he loves me! He is the only person in the whole wide world who truly loves me; everyone else has turned away from me.' Then I recalled his words or just the anxious, warm resonance of his voice, and this was so pleasant and lulled me into such relaxed daydreams that it seemed to uplift me. There was someone after all to whom I was very important and precious even in such a pitiful state.

Next day Melanie, the high sheriff's wife, came to see me. She dismissed her carriage and said she had only come for a ten-minute duty-visit, but was prompted by real affection and as a relative, had my interest at heart. In other words, she was kind, captivating and unfathomable as ever.

'My dear Magda, you won't take it the wrong way if I ask you some almost indiscreet questions, but I'm interested and worried about your future. What are your plans? Could I be of any help to you? Have you in general any small reliable source of income that can tide you over for the time being?'

I felt myself blush painfully, for I knew she must be acquainted with the story of the missing estate funds and other irregularities, the muddled affairs whose makeshift settlement had swallowed up all the current income from the office. I was offended by her interference, but her rapid and bold questions embarrassed me, so I was reluctantly compelled to answer.

'I think all there is comes from some life insurance of long ago, maybe four thousand forints. There's nothing else.'

'Hm. Well that, my dear, certainly isn't very much, though it's better than nothing. Apart from that you've got furniture for eight rooms, haven't you?'

'Well, yes, but that...'

'You couldn't possibly use them all to live in, of course. But I understand that the rent for the house is paid for six months and the lease is for ten years. There are still five to go. Am I right?... Magda, I'm speaking now absolutely from the heart; I'll tell you what I'd do in your circumstance. What about trying to rent your furnished rooms, for example? Let's say, to unmarried officials from the finance department, the court, the railway, and then take in two or three school-children as boarders? You could live in the two rooms facing the courtyard. You could keep your good cook and the maids you've trained.'

I stared at her in silence, with amazed repugnance. I was so surprised I could not follow her train of thought or the possibilities she mentioned. She looked searchingly into my face.

'Or look here!' she said with a sudden thought, 'If you don't feel like doing that, there's something much more clever you might be able to do. But you won't misunderstand me, will you, if I tell you what I'm thinking? You're so clever with your hands, Magda; if you were to give yourself over, say, to a nice, elegant hat-decorating salon, the sort of thing you find in cities... You'd go up to Pest for a while to learn and then, if you're determined to stay here in the town, we women, believe me, would all come and support you as we're able. Not a shop, no, you'd have a room in your own house specially for it, and we'd come and visit you as we always have done for the occasional cup of tea, and while we're passing the time of day we'd select our hats from your advice, the hats we now have sent at random, from a catalogue, from Pest and Vienna. But... now I don't know, Magda, isn't all this upsetting you? Oh, you're terribly annoyed with me!'

'Oh no, not at all... you're infinitely kind, as always. I don't deserve it...'

'Yes, you're right. It's still too early for this. After all, you've hardly recovered yet from all your grief. Do forgive me and don't think of anything for the time being. Only your health is important. How are you? And is your little boy well?'

Hiding her amazement or annoyance, she swiftly and skillfully steered the conversation towards other subjects of various kinds. She was gracious, and assured me of her love in her inimitably kind but at the same time incomprehensibly alien, aloof superior style, and half an hour later she got into her carriage again and went on her way, brilliantly blonde, beautiful, refined and clever, and perhaps never gave me another thought in her life. She had satisfied her would-be charitable, superior nature; she had given me some good advice.

'It's dreadful, dreadful!' I burst out that evening, when Dénes Horváth and I were making our way side by side through the leafless trees in the cemetery. 'I can't endure life! It's got no transition period, it's so cruel! They want me to be a boarding-house landlady or a hat-seller here. Is that conceivable? Tell me! So suddenly, just like that, in the same house! I'd rather go into hiding somewhere, so that they'd never set eyes on me again!'

For a time, we continued in silence along the damp, slippery track between the graves. At Jenő's, seeking refuge, I threw myself on the headstone with a sudden outburst of passionate weeping. Horváth stood behind me in mute grief.

'Magda,' he said on the way home and *now* grasped my hand, pressing it to his lips in silence for a long time, 'you are my every thought, believe me; you know how much I love you and I would gladly lay down this useless, good-for-nothing life of mine for you if that could be of any help. Not for a long time has anything weighed so heavily on me as your destiny now. If only you knew how much I turn it over in my mind! And I've learnt now to curse my own idle, purposeless life up to now, my thoughtlessness, my lack of concern about tomorrow, all of which has made me a helpless nobody who cannot be the mainstay of the person he values most in the world. Have pity on me, Magda, and don't hate me for it! What I possess is at your service, and if you need a self-sacrificing friend in anything, you've only got to give me a nod. Bear with me, don't banish me from your side; I couldn't go away anyway. Maybe something unexpected will turn up to solve everything; fate is sometimes more inventive then all of us. Today all I know is that I love you to no end!'

We were in front of the gateway, and for a long time I felt the warmth of his lips through the glove. Then he unfastened the buckle of the leather glove above my wrist and kissed it there, then again and again. Then I suddenly pulled my hand away and went inside.

At home I found an unexpected letter. It was from my mother's sister in Pest; she expressed her own and her husband's sympathy and with kindred affection invited me to stay with them for the winter, to get away from things a little and together work out some sensible solution to my problem. In a postscript they added that I should bring bed-linen with me and, conditions being what they were in Pest, contribute thirty forints a month towards the housekeeping. I remember being seized then by a fit of caustic bitterness and nausea at it, though, as I can well understand today, it was a natural and proper arrangement. At the time I read the letter again and again in dejection, but at the same time with a trembling, half-cowardly speculation, and some excitement, there emerged in me a desire to be bold, and I crumpled the letter under my pillow. To think out something sensible about my future, to try my luck—or was it just the pull of the unknown city, the spectacle of other people's lives, or did I want to escape from here, from the heartlessness of the Telekdys, the slanders or my own memories? Or was it defiance and the fear of a futile love that prompted me? Next day I made up my mind.

The scenes of my life during those one or two weeks I still had at home come to mind like tangled threads of dreams.

I am standing on the platform at the station; a train departs and the outstretched little white arms of my young son wave farewell in unsuspecting haste from the carriage-window. I can still see his constrained, tearful little smile and my mother-in-law's mournful, suddenly aged, trembling head behind him; then I get on alone into a carriage and the burning, bitter tears begin to flow. 'It's only for a time!' I keep assuring myself, but my senses tell me that I have allowed my son to be torn from my heart.

… Then I recall a windy cold evening when I took leave of my dying grandmother. She lay in the old kitchen-block, in the room with a veranda, beneath the great blackened oak beams, and with vacant eyes I saw once again the old, heavy pedestal table, the sideboard with pot-bellied drawers and the glass-fronted dresser with cotillion-rosettes from balls a hundred years before stuck to it. Childhood years long-departed! A whole world now separated me from them! There she lay, very pale now, her lovely strong face sunken with a thousand parchment-like furrows among the white pillows, the lilac and blue shadows of approaching death already around her nose and chin. But she was still saying farewell and making arrangements, taking advantage of the situation that had assembled most of the family around her that evening. She sent for the solicitor and then declared clearly what not even István had known till then, that in her will she had established a trust-fund for her three daughters for their lifetime, not much of a sum, four hundred forints a year in all, in order that this certain and inalienable little amount might save them some time from begging in their old age. How sensible, how clear-sighted this excellent, strong woman, this female patriarch still was at that time—for she knew how to be more than a *mater familias*, and different too. Why ever had Péter Telekdy rambled on to me about a new type of woman?...

When we were all together, she beckoned István over and in front of all of us pulled her expensive diamond ring from her finger and took off her earrings. 'I'm giving you these now... so that everyone can see, and there'll be no arguments about them... and the house and estate now belong to my son István; now it's free from debt. That's what I want!' And not a whisper could be heard when she let her head fall back on the pillow.

I also remember some painfully brief farewell visits and Ilka Zimán's icy, drooping mouth when we kissed each other. She was perhaps the happiest that I was going away now. I spent a very cruel day packing up my furniture: we piled it all on top of each other ceiling-high in the two little rooms on the courtyard side, including expensive carpets in mothballs and the beautiful gilded dining-room suite with the little cupids. Melanie rented the front rooms from me for some poor mad older brother of hers. As dusk fell, I stood in the deserted courtyard before the denuded, sorrowful garden; I gazed over the bare stalks of the weed-filled flower beds, the sodden lawn with its rust-brown blotches, the leafless trees that poor Jenő had planted, and the black tangled outline of the raspberry canes which only that summer had filled the air with such strong, sweet perfume. How terrible it was long ago!... Then I saw the mad stranger walk along the empty veranda with his nurse.

... At last I was sitting in the railway carriage, and I said to myself, 'Now I'm breaking away, leaving behind all that's existed up till now; Now I can be all on my own and free!' The carriage began to move and I leaned out. Dénes Horváth who had accompanied me from the house was still standing there beside the wooden pillar with bowed head in helpless misery. I took out my black-bordered handkerchief and waved it to him.

XVI.

The dense light of gas lamps, countless shadows reaching out from black iron girders, rumbling, ringing of bells, shouts on all sides, a heavy smell of smoke in the damp air, nothing but confusion, nothing but light and shadow trampling on each other. How I remember the terror of that first minute! Once upon a time, in the first months of my marriage, poor Jenő took me up for a week to go to theatres, go shopping and gaze at shop-windows during those fleeting, brief, buoyant days; threading my arm through his, snuggling against him with the petulant or pleading prattle of a new wife if I needed or fell in love with something, that was how I dashed through this bustling, diverse, gaudily-bedecked city then. Jenő brought a lot of money; we stayed at a smart hotel and with happy, easily-duped chivalrousness he spent freely, showed me things and explained them, dressed me up, guarded and protected me... This time, however, I came on my own, poor and uncertain, living a widow's life, withdrawing from everything, leaving everything far behind me. What was I doing here? No matter what, something would turn up sometime, sometime in the future; the main thing was that I had the strength to come now!... And I sensed something important, almost heroic and dynamic in the fact that I had been able to make the break now. Yes, I had left everything behind me; the tongues of the world could stop wagging. Whatever happened to me here, I had no wish to be in anyone's way or to upset anyone's life. At the same time it was certainly the judgment of those at home, the folk of Szinyér, that to me represented the voice of 'the world', and what gave me a little strength to make the decision was only a feminine feeling, obstinacy in the shape of love and repression. And in the meantime my heart ached and tears choked in my throat—how comforting it would have been to nestle up to someone and hug them in the great alien world, to belong to someone and thread my arm through theirs!

From inside the chain barrier Gida Rácz, my uncle, was waving his arms, beckoning to me; he was the husband of Aunt Marika, my youngest aunt. A porter with a barrow was standing beside him already. He helped me through, saw my baggage loaded and then took me by the arm and we set off on foot behind my baskets and boxes.

'It's not far, you know; why pay one forint twenty for a cab? The porter will be happy with three twenty-fillér pieces! Well, how are you? Have you recovered, you poor little widow?'

But it wasn't nearby; we went for quite a distance in the wake of hurrying human shadows on the wet pavement. I saw a big butcher's window with all kinds of sausages and cheeses in silver paper, and in another one, a vast number of cigars and next to them a newspaper with coloured pictures of half-naked, ugly ballerinas. Then through a frosty, new, silent garden where deserted benches loomed black among the bushes; a good-looking, lanky couple came towards us and the girl in a fur hat was complaining tearfully about something to the boy. We caught up with the porter in a side-street and hurried across perhaps two more. We clambered up to the third floor and Gida had a loud argument with the porter over the cost. Marika opened the door and her noisy, grateful, lively style, her myriad of questions, her sighs and delight, all her gestures and her still graceful bustling around, once more made me feel a little more at home. She was one of us, though she had long broken away; the natural elegance of the Zimán ladies, their confidence and a kind of fresh, humorously charming originality were still to be seen in her behind all the miserable, alien and jarring tempo of Pest.

They had three rooms: in the middle was the dining-room where now paper-thin slices of cold meat adorned the centre of the laid table together with two fingers' breadth of butter and a very modest quantity of serrated shop-bought bread. On one side of it was their bedroom, and their two schoolgirl daughters were asleep there already; into the other narrow side-room Marika had piled the old green corded silk suite with the green plush-covered tables and small cushions embroidered with rose-twigs; so this would have been the drawing-room, but for me they had brought in the iron camp-bed that by day was folded up in the bathroom. Than at last they opened the folding doors to the two side-rooms, since the only heating was from the tiled stove in the dining-room.

That evening all these little things caught my eye and depressed me; I felt offended and almost ashamed by this penny-pinching, constricted, petty official's lifestyle. I knew that

Gida's income was not much less than my poor husband's in his last days. And how we lived on it! They said that they were paying as much for this flat as we did for our last house with all its rooms, the veranda and garden with the raspberry canes... And if only it were possible to sleep, at least! But here the unknown, insidious little sounds never cease, everything can be heard through the walls, from down below the thump of gypsy music reaches here and keeps breaking out over and over again, the horse-trams clang their bells and carriages rattle past. I got up frozen, irritated and curious, and very cautiously raised the iron shutter of the window. Down below it was light as day; there was still plenty of traffic on the carriageway, but the pavement was almost deserted. Music was playing in the big coffee-house on the opposite corner. Now the door opened, revealing the heavy tapestry curtain behind; a party of people streamed out, staggering a little, women shrieked and cackled, and in the doorway a big man in a fur coat held its two sides wide open and suddenly embraced a red-cloaked girl in its silk lining. I crept back among the strange-smelling pillows. Was this how things went on here?...

One benumbed, gloomy, foggy day my first trip out took me to Sándorka, to Angyalföld. And once again I saw my poor, poor little brother's thin face, little tonsured head and blue eyes scared by madness. Only now as I was waiting for him in the poorly-heated, big bleak reception room did the chance thought first circulate in my head, 'Father was already an alcoholic when my two younger brothers were born in rapid succession.' And I thought of the often-mentioned incident when the Jew Lipi, who had speculated on some bankrupt estate of which my father was the trustee, turned up one day with proper respect to see grandma; standing as usual before the alcove-window throne, he announced with the honest concern that characterized his peculiar solidarity with our family, 'Madam... er... it would be a good idea to keep an eye on the master! There are rum bottles on the office shelf behind the bundles of documents!'

They brought him in wearing the hospital coat of rough cloth and the nurse stayed close to him. I sat down beside him with trembling, stifled fear that pierced my very brain and tried to speak to him. It was me, Magda; I'd just come from mother's house, and we longed to see him there, he'd get better. He stared fixedly at me and at the same time into the distance, through me, as if I were made of glass. 'He doesn't understand', whispered the nurse. Then I put my hand on his and stroked it quickly and quiveringly, and I found myself unable to speak as the tears welled up in my throat. 'It's little Maggie,' I began again and the tears broke through, 'your poor sister who always loved you. It's your own Magda! Do look at me!'

'No, no, 'he said in a monotone voice, revealing a sad indifference, 'I want you to be Vulpaverga still and I'll be King Rombertáró!'

'Yes… yes, yes!' I clasped his hand in anguish.

'Except that it's impossible, oh yes…. because under the earth, deep down there's hell, wailing and gnashing its teeth forever and eternal fire… the evil thoughts!… But I'm wearing the robe of the Virgin Mother, the holy scapular over my shoulders… Look, she gave it to me, and whoever wears this she will not allow to suffer damnation. However great a sinner he is, at the last moment, even in the hour of death she will come for him and save him. But here they often want to strip it from me, the evil ones, the hell-hounds who will stand on the left with loathsome bodies. But I don't let them; then they torment me, but it's good to suffer martyrdom for the Virgin Mother! She gathers all this into a garland of red roses and will come to meet me with it as far as the gates of heaven. You, too, you too will be given a robe like this if you pray without ceasing, always, even in the night, and do not submit to the devil. I shall pray for you too!'

'Yes, yes! My darling Sándorka, dear Rombertáró!'

'Then,' he said, suddenly brightening, with a relieved expression, 'then I can love you. You are my sister in Jesus. I love you, Vulpaverga!'

With both hands he grasped my hand, clutched them convulsively and turned the palm upwards where my glove had left a little round gap above the wrist. Now his face was burning, his eyes glittering; with a sudden, peculiar, passionate movement he pressed my hand to his lips, to his teeth, and in instinctive terror, I snatched it back. His face crumpled into an abnormally frightful and ugly smile and once more he reached out with convulsively bent fingers towards my shoulders and waist. 'Quick! Get out!' cried the nurse and confronted him. The double doors slid open at the pressure of some hidden button, a warder came in from the corridor and quickly pushed me outside. I didn't understand it all, but my buzzing head crackled with terror and I was overcome by giddiness.

'A hopeless case!' said the doctor-in-charge sympathetically in the office. 'But it may drag on for years, and he's paid for here by a trust fund, so it's still the best place for him.'

Marika scolded me for this visit. 'That's all you need at a time like this, worrying yourself to death! Can you do anything for him? You've only got to let your health go to pieces, and a fine state you'll be in! Now come along, let's put on our best clothes and go to Hatvani Street and the Radial Road; what hats there are to be seen there now, and Gács's window-display is fabulous! The things they send to you in the country are all out of date, last year's fashions or locally run up; the real Paris models you can see only in Pest. That mourning outfit looks splendid on you, but you must buy a new hat. For tomorrow perhaps Gida can get hold of a cheap box at the National Theatre. We'll do it in style!'

I was still depressed and confused, but Marika laid out my clothes and surveyed them, then she too began to dress. I watched intently to see how attractively she could get herself up. By my reckoning she was then thirty-eight years old, the same as her cousin Ilka Zimán, but she knew how to make herself look years younger. She blackened the bottom of a little porcelain jar from the chemist with a lighted match, then rubbed the soot on to an old toothbrush and lengthened her eyebrows with it; she smeared a thin layer of Vaseline under the powder and even had some red salve in a tube for the corners of her mouth. She laughed at my astonishment when she enclosed her small drooping breasts in a good firm pair of stays whose laces reached right down to the knees and were fastened to her stockings, making her hips fill out. Now she appeared as a good-looking, pretty-eyed new bride of thirty-eight.

I immediately tried out the soot-coated toothbrush, the lip-salve and the Vaseline after her, and Marika brushed my hair into a fashionable Vetsera-knot. But this did not look right, and she too realized this, so we undid it and I reshaped it into my own gypsy style, loose at the front and fluttering. I covered it with a black lace kerchief, and adorned my low-cut neck and arms with black jet jewellery that shone with the colour of mourning.

We did indeed occupy a box, though we were accompanied

by some colleague of Gida's from the bank and his spinster sister. But I sat in front, resting my bejewelled, gloved arms on the velvet of the ledge, and with almost childish transports of amazement took in the light and excitement of the great alien world with wide-open inexperienced eyes. How freshly I saw everything and how well I observed it! The smiles and bows of the women, the stiff aim of opera-glasses raised to flashing eyes, the sly whisperings of frivolous interest—and I was suddenly seized by an avid, bold curiosity to see inside and be part of the life of this seasoned society, which was clearly just as supreme, prominently-active and exclusive here in the real great world as that down there in the town I had abandoned, of which not so long ago I too had been a leading member. My God! How the certainty of provincial pre-eminence shrinks to nothing here! What a total nobody is the person who travels only by a horse-tram and not in a rubber-tyred coach, who stands outside the tiny intricacies of distinguished and wealthy circles! This was a new feeling for me; it irritated me and absorbed my attention. Behind me, Gida was deep in conversation with the other official; they were discussing the tyranny of their chief and petty office gossip. What a proper little pen-pusher he'd become, the former lively, jaunty, leather-gaitered young gentleman who gambled away the last of his little estate at cards when he was already married to Marika! Then he made his wandering way up here out of necessity; he was lucky and it turned out—what a surprise!—that a proclivity to this 'normal' life had always lurked hidden in the depths of his soul. He had changed; perhaps he no longer remembered that self of old.

On the stage they were performing 'Marguerite Gauthier'. The actress flung off a beautifully-cut coloured silk cloak with a grand, fine, free movement, and I felt that with just such a wild and rapid motion, such a convulsive twitch, it was possible to breach and liberate determination, desperate strength, the past, experience and the passing of minutes strained to breaking-point. Except that... I'm more slender than she is and my face has much more character!... And in me, too, sometimes a thousand different strings are strained, confused and inexpressible, when I should like everything, absolutely everything and I believe myself to be filled with the whole of life in all its greatness. In a word, I could never explain all this, but I could pour it out like this in significant gestures and shades of tone. Oh, would this be possible?... How ought I to set about it?...

The great card scene: Marguerite's lover throws the money down in front of her; she screams and raises the imitation fur cloak to protect her face. How studied, how automatic I felt this to be at that moment! All of a sudden I saw how I would do it!

The curtain fell and only then did I realize that Marika was feverishly nudging my elbow. She wanted to draw my attention to a man who was standing at the front of the stalls and with a careless movement had been swivelling his opera-glasses round the half-darkened auditorium during the last scene, then deliberately turning them on me and holding them there for minutes on end. The lights came on and with an elated expression I turned to face him boldly and deliberately.

'It's Losonczy! He's a character! A gambler and owner of a racing-stud: the most distinguished ladies' man in Pest!' whispered Marika. He certainly had the appearance of a gentleman, a thin brown face, dark hair flecked with grey, a gaunt square build and an incomparably well-cut suit.

Back at home, I sat on the edge of the camp-bed for a long time, excited and filled with pleasantly enthusiastic but confused emotions. Then I dressed slowly in front of the large plush-framed mirror, lighting all the candles in the two branched holders. That's how the footlights from below were able to illuminate the face! What should I look like? How splendidly this close-fitting shimmering black silk suits me! It's still one of last year's dresses, from the good old times! At the moment I ought to be wearing deep mourning, but Marika says it doesn't matter in Pest—who knows about it here? It's only compulsory in the elegant world... True, here they, I, we aren't the 'elegant world', we're just small fry with a free box at the theatre. But what about that lanky, Argus-eyed, interesting dark man!... Oh yes, why I too am beginning to think highly of him! The devil! Why, at home far superior men about town had paid their respects to me not long ago! How catching this social-climbing Pest servility is!

And even after that for weeks I was pursued by these doubting, haughty, resistant and turbulent thoughts about my own changed social position. In Szinyér somehow I could still feel that I was the person I had been, even though widowed and impoverished; they knew my past and my family, but here one gets lost in the big crowd, here I was cut off from my natural surroundings, at the mercy of the wind like a little torn-up weed of no value. Sometimes I was almost a ridiculous figure in my own nervousness, and I would leave everything and go out of shops where they called me 'the ladyship' or 'my dear young madam'.

But I was even more annoyed by the elegant stores in the heart of the city, where they serve you in the same way as cotillions are danced at exclusive balls: they do not offer or bargain, and if you make an occasional disparaging comment they shut away the goods with a bang, putting on a refined and ironic indifference.

Gradually I began to grow sick of the amusements that gave Marika such naive satisfaction. Going out to the promenade and staring at all the dresses so much more attractive than mine, sitting in Kugler's confectionery and paying through the nose to breathe the same air as those who with a comfortable sense of belonging gossip, flirt and live their own lives there without noticing any outsiders. I remembered Szinyér, with those insignificant little clerks' wives and the social climbers of shopkeepers' wives for whom the illusion of 'being there' like this was quite sufficient, as we enjoyed ourselves unrestrainedly in a closed group, not taking the slightest notice of them. My God! Could this neutral role possibly satisfy me? If somehow, sometime... I might be on top here too, brilliant and dominating! Might it be possible?

At home lovely long letters from Horváth were awaiting me and this loquacious, respectful, gallant old-fashioned love was balm to me. In his letters, he poured out his emotions entirely without restraint; distance and poetic quality gave him the excuse to justify the beautiful warm commonplaces, the outpourings of a hopeless and stubborn passion. 'You are my every dream and my every thought. Through all the prohibitions, the wrath of fate, even your own will, I love you always, without end, and I can't live without this. What will become of us?!' 'Words that can be learnt, often tried out, piled up with playful ease in moments of boredom and wilfulness—but all the same they're touching. Everyone is incredibly naive in this! Deeply moved, I read them through with pounding heart several times and preserved them like a treasure, a darling talisman; this first, written pledge of my experiences as a woman was precious to me. Before that I had never corresponded with anyone. 'He loves me, he loves me!' I thought; 'So this is the real thing, the great, supreme love of my life! Maybe he's right to mention destiny. This had to happen like this! And who knows what purpose fate still has for us both? It's certain that we belong to each other!'

Old Mrs. Vodicska, my mother-in-law, also wrote: my little boy was well, and no longer cried for his mummy and daddy... When I went to bed that night I wept bitterly at this; the next afternoon I went into a toy shop and had some lovely things sent to the poor little dear, because it was now Christmas week... And that night I watched the joy of other people's children, a stranger beneath the little candles of a strange Christmas tree... Much sadness welled up in me then, as all the desolation of my life and all its despair came flooding back to me. Or was it just one thing that upset me?

'I wonder, is Dénes Horváth celebrating now at Ilka Zimán's house?'... And there was no comfort either in knowing that it was I, after all, who had forbidden him to come up and see me. If he really wanted me, he would not be held back by such a painfully stern, obstinate, resigned, loving prohibition! But was he even capable of really wanting anything?...

It was in this mood that I wrote him a ten-page letter. Then a long, long reply came: self-defence, accusation, doubt, fearfulness, deep emotion, pardon. Each single little complication like this always took up a week of my life.

As I understand things now, I have no clear comprehension of how it was possible—though it certainly was so—that I still gave very little thought or concern to my future at the time. It may be that I had no real understanding of the value of money or of the connection between life and work. While my husband was alive, no large sum was ever entrusted to me, but he provided me with everything; we never talked much about trifling material matters and our house was open to everyone. I could not change from one moment to another or steep myself in worries about the speed with which the little money I had was melting away or fall into despair at the thought of my dependence on the mercy of others. Small lovers' tiffs and letters caused much more turmoil in me.

Otherwise I was living in comfort, without everyday cares

and household duties; there were always new things to keep me occupied; I dressed up and went for walks. And time passed.

'Well, yes,' reflected my uncle over lunch, 'acting isn't to be despised exactly. It's possible you may have some acting ability. It's a bold step, of course, and will cause some eyebrows to be raised down there, but tell me, what have they to offer you instead? Important relatives. Will any of them keep you? If you ask me, it's good to take risks. One's got to break free from all that stupid rustic prejudice if one really wants to become somebody and be one's own master. Only of course you've got to watch out and settle down to it sensibly or not at all. If anyone is ever successful at anything it always means that he was right.'

'But how would I do it, Gida?... They say you've got to study for years, learn how to move, to sit, to stand; and there are all sorts of subjects to learn from books too, like being back at school... And I'm no longer.... young enough for that... maybe.'

'Of course...hm! Certainly it would only make sense if you really had a strong talent for it. You've an interesting face, you have a splendid figure —anyway, you know that, my girl! So in real life you know how to control your expression, your eyes, everything...oh, superbly! But that, of course, is rather different. At all events there's a lot you ought to study; after all, you're a clever young woman, but have you enough energy for it? For anything like that demands all the determination you've got; for a couple of years at least you mustn't think of anything else. Your money would keep you going for that long, and the formalities of the drama-school could be straightened out somehow. Of course, without some good influential backer nobody can start on anything like that nowadays.'

He suddenly changed the subject. That made me realize that he would have something more to say about all this. Over the vegetables he quizzed the two schoolgirls, because apparently some young law-student had accompanied them home from school, news that the greengrocer on the corner had hastened to pass on. When the children took their leave, sure enough he remarked casually as he hurried to get ready for the office, 'Oh, by the way, today I met Attila Losonczy at the Agricultural Society. He recognized me and came over.

'Who's that wonderfully pretty woman I've seen with you a couple of times or so at Kugler's and the theatre? Widowed?' he said. 'She's got a splendid figure. Why don't you come out here and there more often? Her husband committed suicide? Oh, how sad! You ought to give such a marvellous young woman some entertainment. Don't you ever go skating? They're going to hold the great skaters' ball—look, I'll give you an invitation. Mourning? They wear dark clothes to it. I'd like to introduce myself,' he said, 'to your lady wife too. You will be there, won't you?'

He spoke to me almost as if we were old friends, though up to now he's tried to avoid addressing me because he knows very well that we are distantly related by marriage. Petty magnates like him are more haughty than real aristocrats. Yes, well, here's the invitation. Talk it over with Mari!'

We did talk it over for days, Marika and I; we grew excited and had a long discussion about whether I should buy a beautiful little fur cap for 150 forints, together with a collar that went with it and a small fashionable muff. My aunt thought it was a lot of money; she scolded me and sighed, but if I gave up the idea, it was she who began to talk about it again. Finally on the last morning I dashed out without her and brought it home. It suited me superbly.

When I caught sight of the sheet of ice reflecting the hundreds of lights and the swaying of the couples as they danced to well-known gypsy melodies, I was suddenly seized by terrified embarrassment and twinges of conscience. After all, this was a dance, all the same, and it was scarcely six months since my dear husband had died! 'No,' I thought, 'I'm not going skating. I'll just watch.'

I recognized Attila Losonczy in the crowd and waited for him to notice me. He threw up his nervy, dry head like a highly-bred steed and his eyes sparkled. He greeted Gida and waited politely for a minute or two, then made for us. He was already wearing skates. With my usual confidence I offered him my hand. Oh, when I knew that a man liked me, I was always at home, sure of what I had to do throughout my life! And all of a sudden I saw that everyone was watching me, that small groups were whispering together as they looked across, guessing; they were astonished and envious! Yes, this was my true ambience.

Half an hour later I was seated on his sleigh as it flew along, gliding beneath the fabulous glitter of thousands of lights through the swaying, dancing shadows and rime-encrusted branches, enfolded in music and self-oblivion. Once more an intoxicating, delightful hour like those of old! 'You'll catch cold like that! You can't do it! You must put on your skates!' I knew I could do this splendidly, like all dances demanding much movement of the feet and sports to music. It was impossible to resist. With my arm linked in his, I flew along, and around me and in me once again, after such a long time, there gleamed a triumphant evening, an experience just made for me.

I needed conquest, celebration and a big public appearance for my spiritual health. They were as necessary to me as bread; I lived life as long as I had an occasional taste of these things... Otherwise, I well remember, this great gentleman whose life was far removed from mine, with his many women and few words, left me quite cold. I don't even know what we talked about that whole evening.

'When are you coming to Kugler's? Where can I see you? You're staying in Pest till late spring, aren't you?...'

Gida was noticeably pleased by this affair, and somehow it offended me. Once when Marika could not come, he himself escorted me to the rink so that I should not miss it. At the end of February, there was a thaw, with a drizzle in the air, but we still went twice every week to Kugler's. And by now I was annoyed if Losonczy was late. He greeted all his acquaintances in turn, settling down for a little beside the ladies at the tiny tables, then came and sat with us, occupied himself with me and took us home in his carriage. Sometimes I asked myself whether this was proper. Was it right? But after all, my aunt was here as well as a male relation; they surely knew the ins and outs of city life.

Now I was totally confused by all the swift changes in my life. Gida once told me that Losonczy had been chatting with him again, and he had told him briefly of my circumstances and of an acting career as a definite plan. This hurt me to the quick, though I could find no clear reason why, and I was suddenly struck by the impression that at our last meeting Losonczy had spoken differently to me somehow, in a changed tone of voice. With a peculiar and over-bold insistence he kept asking me whether I ever went into town alone, without Marika. And that we should have important discussions concerning myself; he did not know whether he might meet me in the flat or whether this business ought to be dealt with in some other way... At that point he fell silent, somewhat confused, and for a moment or two gave me a strange look of astonishment. And since I myself was frightened to receive him in Marika's salon with the worn green plush furnishings, the business somehow began to be postponed and look rather foolish. In his eyes, I often saw only too well the desire I know how to recognize in men, impatient, angry, almost hate-ridden, a desire they would love to shake off or not entertain, but which will not leave them in peace.

'Tell me, why are you…why are you so obstinate? A woman like you! What do you want? Have you got someone? Confess that you've still got someone from down there!'

This was how things went as we strolled together now along the promenade in Hatvani Street on mild but windy spring evenings, stopping occasionally to gaze into a shop window, and straying away from Marika, the most exemplary of chaperones, as she ignored us. But I went home reluctantly, with feelings that chilled and repelled me. No, I could be moved only through my imagination, never like this! And that brusque, peculiar style offended me. Today, with the experience of all that I have lived through, I can explain the mood of the man too. His illusions concerning me were linked with a beautiful, refined, distinguished country gentlewoman, and all of a sudden it turned out that she was a prospective drama-school student who had come up to Pest obviously to live on her beauty and wanted his patronage. He was disappointed, but now had no mind to abandon the affair; he would have preferred to simplify it.

And then the whole thing ended as clumsily as it had begun. One evening I returned home and unexpectedly found my uncle Hiripy there, Aunt Piroska's husband, the former member of parliament, who was in town pursuing some political speculation or other. Apparently the draining of the marshes was after all beginning to make some progress down there! Except that now it had nothing to do with me.

He was somewhat cold towards me, then after dinner with paternal severity he brought up the subject of what I had done with myself and what my intentions were. He unsettled and frightened me and reduced me to tears, but all the same I felt better for it all. Even for the fact that—though spasms of passionate weeping kept rending me back into the misery of persecution and unhappiness—at last he declared that yes, his solicitor son who lived here had told him the rumour that I was the kept mistress of the notorious womanizer; I was the subject of Pest gossip, I was known and people pointed me out to one another in the street... My God! So this terribly big city is just a little hotbed, after all!

Once again I was filled with disgust and emptiness, with blundering helpless confusion. So what was I now? So quickly... reduced to such a state! What was the right thing to do? Whose advice should I take? Gida and his family were craftily leaving me to my own devices now; they did not defend me. Apparently I hadn't been clever enough... Ugh! But no, I hadn't wanted anything, it wasn't true! What should I know of such things? At home, even if evil tongues accused me, that was only a question of love, of a romantic game, but this...! How nasty the reverse side of everything is! But then how was I placed in this world— it was neither outside nor in: I've broken away from the order that was useful and protective and I can't really cope with liberty, I'm cowardly and fastidious, I haven't the courage, I just can't bear to take responsibility for myself.

Now the winter is over, a good deal of money has gone, and I've not made any progress in anything. Once again I'm on the brink of some fearful abyss that fills me with terror, for old condemnations, from the family or from Szinyér, which ring in my ears as they have done right from childhood, about bad, common, loose women, those kept for money, who are simply 'dealt with'... Oh, my God!

Next day old Hiripy said simply and curtly, 'I'm leaving the day after tomorrow. Come with me, Magda; it'll be for the best. That's all I'm saying. You can stay with us for the summer; we'll find something for you, and it'll certainly be better than what you can do in this Sodom. That is, if you haven't got too used to it yet!'

I fell on his neck, wept and packed, as if it was not I who a couple of months ago had come up here with a great and final resolve. Nothing had happened and now I suddenly withdrew without warning from the life I had hardly sampled. This was my fate in life: it was only by accident and never of my own volition that any great, critical thing happened to me. I had no courage. I was called back by my little town, the observant window-eyes of the familiar houses, the romance of village estates and flat marshlands, the lovely foolishness of close restraints and loquacious, dreamy loves. I hurried back!

XVII.

The crests of the old avenue of poplars reached up bare and sheepishly lanky on both sides of the black muddy road like rows of silent, stern question-marks, and strips of snow still gleamed white here and there among the black rain-sodden furrows of the early spring fields. The little chaise sank down to its axles in the mud; the Rumanian-style hovels in the village with their reed-thatched roofs, blue-painted window-frames and icons leaned to one side with clumsy meekness, proclaiming a vacuous patience and dire, well-nigh animal poverty. The mansion, too, looked denuded now with its rooms musty from the winter and stale with the smell of pipe-smoke, the stifling heat from the pot-bellied stove and the dusty rag-carpets. As for my poor Aunt Piroska, how overworked, withered and neglected she was compared with her sister in Pest and indeed even with my mother. Yet of the three of them she was the wealthiest, she had made the greatest 'fortune', having married into real gentry who had stayed on their own land. In the course of twenty years, she had brought fifteen children into the world, she had put away an incalculable number of jars of preserves and every year five bushels of dried fruit, she had set an incredible number of hens, overseen the weaving of thirty dozen striped Rumanian kerchiefs (kitchen-wear for her little girls in due time) and collected together twenty-eight plump pillows filled with feathers she herself had plucked. Meanwhile her house was a permanent refuge for one and all throughout the family; everyone in trouble, facing or recovering from some crisis in life might hang around there for months on end untroubled; here the changing times had not yet made their ugly, calculating, penny-pinching and selfish spirit felt. Here only the lady of the house was ground down by the monotonous burden of everlasting work, for during those twenty years everything had passed through her and her undying patience; now she would send boxes of food every fortnight by post to Pest to her solicitor son just as she had done to her husband at the time when he was a member of parliament. She hardly went anywhere; one or two expensive silk dresses were growing musty in the wardrobe; by the time she had sent for a hat to match them, she had no gloves or her shoes didn't fit. She took no account of life, and life passed her by.

Here it seemed as if time stood still for me too. After all those big tumultuous changes, decisions, attempts to advance, fearful recoils and vacillating uncertainties, I was now surrounded by peaceful, simple rural days and a kind of unhustled, natural and indifferent goodwill that made it seem possible for me to go on like this to the end of my life if I wanted to. There was no real talk about me and the unceasing, worrying problem of my life, which for six months had revealed itself to me through the querying gaze which everyone had directed at me—what was to become of me, after all? It was the generous, impulsive idea of the moment that had prompted old Hiripy to say, 'Come down and stay with us!' Without a word Piroska agreed to it out of habit and for her own comfort, and a week later the matter was dropped. Here I was, nobody upset me with so much as a single glance or hint, and there was nothing for me to do. The master of the house concerned himself with the ploughing or read the *Comet*, while Piroska created hotbeds and had the kitchen garden re-dug.

A letter came from Dénes Horváth: peculiar, wear-sounding lines written out of stern compulsion, or was it just I who felt them to be so? Love which subsists on mere words goes bankrupt from time to time, it feeds increasingly on itself and agonizingly seeks refreshment. There are hours of exaltation and pulsing ecstasy and valued minutes of sweet, painful yearning, but these peaks are linked only by some spasmodic intention to seek unity and by the frequently, very tiring conclusion that today is just like yesterday. But it was I who perceived all this, and in myself too, though I did not want to admit it. Such is the time when loving rebukes come… He was upset that on my way to Hirip I had spent no time in Szinyér and had not let him know. I blamed not stopping in Szinyér on some gossip concerning him and Ilka. It was a fabrication; I just made it up, but I felt I was not far from the truth. It was certain that he had not broken with her once and for all—after all, he needed a woman and she was on his doorstep, humble, patient and easily satisfied. I must be some kind of red-letter day to him, more respected and more demanding; the ageing old flame was a comfortable, homely, everyday creature for whom he had no need to collect together his words or his spirits; he could be humorous, grumpy or graciously nice to her in small doses; for her that was ample. Not for the world would I have wanted to usurp her position, but all the same I was incensed by the thought that she was there with him.

He must, on occasion say 'I love you!' to her, but does he use a different tone, different words and looks for me? Does he kiss me differently than her?

In one of these contradictory, confusing moments I wrote a brief, cold letter breaking it off. 'Either or!'... I thought; if the great, strong, complete emotions had gone, if we had come to the end of the truest experience of it all, then let the whole thing come to an end! It can be detestable and humiliating to feel my deterioration in someone's eyes, and to see the fastidious consideration with which he tries to hide this. Perhaps we had already said to each other all that was to be said. We must not allow this affair to become something commonplace, so let's put an end to it! Yet to tell the truth I should not have been able to say why I did all this. Was it just nervousness or a gut instinct that prompted it?

For several days I waited for the reply; three times in the following week I walked over to nearby Inácskó on windy spring afternoons for the post. Nothing came! 'That's all right, then!' I thought at the time with sharp but surprisingly satisfying grief. 'It was what I wanted and there you are, I had the strength to do it! Now I'll go on my way, now I really am on my own; anything can happen to me!'

And this strange impetus of obstinacy propelled me incomprehensibly into something for which otherwise I should not have summoned enough strength, from which I should have recoiled in fear in my usual emotional state at that time. I do not know now what may have put the first idea into my head; probably during those days of waiting for a letter I had one or two conversations with the postmistress at Inácskó who, I was told, was an impoverished gentlewoman from the famous Tomanóczy family. She was a well-built, round-shouldered, good-looking big dark woman; her eyebrows nearly met and the teeth in her lively, shapely mouth had a strident gleam. She had beautiful dark eyes with a strong and fiery gaze, but her features had gone to pieces now and looked ordinary; she squatted behind the glass partition uncorseted, in a well-wrinkled red wincey blouse and a fringed scarf around her shoulders, her expression remained indifferent and bored. 'My goodness, even she's alive! It's possible to live anyhow!' I thought, with a chilling, merciless sensation. 'After all, she, too, is a woman, and a beautiful one, and at the most she can only be my age! What right have I to more?... Just because I was once within a hair's breadth of becoming the deputy sheriff's wife? That's all over now; it no longer exists. Everything's finished, and I have to drain the glass of my life to its dregs.'

Yes, I too would be a postmistress in some benighted muddy hole like this and soon be sitting in the same way, faded and resigned, over books of money-orders and other columns. My face would become flabby and my expression grumpy and bored... But never mind! That's life! Or that's suicide... it's all the same! I'll prove that I can do it!...

At Hirip they received it with apathetic good humour when one day at lunch I told them that I wanted to learn about the postal service at Inácskó. 'You can try it!' said my uncle, and Aunt Piroska recommended tall overboots if I really intended going the rounds on foot.

Spring blossomed out gently and unobtrusively. The winds became milder, there were furry catkins on the roadside bushes and a lot of blue in the air, fresh sunlight and the pale shade of green buds. But it still grew dark early and through the open window of the post-office floated gentle evening sounds, buzzing around our two poor drooping women's heads. 'I'll light a lamp,' said Anna Tomanóczy in her hoarse weary voice; 'there's a registered letter here for the priest; I'll show you how to deal with it, because it's rare for a registered letter to come here.' But she waited a little before she went for the matches. 'It's got six ruled lines like this and the counterfoil's different, too.'

I bent over it, forcing myself to pay a little attention, resting my apathetic face in my palm. The door to the veranda opened and the sound of boots approached the threshold gently and hesitantly. 'Is that you, Trajan?' asked the postmistress through the door without looking around. 'Come in front, Trajan, there on the bench; I shan't be long.' Half an hour later they sent the wife of the handyman from Hirip to fetch me because the stars were already out. The peasant lad squatted there on the bench in a heavy sullen silence; he scarcely made a stir to say goodbye to me.

All of a sudden the orchard was in bloom, a mass of rose-pink flowers; the trees went crazy and the fields were resplendent with butterflies and blossoms. I had to hurry, to run when I crossed the avenue because I was so filled with this great preposterous spring and the riot of blossomings. In the post-office garden, too, the lovely little plum-trees with their wide branches put on a show and the lawn sprouted young grass while the evening bell sounded ebbing and flowing above it. It ruffled our half too. It was then that Anna Tomanóczy, poor thing, said slowly and wearily, 'Well, tomorrow they're publishing the banns for the first time. I'm getting married in a fortnight's time.'

'Getting married?' I asked in amazement. 'And it's only now you're telling me? Goodness me! But whomever to?'

'Why, I'm marrying Trajan, of course!'

I couldn't say a word and I didn't dare ask any more questions. 'What's behind all this?' I suddenly wondered and in my confusion reluctantly held my tongue. Was this a romantic novel?

As we merged further into the shade of twilight, she herself began to talk, though it was obvious that she found it difficult. It was as if she owed me an explanation. Only now did it appear how peasant-like and clumsy her speech and her whole behaviour were sometimes.

'Tell me, is it such a big thing? That I'm marrying a peasant—what's in that? He's the son of the mayor; he's got land, a house and grounds. And he thinks a lot of me... his father and mother do too... in their eyes I've got status; even the two thousand forints I've managed to put by is a fortune to them. Some ragged village teacher or notary might have married me for that... it's possible... but do you think that's any better? In any case around here they're all married and ancient.'

'But all the same!... How can you?... Why, isn't it better for you as things are?'

'Don't say that!' she said with sudden mocking harshness in her voice and as she finished speaking she let slip a brief, bitter laugh. She almost snarled at me. 'It really is best for me. Oh, you'll soon know, never fear!... I've been like this for eight years. Oh, at that time I, too, might have found my niche in any refined urban society, fine clothes and fashionable customs. A beautiful, lively and happy girl, youthful and all alone in just such a filthy village. It was the priest who began it—he's almost always the first—and then the squire. But his son wanted me too; butter wouldn't melt in his mouth, the blackguard; when he got nowhere, he betrayed me to his mother, and then there was a great to-do and a lot of mud-flinging; it was a good thing they only transferred me. That was three years ago. Here there's no one, only the peasants. I've always stolen a look at the Hiripys' papers and stuck the wrapper down again. But what sort of a life is it when you don't exchange words with folk of quality for months on end? The Hiripys, you know, have no contact with me… This young man… I don't know how it began…. I remember that at first he just greeted me politely through the porch-door when he came this way: "Good evening!" was all he said. For a long time there wasn't anything more. Then he would stop a little and say something very respectfully. Well, I replied to him and sometimes had a good laugh. By now he would stand in the middle of the veranda, while I was inside, here at the table; that's how we chatted. He's a good-looking lad and leads a decent life. If I was invited to a peasant wedding-feast, I was always seated at the same table as the mayor and his family. Then came those dreadful winter evenings, that hellish silence and loneliness without end. By now I was looking out to see whether he was coming this way and said, "Sit down there on the chest!" After that it didn't take much for him to come inside. I taught him to read. Spring came just like now. What more was needed? In the summer he hung around under my window all night long, and for three years I'd lived like a nun just to scrape a little money together. He's a fine lad; he even became tongue-tied in my presence—and that's something too! Well, that's how things are now.'

'What are you looking at me for? Why, didn't you suspect it when you saw me? Yes, whatever happens now I've got to marry him… Of course now you can despise me because I've made a clean breast of it all. But no matter! One day you'll see for yourself; just try it after me. That's what I want for you.'

'Why are you talking like this, Anna? Have I done anything to upset you?… But for God's sake, are you able to love him? Do you love each other?'

She shrugged her shoulders resignedly, with a movement that insinuated indifference.

'What? I'm in the midst of things here and I don't care. What might I have expected? Growing senile here, stupid and alone? At the time it was summer, such a great mad summer, harvest-time; an untried lad like that really knows how to make love, even swearing and baring his teeth in his infatuation with a woman.

Now, of course… at times like this each one pretends that it's an act of kindness to get married. So I should be thankful to him for it! It's a good job and I've still got that little sum of money.'

I hurried as fast as I could along the spring-filled avenue; the slender line of sweet-scented young trees looked down on me from on high and I felt them close behind me. The crescent moon glimmered through the light foliage. It was here, in this very place, that long ago Endre Tabódy once tried to kiss me; oh, how long ago!… I panted as I drank in all the various great maddening sweet perfumes. Oh youth! If only it would never pass!… Yes, I still had a little of it left; but what was I to do with it? How dreadful it was for poor Anna! And she wasn't any older than I was!… My God! It begins to look now as if I must begin to count my remaining years! Young boys, prospective husbands from the neighbourhood or army officers, sometimes come out to Hirip, for the eldest daughter is over sixteen now and a lively dark-haired lass. She calls me 'auntie' and confides in me about her suitors; everything's going well for her still. Has she too, maybe, scribbled teasing love-messages already on the ancient table in the skittle-alley? As for me, I'm the beautiful widowed aunt who chaperons her. But I, too, still have rights, I must! What a great muddle of a spring!

When I went past the servants' quarters two stout shadows rustled behind me and ran off in two different directions along the moonlit wall, and the branches of the dwarf quinces rattled and crackled. I stopped under them; the blossoms still fell on me where they had scraped against them. I recognized them. It was the teenage young gentleman, the grammar-school boy on Easter vacation, and the little dumpy maid Domnyika, whom Piroska had adopted from her early childhood.

XVIII.

Summer came, diabolically scorching, listless and impotent. At Hirip, we sometimes sat for half the day in the ice-pit with all the hosts of guests. Aunt Piroska sent for an ice-cream machine and everyone came to marvel at it, and then we stayed there in the cool till dusk, spreading blankets on the straw. Apart from this, there was an incredibly large crop of melons that year; sometimes fifteen honeydews were cut open for lunch and those whose aroma was less than perfect were tossed down from the veranda to the servants.

A lot of guests came and went, most of them young boys courting my little cousin, law-students from Pest, young relatives spending the summer nearby, officials, townsfolk. How different this generation was from the one when I was a girl! They lacked seriousness, they were flippant and overbearing and mercilessly comic. They even talked to the girls in this way, particularly aggressive and taunting, with an odd nasal twang or just pretended to be indifferent... Whatever one may say about being 'modern', ten years earlier a more attractive style had been in fashion.

Or was it that I was slowly retreating from the focus of interest and importance, that I had been edged outside, and this perhaps gave me secret pain? 'It's not true! I'm not getting old yet!' I thought, as I grappled with this possibility. 'Things like this can't happen so quickly, from one moment to another. It's only among chickens like these that I look like an 'auntie' and these teenage boys don't dare to say a word to me!' Obviously I was right... but at that time how I kept shrinking back in fear sometimes at such things! And once—it was at the end of August by now—one very starry warm night full of fireflies and the maddening scent of grass, I wandered alone through the garden and the plum trees in the orchard, dashing ever more feverishly along the white paths between the cherry-pie and tuberoses... until I suddenly rushed up to my room and wrote to Horváth. After over two months of silence it was I who wrote first! Just like that, with feminine cunning, a couple of evasive and distant sentences, as if it were long ago that everything between us had come irrevocably to an end, and now we could talk of it as if it were past and over. I used some half-heard gossip as an excuse; they had said something in Szinyér about him and me, and with a little tact and goodwill he could put an end to the gossip even after the event, so that we might preserve some of our cherished memories… I was absolutely certain that this meant encouragement and continuation, and that he would take it as such. For a moment there flashed through my mind my poor grandmother's frequent saying. 'You must never, never call a man back; it's not worth it! Anything rather than that… no woman's yet died of a little fit of epilepsy!…' But I could not bring myself to accept the truth of the old adage. I was impatient and scared that as far as I was concerned everything was already lost. It was I who called him back!

The very next day I, too, received a totally unexpected letter that gave a further twist to my own uncertain and irresolute destiny. I more or less knew that in the autumn something was to be done about me once more; I had been living here for months without any purpose; the forced idea that I should become a postmistress receded of its own accord since poor Anna Tomanóczy, daughter-in-law of the peasant mayor of Inácskó, was unable to teach me anyway: she had taken to her bed in the meantime. But I still had the feeling in those days that I was in a protective and responsible community, my family; on my territory, among my relations both near and distant, who here and out there would discuss my fate when they met, and in due course would come up with something and not leave me on my own with such heartless frigidity as my stepfather would like. And lo and behold, I was not mistaken! So I thought with genuine and grateful delight when my uncle Hiripy showed me a letter from old Ábris Pórtelky containing a message for me. He wrote that if I felt like coming to him not just for the time being but to live there permanently, as long as I wanted to, he affectionately offered his house to the child of his deceased one and only younger brother. He had always been fond of me, and had often marvelled at the order and neat cleanliness of my household and respected it; nor did he wish to keep me out of his charity: rather I was to regard it as his need for me, for his solitary, widower's house needed an intelligent and excellent woman to run it. And I could come whenever I liked: he would expect me in September or at the beginning of October… I was deeply touched by this generous and kindly tone from a man whom everyone regarded as a for-boding old recluse, and who in any case had had a grudge against us for years—against grandma and mother because she turned him down, and originally against me, too, because I had married a Vodicska... So he's got a heart after all! And he is offering to help me, not with words and good advice like the folk in Pest and the rest of them, but with deeds; at one stroke he puts my life back in order! I felt a great burgeoning desire to undertake this role. Yes, of all occupations this was the one for me, for this was something I understood and had been brought up to do, running a household, a woman's work in the home. To be the lady of the house in my own uncle's mansion, see that the servants did their work properly, organize and beautify the house, be given a free hand in everything, work and keep busy, to surprise and touch him with all the delightful changes and... to go from time to time in his carriage to Szinyér, just when I wanted!... For I knew that this summer they had constructed the county highway where streams had been drained or filled in and marshes had been, and since then Pórtelek was no longer in the middle of nowhere; it was only three hours away from the town. I had also heard that the old man wanted to start building, maybe next year. Yes, he was making innovations, and that's why he needed a woman in the house to keep order, tidiness and display his position; maybe now he wanted to play a larger part in the life of the county. After all, nobody was affected more than he was by the present discussions concerning the draining of the marshes. Yes, I really did feel now that of the two of us I was the one more needed by the other.

For September, however, I went down to Szinyér to spend that lovely autumn month there. It was a letter from Horváth that added urgency, though I did not admit this even to myself; his reply was just what I expected and I imagined in advance, suggesting tender, stifled love and pain, sometimes very moving; in other words a letter betokening understanding and continuation. 'How long it is since I've been in my home town, my shabby, miserable, beloved nest! It's almost a year now!' I thought with impatience. That year had flitted away so painfully! It was no use, that was the only place where there was life for me, where every paving-stone, every house and every window could speak!

Without a word, but with concealed contempt I immediately

paid a month's board to my stepfather Péter to stop him talking and to keep him out of the way. All the same I saw clearly that this eccentric was not exactly longing for that meagre sum; he merely wanted to exercise his 'principles' in this matter too. Throughout his life it was his craze to try out in practice every new idea or system he had read about in print. Now his hobby was women's emancipation. Because I had paid him he was at peace with me, and he turned the full force of his dissatisfaction and rage on my younger brother Csaba, who had also been at home now for about two months. His life was beset by troubles. In the south where he was stationed he had fallen in love with the daughter of a very rich Serbian landowner. The girl, too, had lost her heart to the dashing hussar, so the parents reluctantly held the betrothal ceremony. But they wanted him to leave the army and go to live with them, to 'join the house' in Serbian fashion, and to work with his father-in-law on the estate, for they were not going to argue about the marriage-settlement, nor would they let their one and only daughter move away from home... The boy did not ask anyone; on impulse he transferred to the reserve and came home in civilian clothes and with an engagement ring. Really, the uniform of a hussar captain suited him much better, poor lad! And now from odd letters written to my mother and from the whole affair too it came out that he had passed himself off there as a boy with money... Unfortunate child! All the tricks he had been up to as a hussar and... the muddle left after poor Vodicska's death had left hardly anything of those few thousands, and now he was squandering that little here night after night in his grief. In this Péter was perhaps right. He drank a lot and crudely, with anyone at all who would join him, sometimes to a state of blind drunkenness. God knows, maybe he couldn't help it, poor boy!... But his fiancée wrote him totally wild, maddened love-letters filled with more than girlish passion... It was distressing to see this young life here starting on the path to dissipation and utter confusion. My mother sometimes wept for the other luckless one too, and sometimes I thought of my own child: what would become of him, then? But Horváth came and consoled me; he took me for walks and cosseted me more than ever, with more tender and devoted love than before. He almost made a show of it now! He often accompanied me on visits and to relatives, and all of a sudden people began to make kindly enquiries: was it true that we were engaged?

Others congratulated us directly or with malicious laughter whispered how Ilka Zimán was going around now with languishing grief and floods of tears, visiting acquaintances in house after house for coffee, and seeking consolation… All this caught me by surprise, and somehow I felt ashamed; I felt it was impossible to give an answer.

I'm not engaged! Don't I want to get married? Well then, what do I want of Horváth? Secretly offended, I avoided the real truth even in my own thoughts—that after all, this did not depend on me. And anyway, I had no idea why not. Of course, he was up to his ears in debt and forty years old, accustomed to being a bachelor and took life easily; he wasn't suited to marriage. 'Oh, what do I care?' I thought, becoming annoyed again. 'During this short time (only a week altogether by now) I'm not letting myself get upset or be separated from someone who loves me unselfishly!' I deliberately gave myself up to lovely daydreams, the stifling and wearyingly sweet torture of passionate handshakes, silent and timidly desirous embraces and soft kisses in the trembling of the occasional dumb and suffocating minute.

It was only in the middle of October that I went out to Pórtelek and to the open plain.

XIX.

... And once again I saw the big threshing-floor with the horse-drawn mill where once upon a time, as a very tiny child, I, too, had played with the sons and little daughters of the labourers when my paternal grandparents were alive. The ancient house from which the relations who bore my name had originated always lived somewhat confusedly in my memory as if it were a dream. Even much later I remembered the courtyard which always appeared more spacious, and the gabled front of the grey house with its stone ornaments seemed heavier and more imposing, as were the worn stairs and the big squat pillars along the veranda.

Now everything seemed to have shrunk and become more realistic. Nevertheless this was it, the old, old house, where I used to prowl through the rooms uneasily and out of my depth, stretching my two little hands up high to reach the big curly wrought-iron door-handles. I recalled the very large dining-room whose floor eight women scrubbed white with ash and scattered damp chopped reeds over it to stop it from being walked over; only two days later when it was all dry did they sweep it up. I knew that I should find that bay-windowed garden-room where my grandmother Pórtelky, that gentle *grande dame*, kept her spinning-wheel. Everything here was old, so old, maybe centuries old; this was where this hard-bitten little clan of gentry had reigned with recalcitrance and stubbornness in the misty distance of the ages. It was said that they never went where rank, unoccupied lands, alien elegance and important connections were distributed by the alluring patronage of old rival kings and princes setting up new courts. They remained at home here, encircled by the defences of untamed watery marshes, boggy streams and reed-thickets, on this rich little peninsula in the marshlands that was their inheritance; they were little monarchs and they jealously guarded their sovereign status as gentry. This was why they often turned eccentric or secretive, figures of overweening and fierce pride, whose peculiar doings engendered legends deeper in the county.

There was a Stanislas from long ago, an heir of the Gutkeleds and Balog-Semjéns, who cut off his little finger for some woman, so that he could cast it before her complete with a ring—because he had vowed to her that the ring would remain there for eternity.

Another eccentric lived here alone and all his life through never exchanged a single word with a peasant but merely cracked his dog-whip at them; yet in the great cholera epidemic he personally closed the eyes of each dying person. 'Every Pórtelky's got a cog missing!' was the proverbial saying that went the rounds far and wide. After 1848, a distant branch of the family that had put its roots down in Tyukod acquired a barony and became very wealthy, but the rebellious gentry of the true marshland Pórtelkys still did all they could for a long time to disown, despise and disregard the horde of relatives who had deserted, the 'traitors'. But the world went on and forgot, while rank and greater fortune played their part. Why, Melanie the baroness was a high sheriff's wife today! ... And gradually the ancient, beloved rich land was carved up and divided between those who remained here: brothers and sisters had to be given settlements, girls given in marriage; a fine plot on the Gencs side was even in Jewish hands now.

My own father was the first to make a break with his home; he went to study law at Patak and started on a solicitor's career. True, I heard it whispered here and there that he did not really know mercy, that he fleeced anybody he could; certain unfortunate womenfolk, possibly market-women, once knelt down in the dust of the market-square in Szinyér in front of his carriage and shook their raised fists as they cursed even his descendants... My God! That was how it was! It only took him a couple of years or so to gather together the little inheritance for the three of us and my mother; it was then that the craze for drink caught up with him, perhaps he only needed it to stay awake at night and to give himself energy for work at the outset. But he became addicted to it, could not take it, and a year later it was all over... Meanwhile, his elder brother Ábris married some rich and ugly horse-trader's daughter from distant parts; thereupon they redeemed, bought and regulated everything here, but nobody ever managed to see his hand entirely. He had long been widowed; his only daughter was married and lived in Pest County. In recent years, he had even bought swampy inundated land at rock-bottom prices. 'He's a crafty old rogue!' folk would say with incredulity when at one time he began to turn up frequently at the county committee and with an unexpected about-turn called my poor husband 'my dear boy' and visited him when he was standing for deputy sheriff. Now, they said, he was very close with Melanie; and lo and behold, during the summer the county had quartered water-engineers on him and the coach-road towards Szinyér was constructed through the drained water-meadows. It only took me two and a half hours by carriage; that was almost incredible! When I was a tiny child, I remembered, we were shaken to pieces from dawn till afternoon, and there were two ferries to cross. At that time travellers to Pórtelek had still to go right around the Szamos valley marshes.

Uncle Ábris was puffing at his churchwarden on the veranda when I arrived. A maid brought up big earthenware jugs of curds, glazed plates and wooden spoons.

'There are some silver ones too, just a few; you can get them out, though Júlia's taken away practically everything that belonged to her mother. And I don't really buy anything, you know; for ten years I've hardly dragged myself away from here. Though it's true that while I've been seeing about the land-regulation, there's been a bit of toing and froing; it's here that they're making a start, together with the Count's estate and the Kendys'. All the same, I'm not having a swarm of locusts descend on me here! You'll soon get out and see what there is and where. As for me, why, this is how I like my curds!... Good grief, my girl! Is all that your stuff? Two trunks, three baskets! What the devil have you got in all those? Just crinolines? Here you can't wear so many till your dying day! What you need for the garden and the fields is a good twirling calico skirt!'

I gazed at him in astonishment. After all, he'd been a couple of times to my house in Szinyér and seen how I lived and dressed. Was he joking now, I wondered?

The daily round began in earnest: a sudden, muddy wet autumn, rank heavy mists from the watery countryside, lengthening evenings, silence and nothing but strangers around me. Nothing but sullen and suspicious peasants, stern and stupid faces, fixed and pointless habits in this widower's house. And in the evening, sitting in solitude in the big, badly-aired rooms, beneath the light from smoky oil-lamps, I knitted stockings of thick tufted wool for the old man to wear in his boots. He sat opposite me smoking his churchwarden; with its mouthpiece he sometimes parted his big white moustache and spat a long way onto the floor. Sometimes he would talk a little, about old matters, and about who was related to whom and how. For this he sometimes went to the shelf and pulled out the well-worn leather-bound tomes of Iván Nagy's *Families of Hungary* to study the family trees. Whenever I said something, he never really listened and I usually just gave up. But even so, in the silence, I sometimes felt the gaze of his strong dark eyes fixed on me. Then I would steal a furtive glance at his face, his shaggy eyebrows, his bulbous but finely-etched firm hawk-nose, his big dense white beard. How old was he? Maybe sixty-five. But why did I think about this? The wind rattled the window of the plainland mansion, the fine peat-ash kept blowing out from the open hearth, the silence hissed and crackled and the dogs barked outside... Sometimes I escaped for a quarter of an hour, stealing down to the servants' room where the farmhands' wives would spin and sing, and an occasional vagrant gypsy woman, happening to pass that way, would tell their fortune with cards in exchange for ragged petticoats. Their stories droned from greasy tobacco-smelling picture-cards with peculiar illustrations-sometimes for me too. 'I know of a herb which, if you feed it to the one you love, it won't let him ever escape from your hands as long as the world lasts; even if you thrash him he'll come back; you can deceive him, and he'll fawn on you. All I've got to do is to boil something, and when it's bubbling the one your heart desires will appear here through barred and bolted doors and windows or even fall down the chimney....' She panted and whispered the highly-coloured lies and the red embers lit up the whiteness of her upturned eyes.

'Uncle Ábris,' I said in a stifled and almost fearful voice, 'Tomorrow I've got to go into Szinyér.'

'Again? What for? You went there a fortnight ago!'

'That's a long time ago. We need spices, toilet soap and coffee, and for myself knitting wool and other things. And anyway the driver hasn't got anything to do.'

'How should you know about that? Nothing to do? I can give him something to do! What's the point of all this gadding about? Does it make sense? Isn't the soap we make here at home good enough? It spoils your beauty, does it? To keep dabbing at yourself with scented soap! And coffee—caw-fee—as if good fresh milk weren't good at all! All right, just get along there if you're too big for your boots!... Hey there! Damn and blast that cur, the way it howls! They haven't let him out?... Just you wait, blast your eyes!... There now, just hold it!'

But next day I was in the town and I poured out my complaints and had a good cry and rested on the shoulder of someone who was still able to kiss and stroke me as if I were an expensive, sadly-fondled fragile treasure in his possession.

Oh God! If only the spring would come, the spring! Would there never be an end to this dreadful winter? The snow comes whirling down in great eddies, powdering the whole plain, burying the roads, cutting everything off and isolating it. This immense, dead, blinding whiteness! Something that moves and does not utter a sound, silent, noiseless and terrifying! And inside the house the same silence: smoky flames covering everything with soot; only my knitting-needles click and a snowy-bearded flinty-eyed old man gazes ever more stiffly at me... Am I really awake now, I wonder? Suppose all this is just a dream? I think I must have been terribly unnerved at that time.

At the beginning of March, the weather relented, the distant waters rose, and for a time it was impossible to move because of the mud. But at least some preparations began to be made: the postman brought letters from the village, while the old man bargained and corresponded with contractors because he was getting ready to renovate the house, and he also expected his daughter Júlia and her two children for the summer.

Even he seemed to be in a better temper; he bustled about and cursed even more often.

'Hurry up there, you, confound your little ankles! Womenfolk are only good if they're constantly moving!' And the little maids swayed their hips in their pleated skirts and pulled their scarves over their faces, but they giggled and tittered together and their round shoulders shook with tingling delight.

'Just look there! How many stars are out! How clear the sky is! Come here, Maggie, and just look at them! Don't keep hiding yourself away for ever in the corner like a sick cat! There, you see, you can snuggle down by me too for a little! Come nearer, do! My dear, what a good little...'

'Ugh!... You hateful, disgusting old man!... I'll scream this very minute!'

'Don't be silly! After all it's only...'

'Get away, you wretch! Let me go!... You should be ashamed of yourself!'

'Oh how particular you are, my dear! Well, it's a good thing I know the little bride-to-be isn't so hoity-toity with everyone!'

Disgusted, trembling and wretched, I sat in my room and wept. What would happen now? What would he say in the morning? It was awful! I'd no idea that even men as old as that...

He said not a word; it was as if nothing had happened. He talked about other things, giving orders as he usually did, gruffly and bluntly. Then a couple of days later he suddenly blurted out at lunch, 'Well, the decorators are coming next week. And here in the main house there'll only be three rooms that they're not turning upside down; I'll need those, so will my daughter and her family in the summer. But the old farmhouse is empty now—the animals are going back with the shepherds—so you can live there if you like. You can take some furniture down there. It's not a bad place; a lot of folk haven't got anything like it!'

He looked at me long and hard, expecting me to explode, cry and complain so that he might break and humiliate me. 'No,' I thought 'not a word! Come what may! Somehow there'll be an end to it all sometime.'

I took an almost bitter, stubborn delight now in suffering and misery. I had to live in an earth-floored peasant house, and I thought of my old beautiful salon with its mirrors and silk cushions, the flowers and the piano. In the copious spring rains, the water trickled up to my bed at night and once the storm-water flooded in over the low threshold; turbulent dirty water flowed over the mud floor and flung up the shabby table and discarded chairs.

But lovely bright Easter weather came along, dry sunny days, fresh gusty sweet-perfumed winds once again, and the bells from the village could be heard pealing through those blue skies in the refreshing mornings. I went for long walks in the fields and Horváth's hired carriage waited for me at the cross-roads... Apart from him I had nothing and nobody at that time.

In May, Júlia arrived with her two mischievous teenage children. She had no affection for me; I sensed that my presence there was not to her liking and that even from a distance she had been suspicious and fearful—because of the fortune, God help us!... That I would worm myself so far into the old man's

favour that some time perhaps she mighty have to share it!...
Oh, God forbid! I thought. Don't let her believe that I had designs
on it. From then on I was even more cool and reserved; and
now the running of the house was gradually taken out of my
hands as well. Júlia supervised everything and made comments
on it all, while I just gave up dealing with anything in which she
was involved. I had no wish to quarrel, but orders cannot be
given by two ladies of the house, I thought, and in any case it
was obvious that they were doing this deliberately and the two
of them were plotting together against me. She had already
excited the old man completely. All right, I would not go of my
own volition; I would say nothing in case they spread rumours
about me; things would come to a head of their own accord.
Let's just see what they can do! Now I hardly spoke to them, but
it was a very sad, unnerving state that upset me to the depths of
my soul. They also orchestrated the servants against me. And
I had to face such an alliance all on my own.

I often wandered through the meadows, and if I set out for
a rendezvous in my lovely long grey cloak and broad-brimmed,
lace-trimmed sleek hat, I felt refreshed and composed, a town-
dweller once again. No, it would be impossible to spend yet
another such frightful winter here! The young corn was sprouting
now. I often saw clouds of smoke billowing up in the distance
and as it grew dark almost every day, the horizon grew red and
far away plumes of flame scattered sparks. It was an isolated
farm on fire or an inn or the reed-thickets had caught fire in
some distant spot. Gendarmes patrolled the fields; there were
fire-raisers about.

'Times are bad, dearie me! They're hard!' sighed the landlady
at the cross-roads inn where Horváth and I sometimes stopped
and paid too much for the morsel of bacon and bad wine for the
driver. 'The countryside's in turmoil, sir; there are big things in
store here! Why, in Tyukod a cow dropped a monster! And as for
the poor, the folk on the land who've been living off the reed-
beds till now, making baskets, catching loach and fishing—
what's going to become of them now? Where can they go? And
their rights to the marshes, even a whole village's, were bought
three years ago for a hundred forints by Master Ábris... they
hadn't an inkling, poor things, of what was in store for them.
Oh yes, there's a lot of bitterness; you should just hear how they
talk here when they've got a little wine in them. They say there

are men here, among them, from a long way off, encouraging them. They also say that the king's son isn't dead; it was only a likeness that was buried—the one who came to Szinyér three years ago, God rest his soul, poor fellow; he's in hiding here among the people and studying all their problems. And they say he only came then because he wanted to see everything with his own eyes, but the gentry whitewashed the outside of the houses for him and dressed up the people to curry favour with him... But I'm sure he's dead, I am! They're just fairy tales! But suppose these folk do go mad and get hold of pitchforks—what'll happen here? Who knows why they're building at the Pórtelky mansion? Though they're even more angry with the county gentry!... Here's the wine and the cake!'

'I don't know; there may be something in this business,' Horváth would keep saying meditatively, half whispering. 'Though they generally exaggerate such things. After all, there'd be nothing but rebellions in the world if it were possible to avenge every injustice like that... But if that's how things are decreed, there's no way of escaping them.'

I was not comforted by such wisdom. I trembled, my nerves stretched to breaking-point, and I was afraid to stay out in the isolated countryside; most of all I should have liked to take my place among the rebels and profess the same beliefs as the oppressed, the embittered, dispossessed, angry, poor, and the days passed by.

One afternoon in July, a merciless wind roared over the countryside. It snatched at my clothes and tore my hair and once again carried smuts from somewhere into my eyes. A kestrel wheeled and screeched overhead. The landlady of the inn came out to the fence to meet me and asked me, pale and hesitant, 'Have you heard?'

'What? What is it?'

She took me by the hand and helped me over the fence; trembling and silent she came out with me on to the cart-track and pointed ahead with her hand. Far away in the distance there stood a thick black column of smoke; its blazing, blood-red core radiated flashes up to the darkening overcast sky. And the wind roared and howled.

'That... over there?'

'Szinyér's on fire! The town!'

I felt dizzy and hid my eyes in deathly terror. I had no thoughts about anything I had there of value or might lose. In the far distance the dreadful fire swirled terrifying and blood-red like some fate of Sodom over the town, my own town.

The road filled with people; day-labourers at the new water-works came from Gencs, and my Uncle Ábris's bricklayers came too, their mortar-covered flat-heeled boots clattered as they ran panting in mad flight and fell from their feet as they dashed at breakneck speed towards the town. Everything and everyone they had was there.

At last, at long last, the carriage came for me.

'Hurry, my dear, quickly! Get in just as you are! Drive! No, don't tremble! They're all right at your mother's; the Cifrasor has gardens along it, and the big market-place and the park protect it... but the other streets... Your furniture too, and all your belongings. They say Telekdy saved what he could of it. Oh, since noon! I could hardly get hold of a carriage! This is a terrible wind. Some folk saw the mad baron seize a watering-can and sprinkle water when everyone had lost their wits. Firemen are coming this evening on the train from Debrecen. What will become of Szinyér in the meantime? How it's spreading! There, there, my dear, don't cry! Rest your head here!'

We nestled close to each other. We sensed that some very great event, terrifying and swift, was happening before our eyes, and stupefied with excitement, and only half-conscious, we felt each other's presence particularly strongly. He put his arms around me, and his fingers trembled hot through my black lace dress, but we remained almost motionless the whole time.

With smoke, the stifling and fearsome stench of living, burning things, the swirling black smuts in the hellish wind, twilight came quickly. The horses snorted in terror as they tugged at the carriage; they could hardly be held in check. In front of us, a glowing deluge emitting flashes from time to time, terrifyingly mobile, crazy, panting and blood-coloured; streets of firebrands, towers of flame, fiery serpents with blazing tails; it all flowed and snaked like lava, throwing out flames and flashes to the sky all around. And a muffled din, the rumble of crashing walls and mingled shouting in the far distance! All around panting, feverish figures rushed in breathless, desperate flight, their feet wounded and bare, wailing bitterly; some of them grabbed the side of the carriage or clambered up at the back for a moment, but others pushed them off and they fell behind, only waving their fists as we went on.

Now we were in the vineyards; for a time a high privet-hedge hid the awful sight from our eyes; only the blood-coloured sky flashed and the tumultuous noise drew nearer. We moved now at a slow pace, because of the throng of escaping groups of men, women and children.

'Oh dear, oh dear! It's all over now! There's nothing left of the town!' they shouted towards us with marvellously lively gestures as if it were great news.

'Is Börvély Street still open?' asked the driver looking over his shoulder, but he dared not stop in the crowd.

'Oh dear no! It's leapt across it now. The cobbler's storehouse is blazing; you can't go that way!'

'You can get to the market-place from the Kálmándi Gate. Everything's all right in the big market-place.'

We clattered past the cemetery; the light from the fire rested motionless, almost calmly on the side of the white marble grave-stones and the silent grounds. In the little streets low German-inhabited houses whimpered with fear; their inhabitants stood on guard in front of them all prepared, with bundles over their arms and all gathered together in a huddle with heads down like a terrified herd of cattle. Their animals were untethered and roamed freely in the street and yards. At last we saw the square outline of the Water Tower, illuminated and bleak, and the permit-office in the middle of the market-place. That was where we got out.

In the distance of the huge square, a black swarm of people milled around, and the drone of wailing and almost gentle lamen-tation, women weeping, the resigned and dull tone of sorely-tried souls as they watched in an apparently detached way, guessing and learning about the route of the fire and its progress. And the wind died down with just such noticeable suddenness as it had arisen. The whole area was completely filled with alien furniture of a hundred different kinds; bowls and other belongings lay scattered around; if there had been a thief about, he would not have known where to hide them. Groups of strangers chatted like acquaintances and wept on the top of settees, chairs and tables that were not theirs, settling on them all mixed together. All isolation ceased to exist in the community of loss that claimed their almost enthusiastic interest. But other communities and customary groupings lost the ties that bound them too; I remember that we roamed about for a long time, driven to and fro by the tide of moving crowds, and still we could not reach the house where my mother and her husband lived.

The neat courtyards along the Cifrasor and their little gardens were indeed protected and enveloped by darkness, and on the other side the dense black foliage of the Count's park sketched the dark mass of the hard shadow of the trees on the rose-tinted sky in the background. From behind the railings sharp, strange well-nigh human cries could be heard: the noises of the peacocks who having been awoken, were screeching in terror there. There was something unforgettably blood-curdling in those sounds.

'Where did it begin, good people? What do you know? What's burned down?'

'Oh, Lord above! Have you only just come? Everything— well, almost—look for yourself! From the Papszer to the Seven Eagle Feathers Street, the little Hajdú Town, the Brook Side and beyond that everything! Where the poor live, the reed-thatched houses! It ran right through that first of all. Everything's burnt to a cinder there now!'

'And the farmers' quarter, and the craftsmen's too! As far as Little Water Street and Gypsy End, all the lot! And that was only after lunch!'

'Deaths? Oh, how can anyone know now? The folk went out in droves to the fields, towards the villages. Have all the mothers found their children?'

Further away a few peasants stood in a group, propping their stocky, sheepskin-clad figures against the post of the permit-office; they moved in a single mass in the reddish semi-darkness. An arm stretched out on high and threatened the castle with its fist.

'But you can be sure that's not suffering any damage, damn him, the villain! There's no justice in heaven either!'

'Damn and blast it!' thundered another. 'Whoever didn't start the fire there was a fool, once he set about it! As things are, who's he revenging himself on? A fat lot they care about the town!'

One of them caught sight of us nearby, and in terror

I clutched Horváth's arm and pulled him away from the wrath of their glances. Once again we became caught up in a band of lamenting women.

'It's only half of County Street that's burnt! Why, that's a miracle; don't you think it's a miracle? It ran up Elbow Street between the little old Jewish houses packed together there, but the blank wall of the County Hall has been sprayed from the very first moment by the attendants and gendarmes. Only the jailers' lodgings have been burnt in the garden. And there the fire went off to the left.'

'The Zimán house as well?'

'Oh yes, that's for sure. It was the first to go. But it stopped ten houses away from the church... That's a miracle! It turned along the promenade and went right along the line of shops. Oh, it's awful there! Look, it's still in flames. They've taken all the water out of the castle lake. And there are still sparks flashing out of Church Street. Ah! What's that?'

'The firemen! From Debrecen!'

A sigh of relief went up in unison, and a murmuring rumble ran tight through the square.

'Let's go,' said Horváth and grasped my hand firmly. 'The church side of County Street isn't damaged. That's where I live too. Shall we have a look there?'

Slowly and tremblingly we made our way to the foot of the Castle Garden. It suddenly occurred tome that Ilka Zimán's house was over there too, by the church.

'I can't manage any further now. Let's have a rest!' I said beneath the acacia trees on the little 'promenade' and sat down suddenly on a bench. This little square was miraculously deserted now; everybody had withdrawn from here towards the market-place. Opposite, the glorious dome of the church curved upwards, calm and intact, and the rigid stone saints stood in a ghostly line on the ornamented gables. Beyond the trees in the tiny little square, groups of people were still milling about, and then, with horns blaring, a musical flourish of fire-engines came along at a gallop. They turned off towards the shops.

We sat there in marvellous solitude, left to ourselves. Hungry and thirsty, we kept watch during the night; we saw the whole progress of the dreadful tragedy and its outcome, and we did not stir an inch to play a part in it ourselves... Why? It was as if his fatalism had gripped me. To go and join the throng any further, to work myself up in order to find out a couple of hours or so earlier how many chairs or cupboards of mine they had dragged out of the burning house… What was the point? Anyway all that lumber was just a burden to me; if only the whole lot had been destroyed! This thought gave me a wonderful sense of great freedom and lightness! It didn't matter! We two were beggars; *we* had nothing to fear! At least we were together here. I nodded off for a brief moment or two with my head resting on his shoulder, then awoke suddenly, frozen in the chill of dawn, but he kept covering me with his cloak and warming me considerately. Cold dew lay on everything, but the damp wooden benches smeared our hands black with the soot that had fallen so thickly on them. We rose, numbed and exhausted, soaked to the skin, on edge, and with our senses totally depressed and dissipated we set off through the charred and blackened dawn streets.

These are my recollections of that world-shattering, dreadful night. Nor do I know why all this is so sharply etched in my consciousness or where it was linked so strongly with my life. After all, I possessed no house in Szinyér, nor any estate… I had nothing! And as for my furniture, my stepfather Telekdy and his driver pulled out one of two pieces; they saved perhaps enough for two rooms, bits and pieces that were to stay with me and accompany me through life. Those few weather-beaten articles are still around me, even today. What was burnt inside were the silk rep suite with the amorettes, the chest full of carpets and the piano; for all these things, the ostentatious generosity of deputy sheriff Széchy, bestowed on me an abundant share of the disaster-fund subscribed by the whole country; I virtually made a profit out of my loss…. And my old, wrecked home town began to rise in a matter of weeks; new houses with tiled roofs and windows with metal shutters; new shops with glass display-windows; new decorative iron railings and covered gateways. In the course of a year, everything here was renewed and beautified and gained new momentum. But people's lives seemed to have been cut off from their memories, from their childhood and those odd and colourful traditions which mark and distinguish the living things created by them. Very soon an artificial and bogus town was built here with fine straight streets and neat, uniform houses; in the end the standard of living and commerce and everything simply gained from this disaster, but so much of the old indefinable beauty and special attraction had disappeared. And even today I like most of all to walk the length of those old twisting, turning streets that were built up before the fire and have remained as they were.

Now what happened after that?...

I rented a little two-roomed flat looking out onto a courtyard in the Cifrasor, not far from where my mother and stepfather lived, and moved into it with what remained of my furniture. I certainly had no desire to go back to my Uncle Pórtelky, and in any case it would have been impossible now. The old man had spread the news here through Melanie and a few other acquaintances that on the day before the fire, I had secretly left his house and eloped with Horváth, without a word of farewell. As if it was all pre-arranged. 'Elopement!' ... Yes, that was the only name to give to the departure, and the whole affair acquired a particularly intriguing, dangerous, engaging and romantic tint in people's minds. The avalanche of gossip that was set off even during those confused weeks found time to fall on my poor head.

'What am I to say?' my mother said sharply. 'You turned up here at my house at dawn... who knows where you were till morning? Who knows how many acquaintances saw you roaming around at night? I can't say a word against all the gossip. Let him be your protector now, if he's such a great cavalier of yours!'...

Once more I felt that the web of fate was being drawn tighter around me. Once again I was enslaved to it. My poor woman's life!... Once again I was totally dependent on a man, because I must expect from him protection, moral firmness, redress and respect. What else could I have done but desire this from him with all the strength at my command, with complete feminine determination and cunning, concealed intention?

Yes, this was where I lived now and I had no other plans, aims or possibilities. This was where I lived, so that he might be able to come and see me freely every day and I lived only to fan the flame of his desire and love and keep them alive. I saw and knew that he too was slowly becoming involved and that there was no other way out left for him. For public opinion now condescendingly turned against him too. People saw him going in and out of my house; I observed that my window was regularly watched by strangers, passers-by I hardly knew, and we were once again the subject of general gossip. In the street they looked at me with respect, curiosity and fear as if I were a leper.

Yet there was no reason for this!... Certainly all that may happen between a man and a woman did not occur between us, though today I suspect that the boundaries here are not as sharply defined as is generally thought. Often when I defended myself against his desire there arose in me a hazardous passion of some wild, bitter determination, and I thought, 'Oh well! I ought to pay him off and fling everything before him with a defiant and haughty gesture and dismiss him: just let him go! Be gracious and bountiful! Let him go in peace, not feeling humiliated and not thinking that I kept him at arm's length like a rural shopkeeper, making myself important and precious by tempting him into something for which he certainly had no desire or proclivity...'

Nobody ever taught me to think like this, but I felt it would be nicer, haughtier, more humane and aristocratic like this... But I could not do it! My life slid into a blind alley. Everything I tried to do with my own human strength collapsed and failed. Maybe it was mainly my own fault; it appeared that I was not suited for struggle and independence. But instead I could only exist through someone else, through a *man*, whom I desired strongly. Yes, I had to become his wife, a married woman once again, a gentlewoman; to achieve a life that was supported and protected, to run my own household—and *here*, at home in Szinyér again. I almost expected my old life to return. Although Horváth was a different kind of man.... that material things... oh well, things would be all right somehow! And anyway that wouldn't be my concern!... Now all I had to do was defend myself, stand firm, clearly, doggedly and calculatingly. And watch out with eyes wide open and with my own interest in case I got into some terrible plight like that of the poor, downtrodden and humiliated postmistress. No, I did not want that.

It was the other solution I wanted! And I watched and waited as he vacillated and struggled; sometimes he procrastinated with the gesture of a light-headed and pliable person, sometimes he drove himself unexpectedly to the brink of a final decision only to enjoy the irresponsible present again belatedly the next day. In the end it all turned out as I had imagined. In response to something external (old Vodicska wrote me yet another condemnatory letter mentioning my son, who was bearing the brunt of my bad reputation), and to my angry tears he suddenly said with tender emotion, 'All right, come what may, this is what's got to happen!'

Our unexpected betrothal was a great and exciting sensation for the whole town!

And people suddenly became kind, warm, good and forgiving towards me! It was as if I really had made right some wrong, had made amends for something, and they graciously and amicably accepted me once again. Everything calmed down for a time.

What a peculiar menagerie this world is!

XX.

A countless host of years, seasons and days inextricably inter-twined! Seen through the fine mesh of distance, how unimportant is the diligent measurement of time, the changes of a calendar and how many times the sun rises and sets above us. How often nature changed with the return of new moons, floods, snow, rain and the flowers and fruits of the season! Our human life is geared to different divisions, and our fate sketches in the boundaries as it pleases, as on a map. If I consider how many years have passed from my second marriage up to now, why, that is almost half my life! But taken all together, this great mound of years sometimes seems so much of a piece that I marvel at it; all those innumerable days when every single morning I prepared to face life, dressed, talked, saw to things and struggled, and all those years when, as I woke from the turmoil of troubles and worries to an occasional moment of consciousness I would sometimes say, 'Why, the leaves are falling; it's getting cold! We'll soon be lighting the stove!' Or I would sigh with heavy indifference to the sky, 'Oh what a wet summer we're having! Last year the ole-anders made a better display!' Or: 'Here's Christmas come round again already! I ought to get this and that!'... A hazy, heavy and tough dark-hued texture of time, a long, declining, oppressively dull period of life, but one perforated and shredded with so many treacherous, bitter struggles, so many stupid (troublesome even to mention) unromantic, wearing and debili-tating skirmishes in destitution! The years ground me down and wore me away. But would I not have grown old just the same in a life of refinement and beauty, quiet and gentle calm, I wonder? I should be exactly where I am! At this stage I no longer ponder on where I went wrong. Perhaps everyone's life develops according to their nature; or their essential being adapts to their circumstances. Now I cannot imagine myself with a different past and present from those that became part of me and made me what I am.

I had entered my thirtieth year and I was a married woman once again; I myself had willed this and made it my aim, forcing it on myself to support a life that had begun to go downhill.

How should I know now whether it was to revenge myself on my enemies or whether it was for love? It was for all these reasons!

At first sight it seemed as if an age-old period had returned. Once again I had a tiny, three-roomed dwelling for two in a recently built new and clean little street in the Hajdú Town. I moved into it with the brown rep suite rescued from the great fire, the remaining dining-chairs, the varnished beds and cupboards; from the chests I unpacked the sturdy pots and pans I had used long ago, and I also had the oleanders fetched from my mother's and I arranged them in a line along the front of the brick veranda. Once again I had a servant to whom I could give orders and a household where I could sweep, dust and polish to my heart's content, with my old enthusiasm. Except that my fate had once carried me higher, and sometimes I felt the melancholic in this relapse. Never mind, I soon learnt to put up with it all the same!

During long summer afternoons, I sat there, in the wicker chair, on the veranda; the sound of the church bell quivered in the air and the maid sang as she ironed in the kitchen. Now with my nerves on edge I was sewing clothes for a tiny child, stitching rapidly while weighty feminine worries pounded wearily in my head, the usual rebellious fear before the uncompromisingly certain, unavoidable ill. Sometimes I was so painfully oppressed by loneliness that I rejoiced when (as in the old days) an occasional tradeswoman I knew rattled the gate-latch with cautious humility and clambered up the three wooden steps with her knapsack, thanking me gratefully or sighing gently 'Dearie me, madam!'

'Oh me dear, madam, is it really like that with you? Dear God, that was quick! Ah well, that's the way of things. And it's better so, believe me, if that's what you want, have one quickly, so that its father can still have a bit of enjoyment in it too. After all, he's no spring chicken, that's for sure! And perhaps he'll be at home more often, you just see, if there's a little child crawling around him. But look, you mustn't listen to nasty gossip! If only I'd said so at the time!'

'What, Trézsi?'

'Oh dearie me, beg your pardon, it's not proper, indeed it isn't, but there, please don't be angry; I'll tell you. It was when I was taking old clothes in the winter—I always take ladies' silk skirts and used ball-gowns over to Rosemary Street, you see…

to the girls, you know, because they, too, were left with only a single skirt after the big fire. An' then they ask all sorts of questions about what news there is in the town. "Oh yes," says a great big blonde who used to take the money in the Kispipa, "Trézsi," she says, "is it true that that lovely beauty, that widow lady's going to marry that big seedy blonde of a solicitor? Oh dearie me! She ought to be talked out of that! Why, he's a … nothing… just a burden on the earth! A helpless old thing, a nobody," she says.

'There you are, you see, what nasty tongues some people have, don't they? Of course, I wouldn't have let such things pass my lips for the world!'

'It'd be better if you kept them shut now, you old donkey!' I turned on her now with half-simulated anger, because it was only now that my irritation and embarrassment had got the better of my curiosity. She took fright, pleading and wheedling, so after all I had her coffee brought out just as my grandmother had done long ago and my mother and I too now; I made her drink it, then spread out the jumble I had to sell.

'Oh my, madam, why ever are you selling that? I couldn't pay you what it's worth anyway! An expensive theatre shawl, black lace wrap, lace-edged peignoir! You're still young, madam, too young to stop wearing them!'

'Don't argue, Trézsi! Just tell me what you'll give me for them!'

'Oh my, now I understand! Dear me! I daren't promise anything. How much do you want?…'

Another day Náni Spach came with her big haversack; she was panting, her shapeless body gone fat, and the little wicker garden-chair creaked under her. She pulled out the timely swaddling-bands, tiny pillow-cases, knitted bodices with blue ribbon-rosettes. I paid her with the small change I had got for the theatre shawls and pearl-studded mantillas. Yes, that was how I had to look after things… it was no use! As she stirred her little cup of coffee she too recounted what she had picked up here and there. Sometimes her voice faded to a whisper.

'Oh yes, there's a lot of talk about how Mistress Ilka Zimán's still madly in love with the master. That she's put a curse on your life together until death—that's what they're saying, I'm only repeating it —and that she knows some magic too (I don't know whether that's true, I can't swear to it!), some secret craft… casting spells or some such thing… I only know that it includes fasting for nine Tuesdays, and she might be going on a pilgrimage to Pócs,* too; all to stop you having a good life together. But there now, please don't believe such daft talk! Tongues are all wagging like this... There's not a word of truth in it; that's what I say!'

All the same, it became much worse when I was alone. When it grew dark, I became restless; I waited to see whether Dénes would come home. Yet if he missed dinner he always sent the boy from the casino with a polite message not to expect him. For so many, many years he had gotten so used to staying without stirring from wherever he happened to feel comfortable, if by chance a good company of men had come together, or if these men wanted to continue their game of poker or slam. Except that I was not... like this! Oh, how poor Jenő Vodicska protected, pampered and consoled me when I was in this state! Now I myself had to bear all the mental strain too... And on top of all that, the household cares, even such things as the quarterly rent, buying firewood, the garden and getting stores for the winter—all that my first husband had taken away from my usual duties in his tender and meticulous care. It was no use; Dénes was not the man for such things. If sometimes I asked him for something he would buy what was too refined, expensive and unsuitable, and it made him bad-tempered when I became annoyed at it. Then next day he would display his empty wallet with a half-joking, reflective expression.

'Today you do something, my dear! I haven't any money! Some day a Swabian's coming in from Vállaj; he'll bring some!'

At first I didn't know how to take this peculiar, easy-going and smiling irresponsibility. Was this his nature? Well, it couldn't remain like this... after all, he was a husband now and would be a father before long. 'I've got to try,' I thought, 'with fair and reasonable words to make him understand this and accept it.' After all, for the price of the occasional dinner at the casino we could eat for a week here at home. And it would be possible to live quite well from the office, even if we were to keep paying off his debts too, with a little economizing. But how much his debts really were and where everything was I was never able

* *Pócs*: Máriapócs, a village in Eastern Hungary, is a place of pilgrimage to the Uniate shrine of the Virgin Mary.

to get out of him; it appeared that he was not entirely clear about them either and he found it unpleasant to think of them, so he was unwilling to do so.

'I've managed to live with them up to now, dear!' he said, shrugging his shoulders gently, and of the thirty-three displayed pipes in the rack he selected the best-smoked meerschaum with obvious delight. 'Up to now!'... but, after all, he'd married me! True, he couldn't be compelled to do anything like this... he was a man, after all!

A sudden blaze of hostile indignation flared up in me; and it was followed immediately by a bitter sense of shame. That I couldn't hurl that in his face! All the same, I had no other choice! When I was deeply enmeshed in trouble, when the world detested me unfairly, my money was running out and old Vodicska also put his finger in the middle of it all, I know I even said something in my depression about drinking a brew of phosphorus to end it all if my wrecked life were not straightened out...

But if Dénes were really good, really refined and noble, such things ought not to enter his mind now. True, words lead to others and at that time in my condition I was a bundle of nerves. But after all, wasn't it his child that I was carrying, and wasn't he the cause of my sufferings?

In the occasional moment of elation, or if something brought it to his mind, he could still be touchingly kind and tender too, but there was no constant devotion in him. He was one of those more colourful and interesting people who from time to time can wind themselves up like a masterpiece of the clockmaker's art to some delicate and clear-sounding mood or emotion, but in between they forget, retiring comfortably into themselves and cutting themselves off totally as they take their rest. My God! How different the type of man is who makes a good wooer from the one cut out to be a good husband! Dénes was known as a congenial type, soft-hearted and attractively easy-going—as indeed he obviously was—but at times he could be unexpectedly stubborn and even childish occasionally if his spiritual and physical comforts were upset. When this happened, there sometimes burst from him the haughtiness of the petty bourgeois family in his home town, with its penchant for picking on little things, its primitive selfishness and crude mode of expression. True, he quickly calmed down, and with suitable methods and well-devised cunning he could be made to do anything; and if

195

he had any money he would open his wallet generously, without even accounting for it, however much it was. It may be that in this first period, my chief complaint was that I felt he did not love me enough any longer. I seemed to be no longer indispensable to him in body or soul, but perhaps I never was anyway! If I went off, he let me go; if I broke things off, he acquiesced; if I called him back, he came... true, that was how things had been in the past too! And in the meantime he had another woman. He was a pliable person, very weak yet very strong, because nothing was very important to him and he did not allow his peace to be disturbed.

And it seemed as if all the responsibility for this marriage fell on me; that is certainly how I felt it. 'I was the one who agreed to it, if that was all that was needed; so now just see how I fit into it!' That was what all his gestures, his unchanging bachelor-habits and stubborn emancipation from the usual forms and cares of the head of the family seemed to say. Yes, it's no use... men must be given the illusion of struggle and achievement at a great price; the wife must wait motionless like some prize biding its time at the top of a winning-post, increasing her value by being protected and chaperoned, with assumed reluctance and passivity. I, too, might have known this, but then I was so very poor and destitute!... Now I really was at his mercy, and I felt this in my helplessness with a cruel, convulsive and stifled resentment. There often burst from me now an offensive and purblind word, a sharp angry accusation, but with frightened amazement he evaded arguments and he detested battles. When this happened, he preferred to go out and seek company; to dine with other people among happy faces, to feel that he was a free man all the same. And often he was irregular with money for our food, so by now my own tiny fortune had all been used up. After all, I simply had to dress myself properly somehow, though with greatly reduced pretensions.

My first daughter was born in the spring.

XXI.

Two or three years slipped past, it seems now, with remarkable speed. Not like a dream: rather like some heavy sleep with stupid struggles, unconscious and yet deadly weariness. I lived a life, a miserably minuscule, creaking, dull, hard and grinding life. I was scarred and bruised, and I myself became hardened to it. I was not one of those people who develops through humility and suffering into something better and more refined. Instead I was always made more perverse and wicked, which I could never understand.

At that time, I was compelled to remain at home in retirement as I was expecting a child. Hardly had I weaned the second when I had to take her off the breast as the third was on the way. And another girl too; all three were girls.

'They've sucked all the blood out of me, eaten me up and devoured my youth! Oh well, that's the way things are! They're mine, their bodies are my body, the poor, dear little mites! They're lovely and healthy as can be! Just look! The mature blossoming of my own sturdy, richly-endowed stock, of my own belated fertility; a rich burgeoning even from the other declining strain. All the same, was it necessary for me to become such a wreck? Could I have done anything to help my own life? Or if I could, would anything else have been possible? Has absolutely everything, everything got to go through me, and me only?

I no longer breast-fed her. Her firm, resourceful, demanding little lips remained puckered and her diminutive fists remained tightly clenched in her deep sleep. Look! Why, she's such a darling little mite…one could go on looking at her like this for a long time. But the other two are howling and kicking the flush door of the nursery through there. 'Coffee, mummy!' 'Mimi-mummy, kiffee-coffee!' Now they're laughing, the little one repeating after the bigger one, 'Mimi-mummy!' Oh dear, they'll wake the baby!… 'Oh, do keep quiet in there! Just you wait, you rowdy little imps, I'll be after you with the broom-handle!' A moment's silence, soft whispering. 'Toffee!' But where's the nanny, that wretched Rumanian kid? She can't cope with them, or she's slipped out to gossip with the kitchen-maid! Bang! Oh dear! Susie, the little one's bumped herself on something! Oh God! I'll go mad in here! 'So there you are, you rotten little beast! Wherever have you been? How can you leave the two children on their own with a lighted lamp on the wall? What's that you're mumbling? Where have you been? I'll pull that filthy scruffy bun off your head, so I will! Oh dear, her nose is bleeding! Look at her! Fetch some water, you idiot! I'll give you something to remember! There, hold it out here! And don't you make such a noise; Why, for heaven's sake, you haven't broken any bones! There, there, it's all right now!'

Half-ashamed, I lower my voice as in a matter of minutes my bad-tempered fit of hysterical anger subsides; in it all my life's frustrations, my jaded, unsatisfied, subdued and despairing existence as a wife rebels sometimes in an unpredictable, ugly and unhealthy way. In the next room I hear Dénes walking to and fro, tapping clumsily on the pipe-rack.

'Oh dear! There's no light in there! Get on with it, the master's home! Put something on the fire too and then lay the table! And make sure that that glass is clean, that's all I'm saying!'

Oh what a lot of toil and trouble it takes to reach and maintain the old tidiness, the customary shining cleanliness of a household like this, full of children and short of rooms! With a cheap maid, a stupid little thirteen-year-old of a nanny and a husband who demands every comfort with the ingenuousness of a sultan but himself does not lift a finger to help; quite possibly his paralysed fingers would not be able to knock a fallen nail back into the wall... He just sits and smokes his pipe; lost in thought, his big blue eyes stare straight ahead, seemingly fixed on the smoke from his meerschaum. 'It's no use; this had to happen. That's how it was decreed by fate!'... I can almost see him always thinking something like this. And once upon a time I regarded this man as witty, interesting and original!... But in those days he was different too; perhaps, like me, he has been dulled and made commonplace and indifferent by everyday cares, troubles and burdens. Yes, but he isn't right in the midst of them like me! His office is a part of his other life; from there he goes to the casino and plays cards; he's out among people and hears news of what's going on in the town; such liveliness, attraction and thought as he possesses he expends on folk outside. Here at home all he does is eat and sleep and give himself over to the daily reckoning of household expenses in a way suggesting that there is nothing to bind him and that from one day to the next he might decamp without any sense of responsibility. There's no certainty anywhere. I felt as if my whole life were suspended in mid-air together with these three little children; this rootlessness pounded in my brain, harrying and torturing me. All my inclinations spurred me to link myself to someone else, to a man, and through him to exist, to act and to desire. But this had slipped through my fingers and it was impossible to hold on. And all of a sudden the wickedly despairing thought crossed my mind of the news I had received that day of my Uncle Ábris's death. He had left ten thousand forints to his housekeeper, half-peasant by origin, with whom he had also made love. There you are, he died very soon—I shouldn't have had to suffer long if at that time... I'd been able to be a bit more sensible... Pah!

The little ones quietened down; after crying, they whimpered in their sleep. We sat in silence at the dinner table and I fumed with stifled rage when I looked over and saw him poking about reluctantly with his fork in the dish of roast meat.

'You can eat it up,' I turned on him at last, probably hoarse with emotion. 'It's good! Just now and again even a grand seigneur like you may condescend to partake of our humble home cooking.'

'Now what's the matter, Magda?' he asked, staring at me while the fork stopped indecisively in his trembling hand.

'Nothing! I'd only like to remark that you didn't eat much better for ten times the money at yesterday's champagne dinner that's spoilt your appetite so thoroughly.'

'Please tell me what you've got against me! Can't I even swallow a bite of food at home without being criticized? Have I done something wrong to you?'

'Me? Not at all! It's nothing to do with me! It's your own money you're spending; so tell me, what about covering for your unpaid bachelor bills, your unpaid taxes, your membership subscription for the law society—I see a reminder came for it today—and everything else, the peasants' stamp duty too, money for clothes and schooling for these unfortunate little mites...'

'And your domain too... why don't you mention that? The peat-beds, water-chestnut forests, the swarms of loach, imaginary vineyards! Yes, now I'm just such a rogue, a highwayman, a creature who lives off others! And you, of all people, telling me this, Magda! How dare you tell me so?'

'Nobody else can. Your dear table-companions, the flagons of wine, the village dignitaries up for the county assembly certainly won't!'

'Why do you talk such nonsense? In any case, they're your relations, every one of them. A worthy lot; why do you denigrate them?'

'Well, it's true you've got yourself very much into their good graces. Of course, you can drink a lot with them; it's you who finds them female company too, and you even play the violin with your bad hand if they give the word-dabbling in the gypsy Bankó's art.'

'Hm! Is that what your friend the second-hand dealer told you?'

'It doesn't matter who told me! Do you think half the town doesn't know about it? Do you think that although I can't get out, I don't hear of what you've been up to? Shame on you! Maybe you're their buffoon... Oh yes, they weren't fond of poor Jenő because he was a cut above them. They took you up even though they don't know where you came from, or who and what your grandfather was. But they too have come down in the world since then; they're on their last legs; now any sort of man is all right for them. Where's the old pride? Ten years ago they wouldn't have given a glance to a nobody.'

'Like me, you mean. But now listen to me! Just stop it! I overlook what I can, but even if you have a hundred babies to feed, for heaven's sake, if you're mad go and get yourself locked away; you've got a few relations there already!'

'Pah! Shame on you! To keep on bringing *that* up!'

'It was you who began it. You said I was a hanger-on; perhaps your relations paid for my dinner. Well then, know this! If I've had even a single drop at anyone else's generosity...'

'That's just the trouble. I know you're daft enough to do that. And you always lose at cards. They're despicable enough to sit down with you and win money from a hapless beggar like you when they know that his poor family is barely surviving at home. I haven't been able to go outside for years on end; I haven't any decent rags to go out in.'

'Why haven't you? Have I drunk that away too? Where are all those domains now?'

'Only a rake without any sense of duty can think like that… a depraved musician like you…not even a man. You've got three children: have you forgotten? So why do I slave away here sweating blood if I'm not worth even a dress?'

'For all the slaving you do for me, a good maid could do that more cheaply and without complaining. And was it I who wanted the three children too?'

'Do you think it was me, then? Oh, don't tempt the Lord God, you reprobate! If only He'd take them away, poor things! But it was different when Marcsi had scarlet fever; then you dashed from one doctor to another as fast as you could go! And now you talk like this!'

'Yes, indeed, I *am* sorry for the poor things. They only have you to bring them up.'

'Oh you miserable wretch! If only it would occur to you to pay Dr. Jakobi some time, the one who cured Marcsi! It would be better than those champagne dinners and fancy women!'

'Those fancy women again!… Was it Trézsi the second-hand dealer who told you that too? Oho! What a popular lad I've become now! It's no use—you've made me years younger!'

'And that old hag too, your darling Ilka! Do you think I don't know you visit her from time to time? You have a smoke together. That toothless old woman smokes fifteen cigars every day. You have a good laugh at the world together, at me too, the decent fool who's killing herself here. Ah yes, *alte Liebe!* She's got the easier role.'

'If only that were true! If she laughs with me and smokes a cigar with me, at least it's pleasanter than if she were to play the harpy! And anyway she's a relative of yours. It's bad enough that you show your anger with her openly, disgracing yourself in public, just because of such stupid fears and gypsy-wives' gossip.'

'Fearful for you? The devil I am! But it's true that you've made a fine choice of people for yourself even among my own relations.'

'Don't tell me that! Maybe you'd like me to make friends instead with your half-witted stepfather who collects all the dregs of world literature in great heaps and devours them until his brain gets chock-full of them. At the moment he's studying health from a book by some mad quack of a German priest, and every morning the whole market gathers at the fence to stare when he walks barefoot on the grass in the handkerchief-sized garden while the servant walks behind him with the watering-can and keeps sprinkling his ankles. That's what I should do too, isn't it? Or maybe I should keep up a friendship with your famous young brother Csaba, the drunken military officer whose sword and helmet he pawned when he ought to have reported for duty. And now he's even been dismissed by the third notary since he's no good either as a notary's assistant; when he drinks himself silly they pick him up next day out of the gutter. A fine bunch of near relatives you have, to be sure!'

'Just leave them in peace! There are some important and decent people among them too, sober and hard-working, but they don't give a glance in your direction.'

'Of course... István, the excellent István, Mr. Public Notary! Well, he's neatly annihilated his three sisters, and why not? If they hadn't the brain of a hen that at least scratches around for itself. Of course, István doesn't give me a look, but does he look at you, I wonder, or at his mother? Now he keeps company with the great of the land. His wife has become a lady's maid to the sheriff's wife, her intimate confidante, whom she's caused to run up crazy dress-bills and whom she drags off on travels and to spas. That clumsy little goose is going to fly away; her tongue's been loosened already and her eyes opened, and that "upright, sober" husband of hers is paying through the nose. That's the way for one to be able to get on in the world, isn't it?'

'Oh what a stroke of luck! The baroness is my own cousin—mine and not Ágnes Kallós's. While I was Mrs. Vodicska, I can tell you, it was rather she who followed in my footsteps and not the other way around. But now there's no point, I'm sure: a wife is respected for her husband.'

'All right, then, it's pointless! So I'm a detestable creature, a nobody, an outcast who's degraded and dragged you down to my level! It only astonishes me that for the time being you still accept from me this roof and other minuscule remunerations that accrue from my idle and block-head character and my work as a gate-crasher, the money that while I'm asleep you diligently collect every morning, sometimes from the drawer of my bedside cabinet, searching every corner of my wallet with detestation but with the persistence of a magpie.'

'That at least I'm preserving from Rosemary Street!'

'How well-informed you are! Bravo!'

'How am I to buy milk sometimes for your three innocent children? How am I to pay the maid's wages? Or for the firewood? From what you throw at me each day?'

'Right! Now let me just try and see whether I can lay hands on a little extra by morning out of the kindness of one of your distinguished relations. If that's the sort of man I am...'

He had been ready to go out earlier; he knocked out his pipe and slowly gathered his coat and stick with an air of gentility. This platitudinous act was intended to be simply a well-rounded transition, a satirical, disdainful and light-headed conclusion. But all the same he collected his things together slowly as if almost unconsciously or out of old habit he expected to be held back and pacified. 'If only he'd go now, if only he'd hurry up, if only he'd disappear, now that...' I thought stubbornly, for there was no telling, maybe I too was afraid that I would hold him back all the same, or call him back with a gesture of conciliation, or else ostensibly drag out even further the long and tasteless battle of words, while gradually softening my objections, slowly calming and altering the mood to complaint and pleading; or else burst into tears suddenly, with passionate fits of convulsive sobbing to make him turn back from the door and stand over me silently, helplessly, regretfully or appeasingly, and place his soothing hand on my head, slipping it down lower to my waist; or simply stand facing him on the doorstep, flushed from the quarrel, eyes furious and gleaming, nostrils panting, but already getting my breath back, laughing and taking his arm... For I had tried every one of these methods by now and we were beyond that stage. There were four years of marriage behind us. I had become indifferent, as he doubtless was too. 'No, I won't! Just let him go now!'

But when I was left alone, I was stifled with bitter weeping. This is my life! He can find compensation, but I shall toss restlessly here on the hot pillows and that little mite will whimper all night long, sucking milk that is harmful, neurotic and troubled with all the excitement. And to him a whore with a painted face is worth more, or that toothless ancient vixen, his old love, to whom maybe he keeps going to complain about me and his marriage... And for me it is impossible to take revenge or return like for like; I can't even stir from these three nuisances. Oh what provisions life has made for me! And how it exhorts penance from me! But why? Just tell me why?... During these last few years I've suddenly withered away; my figure has gone to pieces with all the children, and everlasting weaning has made me sluttish... Well, now there's nothing coming my way, it's no use! What remains now is only to work myself to the bone, a duty which I've been coerced into.

'How much is expected of me while these children grow up! And there might be more too... oh, God forbid! If I beg him to stay now and hold him back... yes, I can still exercise some influence over him like this. But more children! No I couldn't bear that now. I'd rather die! I've had more than my fill of them.'

With such a man, such a father! 'Was it I who wanted them?' he asked just now. And when they were on the way, too, he treated me and behaved as if I was the only reason for their existence. How different was my poor first husband, with his almost apologetic, grateful, responsible and touching tenderness during this period! He was a saint, Jenő was. A complete, true, conscientious man with serious feelings who knew how to die when once he lost the game of life. He took life on an 'either-or' basis and he lived it accordingly, very seriously and correctly until he paid the ultimate consequence.

This soft-hearted light wrath of a man here loafs through the world more in a 'so-so' way; he gets into everything by accident, just floating above or outside everything; there's nothing really serious in him when it comes to human affairs. What do family, wife, office, work or rank mean to him? All he wants is to feel comfortable both here and there; and in this he's succeeded to this very day! What a man!

And yet despite everything, he was the one I loved. Was this true love, I wonder?... But after all he still fills my mind today, tortures and upsets me and makes me rebel; I need to upset him, I have to hate him. He's important to me. And whatever else there may be, it's from him that I have my healthy, thoroughbred, beautiful children.

There they are, gently snoring in their little warm white beds, their faces lovely, red and chubby, their hair blonde and soft like their father's; their little warm, sweetly-perfumed bodies pant in the languorous half-light of the shaded nightlight. Well, these, these are what life has given me. Sometime they will be wives like me. But I have no wish that their destiny should resemble mine in the least. I shall see to that! At least my own life will still be good for this purpose!

XXII.

Once more years… and years!

Of these times, hardly anything has remained in my mind except that three new pairs of children's shoes had to be bought each season and some little dresses for each one when they went to school, because at all costs… at all costs I was determined to send them there neat and tidy. And what battles and struggles, like getting blood out of a stone, it cost me to get all these out of their father! Often I stole the odd ten-forint piece from his wallet under the pillow when he had had a late night out and slept well into the morning, snoring in a deep heavy sleep. That was probably the best time; for even if he noticed it, he was not sure whether he might have given it to some woman of the streets or some gypsy or other during the night. And he felt pangs of conscience too; he was ashamed of himself in the reluctant moments of sobering-up and only swore under his breath at the washbasin as he puffed and blew, while around him the morning cleaning was going full speed ahead in a burst of wild enthusiasm as I polished and spurred on the maid.

'Oh damn them all! Damn the brigands! The ruffians!… What's become of me? What's happened to me since she got me into her clutches? The serpent! That's what she is!'

This all referred to me, for that is how things were now between us, and even more so!… How had this arisen? How could we have gotten to this state? I ask myself now in the peace and quiet of solitude, the calming influence of old age. Heavens! Slowly, by degrees, our relationship, our treatment of each other, went downhill; and really it was only *words*, ever harsher, nastier, more unbridled, uglier words, that marked this slow descent. But what else can happen to two people living together, what can be more important than how they talk to each other from time to time? In between there may be times of conciliation and even minutes of passionate love too; but not a single word is uttered without leaving its mark. The occasional tense, tortured momentary curse born of hatred or the wicked, cruel blows of reproachful attacks as they strike home at the most painful recesses of the soul or of vanity, or disseminate the bile of profanity or unbridled scorn among the most tortured, tender or valued nooks of the past; and in the end they simply shout degrading curses at each other, baseless, absurd, rebel-rousing charges and muddled, passionate, breathless, quite astonishing inventions of nastiness to make the other suffer and keep on suffering, to open the flood-gates to the pain of stifling revenge, humiliation or slavery—oh, these are all just *words*, it is true, but they have a fearful reaction on the emotions and destroy everything, absolutely everything. An occasional ugly unbalanced scene like this may be followed by a period of calm, a sense of shame and a new rapprochement, but on the next occasion the clash will only be more hellish and more terrible.

At least peasant couples have their scuffles and can knock the hell out of each other; in this way they physically rid themselves of the painful, nervous tensions produced by anger, but for our kind this is impossible. Men are held back from it at the last minute by their upbringing or some other preoccupation, and the sting of anger that remains embedded in them is more harmful than passionate love that is not allowed free rein.

Which of us was worse, he or I? Now from a distance I can see clearly that for a time I was virtually half crazy with nervous, physical and mental overstrain. Rich folk in such a state go travelling, visit spas or nowadays enter sanatoriums; I had to bear the burden of life to breaking point. Here I was in the flower of my womanhood, the zenith of my summertime, overrun with worries and children. I who was used to company and at one time was surrounded with admiration was compelled to retreat into solitude; my appearance was unkempt and neglected, my feminine pride and all my feelings were offended by the neglect I suffered. I know I was also wildly jealous of that man; I scolded him to his face; panting with hatred I heaped reproaches on him, but I waited with frantic anxiety if he was late in the evenings and I suspected him of having affairs with women in the most senseless way. Ilka, the toothless old dragon, his old love… she was the perpetual target of my crazed mind, and if sometimes he defended her against my accusations—possibly just to provoke me—I could no longer restrain myself. Yet even then I felt that these mad outbursts were the reason why I came off worse in the relationship between us. How senseless it was too! A wreck of a man, nearly fifty, unable to do anything with his life… If he sent a message home saying not to wait for him at dinner, I always wrote a note too and sent the boy back with it: curses, threats, suspicion and insults all found their place in the pencil-scrawled shaky lines; his friends at table observed it and smilingly teased him,

'Dénes, here come your orders! How long does your pass last? You'll be kneeling on maize tomorrow!'

He would still be seething with rage about this when he came home drunk at dawn, though now everything was confused in his brain; but at that time he would still pace raging through the three rooms with heavy reverberating steps, reeking of wine, while I with dry eyes that had not slept a wink since the night before pretended to be fast asleep, but I still restrained myself, though with panting nostrils and nerves strained to the utmost; then in one unbearable moment everything suddenly exploded from me.

'You scoundrel! You drunken rascal! What are you doing here? Why don't you go to your den? It's hateful even to see you and it's disgusting to be near you!'

'How finicky you are! Heigh ho! what hoity-toity speech! The only thing that surprises me is that for seven years you've been eating the bread of such a rascal and sucking the sweat of his brow... snake! You suck away at his life like a leech that I can't shake off... like gout from which there's no escape, the plague...'

'Oh God!... God smite your wicked soul! How dare you throw all that at me? Anywhere else they'd pay me a salary and treat me with respect if I worked as hard as I do here...'

'Is it for me you're working? A curse on your every step! We've seen how far you got 'anywhere else'... that's why you resigned yourself to me, why you imposed yourself on me, you wicked witch! That was all I was good for. Why don't you get out of here if you despise me so much? The Pórtelky ancestors are turning in their graves when they see their precious grandchild thrown on the charity of a poor humble townsman like me. We've seen that you haven't been able to earn a penny for yourself. Parasites might at least have the decency to keep out of the way.'

'Pah! Aren't you ashamed of yourself? Tell me! Aren't your eyes burning? In front of your innocent children too! So where am I to take them? Could I leave them here—with a beast of a man like you? To be brought up by the folk from whom you've just come? Disgusting!'

'Even so they'll be in better hands than yours, unfortunate little things! Who knows who was father to which of them? The world... the whole world!'

'Shut up now... for the last time!' I screamed, choking; I leapt up and made for him with clawed fingers. 'You... yes... if you'd taken me! Of course you wanted it... for nothing... that's how you'd have liked it... there's no one else... as villainous!'

In a fit of mad rage I rushed at him; he grabbed a chair to protect himself or else to strike me... he lost his balance and crashed down half on the carpet.

'Dad... Daddy, come along... I'll take you... to a nice little warm bed, just come along!'

Little Marcsi was standing beside him shivering in her little white night-dress; she bent over him with a prematurely aged, serious maternal expression on her little face and struggled to pull his paralysed hand from under him as he had fallen on it. The two little ones were trembling and crying now as they knelt on my bed. He half scrambled up, kissed the child and caressed her with the maudlin affection of a drunkard; then he took her by the hand and staggered into his room; when with her tiny, clever hands she helped him to undress he called her his dear little fairy. Then, when quiet was restored, she, too, crept into my bed, shivering and whimpering.

'Mummy dear! If only you could stop yourself from speaking! Pretend to be asleep—that's what grandma Klári said, too, isn't it? Then he'd put himself to bed, poor man.'

How marvellously sensible, good and pure-hearted these poor little creatures were able to remain in this terrible period of life! Who taught them that strange, simple childish wisdom that made them see both of us as somehow sick at times like this and isolate such scenes from the normal course of life like some reoccurring bad dream? And made them love both of us equally! Sometimes their father did not bother with them for weeks; it was as if they did not exist. Then in a good half-hour he took them out and showed them off and bought a pile of unnecessary toys and things for them. They brought them home, and next day we went to the shop and exchanged them for little pinafores and stockings... In an occasional neurotic spasm

I would suddenly punish them or even beat them for minor misdemeanours; they took this as an act of God and avoided me if they could, or else resigned themselves to it.

But they sensed that I was clinging to them with my last drop of blood, that I was working for them with stubborn and persistent strength of will and I was the only person who cared for them and on whom they could always count. On days following nights like this and among each other or at school, they were healthy, merry, noisy real children who simply brushed us aside. Yes, they inherited a little of their father's recklessness too, but this was a very fortunate mixture in them. They were certainly healthy, sensible and resourceful. It was they who were the success of our life together! My God! So this was what nature or life or whatever needed the two of us for! It was these children that destiny had in mind for us, and it was for them that we had to suffer together for!

We were badly shattered. Certainly he was too, poor man. Now after much thought on the subject I can sense the justice of his side too. He always felt he was in some tight corner, some involuntary trap. He saw the heavy chains of life tangling themselves around him and the bonds tightened ever more closely; he was incapable of doing anything against them, but he looked for a scapegoat and I was there. Yes, after all, when he was a bachelor he managed to live well, easily and pleasantly despite all his debts; and such ugly, rude crudities and commonplaces only surfaced, I think, at the time of his marriage from the forgotten recesses of his nature. He felt that it was I who had made him bad; I had coarsened and ensnared his life; I was sucking his blood, the sweat of his reluctant toil. After all poverty was the main trouble, that was certain!

Things got more and more difficult. Everything became more and more expensive. As the children grew up, they needed more and more. Some new lawyers came into the town; they were fresh, doctors of law and forceful too, though the profession no longer poured out money as of old. The inheritance cases on the marshes were gradually settled and the affair of the drainage was close to conclusion. Now the whole business was in the hands of Imre Scherer, the younger count's favourite, and it must be admitted that he was dealing with it skilfully, cunningly, and swiftly. Those living along the Szinyér valley obtained privileges and most awkward problems were neatly smoothed over. Only the aggrieved peasants remained dissatisfied, but they no longer engaged lawyers to regain the two or three hundred forints of which they had been defrauded; instead they emigrated to America in ever-increasing numbers, leaving not a trace behind. So in this way lawyers were having a difficult time.

Dénes sometimes dealt with nothing but tiny little cases for months on end; or my Uncle István, the public notary would give him the occasional formal appearance which brought in a few forints. But for us at home there was sometimes nothing to live on, and we were afraid of the grocer and the butcher where we had run up bills; and the saucy maid retorted if I dressed her down, 'You'd do better to pay my wages!' But if a rather more profitable case cropped up from somewhere and I got wind of it, I hurried to entice money from Dénes—by extortion, theft or getting the children to beg for it, and as much as possible, for clothes, shoes, varnish for the floors, cheap and tawdry but showy decorations for the rooms (God forgive me!), flowers, coloured peasant embroidery; for I clung tenaciously (and still do, to this very day) to this poor but nice little reckless touch of beauty in life, to clean, fresh-smelling attractive rooms, a table pedantically laid with a fine white cloth, with nickel-silver forks burnished silver and spotlessly clean glasses. And after all, this was what still bound Dénes to his home, this welcome orderliness to which he was accustomed at my side, whether he liked it or not, the fresh bed linen, the dignified service at the table, his pipe-rack kept in order and the paper-lined spittoon replenished daily with fresh sand... and the good cuisine, my ample and excellent cooking, however desperately I fought for it and got hold of it. I knew this, too, and had no qualms about picking up and spending his money, if there was any. 'He'd only put it to worse use anyway!' Who could have imagined any economizing or putting money aside in our home? We were glad if no bailiff came along, if we did not pay legal expenses too when (always at the last minute) he managed to conjure up a little money from somewhere and once more there was a week of peace, a lull in the storm. I did not know how much he earned, to whom he owed money and how much, or how much money he hid from me in order to fritter it away... how could I have taken his side firmly in matters like these?

So it was almost a foregone conclusion that once I went the

rounds begging and canvassing for him. By that time everything was going very badly indeed and I believed that somehow it would soon be all over and the problem solved; things could not stay as they were, and we could not drag things out like this for a whole lifetime. My whole long married life with Dénes was characterized by some passing emotion like this. By that time people tended to take my side; they pitied me for all my sufferings and the cruel struggle, and praised me because in spite of everything I was able to provide proper education and clothing for the children and keep a decent household and everything, all by my strong and tenacious willpower. It seemed as if the world now felt that I had done enough penance. And others, strangers, were struck by the thought that an election was in the offing and there was a vacancy for a deputy notary; that unfortunate man ought to be put in! Then at least he would have a little regular income. And his friends from the countryside, whom for ten years he had helped to go pleasantly to ruin with their carousing, whom he had often reduced to tears with the violin in his damaged, fumbling hand, who for some time now had sat down pityingly and ill at ease to play cards with him and were afraid to win his last forint—these friends now tried to help him all the same. He was elected by acclamation that was fine, moving and unanimous—just like paying respect at a funeral. Poor man! He was able to remain amiable, pleasant and easy-going with everyone even at the time of his impoverishment and decline; only to his family was he bad, and it was only his family that he took with him down to the depths. He simply was not cut out for it.

I took the news to my mother. Well, after all I had become a county lady, poor me! The irony of life!... I was reminded of another election, of old dreams and hopes... oh well, that held no meaning for me now. The town was almost a foreign place to me, it was so long since I had been out of the house... After the fire new streets and shops had been built; there was the row of old houses that had survived intact with their ancient twisted acacia trees—why, there was the one where my late husband and I had last lived! How those trees had grown! It was he who had planted them in front of the woodshed. I went slowly past the gateway with its trellis. There is the foot of the Castle Garden; behind the iron railings the dense mass of the huge old trees, the peace of the woods, that monotonous, unchanging, distinguished and isolated calm that remains untouched by life! How much has happened to me, how much have I changed since I walked here so long ago on Dénes's arm, my intentions verging on illusion, cherishing hopes of a great love! And the little gardens along the Cifrasor with their coloured glass globes are all the same, the Permit Office and the Water Tower, and over there across the green bank of the ditch the cemetery where poor Vodicska's grave has begun to cave in and the marble cross with its gold lettering 'In memoriam: his disconsolate father' is tilting.

How much there is that has not changed, that was once part of my life, on which I looked long ago with different eyes! Ah well, it's all the same now; it would all have passed away anyway! Now the only task is to bring up Marcsa, Zsuzsi and Klári so that they do not continue on the downhill path, so that my offspring at least may stand on their own feet and strive for their place in the world!

'Permission has been given now for girls to attend grammar-school too. That's what I want for them whatever happens, if I live to see the day! Let them go and be doctors or teachers! Let them have the same chances as men!'

Péter Telekdy gazed at me from his sickbed with a sour smile on his yellow, wizened face.

'That's madness! The mania of the ignorant, with no basis in fact. The woman will always remain inferior; things can't be otherwise. After all, two thirds of their life-span are occupied with unconscious animal cares and duties that go with the maintenance of humankind, and instincts guide their intellect. If they liberate themselves from these, they become wayward, mongrel figures who can't find their own place; they're clumsy and unhappy. The woman is a blind tool in the purposes of nature; she has not reached the stage of self-awareness, she is still finding her roots, a being with the life of a plant, whose whole value is involuntarily charm and beauty, the beauty of flowers and the silent, undemanding, expectant productivity of seeds. All the philosophers, Plato, Spinoza, Kant, Schopenhauer and Nietzsche agree. Only the sick culture of today struggles to play with the idea that women should be taken seriously.'

This was how he spoke now, and it obviously did not occur

to him how different his creed had been some time before. Poor dreamer! He had been in bed now for two years, surrounded by a plethora of books, his sick face yellow and puffy, his sores ugly and suppurating. He had picked up this illness in the course of his mania for health: at that time he was addicted to hydropathy as taught be Kneipp,[*] he did physical exercise and drank infusions of blood-purifying herbs and fresh milk straight from the cow, even when he was on official duty for the land-registration office, as he passed through villages. And the scores of illness which germinated with virulent destructive force in his poor, decayed, degenerate, wrecked and hybrid-blooded body are discovered in human organisms only once in a hundred years by doctors. It is a cattle-disease, and it reached him through the untreated milk.

My mother attended his needs quietly, with a kind of indifferent, cheerful patience. She became accustomed to having him there in bed, and he gave her little trouble. They just subsisted peacefully on a pension, an annuity and debts. He read and read and would launch into explanations to mama, who nodded off in the meantime; then, always inclined to quackery and with the born instinct of a wise-woman, she bandaged, cleaned and doctored the suppurating sores, or with intense delight cooked old Hungarian food mixtures for him, or light dainty delicacies with a hundred flavours that he would dictate to her from recipes in crazy old French cookery books.

'Let him have his pleasures, poor soul; after all, it's only his tongue that desires them; he can't digest them any more, poor thing!'

... I often marvelled at my mother; neither her spirit nor her old humour had deserted her yet. She never took life too seriously. Yet how many catastrophes had assailed her! One of her sons is in the madhouse and knows nothing of her; the other one turns up sometimes, but there is no joy in that. Csaba is totally dissolute. Sometimes he goes the round of the villages begging along the highroads; sometimes he is discovered in a ditch in a delirious sleep and half-frozen. Then they cure his ugly diseases in some hospital, bath him, and feed him, and at that stage some ambitious doctor or other, learning who and

* *Kneipp:* Sebastian Kneipp (1821–1897) was a hydropath whose aids to health included baths, cold-water compresses and walking barefoot in wet grass.

what he was, begins to experiment on him with his anti-alcohol cures and give him his old suits; for his good breeding and good handwriting they still keep him there, sometimes even employing him, encouraging and spoiling him. This goes on for a month or two, then the craving for drink suddenly seizes him and he escapes; he pours alcohol into himself in the sleaziest taverns, and they take his shirt and coat when he is no longer able to pay, then he turns up at home in a ragged overcoat covering his filthy naked body full of mites and dirt. Oh what a heavy burden this was on my spirit too! I was tortured, scared and tormented by a mixture of pity and detestation for him; in nightmarish dreams I sensed weeks in advance that he would suddenly appear here again and I should have to watch, feed and bear with him for a time until his wanderlust once again caught hold of him. Then he would weep and implore us; at other times he would boast and bitterly reproach everyone or else play stupidly and childishly with my little girls and eat like a horse. Once the rumour reached us that he was travelling with some Rumanian gypsy caravan and had married into the tribe; he had taken one of them called Dilina to be his wife.

'Bravo!' said my mother with a hearty laugh. 'If only my daughter-in-law would come and see me some time! I wouldn't begrudge her one or two coral necklaces and kerchiefs!'

My mother was able to talk about it like this; was she indifferent, or was it her easy temperament that helped her?

'My dear little girls, darlings! You just study! Whatever the cost, whatever happens! Don't do anything around the house; I'll do the cooking, sweeping and cleaning; my hands are worked to the bone and my body's neglected and gone to pieces anyway, so it doesn't matter. All you've got to do is to prepare yourselves for a better, triumphant and independent life, to be your own mistress, not to humble yourselves before any man, and not to be a washerwoman at anyone's mercy, or a dog to be kicked around by anyone! Just study everything, even if I have to give my last pillow for that cause!'

I gave an excellent poor student free board so that he could tutor them for grammar-school. Marcsi and Zsuzsi had already taken their examinations. Klári had inherited her father's instinct for music, so I got her an old, rattling, rickety piano on five-forint monthly instalments. And I did the work, now once again with a servant, panting and struggling till I dropped. But we ate well and copiously. Dénes demanded this and gave even more money for it as his stomach became increasingly important to him. He put on weight; he sat and smoked his pipe, and now he would drink wine even at home; sometimes his puffy face was almost blue, his eyes bloodshot, his mouth sagging. Often he went off to sleep in the armchair and this daughters undressed him and put him to bed.

'It's not worth while quarrelling with him now!' I sometimes thought then, and just left the unfortunate man alone. Sometimes we hardly exchanged a word for weeks.

XXIII.

After this, I measured the passage of time, the years and seasons only by the growth of my children: that now Marcsa's flared skirt was reaching down to the top of her shoes over her slender waist and lovely schoolgirl hips; that the young tutor blushed to the roots of his hair whenever Zsuzska's beautiful eyes rested on his face for a time with mischievous feigned attention; that twelve-year-old Klári sometimes sat at the piano with pale and drooping fingers and said, 'I'd love to play on one like Auntie Ágnes's girls. What a different tone it has, and how many expensive scores they've got! But they're tone-deaf!'

They grow and grow. Meanwhile who bothers about my greying hair, the dark creases in the sockets of my deep-set eyes and the deep lines around my lips? It's such a long time since I've expected of life anything that can give me a youthful appearance and preserve and care for my beauty; my own imperceptible ageing has gone unnoticed by everyone.

'But of course I now have a big grown-up son, a law-student in Pest!' I thought occasionally, surprised and somewhat confused. True, my son István, who was brought up by his grandparents, wrote from there to me two or three polite, amicable and informative letters each year, precisely for the new year, my name-day and after his examinations. Just as he did when he was a little boy, from the time when he was taught to write, and the letters of today were merely more advanced exercises in style than those, neither more spontaneous nor with any more human warmth. But could I expect anything more, and if so where from and why? For many years, old Vodicska, his grandfather had brought up his grandson and heir alone, surely with his own old man's stubborn prejudices. Could he have taught him to love me, his unknown mother? Would he not almost unintentionally have had to estrange him from me, whom he had always hated? I, too, sensed that this old man was the evil spirit in my life, and yet I had allowed him to take my child. I know I could not have done anything else at the time and it was better for the child too. His grandfather declared that he would care for him and leave him his fortune only if he could bring him up as he wished without any intervention from me, as a son in place of the son he had lost. So could I have stood in his way? Could I have brought him here by force, into this poverty, as a stepson with an uncertain future? 'Ah, but there's no bargaining, no arguing with the heart of a mother!' sentimentalists would say, their view of life picked up from mawkish books. Well, yes, now I dare to think right through what a whole life has taught me, its unvarnished, tangled, harsh and hard truths. Yes, motherhood is not just instinct; after all, we are not entirely animals. It is partly a social sense too, determination and duty; and then a lot depends on the character of the child too—after all, we enter into marriage with a stranger, and our child is his blood, his being, his heritage too… Oh one occasion, on the death of my poor mother-in-law Mrs. Vodicska (they passed through on their way to Pest where she was to have an operation), they left the little boy in my charge, and his visit here then lasted about ten days. He must have been twelve years old… and the girls were still quite small. I remember how searchingly, how expectantly I looked into his changed, almost forgotten childish face then, how I sought and pursued in myself that painful, great tragic maternal affection—but it was only with astonishment and cool respect that I watched the proper and somehow always deliberately well-intentioned activities of the formal little stranger, the trained model child; though I struggled against it in vain, this reminded me of my old instinctive and enthralled antipathy, my unworthy, bad but natural aversion at certain times to his poor father… Yes, yes, he resembled his father, but most of all his grandfather. I wept again when I said goodbye to him; I was weeping for my own illusion of love towards him, something that distance had left intact till now. But in my soul I almost breathed a sigh of relief when once more I was left alone with *my own children*, the girls, to whom I had come of my own volition, not by chance, as an adult, a wife, at an age when I had matured into a mother with a long-suffering spirit and a resigned body; which for me gave life its content, duty and respect; they were a link with my destiny, even at that time, and later too, all the way through. They grew up… and it was at my side that they grew up; my care, my labour, my will all went into them, and they were my own pride and my own success.

When they grew into their teens, once again I had to summon up all my energies and calculating good sense in order to settle

217

their future. For their father declined rapidly; day by day he became more of a nobody. Worn out and weakened by a tumultuous past, his mind was failing too; he was a pitiful, tottering old man. We went around side by side in obstinate and silent hatred; the stifled rage of contempt sometimes surfaced in the occasional word we hissed at each other. But we ate at the same table and our children surrounded us with simple, happy and forgiving affection.

The office, of course, was a sinecure to him; after all, nobody had expected anything else of him. He tottered off around noon as far as the County Hall and exchanged a word or two with the gentry there; sometimes he dictated something perfunctorily to Mr. Kricsák the old clerk, who knew the job better than he did anyway and quietly, patiently and precisely did the work in his place. By that time Mr. Kricsák had married the noblewoman Zsuzsanna Képíró, my one-time cook. For years he had lived with that fine woman; she had washed and cooked for him; so now in his old age he rewarded her for her fidelity and made her a lady of quality. And Zsuzsi sometimes came to visit me as in the old days when she was a daily help, to pay her respects and humbly exchange a few words. But the way she related her life with her husband really turned it into a good dressing-down.

'So, begging your pardon, I always take the whole of the fifty forints on the first of the month. Apart from deductions I leave him with two forints fifty to spend: that leaves forty-six. Out of that I immediately put aside fifteen for the quarter's rent: that leaves thirty-one...' Zsuzsanna Képíró stroked her gleaming flat cheeks from top to bottom with her chubby hands, then sniffed and sent a priggish, insinuating, proud glance in my direction. 'But we don't owe anyone a single penny; God grant we never do, I'd die of shame! Since I've been with him, two hundred forints have gone into the Savings Bank!'

'Well I never!' I thought with a wry smile. 'With the best will in the world I couldn't economize like that; Dénes's salary is tied up for decades to the permitted limit. The moment he had a small secure income, his creditors all fell on it.'

That was how we were. And the girls could not stay at home and study much longer; they had to continue in Pest. Where was I to lay hands on some money for board and expensive tuition? My God!... Then I settled down to the kind of work my whole being protested against: I wrote begging letters to Jolsvay, the former high sheriff who by then was a notability up there and expected to be appointed a minister, to my uncle Hiripy's son who was a councillor, and to one or two other distant relatives; I had made enquiries about all of them and sought out what they had become, what their connections were, who were their relatives and what families they had married into, who depended on them or were indebted to them. And with painful humility I reminded them of my existence, laid bare my situation and lamented my lot in heart-rending terms. I read them through two or three times: were they sufficiently respectful, modest and yet self-assured? What a big task it was! How many times did I tear them up and begin again! As far as Klári was concerned, I wrote to Terényi, the old violinist with whom Dénes once roved around abroad. Now he was director-in-chief of the Academy of Music.

Then someone told me that the other two could get scholarships if the old Countess Szinyéry would write a couple of lines commending them to the minister. All right. I did it. I went to see the dowager countess.

The gate into the park opened before me and for the second time in my life I passed through the dense woods of great beech trees and the dark green hosts of stiff grave pines. The silence of woodlands was here and the many gold-coloured dry leaves rustled and crackled under my feet; the sad autumn sunlight rested motionless and languid on the surface of the white roads. It was about twenty-five years earlier that I had walked here when poor Jenő brought me on a reluctant introductory visit. How difficult it is to plead, complain and humble oneself! What a bitter cup! The estate officials would all know that I was going there to beg from their mistress!

She came to meet me; she smiled gently as old people do and kept nodding her trembling, white-haired head towards me. She said she expected me and was delighted to get my letter asking for an audience with her. She sat me beside her on the little sofa with gilded legs, and I noticed the discreet perfume of her pale grey silks. She placed her little manicured hand in my own roughened palm.

'What a long time since I've seen you! How are you? What's your dear husband doing? Oh, my son Lajos is very fond of him; he has a high regard for his services. Or... oh yes! Do forgive me! Yes, it's your second husband. Poverty... of course, of course!

You mustn't take offence. Sometimes I get things and names muddled. I'm eighty years old—just imagine it! That's a lot, isn't it? Yes, you're right, the children, they're the only ones who are important for us now! For us?... Don't say that! For someone still as young as you, my dear! But later on they too go way, they go far away from our heart! And then there's only religion left; we can put our trust in heaven. Do you go to church? You see, they no longer give to us old folk anything of what was beautiful, but church still remains and it's so lovely! The new little chaplain at the Piarist College, he's really got a silver tongue, hasn't he? I always go to him for confession; he's the only one I can confess to now!... The letter... Oh, of course, I'll write it myself this very day in your interest. And what's the name of your new husband? Horváth? He's of noble birth, isn't he?'

I felt relaxed and touched as I strolled towards the big wrought-iron gate; the footman shadowed me in silence as far as the gardener's house in case I lost my way among the winding paths among the trees on whose rich foliage and huge girth, or snow-covered, frost-decked tops I had gazed so many, many days of my life from outside the railings. How gentle, tender, generous-hearted these great aristocrats are able to remain a whole life through! With their charity they ask God's pardon for their great wealth and for never being touched by the rough, mean, common miseries of life. But, I wonder, can these people comprehend earthly life and people?...

I went towards my mother's. Poor Péter Telekdy had been very close to death for weeks now. 'Jakobi says it can only be a matter of a couple of days!' whispered my mother on the veranda. She was not weeping. She came and went softly, with quiet apathetic sadness, in the mellow autumn afternoon; she made coffee and we drank it under the mulberry tree. The withered leaves fell slowly on to the tablecloth before us.

'Let's go in for a little and see him, poor soul,' she said and shook the crumbs from her apron.

The weak, reddish evening light fell slantwise across the sick-bed; the pale autumnal rays did not dance on the white pillow, but motionlessly garlanded his shrunken shoulders in the limp night-shirt and his skeletal old head, which seemed to be only the size of a fist. His shaven face was yellow and still and his knees were drawn up tightly so that the worn eiderdown sketched a conical hill over them. He lay there on his back in a heap, gentle and innocent as a poor little child. He had lain there like that for almost four years.

We sat quietly at the window, thinking that he was asleep. I learnt from my mother that he had been silent like this for days; before that he had remarked on everything, made arrangements and frequently repeated his last wishes. That he wanted a wooden coffin, so that his body might be taken over all the more quickly by peaceful decay, by the earth; but all the same he desired the Calvinist minister from Telekd, his old classmate and companion in foreign universities, to give the funeral oration. And there were to be no wreaths or flowers on his grave, and they were not to erect a marble headstone on it; and they were certainly not to take him home to the family crypt. He seemed to derive some pleasure in making these arrangements; nothing else in the world really interested him now. For four years he had gazed at the same decorations on the ceiling, and in the meantime he had read and experienced the whole of philosophy and every great human thought.

Suddenly he stretched out his waxen white hand; we saw it fluttering hesitantly like a ghostly bird in the gloom, searching over the little smoker's table. Mama quietly went over to him, lit a cigarette, put it in his hand and sat down at the head of the bed in silence. I saw the intermittent little glow struggle and smoulder into light in the ever denser twilight…

'Have one yourself, dearest,' I heard him whisper in a sad, soft and submissively gentle groan.

Now the two of them were smoking, but I could see that my mother was only pretending, and she watched the sick-bed intently. The pillow and sheet stood out in dreamy soft whiteness, like a strange cloud, in the evening light of the room. And there was deep silence.

Then my mother suddenly stood up, walked over to him and stroked his face and eyes gently and softly with her hand. She stayed like that for some moments, then turned round and slowly came to me in the window. 'He's cold already,' she said in a whisper and bowed her head, and I could see that tears had long been trickling from her eyes. In her drooping hand she held the half-smoked cigarette that she had taken out of his stiffening fingers. With very great care and attention she put it into a little drawer in the desk to preserve it as a sad treasured relic all her life through.

He was buried in accordance with his wishes; many of his acquaintances from the town escorted him and quiet tears fell at the graveside. After all, we had all long ago become used to the idea that Péter Telekdy did not exist. He was no longer young, and his former colleagues in the office had forgotten him since he had retired; and as for mama, everyone knew that her small yearly income would protect her from starving to death. They praised her fidelity and patience, and sincerely wished her a little undisturbed rest and relief at last.

'That's the way our turn comes!' muttered Dénes to himself that evening, filling his pipe with trembling fingers. 'A lot have passed on already. They're in peace there now! It's no use… one's just got to wait in peace for it; it will come as it is predestined!'…

But he still puffed away cheerfully at his pipe and enjoyed the pleasant table wines, clicking his tongue; when as the result of the expenses of some small case or a permit to sell liquor he gained access to a small barrel or two, he would settle to it in a festive mood, raising his glass to the lamp to keep looking through its golden colour, and sometimes I watched in astonishment as he devoured portions of roast and noodles for dinner with great gusto.

'That wolfish appetite's an unhealthy sign!' I thought, glancing at his reddish-blue face and swollen, thick neck… If weeks of penury came again, so that he could scarcely give me anything for food, he would suddenly not come home in the evening and stay out again. 'I wonder who he's sponging on; after all, he hasn't got a farthing!' I thought wearily.

And on the morning following one such day I suddenly heard the sound of a gypsy band outside our front door. 'Oh, God strike him dead! Whatever now!' I burst out angrily, and started up post-haste to chase it away. It was a bright morning and the maid had already gone out to get meat on credit. I was dressed for cleaning, with a tattered canvas apron and a dusty grey kerchief tied round my head. 'Mummy, don't go out like that!' Marcsi called back from the window as she peered out.

But I had not heard what she had said. As I stepped outside

the younger Bankó struck up my own tune of years ago, 'See, the vine-leaves' veins are blue…,' the tune I had made his father play for me in the days long gone.

'Many happy returns of the day!' one of the accompanying players shouted through the tune as he ornamented it. Lord Almighty! whoever would have remembered that today was my name-day? Had Dénes gone completely mad?…

'Since a man I've grown to be…,' sang a pleasant hoarse male voice behind them, a voice that was vaguely familiar. Leaning sideways against the door-post beside my husband stood Endre Tabódy.

It must have been at least ten years since I had last seen him, and then only in passing, on the day of a county assembly or driving past me in the street, crouched in his little yellow carriage; since then maybe I had not met him face to face for, oh, who knows how long? Now he raised his eyes to me, bloodshot and tipsy with drink, then reached for my hand and kissed it (oh dear! my palm is rough and my nails neglected!), and in his wine-sodden, hoarse, delightful voice he sang that old, old song of mine, But since a man I've grown to be, Women I love eternally!

How many wrinkles there are in his brown face, how many furrows! How stubbly and bristly is his chin! And there are gaps in his teeth…

All three girls suddenly appeared outside, surrounding them and inviting them into the house. The band followed them. Aha, this affair caught the fancy of my three naughty little maidens! Songs, music, mother's old flame all made for a good time! Marcsi laid a table under the two acacias in front of the veranda. And whatever was Zsuzsi up to? She sent the girl off in a hurry for wine and I saw that for money she slipped something screwed up in paper into the shopping basket. Why, wasn't that her little ring with the blue stone that she was sending over to the pawnbroker?… Klári was inclined to put on airs about gypsy music, saying that she couldn't stand it, but now she too fell under its spell; she made black coffee on the open stove for the men who had been drinking. I ran in to put on something decent to wear and discovered a little stock of rice-powder remaining in the bottom of a box in the mirror drawer.

By the time I emerged they were drinking beneath the

yellowing acacias in the fresh autumnal morning. The girls were sitting among them too, and I held out my glass to Dénes for him to fill, then I touched my glass against Tabódy's.

'Oh my lady, my lady!' he kept saying with tipsy melancholy, looking sadly and enthusiastically into my eyes, resting his face on his two fists. 'Is this really true, tell me! Is it really we are facing each other here like this?'

'Or perhaps it wasn't true, Endre, that we ever saw each other. Or at least never like this, by such… bright morning light.'

'See here… there's something in what you say. Hm, Magda. It's very odd. Yet perhaps this would have been the real thing.'

'Heaven forbid!'

'Who can tell, Magda?'

Dénes stretched over for the wine bottle and poured some out with an unsteady hand, missing Endre's glass. 'Ah well, just let the young folk laugh at us… isn't that so, Marcsi, Zsuzska? Don't bother your mother just now!' And an ingratiating, pleasant, cunning smile spread over his red shining face.

'All the same, it's easy for you, old chap!' the guest called over to him. 'After all, we've all grown old and that's the truth, but here you are sitting with your three lovely good children. I had no such luck, you see. In the two years since my poor wife passed away, I've been living, I swear, like an animal in the wild. What abundance there is here! What an attractive homely household!… Ah, in this you're the same as ever you were, Magda! Everything around you is beautiful, clean and attractive; the yard, the garden and the veranda. And look at the way those rubbishy hunting trophies are arranged above the veranda door on the wall and how this tub of oleanders is painted green and this garden seat red. Even the flowers bloom more beautifully here than elsewhere!… Oh, what a woman! There's nobody to match her, isn't that so, old chap? Why, if you can't even appreciate this, if you've got even a single word to say against her…'

'Come, come! After all, we're managing, that's all, through thick and thin,' Dénes nodded and at that moment probably felt so too.

'It's with a wife like this that you've spent the best of your life!' Endre worked himself up into a fit of sorrowful enthusiasm, elated by inebriation. 'And three such lovely creatures, my God! Why, even the smallest is as big as her mother already! But this one, the middle one, is most like her mother… with her white gypsy face. Well, for goodness' sake! Come on now, drink up, Dini.'

Klári brought out a warm blanket to put over her father's gouty knee. 'It'd be a good idea to pull that cloak closer round your shoulders, Endre. It's a chilly morning now,' I said quietly, and I too tied my knitted head-scarf more tightly. Then we had a good look at each other, nodding our heads in peace and quiet like folk who share a single thought and understand everything now… and after all, there's no point in moping over anything.

Once upon a time, I mused to myself, we thought about old age as we parted. That things should just stay as they were, so that memory might one day be our treasure-trove and that we might be able to think back happily over it all at some time in the future. Well now… here was the memory, here was the fine moment; we were looking at each other with the old eyes from these two furrowed faces. And, well… there was nothing! Was it worthwhile for this, I wonder?…

The gypsies had feasted well on cabbage soup and plied themselves with hot coffee, and they set to work again with renewed energy. Tabódy struck up the tune with them, and his voice, the old, hoarse, vibrant warm male voice, suddenly rent my soul asunder with some dear, tearful emotion from the past, something that had existed only once, all the same… For a minute I buried my face in both hands and just listened, as I had once upon a time at a ball, after a wild, rose-tinted night full of dancing.

'See, the vine-leaf's veins are blue,
Fair women have fair daughters too!'
Hey, Zsuzsika! Lovely cherry blossom, little bud, miracle, all that smells lovely! Turn your beautiful little witch's eyes this way! Yes, like that! Don't begrudge them to an old man!'

I raised my head and laughed out loud. Oh, the old fool!

'Why are you laughing at me, madam? Do you think it's not you I'm making love to when I surround this lovely young offspring of yours with such prayers of devotion from the litany? I shan't do her any harm, never fear! It's your two spellbinding eyes that gaze out of that rosy face; they reflect you… no, it's their ancestral grandmother's look, her dazzling charm, her embrace, her protestations, her allure, her cruelty—all these things flash out from those two witch's mirrors. Those eyes are like some deep, deep well that goes down to the centre of the earth…'

'Well, just go on looking at him, Zsuzsa my love, let him go on talking! He'll strike up a tune; we deserve one, for sure!'

'Magda, how time's passed! We've been driven apart. Or was it just by chance... and why?... It seems as if we didn't think *that* to be very important. And you know'—don't laugh!—that's not the chief thing either, Magda. Look, it often happened, when I wasn't thinking about it, that I closed my eyes and without any warning I saw your two eyes all alive. Or not even that... but if the words 'wife, woman' came into my mind, they invariably meant you, even unconsciously. Compared with that, what does it matter that it wasn't with you that I've lived for the last twenty-five years? Life, a single life, isn't such a great thing; but somewhere, once or several times, we must have been very much together. All the embraces of your grandmothers bewitch me in the two eyes of your daughter.'

'This is all very poetic, Endre! But you do well to say so. It's beautiful! It's good! Life really isn't a very big thing, for it has the same end. However our affair might have turned out, growing old scarcely comes much better. God forbid that we should have lived together! But what people can say to one another like this, you see,—I know it's the most of all. The greatest human gift: words, words!'

I stood up to get on with the housework, and I longed for the pleasant warmth of the kitchen stove, for the morning was chilly outside, the grass was damp and my shoes needed soling. The sound of the quick movement of a great wild csárdás filled the air when I went out again. The sun was shining too, and the air was warm. The two former student-tutors had appeared from somewhere too; they were now young teachers in training in Pest, and the young folk were dancing, treading the frost-speckled grass in the garden beneath their feet. I saw normal busy folk passing in the street on their way to the office or market; they stared through the palings and shook their heads. The local paper was always carrying notices of some bailiffs' auction because we had defaulted; my Uncle István would buy our little bits and pieces in theory and keep claiming them back, and the shop-keeper told everyone that we were in debt.

'Never mind, Dini! What was it the woman from Kaba said? Drink! Look, I'm drinking too! Put it in your pocket, Bankó! What are you looking at? Your father tucked bigger bank notes than that in his pocket! Eh, who knows how long?... They say, Magda, that your mother put a curse on Telekd when they left it; she cursed it saying that never would an owner of the estate remain there until he died, that all of them would go bankrupt. Well, if that's true, the curse will soon be fulfilled in me; I'm on my last legs. But why bother? You'll bring me in here to do something at the County Hall. There's no one to worry about. Let's drink, devil take it!'

I stood up once more to go inside. Yes, I was afraid that he might possibly wreck this lovely, peaceful mourning mood of mine by something that he said. 'But then if they begin to talk filth, just come inside!' I warned Marcsi, the most responsible of the girls.

There followed a heavy overcast afternoon. The girls went back to their books with drooping spirits. Dénes lay on the divan in the dining room, his face swollen, and his mouth wide open and wet, snoring deeply.

I was in such an extraordinary mood that I just went to and fro tidying up; I picked up things to darn and dropped them again, as if something else ought to be in store for me that day. And since noon I had not picked a quarrel with anyone, not even the maid. Whatever was the matter with me, silly old fool that I was!

A dense grey nightfall came early, and the little room with the brown rep suite, the cheap vases and woven tablecloths relapsed into a deep blank shadow; for a good while I had not been able to see to sew. All of a sudden I got up and went over to the piano. Poor old instrument, it bared its row of yellow teeth at me. And fearfully, furtively, bashfully I ran my work-stiffened, unhabituated, rough fingers over the keys. How hard it was! I had not played for years. But all the same something would come of it; yes, something was coming to mind. It was a well-known aria, a strange, wistful Polish dance that I had played at one time. When, I wondered? Oh, I remember now, Dénes Horváth brought me this score when he first began to come to our house, and it was he who taught me to play it properly. At the time I studied it with enthusiasm; I wanted to please him with it. And lo and behold! I can still play it!... (Semi-consciously I heard him shuffle slowly into the room; had he gone out, or was he sitting on the divan behind me?) Just listen! I still know the little Polish song: that's a wrong note, and that's another one: now that's the right one! It's refined, soft and

227

pleasing like the gentle warmth of a stove, as if some quivering old musical clock were chirruping with playful, sad, grand-motherly charm a minuet danced by powdered wigs and silk-rosetted ankles; oh, once upon a time I saw a picture like this in the cotillion rosettes in grandma's old cupboard... Tralala!

Once I looked back. He was indeed sitting behind me on the divan in the corner; he was holding his handkerchief to his eyes and weeping softly but convulsively...

Oh my God! He's weeping...

What's the matter with him: Why, can he still *feel* such things—or anything—, the misery of his life? Or is it only alcohol, old age and decrepitude that fill his eyes with tears?... Poor man!... Perhaps now would be the time for me to go to him and stroke his head and hands... Yes, that's it! So that tomorrow, or even still today, we may rake up our show of emotion and mention it to each other with devastating, cruel irony!... No, now we can't grow any closer through *words*. We have felt this lovely, crazy moment; we have been in it together, and we shut it up and isolate it; and tomorrow or even today, we shall still go on quarrelling... And what would our children say if by some miracle we were now to try to reach some understanding? We had gotten used to things as they are; now there is no way out.

Two poor unfortunate souls that we are!

XXIV.

Suddenly, all that might have served as a bridge, a balance, a direction, the excuse for our life together and its meaning disappeared from us, that which for decades we had thought was the only thing that kept us together. All three children left home. But by that time it mattered so little to either of us that we might just as well stay together. Before that we had often lashed out with, 'All right then, divorce me!' 'Very well, just go!' But now there was no question of this, and in general we exchanged very few words anyway. But all the bad things we had become accustomed to became part of our nature; we could not even imagine ourselves having a different life.

In any case, Dénes was no longer a person with whom it would have been worthwhile talking about serious matters. He visibly went downhill from day to day. Now he often sat with his eyes in a glassy stare and the stem of his pipe fell from the lips he had left open. Since I saw him every day, I did not really observe this rapid deterioration, but when others, strangers, came, they were shocked and shook their heads, saying, 'Hm, he's not going to last much longer!'

'The spring of life is growing slack, the machine's stuttering, stopping and starting and getting irregular,' explained old Jakobi thoughtfully; the dear little old doctor who was now white-headed, but still spoke reassuringly. He was not really practising now, but simply went on his rounds and theorized about illnesses.

Meanwhile, I looked at this human wreck in front of me and was overwhelmed by a nagging worry that had long occupied my mind—a worry about my own life, yes, and—maybe this is ludicrous—my future. To become a widow once again, to start all over again the old, unsuccessful chase for life of such bitter memory, all for myself and my daily bread? No, a pang of real terror shot through me at this; it became an obsession, a permanent, nerve-racking, all-compelling subject for my mind. Almost twenty years separated me now from that time; since then, making ends meet had simply become more difficult, while becoming ever more tired and worn-out. What could I do? It was a long time before the children could stand on their own feet, even if they were provided with passable free places and scholarships; but later on—to have to depend on them;... Or on relations; had the famous old solidarity in our family so fallen apart and crumbled away (or is it the same with every family, and a product of the age?), that now I could not count on a few months' hospitality anywhere?

Shortly after Telekdy's death, my mother moved to Pest. My Uncle István and his family had already gone up there earlier to retire; they left without fuss and sold Bere here beforehand. Well, it's true that all the children can be brought up there better and at less cost, and Ágnes may have been attracted by Melanie too, whom she surrounded not with friendship but with fervent devotion. But to let Bere, that estate, slip from under their feet, that firm base for which poor grandma had struggled her whole life through with the sweat of her brow, hard work and cunning shrewdness! After all, they could not have had many debts, though at the same time they certainly lived in great style here, and the news spread right through the town that Ágnes had travelled with Melanie to Karlsbad and on the way, they had slept in a sleeping-car and eaten in the restaurant-car. Here in the home of plenty, with its tradition of abundance and well-being in which the family circle was nurtured, this form of luxury was unheard of... But it was out of the question for them not to have been able to maintain Bere if they had really wanted to.

'Believe me, I'm not sorry about it,' said Ágnes when she took her leave. 'I haven't a single happy memory from it. It just meant trouble and worry; turning out every spring with the whole rabble to go to the village with its stench of dung, stifling heat and dust, to vegetate in a mixture of frenzied work and rushing around. To spend a couple of weeks cleaning, decorating, putting things straight, bottling and drying fruit for the winter, and if there were guests, nothing but worry and bother, but if you weren't working the monotony was deadly and paralysing. While my poor mother-in-law was alive, I lived a life of continuous oppression; I had a child every year; later when my life was a bit more free, I too blossomed out a bit more, it's true: a little dressing-up, running around, flights of fancy—it came to me later than it did to you, Magda, but to every married woman there once comes a share of it. Well, after that I fell in love with town-life, indeed I did, with people and life all round me, and the whole of Bere, the summers out there and the idyll village, simply became a burden to me!'

That was all there was to it! And those feelings were shared by many others in our family too, I saw; I heard that the Hiripy children too divided the estate after their father's death; there was no longer anything that bound them to the patch of land where they had grown up, or for which their forefathers had sweated, cheated and gone to court, sometimes with a lifelong passion. All of them longed for the town, so up they went to Pest, to noisy streets, theatres, households free from work, and a life of idleness, cheapness and easy semi-starvation. Why, even mama, old as she was, cheerfully found a niche for herself there! In a letter she wrote to me, she told me about the wonderful and exciting life of the city.

'Believe me, this is the most wonderful place!' she wrote. 'The whole population of the country is gradually drawn to it, family by family. Those who win in the lottery come to spend their money in luxury, those who are reduced to begging come here to rough it, those who have embezzled or got themselves into trouble come here to hide. Anybody who wants to make a bit of money from their brains, beauty, roguery or any little knowledge you like, has got to come here. They make a living from making flowers, selling papers, writing verse, enticing men—you can't imagine what else! I'm doing quite well here, believe me, on my little annuity of forty forints a month—thank God for the wisdom of my poor mother, dust and ashes though she is! I rent a little room by the month from a family; it's very good (if only there weren't so many insects here, damn them!), and I'm hardly at home during the day. I spend the time with one relative or another; I'm only careful not to eat with any of them, believe me, because that's all taken into account here! We go from time to time and sit in the park and watch the carriages driving around—oh, there's so much to see here, a real feast for the eyes, while down there they still preoccupy themselves with their stomach. On Sundays we go to a coffee-house. No woman in the country would ever dream of daring to go there, as if to a casino, with her woman-friends for a cup of coffee; for thirty kreutzers you get a lot of whipped cream, fashion journals, electric light and good warmth, while three waiters hover around you, and through the glass window you can watch the street where there's always a crowd of people going to and fro and you don't see the same person twice. What interesting little romances you can observe here! And when you do see a familiar face from home, you're overjoyed and grateful and ask, "What are you doing up here, my dear?" "Why, we've been living here for six months now!"

'And there are always more and more. Oh yes, the other day in the very middle of the ring road, my way was barred by a lanky, grey-haired, ragged man with a sheaf of newspapers under his arm. He looked at me, gave a delighted roar of laughter and then recited this ditty:

> Klára Zimán, rose of gold,
> Now your shining face grows old;
> Gone the sparkle from your eye—
> All paid in tax to destiny.
>
> Yet, you know, through right or wrong,
> You're the subject of my song.
> Just for you, as you must see,
> A shepherd-dog I'd gladly be!

'Can you imagine who the old fool was? It was Jánoska, who was once Széchy's groom, the one who brought all those bouquets of camellias to me all of thirty-five years ago! The old chap's a newspaper-seller here and a socialist; he's also a folk-poet under the pen name of János Hazaffy. He earns his living here from making up such ditties; he wrote this one down for me on the spot and pressed it into my hand. I gave him one of my last remaining five forints, but in such a way that it looked as if I'd still got a lot more. Just imagine, he recognized me!...

'And what are you doing? How's Dénes getting on? Marcsi and Zsuzska came here yesterday; they say he's not at all well. See here! The important thing is that he's been at the County Hall for ten years, so they can pension him off if he's incapable of working now. Like my Péter. Except that if they do that the wife doesn't get anything after that, and unlike me you haven't got this little monthly income. What will you do then, my dear? Just pray that if God really wants to take him away, then rather... though to write something like this is a sin, but it's possible to explain it in prayer. Oh, wouldn't it be nice if you, too, could come up here some time! We could move into a nice flat together and we'd lead a merry life, two independent widows! And a woman deserves a bit of a break if, like us, she's served two husbands. Well, better luck, heaven be with you.

'Love, Mother.

'P. S. Look! Those seven sacks of rubbishy books that my poor husband Péter left behind, the ones I left with you in the attic, just give them to the Piarists for their library, will you? They mentioned two forints per sack; that's something too! The shop-keeper would only promise fifty kreutzers to use them for packaging. Love, Mother.'

Mama was like that. She was not bound to any place or thing by any very strong unbreakable bonds, so she easily and quickly found her place in each new situation. People everywhere soon came to love her for her humorous pleasant manner, her still good and genteel appearance and her expansiveness.

'Oh,' I thought to myself, 'I don't want to move anywhere from here, to begin a new life, to grow accustomed to things and accommodate myself to them... they're not for me any longer. I'm older than my own mother!... But what shall I do with what remains of my poor life, where shall I turn if this man lasts out half-dead like this until... My God! It's a sin, a great sin, to be terrified of that, but everything depends on it, after all. I wouldn't have the strength to bear the loneliness, the struggle with life, the subjection to others all over again. At least with Dénes I've been my own mistress even in poverty; in my house I alone have managed and ruled. He's never interfered in anything anyway, poor man. And now it's as if he's never existed; for over six months he's not been to the office, except very, very occasionally; he's sat in the armchair with his head drooping; even his pipe doesn't always give him pleasure, and he's not been particular about his food, but just eats bad, cheap meals fetched from a restaurant, devouring them greedily. We live on the sixty forints per month that was left of his salary after stoppages and pension contributions.'

But in the house there was silence such as there had never been before in our lives. No children, no servant, no quarrels. Here I preserved this living corpse; I busied myself around him, cooked, washed and cleaned for him, but with a new, gentle, nun-like resignation instead of the old, furious, tortured passion. A new vision began to fill the chaos and torment of my existence—religion, ethereal hope, a kind of utterly weary dependence on a higher providence that was gentle, forgiving and full of sympathy... Yes, even this came along!... My womanhood survived the years of crisis, my nerves calmed down too, and I sensed people's respect and sympathy; they visited and comforted me and this all affected me and moved me deeply. I had thought a good deal about my life and I began to see it as a whole, from a distance, with everything a little dulled and blurred. It was only then that the significance of a lot of things began to take shape within me. And then I saw this: so often it was not I myself who lived, regulated and acted; some outside, unpredictable, higher authority bore me along and a mysterious somebody always wanted and intended me to do something, but it was only afterwards that one realized this. Why call it chance, fate, universal order? 'God' is only a word too, but at least it always has the same meaning. And this is the important thing: can we still obtain a little illusion from something once other kinds of dreams, excitements and significances have deserted us? That death is simply a transition, a dream; life is not important, and when we think that everything is behind us, the future suddenly opens before us. Unknown, undefined, but beautiful, fabulous, refined and endless: the kingdom of heaven. To rise with a rejuvenated body, a soul that has done penance in suffering and is innocent, pure and perfect, to see again those we have loved, those we have offended, or did not understand, or those who tormented us; but only in unity, with sins absolved, in understanding and love; and from somewhere high up and far away to look down smiling, sad and forgivingly upon our past life and the vale of tears. For those of the Blessed Church who have arrived, holy tears glisten in their eyes at the recollection...

Yes, this was how Father Rozverits, the well-known young chaplain to the Piarist school, talked to me in his enthusiastic, quiet, meaningful tone in the course of several very peaceful, lovely evenings. This priest won over to the faith the whole of genteel society in the little town at that time. The women listened with longing hearts to his beautiful orations at high mass; since he was confessor to the patron, the Count and his family, it was elegant to receive him and be seen with him everywhere. He organized an altar guild and the old dowager countess, my benefactor, became its patroness; sometimes the Catholic women and girls in the town met there and embroidered altar-kneelers and pulpit-falls, and Rozverits read aloud or told them legends of Francis of Assisi, Catharine of Alexandria and Mary of Egypt who gave her young virgin body to seven ferry-men so that she might cross to the far bank where Jesus was teaching. And he talked of Jesus, who grazes his flock among the lilies and whose name has spread abroad like expensive ointments, who is seen as the dawn; he comes up like the sun, is as beautiful as the moon and as terrible as an armed camp... I remember that in those days an enthusiastic wave of devotion swept over the town which, after all, was still the same old excitable, romantic, ardent little eyrie; the strangers who had moved there were also cast under the spell of this mood; to be a Catholic then meant possessing distinction, a role in society, a presence in everything; it was the fashion. And the Protestant women, who were left out of everything, fumed with rage among themselves at it all.

And I, the debased, impoverished, played-out housewife, found my way into that current which linked me in tender and sacred sisterhood with the women who were now playing an active role in my town, with the whole of social life. It was incredible! With my one and only shabby black dress and work-roughened hands, with my shameful and widely-proclaimed poverty I became one of the inner circle, as a secretary of the altar-guild.

Rozverits was my mentor; it was he who carried me into it and inspired me just like the rest. My girls took their examinations at the Piarist grammar-school; he knew them, and maybe the good countess also drew me to his attention. He called on me, consoled me, converted me and conquered me. But I felt in my case this was no fashionable fad, but an inner spiritual need.

'The Lord calls you!' said the priest, and it was so sublime, welcome and uplifting to feel this. It was my good fortune that I was not brought up in a religious atmosphere in childhood; so all the beauty of the ceremony, its fantasy, the secret charm of its words, the poesy of tradition and the dogma that was crystal-clear and beyond the intellect came all upon me as new and surprising, without the boredom of habitude, and filled my weary soul with fresh amazement after it had pursued such different paths. In the midst of my worries and terrifying cares, faith was liberation and beauty to me. On some peaceful evenings there came a young friar, his lips pursed, his eyes serious and enthusiastic, his expression pale and holy; he was acquainted with every secular science, art and literature, and had not parted from his faith, indeed he was fanatical about it. And from his vocation and Christ-like love he unselfishly occupied himself with me, and it was important to him that I should be converted and saved. His whole being was incomprehensible, miraculous, sublime and stimulating to me, as were the community of saints, the way of perfection or the love of one's enemies. Into my dried-up, lacklustre soul came ideals, poesy and emotions with triumphant trumpet-blasts.

Faith, he said, is within us and not in the verity of things. Faith is the state of the soul, the deliberate surrender of the heart; it is humility and devotion. This is the important thing. You believe that the earth is round and revolves round the sun. And this faith requires no less respect for authority or acquiescence, and belief in it presents the soul with nothing more than if you were to believe the opposite. But even if our faith were to move mountains, says St. Paul, if we have no love we are worth nothing... Why worry about the troubles of life, bread or position in society? Why, are all these important if our spiritual life is independent? The first holy Christian bishops were slaves or artisans as far as their social status was concerned. Who clothes the lilies of the field? Humility and modesty will help you through earthly life unscathed, an uplifted glance will release you from every anxiety. *Nolite timere—alleluia!*

I nodded as I bowed my head with a wonderful feeling of relief. The yellow-shaded oil-lamp crackled in the silence of the room with its rep suite; outside in the little street the hurried footsteps of passers-by pattered softly in the thick fresh snow... How many such intimate, warm, wintry evenings with an atmosphere like this had there been in my life before, I thought suddenly.... The heavy snores of the man asleep could be heard from the next room.

I started attending church; I went to confession and communion regularly. When my daughter Marcsi was at home not long ago, she told me that now there is some new kind of cure for nerves that calms and cures them through questioning, confession and talking... Well, I think the Church discovered this a long time earlier and practises it more cheaply, more effectively and in a more popular way. I bent my head on to the violet velvet rail of the confessional and poured out my life, my emotions, deeds and troubles—effusively, completely, without reservations. And I felt to the full absolution, relief and peace! How sensibly, delicately, earnestly this wonderful servant of God tended and cured my soul! I felt that I was totally dependent on him as on a doctor, a support and guide along the way.

With head thrown back and half-closed eyes I sat in one of the rear pews in the church and gazed at the incense-clouded semi-darkness, the lengthening distant shadows of the arches, the heavenly spell of the coloured swathes of light through the emerald and ruby glass of the windows, rays that were shattered into fragments on the mosaic of the stone floor, and at the saints with their garments in folds. Or far away, inside the church, at the high altar, with its dreamy white lace, the deep pale golden glow and the ethereal radiance. There Rozverits moved to and fro, his slender figure and delicate shoulders bearing the church's dreamy-coloured robes in yellow and white; he glowed as if in some soft cloak of light, noiselessly stepping, turning and inclining his head, his silky voice hypnotically murmuring the unchanging, secretive foreign words...

One foggy morning in February as I stepped out rather stiffly into the street that was white with snow and profanely light, an old woman in a moiré mantilla was making her way in front of me, pattering swiftly along. I recognized her by her old pearl-studded weather-beaten hat. I caught up with her and greeted her softly. It was Ilka Zimán.

'Good morning, my dear!' She took her cotton-gloved hand out of her moth-eaten muff and offered it to me. 'Oh, Magda! How long it is since I've seen you... Why, it's you! Well, you see, people who go to church do meet each other after all!'

I nodded and looked at her wizened face with its thousand wrinkles, her matted greying hair, at the whole of the slipshod, flustered, whining and coughing little old woman. Good God! How she had lost weight! Does time pass as quickly as that?...

'How are you all, my dear, my little girl? What's happening to that poor unfortunate man?'

'He's no man any longer, Ilka. He finds it hard to speak now and hardly understands anything. He just eats and breathes, that's all. Come and see him, auntie, if you're interested.'

'Why ever should I do that, my dear Magda? I still have memories of him when he was different. Why should I see him in such a state? You've certainly had a hard time of it, poor woman! You look after him and watch over him, but see here, sooner or later you've got to work for everything in this rotten world. Poor soul, he lived a lot and knocked about a lot all over the place and spoilt himself with too many good things long before we knew him. But he might have lived longer! He's sixty—one... no, he isn't, sixty-two. He might have lived on quite nicely, mightn't he? Ah well, God bless you, Magda! It's nice, all the same, that we've met each other this once on the way out of church.'

Her bloodshot, lacklustre eyes were swimming with dank tears; she blew her nose red, sniffled and coughed. And we clasped each other's hands yet again... one wintry morning on the way back from church.

That winter too passed by, spring too, and the summer came. 'He's only got a week or two at the most,' Jakobi said at last. And some great heavy stone fell from my heart, and I gave a sigh of relief. (God is good to me, after all!) And all of a sudden I tended and cleansed the poor, helpless, paralysed human corpse with increased readiness and pity. Well, after all they had not pensioned him off, they had some regard for me... and now he was going, poor thing... and after that I should be released from starvation, all the same, with my little pension of six hundred forints a year. My God! So this was the end! Oh, why could we not have been better to each other? Just a word of appeasement, a farewell explanation, if that were possible! But now he can't speak, nor can he understand...

That spring something else happened too: Rozverits the golden-tongued chaplain left the town. They suddenly transferred him! I don't know whether there was any basis for all the wicked, scared, insinuating or supportive gossip that linked this swift departure with a woman, a still beautiful, pure-faced, earnest girl of thirty, who lived only for devotion and charitable work; she was the other secretary of the guild. That he lunched and dined with her too much, that every day he explained the way of salvation till midnight... that (God forgive me!) he would even keep accompanying her in the street, all the way down it.

'To the shop, why did they go together into the draper's to buy clothes for poor children?' Protestant opinion enquired with triumphant scorn as it suddenly gained the upper hand.

'For two years now he's been turning the heads of the town, poisoning the old harmonious relationship between

238

denominations, and driving the women crazy because every single one of them has fallen in love with him, and Christ our Lord is only a procurer of hearts here!'

So declared the loud mouths in Magyar Street, but obviously the whole thing might have been smoothed over, obviously this clean-living man could have triumphed with his truth, but he did not put up a fight, he did not oppose it all, but swiftly demanded to be transferred, and the dowager countess, unable to dissuade him, regretfully arranged this for him. Was there really, I wondered, some emotional basis, a refined, ethereal, sacred beginning to it, a fear or struggle for what the furious company of the ignored whispered with foul mouths but not believing it themselves? After all, we're only human! Perhaps he ought not to have given up the struggle and run away like a coward. But who knows what went to pieces, what silent tragedy was played out in this hard, stern and militant young soul? And now that he had gone this town, which could be crazy, excited and enthusiastic and yet suddenly become hideously and maliciously disillusioned, immediately shook off all that he had clothed it with—a cloak of devotion and a burden of duty—with those wonderful, heart-stirring words.

'The whole lot were in love with him!' guffawed the men, the Lutheran women and the society in the neighbouring town in chorus. And the women here were ashamed of themselves and held their tongues, then later themselves joined in the mockery, like the cowardly host of disciples who betrayed Jesus. It was a fashion, a fad, a sport for two boring seasons! All of a sudden everything returned to the old ways: cynical talk, ambiguous conversations, indecency, good humour, loud-mouthed naivety. It's impossible in such a short time to transform, refine and deepen a few hundred souls. Now he is sometimes mentioned with pity or deprecation; they are ashamed that they came under his influence and played at being holy.

In my case things were different. At the time I was startled too, and stricken, and thought, 'Is it really possible that *this* enabled him to reach the point where we sensed the man behind his harmonious words and steely incandescent will? Maybe it was... and perhaps I felt it too! I was long, long past that age... but it is not such a simple business, it does not depend so clearly on what is corporeal, and it is impossible to separate emotions so boldly and give them names. Loves—I sometimes smiled sadly—and my own life! Who knows which was the truer, the less deliberate of my loves, the more independent of everything simply because it was unconscious? It may well be that in my life I have never known that really great love, the one which is above all others! Poor Rozverits! Yes, after he left, my own spiritual life too reverted to a more ordinary, greyer, more worldly course. But all the same that was a lovely time! I still went to church (and I do today; that much has survived), but my faith was no longer vivid elation, a high-flown, dynamic, feverish state, a peculiar deep emotion and wonderment.

Later my scholarly daughters came home for some vacation or other; they talked and explained one or two things; Marcsi often sends me books even today; I've read a lot and come to realize that other explanations of the world are more interesting and of a hundred different kinds, though sadly aimless, but learning is a sacred human struggle. But faith and ardour were *beautiful*. Maybe it is a pity I could not preserve that mood till my dying day, but doubtless, there was insufficient imagination or devotion in me for that; it had not struck deep enough roots in me. But before I die—and I feel this for certain—I shall send for a priest and make my confession. For at that stage there's nothing more to argue about!

Poor Dénes! When with great difficulty Zsuzsanna Képíró, who volunteered her help, and I lifted his heavy body, now growing cold, onto the bed ('He'll haunt you if he doesn't die in bed!' warned Madam Zsuzsi), he gave a snort and looked hard at me; his long stupid and expressionless eyes seemed to recognize me with some sudden return of a glimmer of understanding. He grasped my hand and strove hard, struggling shakily and clumsily to lift it to his lips... Did he want to kiss it or perhaps bite it? What did it mean? It was the semi-animal, indecisive, unfinished movement and intention of a paralytic.

But I felt a sudden icy panic and snatched my hand away with all my strength; my knees trembled and I ran out into the next room. To the living, this death's head of a human being meant a ghostly other-worldliness and incomprehensibility. Later I calmed down, but I did not approach the bed again; it was only from the doorway that I looked at his closed, puffy eyes, his dropped jaw and swollen belly beneath the blanket; and I listened to the characteristic heavy snoring that had filled the house without interruption for weeks now, together with the almost unbearable stench of the sick body.

That, too, was a lovely gentle autumn. In the mild sunshine I went to and fro in a quiet daze; I kept going inside for a little and sat down on the rep divan in the drawing-room, reciting a few Lord's Prayers with my hands in my lap; then with noiseless steps I would pace the brick veranda, pulling the red woven kerchief close to me; I laid the table for a little morning coffee, all neat and clean on the gleaming paintwork of the tiny garden table, then looked far away into the blue and white sky. 'Well, today it will come to pass!' I thought with gentle calm. 'Where will he go? What will become of him? Does he still *exist* now at this very moment? How does one pass away, where does one go…'

How many unspoken secrets! But now all this seemed so simple, so near at hand. After all, it's not *today* that he will die; for years something in him has been dying every day, who knows for how long? Perhaps we gradually die from birth. And what becomes of the flowers that wither and die? After all, they also live, bloom and *exist*. I stood up and slowly, one by one, I picked the mallow, pansies, basil and hollyhocks, all there were; I went inside for a kitchen-knife and stripped the oleanders of their still perfect rose-coloured blooms to decorate the bier. In the meantime, I often had to go to the gate because almost everyone who passed by, servants of acquaintances out buying meat, women from the villages selling milk, market-women and gentlemen off to their offices, greeted me and asked after the sick man… When Zsuzsi called me inside around eleven o'clock, his chin was already done up with a white napkin and there were two heavy silver forints covering his eyes. Zsuzsi had taken them from her own pocket and placed them there to close them nicely.

*

A good three years have passed since then. Now I sit here in this little Swabian house; the only room facing the street belongs to me, and in it are my old brown suite and a lot of thirty-year-old odds and ends, all polished to death, that have accompanied me all my life. But here too are the oleanders, still those that were cut from grandma's bushes, and a few little flower-beds too, basil, red holly-hocks and mallow. On summer afternoons, I sit from time to time among them, as I hear the sound of the bells. I do a little reading and make good little cups of coffee for myself and offer them to the occasional good old charwoman. But sometimes nobody calls at my door for weeks on end.

My daughters are doing well. Marcsi is an outstanding teacher at the girls' grammar school in Pest. Szerén, the daughter of the old factor Lipi (today a wealthy property-owner in Pest), also became a teacher and they are together. They were bosom friends even when they were at school; at that time I was opposed to their friendship, but since then this 'Szeréna Szinyéri' has become a famous poet. She writes beautiful, strange love poems. How much a Jewish girl like that knows and dares to do! My daughter Zsuzsi trained as a dispensing chemist ('Because you can only do that in male company,' the older one mocked sometimes), and not long ago became engaged to her chief in one of the larger country towns. Marcsi is supplying her trousseau; she is also the one who most often keeps helping me, though I don't really want her to; after all the little I have is enough for me. Klári, too, has finished her studies; for the time being she makes a living from giving piano-lessons, but she has been promised a post in a school in Pest. Marcsi believes she's in love with a former teacher of hers, some great artist. That's nothing to worry about! She has plenty of time for such extravagance; she hasn't any need to rush into marriage for her daily bread… So they're provided for; for some time now, they've had no need of me, my care and affection. They write sometimes, and their visits home are increasingly rare.

I am surrounded by a deep and pleasurable tranquillity; I can hear the bells clearly, and with my hands in my lap I can sit in the same place, alone and for hours on end, reviving memories in a thousand different ways, making various connections and coming up with various explanations, thinking about the distant, very distant affairs of life.

Printed in Hungary